11/10/95

To my darling Susan,
a friend of
my heart
with all
my love and
awe
always,

[illegible]

MARRIAGE

Also by Gloria Nagy

LOOKING FOR LEO

A HOUSE IN THE HAMPTONS

RADIO BLUES

NATURAL SELECTIONS

UNAPPARENT WOUNDS

VIRGIN KISSES

MARRIAGE

A NOVEL BY

GLORIA NAGY

LITTLE, BROWN AND COMPANY

BOSTON NEW YORK TORONTO LONDON

First Edition

Library of Congress Cataloging-in-Publication Data

Nagy, Gloria.
Marriage : a novel / by Gloria Nagy. — 1st ed.
p. cm.
ISBN 0-316-59675-2 (HC)
I. Title.
PS3564.A36M37 1995
813'.54 — dc20
DLC
for Library of Congress 94-43191

10 9 8 7 6 5 4 3 2 1

RRD-VA

Published simultaneously in Canada
by Little, Brown & Company (Canada) Limited

Printed in the United States of America

For Julia Budin, my mother, and Ann Walker, my friend.

Marriage is like a garden. It can work with one flower and one gardener. It can work with two gardeners. But two flowers — that's really tough.

— Mike Nichols

The heart wants what it wants.

— Woody Allen
Time, September 1992

ACKNOWLEDGMENTS

I DEEPLY THANK my agent Ed Victor for his faith, my editor Fredrica Friedman for her invaluable guidance; Patricia Soliman and Patricia Aburdene for everything, Victoria Polk and Kirstin Zettmar my angels, Jane Rosch and Hannah my rock and my joy, Elyce Goldstein my other daughter, Tony Wurman, Dr. Josh Wurman, Mary Beth Heim, Blanca McGee and Bonnie Strauss for really being there, Reven Wurman for making me look good, Chip Benson and Barbara Benson for reading everything and those lunches, David Sume for cheerfully bringing immaculate order to semi-chaos, and Mary Sheekey and Tim Sullivan for doing the same thing for our lives, and always, Richard.

MARRIAGE

PART 1

FOR BETTER OR WORSE

PROLOGUE

A SLIVER OF TURQUOISE NYLON. Not even silk — nylon with 10 percent Lycra spandex. It was less than a bikini, but more than a thong. It was on the floor of her mother's Range Rover (backseat driver's side to be precise). A pair of panties. They were not, Ella was sure, her mother's. (No tummy-control panel, no reinforced cotton crotch) and *turquoise?* No way. They certainly weren't hers, and she and Toby had arrived together. (Actually — he was almost twisted enough these days to make such a purchase.) So? She was not *that* naive.

Her dad must have used the car. Her dad had fucked someone with no taste, tight stomach muscles, and not much money (not pure cotton or, of course, silk). Someone . . . young. Someone in the backseat of her mother's car.

She picked up the turquoise intruder and stuffed it into her pocket. She'd had this feeling all day, all the way from New York. A slipping feeling. Something sliding underneath her. That the something could be her family, her earthquake-proof and steel-reinforced family, had never entered her mind.

Her fist closed around the panties, curled deep down inside her brand-new winter blazer, as her mother, chatting innocently, swung the car into the long, gravel drive.

Home, she thought. Shit.

MICHAEL JAMES WILDER, Emmy-nominated star of the gritty crime series *War Zone,* is as unlike Detective Jake Jerico, the cocky, gum-chewing wise guy he portrays, as day is from night. His TV character is a divorced, childless cynic, while the real man has been married to his childhood sweetheart, Annie (Diana) Miller Wilder, for almost twenty-three years. The vivacious Annie, a travel writer specializing in country inns, has been called "the baroness of the bed and breakfast" with her enthusiastic columns and articles on American rural hideaways. Since moving to Montecito, California, from their native New York five years ago when the series began, they have become ardent California boosters, biking, hiking, and walking the beautiful Santa Barbara shoreline.

Says Annie, "We chose Montecito even though it means Michael has to commute when the show's filming, because Los Angeles just seemed too overwhelming for the kids and for us. Also, there are an enormous number of left turns to make in L.A. and I have never been too great at left turns."

The Wilder family includes their

two handsome kids, son Toby, a freshman at Brown University, and daughter Ella, a recent graduate of NYU. They live with their dog, Portia, "a slobbering, foul-smelling beast of dubious origins," jokes Michael, in a lovely Mediterranean home that boasts a restaurant-quality gourmet kitchen, an office exercise room for Michael (Mickey to his friends), and a small study where Annie writes.

War Zone's temperamental creator, Stan Stein, has been battling network executives over ratings drops since shortly before the new season's shooting began, and rumor has it that *War Zone* may be headed for the end zone. Either way, the future looks bright for this happy family.

"Annie and I practically raised one another—we had our kids young too, so we have all grown up together in a way. Series come and go, but my family is forever," adds Mickey.

What a refreshing breath of air the Wilders are in polluted Hollywood!

—*People*, March 1993

IN AMERICA, there are places to live that might be called paradise places. They are usually towns, sometimes villages — but never cities anymore — where lucky people live. Lucky people with gunite pools and German sports cars and someone to mow the lawn, bring in the paper, and let out the dog.

People who are fortunate enough to live in these places are often envied. The independently wealthy, the affluently retired, the creative who have the freedom to work anywhere. But the reality is often something else. And the reality of this last illusion of the twentieth century is that there is no longer anywhere to escape for long. Empty boutiques, too many For Sale signs, bag ladies and homeless phantom people, drug addicts and thieves; the sore thumbs of society are everywhere now.

Montecito, California, is a paradise place. It appears to the casual eye to be a rather newly created place, springing up behind the grand old Biltmore Hotel as a reaction to the small city it is attached to. That city, Santa Barbara, an old mission town with fine Spanish architecture, a lovely sea-fronted site, and several fine restaurants, has an underclass and homeless population to rival many less romantic places.

Tiny Montecito is the place to be in Santa Barbara County. The time of the fax machine, cellular communication, and environmental obsession has come, and for people who have a choice, Montecito offers to Los Angeles what the Hamptons have offered to New York City. Everyone wants to be there because they can be somewhere scenic and laid back and still be in the game.

This is a recent stampede. A nineties trend. Life is too short is the mantra at the lip of the millennium. The cities feel this betrayal by those who built them up, puffed them up with energy and arrogance, overstimulating them until they careened out of control; too big, too poor, too angry, too old.

The paradise places know this. They know that those who come from the cities having stripped them like stolen convertibles on Saturday night, will do it to them too.

The Wilders were gentle guests in their paradise place. They came as innocents, knowing absolutely nothing about the West, Father Serra, Spanish architecture, Mexican food, freeways, oil rigs, seagulls, or non-urban places. They had never lived anywhere but New York City and had only that on which to base their comparisons. This made some things easier and many things more confusing.

Annie Miller met Mickey Wilder when they were six years old. Her father, Joseph, a well-known but marginally successful theatrical agent, and her mother, Sara, who was only that, moved into the top floor of a converted brownstone on MacDougal Street in Greenwich Village. Mickey's family lived on the first floor.

Annie had a younger brother named Martin, and Mickey had a younger brother named Jackie. Sara Miller's excitement about the new neighbors with children of similar ages and all the benefits of that sort of young-family neighborliness lasted until she actually met the Wilskis (Mickey's real name) face to face.

Mickey's family was not your regular fifties family, even for Greenwich Village.

They were, as Sara Miller whispered to her husband after dragging Annie and Martin downstairs to introduce themselves, "radicals." Mickey's mother, Ida Mae, dressed in black, rode a motorcycle, and collected African art. His father, Moe, owned a Harley-Davidson dealership on Eleventh Avenue. Ida Mae ran him, the boys, the house, and the neighborhood. She scared Sara Miller to death, but Annie thought she was wonderful, and she thought Annie was wonderful, even after Annie and Mickey fell in love.

They were friends for a long time before this happened. They walked to school together every day and home together most afternoons. They plotted against their little brothers together and shared their mutual frustration at their parents' blindness to the flaws of the younger creatures. Neither of them ever understood why on earth their parents had wanted anyone but them, and as their brothers grew up no new information was presented to soften their outrage.

The first time Mickey kissed her they were ten, and that was pretty much that.

Every once in a while such a thing occurs in life. Two children find their soulmates. Mickey and Annie did not think about this privately or say it out loud to one another for many, many years; but they accepted their connection to one another as what life was supposed to be.

It drove their families crazy. It drove their teachers, their friends, and their relatives crazy. No one believed that you could meet someone when barely more than a toddler and cleave unto them and them alone from that time forward. They were inseparable. Even the ease with which friendship became romance — and romance it did become and not mild, pal romance, but intense, erotic romance — annoyed everyone. No one ever thought that it could last. But it did.

These were not two reclusive or unattractive, odd or in some way peculiar, young people, either. They were not clinging together out of shyness or maladaptation. Mick ("the Stick") Wilski, long before he became Michael James Wilder, television star, was the best-looking, most athletic kid in his class. He was voted best build, best actor, and best sense of humor when he graduated from Elizabeth Irwin High School (a fifties bastion of free-spirited kids if there ever was one). And Annie was his equal. When she was seven years old (her father liked to tell her), an old man sitting next to her on the subway became so entranced with her bright orange curls and freckle-dotted face that he struck up a conversation. "What's your name, little girl?"

"Annie," she said, but the old man had trouble hearing over the subway noise.

"Anna? As in Karenina?" he asked.

"Nope. Annie as in 'Little Orphan,'" she replied.

Annie was a bright penny. A funny, spunky little girl, who grew up intact.

Annie and Mickey graduated from high school together and they went to NYU together. They majored in theater together. The only difference in their courses was that Annie minored in dance.

The women in Annie's family had always danced. Not for any reason (exercise or health) or with any real skill (or grace for that matter). They just loved moving to music.

Annie danced to anything and on any occasion. She began with the Maypole in kindergarten; she did the hora in grade school and the box step in junior high. She rocked and rolled through high school. She twisted, monkeyed, frugged, and discoed. She danced in the dark and cheek to cheek. She did it dirty and slow and alone and with others. She did it when she was happy or because she was sad. And always when she felt romantic.

"Maybe we'll grow too old to dream," her aunt Bessie used to say, "but never to dance."

Dancing was all about the tickle inside life.

It was when she was at dance class, and only then, that Mickey and Annie were not together.

In Annie's senior year, an artery in her mother's head exploded. She was standing at the sink in their apartment making tuna-fish sandwiches with pickle relish and onions for Annie and Martin, when she stopped talking. Her feet shuffled back and Annie thought for a minute that she was going to dance. They often did that, she and her mother; they would just suddenly respond to some tune in their heads and do a little dance step. Her mother shuffled back; the knife in her hand dropped to the floor and her mother went with it.

If her mother hadn't died, maybe she would have waited, but her mother did die and Annie dropped out of school and married Mickey.

A year later Ella was born, and Annie moved aside and let Mickey pass through. Mickey had the aura of success about him. He had presence. Everyone at NYU thought he would go places and he did. He worked steadily off-Broadway, on Broadway, in small roles; he did commercials and voice-overs.

They bought a brownstone on Barrow Street and he went "out to the Coast" to do guest shots. He did a short-lived series in New York and several more plays.

Considering that Mickey was a moderately successful actor, they lived an entirely normal life. Working actors who are not famous live far more ordinary lives than most people think. Once in a while he would be recognized, but not often enough for it to be anything but a pleasant ego boost. Annie started writing her travel pieces and in between jobs Mickey would take off with her on her B&B excursions.

When he wasn't working he was home a lot, and they were always together. She helped him with his lines, went to auditions and rehearsals with him; they even took exercise classes together.

Their lives moved forward with the normal wear and tear, aggravations and disappointments, fighting and making up, sick kids, and bills to pay as everyone else.

What made them special to those around them in the New York City theatrical world was their endurance. Through the seventies and the eighties, when relationships were crashing like cheap pottery at a Greek wedding — human beings smashing and breaking apart; infecting one another with terrifying diseases; betraying, lying, incesting, child abusing, deserting one another as if an epidemic of antihumanity had consumed the planet — they endured. They were the envy of everyone.

They did not understand their good fortune any more than anyone else did. People thought that they were just blessed, but that wasn't fair. They worked hard at staying together, maybe because having always been together, they could not even imagine being apart. They went forward, trying to be decent and raise their children in the midst of the madness.

There were many things that they had given up by being together, adventures not taken, other lovers not explored. But they were still young enough not to feel regret and frightened enough by the human rubble encircling them, and they clung to one another as shipwreck survivors cling to the mast. They seemed by the eighties to be the last couple still standing on deck. Everyone else had sunk.

Their children were unique in their classes just by living in what the school called "an organic family." Maybe Annie felt a little smug about this; so many women had passed her by, this was her little piece of the rock.

And then California called again. Only this time it wasn't for an "episode," one week and Mickey was home. This time it was serious. He was thirty-nine years old and he had not become Al Pacino. They had kids to put through college, and this was Mickey's chance and their chance not to end up hanging out at the Stage Deli rereading the yellowed clippings.

So they went to California, strangers in a strange land, and every dream came true for a while.

CHAPTER I

A LETTER to Annie Wilder from Annie Wilder on the eve of her forty-fifth birthday *and* Thanksgiving:

Dear Me,

Well, it looks like I made it. I have now outlived my mother.

Is this reason to celebrate or mourn? Actually it's only 11:40, so by saying this before midnight, it is still possible that I could trigger a massive cerebral hemorrhage or my estrogen level could suddenly plummet, throwing me into instant menopause and cardiac arrest, or a serial killer who has been thwarted by our alarm system and Portia's horrifying smell has found an unlocked window and is at this very second racing toward my bedroom door with an ax, an Uzi, and my favorite carving knife. But what the hell, I'll risk it. So, Birthday Girl, where are you?

Not back in New York, where Mickey promised I would be by now. Of course if the show's canceled that could change very quickly. I'm so mixed up about this. Renewal represents another year of security, money I can stash for our old age, and Mickey out of the house every day. On the other hand, it means staying in California.

The fact is I have no control. This fact was made increasingly clear to me after picking Toby and Ella up at LAX.

Maybe it would be easier for me to deal with the "separation issues" involving an eighteen-year-old son and a twenty-two-year-old daughter if my mother had lived long enough for me to have gone through it myself but I don't think so. I do have a brilliant idea for getting through Thanksgiving with them and the rest of the family. I am going to mash my lips together with Elmer's glue and cover them prettily with my new Winter Pumpkin lipstick. I will communicate only by enthusiastic nodding, and as a perk I should also lose several pounds.

If I can just keep my big mouth shut I will emerge unscathed. It seems that nothing that I have said to either child or Mickey in the last six months has served any purpose but the most perversely sadistic pleasure I might derive from seeing those closest to me roll their eyes, grit their teeth, and pound on any available surface. Elmer's it is.

The only justification I can find for whatever madness drove me to another Marilyn-Quayle-on-quaaludes Thanksgiving is that I was planning a survival celebration. Some really rather sweet, however demented, reaching out to *The Entire Family* on this major birthday.

I really do want to go *home*. I was a more chipper person on Barrow Street. Of course I was not outliving my mother and turning forty-five on Barrow Street. I was not married to a famous TV star on Barrow Street. My children had not grown up yet on Barrow Street. I did not have a fibroid "the size of a cantaloupe" hanging out in my uterus on Barrow Street.

How ironic that I should feel like I'm shrinking and the damn fibroid is getting bigger. Maybe I should stop denying that having the damn thing in there is freaking me out. I want to believe that my New Age gynecologist, with her herbal remedies and antihysterectomy bias, is right. It's all so P.C., and far less terrifying than a scalpel in the abdomen — but I don't know — the cantaloupe tumor idea is not so amusing. I guess the truth is I'm so terrified of dying like my mother, I'll do anything rather than face a hospital and all those health-care types. I'm still hopeful about the homeopathic stuff she gave me. My cantaloupe may well become an orange by New Year's. If not — I'll deal with it *after* the holidays. I promise.

The other thing I'm thinking about is how I ended up buried under all of these other egos. What happened to mine? I started out basically even with Mickey. How did I end up still at the starting line? Okay. That's a little too breast-beaty. I have a wonderful life, a great husband, and two kids I adore, and I have had a pleasant career or I did until last month.

Okay — I'm going to say it straight out — I *hate* bed and breakfasts. From that very first one in Virginia to the Victorian in Mendocino with the black velvet walls and the empty bird cages. I cannot write one more insincere adjective about one more weekend in someone's converted stable. I can never make love in a B&B. I just know the owners are listening with a glass to the wall in the next room. All of those horrifying tchotchkes everywhere and the little lists of Do's and Don'ts. Making small talk with total strangers at breakfast! Little crocheted covers for the toothpaste tubes. Antique dolls with those dead glass eyes posing on top of the needlepoint toilet seats. The horrible hosts ("Marge and I just love making new friends!"). What they really *love* is an endless audience to applaud their decorating delusions and collections of farm animal icons. Porcelain cow pitchers, wooden ducks, ceramic sheep. It's idol worship if the truth be told. If I never see another copper pot stuffed with dried flowers, walk on a hand-hooked rug, or eat a homemade carrot-and-zucchini muffin again it will be too soon. I can't even *mouth* the word "quaint"! So — I guess I am now careerless. Except for running our overly complex lives and managing our finances (with Leonard's help, of course). Who would have thought that a kid who still counts on her fingers would be in charge of our *life's savings.* I know I couldn't do it without Leonard, but still, I've had very good investment ideas — and unless the world falls apart we should be okay in our waning years, and that's something Mickey has had no part of. The only financial news that interests him is on the front page of *Variety.*

This is not how I want to feel tonight. Every magazine I pick up is chirping at me that this middle-age thing is all in my mind. Gail Sheehy says that "fifty is the youth of middle age," so I am just a puppy. All those articles keep telling me that I don't even have to age. No woman interviewed by any women's magazine that I have personally read in the last five years has admitted to anything but oozing sexuality, supreme self-confidence, and endless energy.

Where did I read that Raquel Welch gets up at six every day, performs ninety minutes of weight training, yoga, and aerobics, has a slice of whole-grain toast, oat bran, and Evian, works on her career, eats a small fruit-plate for lunch, does another hour of something exhausting, has a rice cake, works some more, has sprouts and water for dinner, and calls it a day.

If all the women who say they live like this were telling the truth the suicide rate for women over 40 would be equal to the national debt.

I have never known any woman in real life who looks, thinks, or acts like any of the women the magazines seem to know. Even the ones that I read about and really *do* know. It's like reading about Hollywood marriages in *People* magazine. I mean, they did *my* marriage. We made Jack and Jill look like Bonnie and Clyde. But still, all evidence to the contrary, I buy into it.

I read about all of these perfect Out There Gals. But the truth is that I know some happy men (ignorance being bliss and all) but I do not know *any* happy women.

Sometimes I really believe that men are put on this earth for the sole purpose of driving women crazy. Not in any great big premeditated evil way, just inch by inch, infuriating habit by habit. However, I also believe that men seem to be getting softer and women seem to be getting harder.

There are no men that I know who intimidate or frighten me.

There are several women who do both.

Once you figure men out they are relatively easy to deal with. You can never figure any woman out including yourself.

Men's anger doesn't bother me. Women's anger scares the shit out of me. When two women really let it go, there are no boundaries. They, unlike men, know exactly where to strike. Maybe that's why women try so hard to be nice. Maybe that's why I do, too.

Maybe it's the fibroid causing all of this angst. I mean, it is a really weird feeling to know that there is something "the size of a four-month pregnancy" growing in your uterus that is never going to go to college.

I think this depression really started after I went to the girl-child radiologist to have the tests, lying there with those merciless lights burning down on me and these twenty-something, red-nailed, diamond-covered fingers palpating my poor lumpy middle-aged breasts.

Those were not the hands I wanted on my boobs and poking the ultrasound dildo up inside my overgrown womb. I wanted a kind, liver-spotted, been-around-the-block, "there, there, my dear, everything's going to be fine" kind of hand. Maybe with a thin gold band that had been on its finger for so long that it was embedded in the creases.

It is now 1:30 a.m. I *have* outlived my mother. The serial killer has gone next door to attack the O'Brians, who are Irish and never lock their doors. Any serial killer worth his salt should know never to try attacking a Jewish family. Triple locks, bolts, lots of screaming and crying and blaming God.

I saw an article in *USA Today* yesterday about how some top scientists have been studying the way that yeast grows and have come up with the theory that within the next three decades people will be able to live as long as *four hundred years*. Things like this really irritate me. What does that mean? Since there is only so much one can do (even Raquel) what with gravity and cell division and all, only so many lifts and tucks you can have, what would this four hundred years entail? Wandering around for, say, three hundred and thirty years really looking like shit?

Sometimes I really think that our mothers had it easier (generally speaking — certainly not my poor mother). I'm not sure about this idea, but maybe our mothers got a break. They just lived their lives. They didn't know from plastic surgery and Stair Masters. No one expected them to look twenty when they were fifty. No one expected them to do anything other than what they did: be mothers and wives and whatever. And those standards were not so high, either. Most of them were fairly terrible cooks and raised us more by the benign neglect "that's nice, dear, go out and play now" school, than the Yuppie child-as-sacred-object academy. They seemed to be more accepting of themselves and with almost no therapy or recovery programs. I may be in real trouble here, but as long as this is for my nearsighted peepers only, here goes . . .

At this moment I do not believe in my heart of hearts that I will ever recover from my children growing up. I have been wandering around in a daze since Ella went to college. I cannot quite believe that that part of my life, heart of my life, is over forever. *Forever.* Not that it was all so wildly wonderful. We all know better. But it was all about building, reaching up, watching things grow. It was my safety on this earth, it was my completeness. My babies, my husband, my house. I feel as if I have been halved, withered in some way.

I am lost in this loss, and as wonderful as they are now, so good-looking and funny and when they are not insane, fantastic to be around, I still cannot quite believe that they will never be ten years old again. Three years old. Eight. It is all over. I cannot dress my fibroid up in a darling little sailor suit and march it off to kindergarten. I will never be a mother and we will never be a family in that way again. Sometimes I feel just hunky do about that and The Future and my new freedom and all, and sometimes I feel as if the pain of that loss, the loss of that part, in many ways the best part of myself, is just quite simply, unbearable. There, I've said it.

I haven't heard from Mickey, which either means that the wrap party turned into an orgy because the series was renewed, or it was canceled and he's too depressed to tell me. He just better be back here before his mother arrives. (His mother, *my* father, his brother, *my* brother — I must be out of my mind!)

I'd better work on *the family* and prepare myself a little.

I will let my father go on about the old days in the Theater; let him lie, exaggerate, brag, recite, name-drop every show he produced, every client he represented. I will listen to the same stories for the eight thousandth time with my pumpkin grin. I will not tell him any bad news (me and my fibroid strolling down the avenue). I will not expect any depth.

I will not get defensive with Ida Mae. She and my father can do their simulcast monologues. He will talk about the first New York performance of *The Front Page* and she will talk about the Hollywood Five and James Dean as a symbol of Our Lost Hope.

I will not be self-righteous with Jackie about his shows or his love life, I will be nice. It's so perfect for Jackie to produce tabloid TV! He really was a voyeur at eighteen months. I remember him lying on the floor outside Ida Mae's room trying to squeeze his eyes under the door and his little fat fingers getting stuck and Ida Mae throwing open the door, bashing the little weirdo in the head or stepping on his hand. Maybe that's what's wrong with him.

Martin, Loretta, and Bentley. Imagine naming a little baby *Bentley.* I never know whether to polish him or ask him to bring the Witherspoons another martini. *I will not try to bond with my brother. I will not react when I see him ever so slyly scanning my freckles for signs of melanoma. I will nod cheerfully when he reminds me that freckled redheads must take extra precautions out of doors.*

I am convinced that Martin really believes that no one should go outside. It's those vampire genes from way back in the middle Europe days of our ancestors. He *is* as pale as Casper the ghost. Pale looks great on women, but really bad on men. I have never seen a man who does not look much better with "a little color," as my mother used to say. It is one of the only things women are fortunate about physically.

I know how this sounds, sibling rivalry, yah, yah, yah. However, my brother *does* spend most of his life in a sterile, artificially lit little room removing gross disgusting growths from gross disgusting grown-ups, and my poor sister-in-law *does* spend most of *her* life in a sparse, artificially lit little room removing gross disgusting grown-ups from one another.

I sound so caustic I could scour copper with just the moisture from my fevered brow. I *will* be nice. I *will not judge them.* I am no A.P.A. poster girl myself.

I had a fantasy this morning driving to the airport to pick up the kids. Everyone is sitting at my beautiful antique oak table waiting for The Turkey. The kitchen doors swing open. Two carts are wheeled in. The turkey is on one and I am on the other. We are both golden brown (though my color is the result of our recent trip to Hawaii and not the oven).

The turkey and I lie on our backs side by side. My hands are trussed, giving me a fantastic reclining bust line. My legs are tied together in a discreetly ladylike, reverse S&M position. Mickey will stand up as usual at this point and recite a poem appropriate to the occasion. Frost. Probably the "miles to go before I sleep" one. His mother will sigh in Oedipal ecstasy. My father's eyes will fill, thinking of opening nights past.

The turkey and I will wait patiently. When Mickey unties my trusses, I will leap up on the table and belt out the entire first act of *Funny Girl*. And they will have to sit and listen, it being Thanksgiving *and* my Birthday. And when I am through I will dance. I will tap dance. I will hoof my way down the table tapping on the china plates. I will leap into the air and land on my Mexican-tile floor and tap my heart out. Down the hall, across my hacienda-style living room, I will dance myself out of this funk. I will stomp myself into shape, into an appropriately upbeat frame of mind from which to face the next forty-five years, or at least the next forty-five minutes. Good night Annie Wilder and good luck.

The phone rang, forcing Annie into the first morning of her forty-fifth year. She was having her favorite dream. In this dream she is running down a beach with her children. She is in the middle and they are holding her hands. They are small, small enough to still be running down a beach holding hands with their mother and not be mortified by such an act. The wind is blowing their hair back and the sea spray has dampened their faces and legs. It is very warm and easy to move; the sand is not heavy, but slick as marble, and they glide along, their bare feet hardly touching the ground.

It was her very best dream. Actually, the only really fun dream she ever had. Usually her dreams involved being chased by a madman and screaming soundlessly for help, or the garden variety "trapped in high school and unprepared for the final exam" dream. There was also the "Mother is still alive and comes to live with me and I don't know what to do with her" dream and the really kinky series where she is always in some brothel in Tahiti or somewhere. She hadn't had the beach dream often, and not for a very long time now, but when it came back it always made her feel better, as if her unconscious was not such a tangled web after all. She did not want to surrender the dream quite yet.

"Hullo?"

"Happy birthday to you, happy birthday a-to a-you a —"

"Hi, honey. I was dreaming. What time is it?"

"Eight a.m. I thought you'd be well into your turkey trauma by now."

"Omigod! The alarm didn't go off!"

"It didn't go off because you forgot to set it again, right?"

"I'm losing it, Mickey. This is the third time this month. Have you ever in our entire lives known me to forget to set an alarm? God, that makes me feel so out of control."

"It's your birthday. Maybe you just needed a break. Everything will be fine."

Annie sat up and pushed her quilt down. "Where are you? Why didn't you call last night?"

"Wrap party. We all got wrapped. I didn't get back to the apartment till two. I thought you'd be asleep. Sorry, Bunny-bunny."

"Please, no baby talk; I haven't decided whether I'm mad at you or not. I was worried. What happened? Are we unemployed?"

"No beating around the bush for my wife." Mickey sighed.

Annie swung her white, freckled legs onto the polished maple floor. "What's with the sighing. Since when are you sighing? Tell me!"

"Jesus! You've only been conscious for three minutes, where do you find the fury? I was making a left turn, so I paused for a second. I don't really know. They told us at the party that the final decision hasn't been made yet. I think they're waiting for this week's Nielsens. But no news is good news. Frankly, I'm relieved. It'll make Thanksgiving nicer. Are the kids there?"

Annie patted her chest. Her heart was pounding. She realized that she was far more anxious about the show being canceled than she had wanted to be. She had gone Hollywood. That's what it was. She had gotten used to the fancy house and the nice clothes and the pool and not worrying about money all the time. Corrupted. She was corrupted and now she would turn into one of those Hollywood

Wives, pushing her husband and networking and entertaining compulsively and having trendy conversations with agents at cocktail parties while her eyes roamed the room looking for someone who would be more statusy to talk to.

"Annie?"

"Oh, sorry. I was accelerating a little bit."

"Please, no shrink talk. I thought you'd gone into a coma."

"I was, I was . . . accelerating. There is no other way to say it. I had a negative thought about starting to . . . you know . . . getting used to all the goodies, and being corrupted and not being able to let it go, kind of thing. I just had a moment of acute irrationality. I'm fine now."

Mickey laughed. "Whatever living with you is, Spots, it is never boring. Did you hear my question?"

"Yes. The kids are here in the body sense. Mind-wise, I'll know more later. Toby spent the entire ride from LAX with his Walkman on, turned up so loud, I could feel the vibrations in my teeth. That horrible rap music. Something about fucking whitey and shooting The Man — or maybe it's the other way around. He just nodded and snapped his fingers and I basically talked to myself. Something's up with Ella — she's in one of those 'quiet moods.' I can hear everything I'm saying through her ears. I mean, everything comes out sounding really dumb, like I'm trying too hard to please her. I hate that. Nothing I say is right. I was looking at pictures of her from graduation and I said, 'Honey, look at this one. You look so sexy and petulant.' She practically ripped it out of my hand. 'I look fat and mean,' she said, and she tore it up. Something's wrong, but I'm afraid to ask."

"Well, did she?"

"What?"

"Look fat and mean."

"Oh, funny. You never answered my question — where are you?"

"I'm at La Cienega and Sunset heading toward the Sunset Plaza hotel. Ask me why!"

"I'm afraid to. Are floozies involved?"

"I'm going to pick up *my* mother and *your* father. They flew in two days ago and have been having a little 'adventure,' is the way my mother described it."

Annie sat down again. "You're making this up."

"Nope. I had a message on my machine last night. They sounded like two nine-year-olds making their first phone call from camp. I think it's great. They went to Universal for the tour. I could have gotten them VIP passes, but they wanted to do it themselves."

"She just better not put Pop on any motorcycles. Remember the last time?"

Mickey laughed. "I think they've learned their lesson. Anyway, I'm almost there and I'll hit the freeway right afterward. I don't have to wait around for their plane, so I'll be home early to help my aging birthday girl with her wifely duties."

"I just thought of something, Mick. We are NINETY YEARS OLD. I mean, together. We are *ninety.*"

"Well, that is a really unique way of turning a happy birthday into the slough of despond. I'm the one who may be canceled and over the hill. Why are you so morbid?"

"I dunno. I worked on that one last night to no avail. I've got to get on the stick. Drive carefully."

"Hey, baby. Watch your words. You are talking to Mick the Stick, and this is the only stick you be gettin' on, girl."

"It may be time to shift, dear. 'Bye."

Annie pulled up the white Egyptian cotton duvet cover and shook out the European goose-down pillows. It was so easy making the bed when Mickey wasn't there. Was that a bad thought? She was a tidy sleeper, hardly moving at all once she had her pillows right and the sheet just so. Mickey was the total opposite. Sleeping with Mickey was like sleeping with a combustion engine. He snored, he did some really annoying whistling thing with his teeth and tongue; he thrashed around (and she had the bruises on her right leg to prove it). He didn't so much sleep as do slumber improvisation.

When he was in L.A. filming, many times it was a relief for her. She had been alone so little in her life, going right from her parents' house to Mickey. It wasn't really until he started to work in Hollywood that she had ever been alone. Now she enjoyed it. It provided her with time to connect with herself, as she was now, not as anyone's anything. When the kids first left she had been afraid that it would be too lonely with just her and her dog and Juanita in a big empty house, but she loved it. It was like being in a hotel room by herself. It always made her feel completely independent and slightly illicit.

She padded into the bathroom and turned on the shower, slipping her nightgown over her head and looking at herself in the mirror. The light in the bathroom was harsh California sun, making her face look drawn. She turned on the lights over the sink, which were pinker and more flattering. God, I'm going to end up like Lina — soon I won't go into any room where the lighting isn't right. She turned sideways and sucked in her stomach.

Ninety. She couldn't even think of her *age* without attaching him to it! Actually she probably looked fifty and he looked forty so it wasn't even a fair test. Was that true? She couldn't tell anymore. She was far too close to him to see him objectively, even when she watched him on television. Maybe especially on television, because the way he was lit, he looked fantastic. How had she ever had the courage to marry an actor in the first place? Probably only because she had known him from when he was six years old and hadn't really thought about him as anything but her Mickey until so much later.

Not until the fan letters and stuff, and seeing women look at him and come on to him. The kids thought it was hilarious. To them he was the guy with the torn terry-cloth bathrobe and the baggy eyes and stubble on his face. After all, he wasn't Redford. He never had played parts like that. He was really more of a character actor. His hair was receding and his nose was crooked. But now that look was in. Mickey was in, even if he was *ninety*. There it was again. If she still lived in New York she would probably be feeling okay about how she was holding up to the test of time, but here, forget about it.

Also, she was the only woman she knew her age who had grown children. There were all of these forty-something women with toddlers! She would see them at Gelson's or the Montecito pharmacy with that "We've just invented motherhood!" attitude. But *they* had babies so *they* were still young? How did that work? Someone changed the jukebox on her quarter. Now it was weird to have babies in your twenties, but perfectly okay to have a new uterus grafted on and have one at fifty.

Sometimes when she talked to these mid-age moms, they would say something oversolicitous like "You're so lucky to have all of this out of the way and have your freedom back." Well, fine. But freedom to do what? I mean, what exactly did that mean? Should she shoot drugs or join the roller derby? This is what she must figure out. What to do with this freedom. Unless, of course, she and Mickey were suddenly unemployed. One of the things she had done was take charge of their money. They had invested enough (actually just about everything — every possible extra cent) so that they should be okay for a long time. She must make a note to call Leonard after the holidays and check in with him.

That had been a really scary decision, turning all of their savings over to an outsider. "Investment adviser to the stars," Lina called him. Well, Lina was tight as a tick, and had a notoriously paranoid aging-actress phobia about her money, so if she trusted Leonard, then they probably could too. Almost all of their friends used Leonard. But it had still been a stretch. Annie thought that anyone named Leonard would have had such an unpleasant childhood that they would harbor a lot of deep-seated resentment toward other people. There was no nickname or anything. Imagine being a six-month-old named Leonard. Imagine a parent who would like that idea.

What they had done (at Annie's urging) was befriend Leonard and his wife, Bambi. A couple that would never have crossed their paths any other way. Annie felt that it was wise to keep the people who held their security as close as possible. Leonard had done very well for them. At least they had built something after all their years of struggling. They had their nest egg, no matter what. And at *ninety* that was a very good feeling. She grabbed her shampoo and jumped into the shower.

When Annie raced into the kitchen fifteen minutes later, she was greeted by a large bunch of roses with a note pinned to the vase: "Happy Birthday from Your Bundles of Joy." Portia lunged for her, slobbering and drooling, her breath as vile as ever, and Juanita handed her a cup of coffee. Toby and Ella, who were watching their uncle Jackie's latest morning tell-all show, jumped to their feet. "Yo, big momma. Happy happy," Toby said. Annie burst into tears.

"Hey, Mrs. W, why you cryin'? The kids sing good. It's a good day. You got a good day for to be born. Nobody ever forget your birthday. I gotta lousy birthday. June, uh, twenty-three. See, even I myself got a hard time remembering it. You born on the giving thanks day. Be cheerful."

Ella came over and hugged her. "What's the matter?"

Annie hugged her back. "Nothing. You just made me feel so happy. I was so touched. I mean you're up and everything."

Toby reached around and encircled both of them with his long, well-muscled arms. "See what they think, Ell? They have such small expectations for us that all we have to do is pull ourselves out of bed and it causes hysterical relief."

"No, no! You know what I mean. Don't give me a hard time. I've got zillions of things to do and I'm already running two hours late."

Toby squeezed harder, crushing them together. "We love you, Momma. We're going to make you laugh and forget your troubles."

Portia, feeling neglected, pushed her head between Toby's legs, slurping against his jeans. Toby let go.

"Mom, can't you do something about that hound? I'm serious, she really smells. I mean it's really revolting. No one but you will even touch her anymore. Maybe she's sick or something."

Ella went back to her breakfast. "Nice, Toby. Make Mom feel even worse on her birthday."

Annie took a sip of coffee and picked up her To Do list. "She's fine, Toby. She's just old. Her gums are bad and she has this sort of dog halitosis. It's not her fault. Is that how you'll treat me when I'm old and smell bad?"

Toby leaned over and kissed her cheek. "Only if you start butting your head against my calves and slobbering on my Calvins."

"Maybe one, but never both."

Annie opened the refrigerator and lifted out the turkey.

"By the way, why do you both think that I'm so upset about this birthday. I mean I'm only forty-five. You didn't act like that last summer when your father turned forty-five."

"It's different for men," Ella said and turned up the sound.

One of the blond women who ran daytime television was standing in an audience of housewives.

> "Today we are talking to women who are embarrassed by their husbands. Dorothy's husband licks his plate in restaurants. Martha's husband dances like a wild animal. Joan's mate is a terrible dresser. We'll hear from them and their partners after this."

"I am never getting married." Toby clicked the channel back. "I want to watch Uncle Jackie's new show."

> "In this morning's news, a high-ranking member of John Gotti's mob family described yesterday how his boss, 'Sammy the Bull' Gravano, chopped his brother-in-law into little pieces and buried him in the yard. The family dog dug up the hand, for which a funeral was held."

Annie patted the turkey dry. "Will you get that insanity off there, Toby."

"Wait a minute. This is interesting. Maybe that's why Portia smells so bad. Check the yard."

Ella grabbed the remote. "I was watching Sally Jessy."

An "expert" was on the stage talking to the embarrassed wives.

> "Feeling embarrassed by your husband's appearance or behavior only means that you are insecure about yourselves. He is no reflection on you, and so it shouldn't bother you. Give me some examples of what your mates do specifically that embarrasses you."

"He wears Hawaiian shirts, bright yellow shorts, and black socks, everywhere. To church even."

"He has a pair of fake glasses with eyeballs that roll around, and he makes faces at people at traffic lights."

"He wears smelly sweat socks and his baseball cap when we make love."

"Just the one thing, as I said before. He licks his plate in public."

Juanita moved closer. "This I've gotta hear. My men are always fontostic. No creeps like these guys."

"We know, Juanita." Annie winked at Ella.

"Well, ladies, I can only repeat that marriage is give and take, and I'm sure you all have many annoying habits of your own that these fellas put up with, so I can only suggest that in the bigger picture, these are not worth arguing about."

Annie poured more coffee. "Ella, if you marry someone who licks his plate in public, I will never tell you it's an ant on the big behind of marriage. We'll cut his tongue off."

Ella gave the remote back to Toby. "So unbelievably sicko. How desperate are women? Can you imagine marrying someone who thinks making faces at total strangers on the road is funny?"

"Maybe he's a billionaire scientist or something. No one's perfect."

"Well, you would certainly know all about that, Tob." Ella reached for a piece of toast.

Toby pulled the butter toward his side of the table, knocking her toast out of her hand. "Sorry."

He reached across for the jam, smashing the butter with his arm.

"Toby, your table manners are disgusting. You eat like a three-year-old."

It was the one-two punch. "Look who's talking. Are you now a dainty little woman of the world? Since when are your manners so great? I remember years of belching at the table." He was hurt. His face was red.

Ella stopped. "I'm sorry. I know I've been acting like a bitch lately."

"Lately!" Toby wiped the butter off his arm. "You've been a bitch since you were two years old."

"You weren't even alive when I was two years old."

"Others were."

"Oh, so now you're saying that Mom and Dad told you that I was a bitch when I was two years old?"

"Is it a bird? Is it a plane? No! It's . . . BABY BITCH!"

Annie finished cleaning the turkey. "Okay, enough. You want me to cry again? I would like to try for one family weekend that doesn't disintegrate into Jewish Eugene O'Neill, please. We won't be together again until Christmas. Mightn't we try?" Annie thought she saw Ella's face tighten.

"Okay. I'm sorry, Tob. Maybe I am just genetically FUBAR."

"Yeah, maybe." Toby smiled, always so willing to forgive her.

Juanita picked up their empty plates. "What is FUBAR? My English is fontostic, but I never hear this word 'FUBAR.'"

Ella smiled at her. They teased Juanita a lot, because Juanita was one of the world's greatest characters.

She had started working for them when Toby was still in diapers and she had just arrived from Puerto Rico. Juanita was as round as she was tall, which was maybe five feet with stilettos, and she had never married or had children. But she had an endless series of boyfriends (at least according to Juanita, they had never met any of them) all of whom, as Juanita described them, were handsomer than film stars and madly in love with her, and all of whom died tragically. Annie thought that Juanita had the most self-esteem of any woman she had ever known.

"FUBAR means Fucked Up Beyond All Repair. It's just a saying going around."

Juanita laughed, her gold front tooth gleaming in the brightly lit kitchen. "I like that one. FUBAR. That's cool."

Toby found what he was looking for. "Mom, it's Uncle Jackie's new show."

"Good morning. I'm Connie King. Welcome to *Under the Covers*. We have a most unusual story for you today. We will take you into the world of two men, whose faces and voices will be altered to protect their identities. These men are father and son-in-law. After years of marriage to his loving wife and the birth of three precious children, Dan came face to face with his own shocking truth. He had fallen madly, passionately in love with his wife's widowed father. In an emotional confession, he found to his amazement that his feelings were returned. Now all these two tortured men want to do is to live their lives together as a couple. How do they tell their devoted wife and daughter their terrible secret. Stay tuned for 'The Love That Cannot Be Denied.'"

Juanita made the sign of the cross. "FUBAR! These guys is absolutely FUBAR."

Everyone was laughing at this latest addition to the cultural dementia. The underworld of seemingly normal and respectable people who willingly appeared on television to display perversions and admit secrets, shames, and abuses, eagerly revealing bizarre personal behavior and pain to masses of faceless, nameless voyeurs.

Annie often wondered where it would all end. How much further could the tabloids go? She and Mickey were old enough to still be unnerved and astonished by what could now be seen and said on television. Their children, however, had never known the world before. One channel has *Sesame Street* and the one next to it has a live interview from the Clit Club, famous lesbian hangout on West Fourteenth Street. What worldview could these kids have? Not theirs, for sure.

"Hey, Mom, how about this as an idea. Dad and Grandpa — caught in a clinch, throwing themselves at your feet and asking for your blessing."

Annie handed the turkey to Juanita. "That is a truly hilarious idea, though I hate to admit that anything Jackie does could make me laugh, intentionally or otherwise. The man will stop at nothing. No wonder he's blown three marriages. Can you imagine living with a guy whose mind works like that? When he was five years old he used to sneak into my parents' room and hide under the bed trying to listen to them."

Ella looked up from the paper. "Listen to them doing what?"

"I have no idea. Most of the time he fell asleep before they went to bed, and my mother would hear him breathing, drag him out, and carry him downstairs. I can't imagine about the other times. All he probably heard was breathing and coughing."

Toby loved conversations like this. "I didn't know Jackie was getting another divorce. I liked Candy."

"*Sandy.* I did too. But she's moved on."

Annie opened the oven for Juanita. "Push it straight in, so it will cook evenly."

"Same as every year, Mrs. W. Always tell me the same thing."

Ella looked out the window. "Molly's coming." Molly O'Brian, their next-door neighbor, and two of her twins were climbing over the wall between their houses. It was only a few steps longer to enter the Wilders' the proper way but the O'Brians always came in over the fence. The O'Brians never did anything conventional.

Molly O'Brian and her husband, Billy, were the Wilders' best friends in Montecito, maybe in California. Molly was a Southern belle, a trust-fund baby, who had inherited a large amount of money shortly after marrying Billy. Billy was a lawyer of sorts.

Mickey called them "floaters." They bobbed around on the inflatable cushion their money provided, going where the current took them. They traveled and sailed, raised herbs and flowers and orchids, played golf and tennis, rode horses, and cooked lavish meals for other floaters like them. They had two sets of fraternal twins, one female and one male. One aged eight and one aged ten. They all looked alike. Molly and Billy looked alike and all of their twins looked like them. They all had Dutch-boy-cut straight blond hair, blue eyes, pug noses, and slender, lanky frames. Toby and Ella called the twins "The Pats" after the *Saturday Night Live* character of indeterminate sexual identity. They could never tell any of the twins apart. Annie couldn't wait for their puberty, when at least the girls would be definable.

The O'Brians were as different from the Wilders as couples get, which was why the friendship worked. They were in no way competitive. Annie thought the O'Brians were the most relaxing people that she had ever been around. Everything and anything was fine with them. The kids loved eavesdropping on Molly's visits because Molly, as she was likely to say apropos of nothing in particular, didn't "give a tinker's tit" what anyone thought of her.

If anything, Molly went out of her way to be as outrageous and provocative as possible. She was known for wandering around the one shopping street of Montecito dressed in her uniform of floor-length Victorian silk dresses, little straw hats with real flowers from her garden pinned to their brims, and no shoes. She always carried a wicker basket, as if she were a character from E. M. Forster, lost on her way to pick wildflowers on the moors.

She didn't so much raise the twins as gentle them; in her murmuring, giggling, seductive way, she just ever so slightly, constantly reset their course. Underneath it all, Annie knew there was a wrought-iron will, but it was well hidden. As for Molly and Billy, Mickey thought their weak spot was in the bedroom. "All that unearned money," Mickey said about Billy, "is hard on the *cojones*."

Toby waved and went to open the door for them. "She's wearing her nightgown, Mom. Why don't you ever do anything cool like that."

"I read *Great Expectations* too many times. Besides, your grandmother believed that anyone who wore a bathrobe or nightgown after nine o'clock in the morning was either insane or terminally ill. Those rules die hard."

Molly breezed in, her bare feet wet from the lawn, tiny pieces of grass sticking to her long bony toes.

"Happy birthday, my little redheaded friend. Happy turkey day to y'all. We have sweet potato pie, oyster pie, and wild greens and okra for your party. I have been up all night just cookin' my Southern heart out and the twins have been with me since four in the a.m. Perfect children. Little lambs from Lourdes."

Juanita waddled over and took the pie from Molly. "Why, Juanita, you darling thing, you've lost some weight. You're lookin' very Dolores Del Rio to me these days. Must be a new man in your life."

Juanita took the plates from The Pats, who were still in their pajamas, and set them down on the sink. "I know everybody famous, I don't know this Del Rio."

Molly poured herself some coffee, carrying it to the liquor cupboard and dropping a shot of Amaretto into it. "She was a true beauty. Mexican, I believe. She made several movies and then she married someone fabulously rich and retired."

Juanita flashed her golden smile. "That's me. I gotta new man. He have the body of the Schwarzenegger and the face of the Regis Philbin" (Juanita loved Regis and Kathie Lee). "He is fontostic. He ask me to marry with him every day. I tell him I have the curse but he won't take it for an answer."

Toby and Ella looked at her. "What curse?" Toby asked.

Molly sat down at the table, stirring her brew. The twins sat down on the floor with Portia, who expressed her joy at the company by drooling all over their pajamas. "Now, Juanita dear, you know what I told you. It's all in your *mind*. You can certainly marry this Regis Schwarzenegger if you choose."

Annie wiped pie crust off her hands. "Juanita, what is this curse business?"

Juanita handed her a fresh towel. "You know, Mrs. W. All my men, so crazy for me, they all die. They propose, I say, 'Give me some time, I have my Wilders to consider,' and while I'm deciding they are going to Jesus. One hit by a bus. One knifed on the subway. The last one, the most perfect, with the body of Mr. Universe and the face of Billy Crystal" (Juanita adored Billy Crystal); "he eat some bad cheese, he puke for a week. He die. It's a curse. My cousin Lupe is a witch. She told me, 'Never marry with anyone. You have the curse.' But the guys go crazy for me. Mrs. O'Brian told me it's all in my mind. So I am trying again."

Annie looked at Ella and rolled her eyes. They had never believed any of Juanita's stories of torrid romance with her bigger-than-life swains, but for Molly to be having these little over-the-fence chats with Juanita about her love life seemed inappropriate to Annie, and somehow not very nice.

"Juanita, I think it would be fine for you to invite your friend over for pie and coffee tonight. It's high time we meet one of your beaus. We will be glad to tell him that you are the least cursed person we know. Right, Molly?"

Molly sipped her brew. "Absolutely." Molly always knew when to quit. It was one of her strengths.

"Okay. Now, Ella, I need you to set the table. Use the lace place mats and those orange and green napkins and the crystal glasses. Toby, I need you to pick up the fresh shrimp at Mr. Lee's and get some whipping cream and vanilla. Oh, and more wood for the fire. Juanita, will you pick some roses for Mrs. Wilski's room, and make sure there are sheets on the beds in the guest room and check the bathrooms, too. I don't think anyone but Pop and Ida Mae are staying over, but let's be prepared. Ella, if Uncle Martin and Loretta stay, you and Toby will have to share your room."

"Great."

"Don't turn teenage on me. We're talking about *one* night. Now everyone move."

The twins jumped up. "Can we go with Toby, Momma?"

"Fine with me. Ask him."

Toby was caught off guard. "In their pajamas?"

The Pats shrugged. "Fine with us."

Toby laughed. He had no idea if they were the girls, the boys, or one of each. Having spent his entire life as the youngest, he rather enjoyed having younger kids around. "Okay, let's boogie."

Molly blew kisses. "Seat belts, sweetiekins."

Annie took a deep breath. Quiet. She loved a chat in a quiet kitchen. She pulled a bag of green beans out of the refrigerator and dumped them into a bowl. "I'm snapping, now talk to me."

Molly lit a cigarette and put her feet up on a chair.

Annie smelled the smoke and turned around. "I thought you quit."

"My friend Samantha's here. I'm only smoking because she is."

"Well, I'm glad Samantha isn't murdering someone."

"Very funny. See what you did? You made me defensive. I hate that. I am *never* defensive." Molly put the cigarette in her mouth and went back to respike her coffee.

"Where's Detective Jerico?"

"He's driving my father and his mother up from L.A. where they have been painting the town red."

Molly plopped back down and crossed her grass-stained toes, making a chaise out of the two chairs. "Together?"

"Molly, they've known one another for almost forty years. They buried spouses together. They're pals. They still live in the same building."

"Wouldn't that be romantic, if they got married?"

"No. It would be the worst of both worlds."

"What do you mean? I thought you liked Ida Mae. She's almost been a second mother to y'all. I think she's a hoot."

"I do like Ida Mae. I don't know what I meant. The perversity of the idea caught me off guard. I've never thought of them that way."

Molly giggled. "What way are we talking about? Biblical? I think it's darling. She could chase him around naked save for her black leather jacket. I see a bit of dominatrix in Ida Mae. Though actually I wouldn't be surprised if she was gay."

Annie brought the bowl over and sat down next to Molly. "You think everyone is gay."

"Not everyone. Just *most* everyone. I am, I'm more and more convinced."

Annie laughed. "Is this new? This concept I haven't heard from you before."

Molly sipped her coffee. "Samantha triggered it. I do lust after Samantha."

"You do?" Annie was trying to act blasé and sophisticated.

"Billy and I both do. It's very sensual having her there. It sort of renews our sexual tension. She's quite powerful. She's started up this cult in New Orleans. She calls herself the new Delphic oracle. She has this really upscale following. She's re-created the whole Greek ideal of the old woman as high priestess, people journeying from thousands of miles to hear her wisdom. She has tapes and books now. She's going to make a fortune."

"Is Samantha an old Greek woman?"

"Oh, Annie. You are soooo bad. Of course not. She's a ripe Louisiana beauty. She was runner-up to Miss Baton Rouge in the Miss Louisiana pageant some years back. That's what makes it so great. She embodies the spirit and the ideas, but she looks magnificent."

"Is she gay?"

"She's beyond all that. She's on a higher plane. But she sure triggers some powerful energy. She gets my hormones just pumping to beat the band."

Annie snapped on. The conversation was drawing her forward, enticing her and making her nervous. "Doesn't it scare you a little, having someone like that in your house turning on your husband?"

Molly inhaled deeply. She loved to get Annie going like this. "Unh-uh. I find it very refreshing. I mean we have been married *so* long. It does get a tiny ho hum, don't you think? I mean, most of the porno is so awful. If they would just stop trying to be 'filmmakers' or, worse yet, comedy writers and just pack the things with lots of nasty sex. But they insist on all of these really inane story lines with all those cokeheaded lamebrains trying to act, I get so bored. By the time they get to any sex, I'm usually asleep. And Hollywood's eros is truly pathetic. Every sex scene in every R movie involves fucking on hard surfaces. The gentleman is always knocking the lady back onto a kitchen table or slamming her up against a wall, usually just outside her very comfortable bedroom. It's just so silly. I mean couches are sexy, but kitchen tables? tile floors? I can't get turned on anywhere anymore. Billy and I have plumb run out of fantasies. So having Samantha around for a few days here and there is very enlivening."

Annie looked concerned. "But what if it got out of hand. I mean, what if something actually happened?"

"Oh, Annie-Fannie, you are so guileless for a cynic. How do y'all know that it hasn't 'got out of hand,' as you call it. What's so bad if it did?"

"It threatens your bond with Billy."

Molly wiggled grass off her toes. "You have this idea of life as some sort of *Saturday Evening Post* cover, but it's not like that."

Annie laughed. "Yeah, you're right about that. I am most certainly not a woman of the world. I realized this morning that I have now been married longer than my entire life up until the time I got married. And I've been a mother almost the same. So if you figure that the first five years you're alive are sort of a throwaway, my whole conscious life has been lived in basically a very large shell."

"Maybe what y'all needs, lovey, is a nice fat snail."

Annie blushed. "You are so wicked. If Mickey could hear this he would pass out."

Molly reached into the bowl and pulled out a handful of beans. "Don't be so sure, darlin'. We always think we know our guys so well, and the fact is we mostly don't really know what goes on inside their little beanies any more than they know what's going on inside ours."

They sat quietly, listening to the sounds of beans snapping.

"Did you ever see that excerpt from Hurley Gurley Brown's last book, *Creative Places to Make Love*?"

Annie nodded. "I read half of it. I stopped somewhere after 'In the locker room of the New York Jets' and 'On the Cyclone roller coaster at Coney Island.' Somehow I couldn't relate."

Molly giggled. "I liked in Edgar Allan Poe's bed at the University of Virginia and on the chairlift at Vail."

Annie dumped all the snapped beans back into the bowl and carried it over to the sink. "Not only have I never made love in any place remotely associated with her list, including a pool table, a sauna, or in a marble bathtub without water, but I've never even wanted to."

Molly finished off her coffee. "Well you sure inhaled the list for someone so uninterested."

Annie ran water over the beans. "Yes, ma'am. You're right about that. Another middle-aged victim of the marital muggies."

Molly yawned, stretching her arms up over her head, purring like one of her kittens. "Tell the truth, have you really only slept with Mickey in your entire life?"

Annie turned off the water and faced her, leaning back against the sink. "Yes. I mean I had a few heavy petting sessions with some other boys, but I always had this thing about belonging to Mickey. Pretty dumb, huh? How about you? You've been married almost as long as I have and you're six years younger."

"Yes, but I was a little slut. The school whore. I married Billy because there was no one left to fuck in New Orleans. Lucky for me it was way before the Age of Diseases, or I'd have 'em all."

"Oh," Annie said, her voice small and wistful.

A car pulled into the driveway. Annie turned and looked out the window. "Well, Mickey and The Love Connection are here." She looked at her watch. Nine-thirty. She was okay. Maybe she had time to sneak off for a walk. There were too many things still floating in her mind.

Molly stood up. "I've got to get some sleep. Billy's entire family is coming in and Samantha's invited some of her Santa Barbara converts. It's going to be a nightmare."

Mickey came in followed by his mother and Annie's father. Ida Mae had on a blond wig and black leather jodhpurs. Her father was wearing his uniform, carefully waxed goatee, tweed beret and jacket, blue shirt, and polka-dot bow tie. She turned to catch Molly's eye, but she had fled. Molly had her own agenda about socializing. When she wasn't in the mood, she felt no obligation to perform.

"Was that Molly running away in her nightgown?" Mickey leaned over and kissed her cheek.

"She's been up all night."

"Then we won't take it personally."

Ida Mae wrapped her arms around Annie, her leather squeaking against Annie's sweatshirt. "Give an old broad a hug, you little doll, you! Mick, she looks good! All this capitalism agrees with her." Ida

Mae let Annie go, settling into her favorite position, her hands planted low on her high round hips. "Look at this kitchen. I forgot how big this kitchen was. Look at this, Joe, it's bigger than my apartment. People sleeping in doggie bags and others living in mansions. Ain't life a pisser."

Mickey put their suitcases down and poured some coffee. He looked tired, Annie thought. These two could wear out Superman.

"Ma, this is hardly a mansion. Will you give the Socialist Party a day off. Most Jewish mothers would be beside themselves with joy."

"Well there is not now nor has there ever been a 'most' attached to your mother, right, Joe?"

Annie's father came up beside her. He never touched her first. She put her arms around him and kissed his cheek. He looked smaller to her. Funny, she thought, how when you've been away from your kids they always look bigger than you remember them, and your parents always look smaller.

"Good to see you, Annie dear. So nice of you to have us." Annie flinched. She had forgotten the stiffness. The theater formality. Her father was one of those men who escorted people like Kitty Carlisle Hart to benefits, always charming and erudite, having the smart bon mots, knowing all the latest gossip, familiar with the wine list at the newest chic bistro. All of it seemed increasingly superficial to Annie. Her brother, who was in many ways very much like her father, despised his affectations even more than she did — a dark mirror of himself, perhaps.

Mickey put his arm around her as if sensing her discomfort. "Guess what I've gotten you for your birthday."

"A Shetland pony."

Ida Mae patted her wig. "See, Joe. They come to La-La Land and they become animal abusers."

"That's a joke, Ida. I can't guess. Why are you telling me now, anyway?"

"You know how I am. I can't ever wait. Besides, you have to go choose it. Tomorrow or this weekend if you want."

"Choose it?"

"One of Ivy Clare's pots. I was at Stan Stein's last week and he had a fabulous one and I called her and arranged it. You just have to go up to her house in Ojai and pick the one you want."

Annie's eyes filled. "Oh, Mickey, that is the best present! I love her work!" She hugged him, resting her head against his shoulder.

Ida Mae picked up her suitcase. "Come on, Joe, let's unpack. Leave the newlyweds alone. All these years, they're still like a couple of teenagers. We should have been so lucky."

Mickey let Annie go. "Let me carry those."

Joseph Miller waved him away. "No, no, my boy. We're not that old yet. We'll just freshen up a bit."

They watched them struggling up the stairs with their cases. "Good idea." Annie put her head back on Mickey's shoulder.

Mickey picked up his coffee. "They slept the whole way up. I thought, this is like reverse childhood. Remember when we were kids, falling asleep in the back of their cars when they drove us home? Now *they're* asleep in the backseat and I'm driving *them* home. Pretty weird feeling. How do you like the wig?"

"She looks like The Little Old Wine Maker."

They laughed together.

"I missed you." Mickey smiled at her.

"I missed you, too."

"Where are the kids?"

"Toby's doing errands and Ella's in the dining room setting the table. Or at least that's where she's supposed to be. Would you mind if I went for a walk to the village? I want to pick up a couple of things I forgot to tell Toby about, and I could use the air."

"Go on. I'll make the stuffing. See? I didn't forget my assigned task."

"Great. I taped the recipe to the refrigerator. Everything you need is on the chopping block. I'll be back in half an hour."

"Jackie said he'll be here around five."

"I told Martin and Loretta five-thirty. So we're in good shape."

"Considering," Mickey sighed.

"There you go with the sighing again! You're starting to sound like my aunt Bessie. What's up?"

"Nothing. Actor's angst. I'm fine."

"Considering." Annie kissed him again and picked up her list.

"Hey, Mick. I love my present."

"You deserve it, Spots." He watched her march down the driveway with her springing, graceful stride.

CHAPTER II

MICKEY PICKED UP as many dishes and cups as he could carry and took them to the sink. Where the hell was Juanita? The stuffing he would do; the dishes, no way. He found the recipe on the fridge, all typed out in Annie's precise prose. Step by step, so that even he couldn't mess it up.

Everything was either on the sink or in the refrigerator with little labels, so his usual fridge blindness could not be used as an excuse. He laughed. All the effort preparing the path for him, she could have made it herself.

He put the margarine in the micro to melt and ran cold water over the celery. He opened the bags of corn bread crumbs and poured them into a large plastic bowl. He was tired.

All he really wanted to do was go upstairs, take a long hot shower, and crash for a couple of hours. He could never have imagined how exhausting it was working on a weekly series. It made him feel edgy and disconnected from his family when he came home. It took him a full day to reconnect, and then it was time to turn around and go back down. There was always a script to memorize, producers to talk to, other egos to maneuver around, and of course the knowledge, never more than a millimeter away from consciousness, that every Monday he had to get it all the way up and keep the fucking thing hard all week.

He took it out on Annie, but it wasn't her fault. He just felt lonely and so damn tired. Being tired scared him the most. Who said that acting was 10 percent talent and 90 percent stamina. Olivier? Yeah. Annie teased him about all his actor indulgences. His nutritionist, his trainer, his health and exercise regimen.

Didn't she know that he would like nothing better than to kick back with a bottle of tequila and a couple of Big Macs and watch football for a year or two? He couldn't. More and more he felt the years catching up. Lines were harder to learn and by the end of the shooting day he was dragging his ass. He needed all the props he could find.

Was he complaining? Certainly sounded that way. Where was the guy falling on his knees before the Nielsen god, thanking him for his good fortune. Where was the dude holding forth with Mary Hart: "I am one of the happiest men on earth. This series is the most fabulous surprise an actor could have."

What had Jackie told him about Mary Hart? Some woman had called his office wanting to be on one of his shows because the sound of Mary Hart's voice had triggered her epileptic seizures. Jackie told the woman it wasn't Hart's voice, it was her *clothes*. They were the true offenders.

Jackie was right. That woman wore some weird shit. Lots of sweaters with sequined animals and birds and things knitted into them. Furry tops, big jeweled ear things, and heavy on shiny royal blue and pink. Not at all like Annie. Annie had fabulous taste. None of the actresses he knew had taste worth shit. If someone dressed them for a part, they looked good. But off-camera, forget about it.

Most of them had no real identity off-camera, so how could they dress a person they didn't know? Without their lines to say and people running around pampering them and creating their fairy tales, they were like lost souls in one of those made-for-cable movie scripts he was always getting. The truth was, he didn't much like actors. He didn't have anything to talk to them about.

What did that mean? Mickey chopped the celery and mixed it with the onions. Tears sprung from his eyes, the onions stinging his senses. He sneezed, picking up a towel and holding it over his face. No wonder Annie always gave him the stuffing to do. Annie could hardly even look at an onion without all hell breaking loose. All that redheaded fragility. Watering eyes, red twitching nose, turning her pretty face into Roger Rabbit.

He had been thinking about being an actor a lot lately. Maybe it was burnout, and potential bad news hanging over the set was sure as hell no help. Success was the biggest fucking booster rocket Mickey had ever ridden. God, how sweet that was, having *War Zone* become a hit! All of his career, though he had never said it out loud, not even to Annie, he had wanted just once to have something go through the roof. Everything he had done had been "a qualified success." Year after year he felt like Sisyphus. Well, maybe that was too dramatic, more like a backpacker who kept hitting plateaus but still could see the top of the mountain.

All of a sudden. Pow. The fucking Matterhorn. He was famous. In a month, he was a household word. The best and worst of America. He had his fame fix, and it had been sensational, far beyond his dreams, because by the time it came he was grounded in his life and his family. He had already let the dream drift off. He had traded the hunger, the bitter knot of frustrated energy, the envy of the others who had already been struck by the luck laser, for a great family life and a good night's sleep. So when the beam hit him, he did not need it to justify his life. Or did he?

Mickey took the softened margarine from the micro and put it in a frying pan. He added the onions and celery and stirred with one of Annie's special slotted spoons.

Maybe that was all just self-rationalization. Who the fuck knows what would have happened to him, to *them,* if *War Zone* hadn't dropped down from the show biz angels. Where would he be now? Not sitting in the lap of luxury in the "in" town of choice. He had made more money in the last five years than in all of the years of his career before that. Every hiatus, he pushed the bag doing movies and guest spots. He never said no. And Annie, bless her heart, never said no either.

Did that make him angry? Sometimes he felt like the prizefighter with the greedy trainer, like Tyson and King. Annie indulged him, pampered and comforted him before every match. "Go out and kill 'em, tiger." The more he worked, the more she socked away, trotting the checks and residuals over to Leonard like a campfire girl, bringing her bead strands in for her badges.

Okay, that was probably unfair. He had loved every single second.

He loved the interviews and the attention. All of a sudden what he thought about AIDS, the future of the cinema, abortion rights, was of interest to reporters and the public. Unfuckingbelievable! It was all such a joke. I mean, *actors'* opinions? Who were they to express opinions on health issues or world events. Was the public really that backward? He had heard actors who could barely form sentences and to his knowledge never read anything but *Variety* sound off on the famine in Somalia and free speech in China. It was all too ridiculous for words. But there he was, mouthing off with the rest of them.

Mickey looked at Annie's recipe. She had the spices all lined up by the stove. *Chopped parsley.* Shit. He had forgotten. He turned down the heat and went back to the refrigerator. The parsley was right in front, with a little stickem that said "Don't forget the parsley" and a cute little Annie face penned in. Okay, so sue him, he always forgot the parsley. It still made him mad, being treated like the "slow" child. Maybe what made him mad was someone knowing him that well. There was no place to get a break anymore. All week he was under one kind of microscope and all weekend he was under another.

This heightened attention to his moods, tone of voice, and word choice had gotten worse and worse since the kids had gone. She had nothing else to pull her attention and now, since she wasn't writing anymore, he was on first, second, and third.

This was harsh. He felt ashamed of himself. All those years that he was never working full time, he had acted like a spoiled brat. He had wanted her with him, needed her continual support, reinforcement, and companionship. He never let her alone. It was really amazing that she had managed to raise those kids, build a career all by herself (he had certainly not helped), and given so much time and energy to his needs. He knew that he drove her nuts when he was home like that. He had even pushed his way into her roles. By writing stories and making her edit them! (Where was that story about the actor he had written? Gotta give that to Stan Stein. Could be a *Movie of the Week* with a little work.) He had even started to cook and pushed her out of her own kitchen. He would infiltrate her domain, cut her off from her friends, manipulating her into canceling dates if he was home ("Mickey's not working, can we have lunch some other time?"). He would entice her with matinees, tap lessons, anything that kept her attention on him. Then the minute he had a gig, he deserted her and she had to restart her own life all over again.

Okay. He was a selfish prick. But that was then. This was now.

Things had changed, *they* had changed. He had changed. Must he completely ignore his needs because of how selfless she had been ten years ago? She was not exactly suffering from her investment in her "boxer." She enjoyed the perks as much as he did. So why should he feel so guilty about wanting a little time alone?

Mickey tossed the chopped parsley into the onions and celery and sprinkled more salt and sage in the pan. He turned off the heat and put more margarine in the micro. He sliced a lemon and squeezed it into a small bowl, and picked out the pits. The buzzer on the micro beeped. He took out the margarine and put it next to the chicken broth that Annie had already prepared. He pressed the buttons and stood watching as if it were a television screen.

He was really beat. Of course all of this discontent might evaporate if they were canceled. He had already asked Leonard, who served as much as his agent these days as his business manager, to start putting the feelers out, and at least Stan Stein still loved him. Stan was working on three new projects with the networks, so he might strike gold twice. Then again, even at a much loftier level, it was back to the hustle and the uncertainty of the actor without a day job. He had seen more than his fill of Benzes and Beemers at the unemployment office parking lot.

Anxiety crept up his spine, starting with a tingle and moving up into his stomach. He felt dizzy, the smells of the turkey and the buttery onions sickening him. The panic swelled, crawling out of his stomach and up into his chest. It was hard to get his breath.

The micro beeped. He pulled out the chicken soup and placed it neatly beside the patiently waiting margarine and lemon juice. He wanted to bolt, to fling open the kitchen door and tear off into the wind. To stretch out and breathe. *Just finish the fucking stuffing.* He poured the broth over the crumbs, stirring with the special spoon.

He stopped pouring and stirred, the motion calming him. He added the margarine, watching the corn bread turn soft and shrink under the liquid. He felt sad for the corn bread, losing its crustiness like that. Was *that* where he was? Projecting onto bread crumbs?

He really was tired. He added the lemon juice and tasted. Good. A little more salt. No oysters this year. Probably some horrible health scare about smoked oysters. Pretty soon there would be nothing left to eat. Or at least nothing left that anyone wanted to eat. It was already pretty close. That's why he loved Thanksgiving so much. No one would ever give up Thanksgiving. Well, there were some. His costar, for example. They were having some macrobiotic Thanksgiving. He couldn't imagine such a pretentious, self-righteous crock of turkey shit. They would all probably die from some rare cancer caused by fava-bean sprouts.

He had practically starved himself all week getting ready for his favorite holiday meal. He would have it all. Skin and dark meat and sweet potato pie and three slabs of stuffing and all the wine he could swallow. They had Friday off, a whole extra day off, a day for sleeping and eating leftovers.

Why did Thanksgiving leftovers seem so much more appealing than all the trendy restaurant food? What was that restaurant he and Annie had gone to when the waitress was describing the pasta special — "A homemade spinach pasta with a sauce of raisins, tomatoes, Gorgonzola cheese, and pignoli nuts" — and her whole body had shuddered involuntarily?

He knew. He was getting old. He didn't know three quarters of the new rock groups. Even old mainstream *People* magazine's cover story of the 50 Most Beautiful People — a third of them he had never even heard of and another third he thought were ugly. All he wanted was something tasty and comprehensible. A long way from Mercutio and *Waiting for Godot,* pal. No more cumin-crusted, rare, duck breasts and braised skate for Mick the Stick.

He was through. He covered the stuffing with plastic wrap and put it back in the refrigerator. He poured a glass of water and sat down for a moment. He should work out, but he was just so damn tired. He reached for one of Toby's abandoned bagels and tore off a piece. He hated the way his kids wasted food. He was his mother's son, after all.

How had his life turned into such a Grand Guignol? He had always avoided any subtext. But nothing was the same anymore.

That is why he needed some time to think. Even if *War Zone* got axed, he would still try to take some time. He had to be alone to figure everything out.

If the weekend went well, he would try to talk to Annie before he left.

He stood up, feeling guilty about leaving the mess, and went to Annie's kitchen desk. He pulled out one of her colored markers and wrote a note: "Stuffing is in fridge. Love you."

He did love her, didn't he? How much of their relationship was just habit, knee-jerk reactions to a lifetime of endearments? He could no longer even be sure of that.

By the time Annie returned from her walk, the family was in various stages of pre-Thanksgiving snacking. One of Jackie's shows was on in the background. The turkey aroma was starting to fill the kitchen.

"Where's Juanita?" Annie put down her packages and joined them.

Toby looked up from the *New York Times*. "She took Portia for a walk."

"Give me a break. Juanita has never taken Portia or anything else for a walk."

"That's what she said. Maybe she's meeting some dude."

"This is really peculiar. I need her to baste."

Mickey turned up the volume. "I'm trying to hear this!"

> "And how did you feel, Mrs. Morgan, when your son dropped out of medical school to become a Joan Rivers impersonator?"

Annie reached across for one of Mickey's strawberries. "'Why, I felt great! I mean, lots of boys can go to med school, but how many can impersonate Joan Rivers?' Mickey turn that off. I cannot take one more morning of it."

Ella pushed her bowl away and Annie thought she saw tears in her eyes. "Why is it so awful if someone decides to be a Joan Rivers impersonator instead of a doctor. All we do is judge, judge, judge!

"I mean there is just so much pressure. You graduate from college and for like about ten minutes you get a break, people are proud of you; I mean you made it. You didn't end up a crack addict or frying spuds at McDonald's, and then, bang, it starts all over again! What are you going to do? Who are you going to be? You guys make fun of these poor people because you've done well. You've got your careers and your nice house and everything. Well, it's not so easy for us. It's awful."

Annie let her eyes slide ever so slightly toward Mickey. Parental warning light. Approaching unmapped minefield. That is the way family fights worked. During the years of adolescence, parenting was all about learning the minefields, trying to anticipate the ones that they always hit too late, after they had stomped a big clumsy boot down without thinking. In dealing with growing children there were no scouts running ahead to warn them, no helicopter patrol calling in, "Minefield straight ahead, avoid conversations concerning achievement, circle around until safe ground is found."

The rules of how to conduct oneself in these minefields were the same as in any battleground. Stay quiet, move cautiously, poke around with your bayonet before entering suspicious terrain. If all efforts fail and you have stepped onto a mine, stay still, don't panic or overreact, wait for help. They now had years of experience and were seasoned Purple Heart recipients. They waited.

Ella wiped her eyes. "I've decided not to take the LSATs. I don't want to go to law school. I don't want to be a lawyer."

Mickey risked a step. "Any particular reason?"

"I don't know. I just decided that most of the really revolting people in politics and in the news are lawyers. It's like criminal law was the only law that I was ever interested in, but after my undergrad classes, when we'd go to Center Street and sit in on trials . . . Well, I could *never* be a public defender, because most of those defendants were total scumbags. I wouldn't want to be physically near those creeps, let alone get them off for things you just knew they were guilty of, and I'm too young to work for the D.A.!

"I mean, you're supposed to begin innocent and believing in the underdog and then grow cynical and switch over, otherwise it's like starting out as a Republican! Really depressing. Then I started thinking about famous lawyers like Alan Dershowitz, Johnnie Cochran, Marcia Clark. I mean everyone's not so together, and they've been ripped apart by the press."

Annie poked her bayonet around. "What about Sandra Day O'Connor?"

"Oh, pa-leeze. I mean imagine spending the next thirty years sitting between David Souter and Clarence Thomas!"

Toby, who was not a parent and therefore not privy to the rules of the minefield, jumped in. "Only *my* sister could leap from not even having taken the law school *entrance* exam to worrying about who she wants to sit next to on the Supreme Court."

Ella stood up. "I knew none of you would understand. I guess I'm a failure in your eyes, but I don't want to do it. I'm working. I'm paying my rent, so it's really none of your business, anyway."

Mickey got up and moved to her, encircling her in his arms. She tensed, resisting her vulnerability, a new recruit trying to stand alone and fight her own battles. "Hey, baby. It's okay. We're not the enemy. It was your idea to go to law school, remember. You're talking to an *actor* for chrissakes. Your mother never even graduated college. She was already pregnant with you when she was your age. Who's judging? This is an inside job, princess. Really."

Ella relaxed against his chest. A moment's rest. A tiny girl's reprieve from the life of a newly grown-up woman. Annie watched them, thinking that one advantage of being a woman was that even when they grew older, such moments were still allowed them. Men never got the same. She reached out and covered Toby's hand with hers. Her entire hand barely covered his palm. She could feel the pressure of the loss pushing against her heart. *Remember the game,*

Toby. You'd hold your hand up against mine to see if you'd grown. Look at it now, baby boy.

Ella stiffened again, almost pushing her father away. Mickey and Annie looked at one another. This was new behavior.

"Hey, since when does my daughter turn down a hug from Detective Jerico, every woman's best friend?"

"I'm just not feeling very cuddly right now. I'm sorry, you guys, I'm overreacting. I guess I didn't know all of that was inside. I thought I was okay about it. I was going to talk to you later."

Ella reached behind her chair and picked up her jacket. "I think I'll go for a walk on the beach."

Annie watched her. "Honey, your nose is running."

Ella sniffled, thrusting her hand into her pocket for a Kleenex. She pulled the Kleenex out and blew her nose. Something dropped onto her yogurt.

Toby grabbed it. "What have we here?" He was dangling something. Something turquoise.

Ella's hand shot out and took hold. They tugged the tiny turquoise thing back and forth, like taffy pullers on the boardwalk.

"Give it to me, Toby!"

Toby stood up, towering over Ella, and held the nylon alien high over his head. "So this is what happens to young single women living on their own in New York City. They take to tarty undergarments carried in their pockets in case of an unsafe sex opportunity — say, on the beach."

Ella changed tactics. She sat back down and ignored him. Annie and Mickey, having completely lost their sense of direction and fearing shrapnel all around, said nothing.

"Never mind. Have your little joke. They're not mine anyway and I don't have to justify myself to you."

Toby tossed them back onto the table, losing his edge. "Do you often find strange unclaimed pairs of panties in your jacket pockets or is this a unique occurrence?"

Ella kept her head down. She blew her nose again. "Just shut up, Toby."

"Why are you acting so weird?" Toby touched her arm. "Ella, what's the big deal. It was just funny to have them fall on your yogurt. Who's are they?"

"I don't know. I found them."

Annie moved, forgetting to test with her bayonet. "You *found* them?! You mean that you picked up a total stranger's underwear that could have been on anybody, doing God only knows what while wearing them, and put them in your *pocket?* Ella! You're the girl who washes her hands when she gets out of a taxicab. What's with you?"

"What's with *me!*" Ella jumped up. "They were on the floor of *your* car. I was just trying to . . . to . . ."

Boom.

Annie inhaled. Mickey was staring at the television. Toby's face looked funny, as if he might cry, too.

Annie stood up and gently lifted the panties from the table.

"They're mine," she said softly. "Part of my midlife crisis. They must have fallen out of the bag."

Ella watched her, searching for the truth. "Really?"

Annie carried them over to the laundry room and tossed them into the hamper. "Sure. Time to loosen up my image. I've never had frilly underwear and now that your father's a sex symbol — well, what the hell. I splurged."

Ella was bolder now. Her father had glued himself to the set, avoiding all of them.

"Splurged? They weren't even silk."

"I bought several expensive ones and a few fun ones. What is this, night court?"

"Where were the tags?" Ella asked, her voice as light as rain.

"That," Annie said, turning her back and heading for the stairs, "is none of your business."

Ella watched her mother go. Her jaunty little steps bouncing her along. Her mother had never talked to her like that, in that cocky way before. Her father had completely flaked out, hunching over the TV with intensely phony interest, as if he were watching a space launch or waiting to see if he'd won an Emmy or something.

Was her mother lying? Her mother never lied. Her head hurt. She was so disappointed in herself. She had wanted to come home really together and mature and show them how well she was doing on her own. Now she had made a total fool out of herself and in addition, acted out some anger at her mother and maybe destroyed her marriage.

Ella reached for the door.

Toby, who was still standing by the table looking helpless and confused, followed her. "Where are you going?"

"The beach."

"I'm going with you."

They strode out of the house, leaving their father alone.

When Mickey opened the door to their room, Annie was sitting in her favorite, muslin-covered chair by the window, her hands folded demurely in her lap, her legs crossed neatly at the ankles, like an employment agency applicant for the secretarial pool. The early noontime light streaked in through the shutter, crisscrossing her face and haloing her hair.

He was surprised to see her, though he didn't know why. She had, after all, left the kitchen and gone upstairs. Where did he think she had been?

"I thought you went out," he said, as if apologizing for not seeking her sooner.

She shook her head as if not ready to be wooed from her reverie.

He stripped off his sweats, kicking his Top-Siders into the closet. "God, I'm dead. I need to sleep for a while or I'll be a zombie during my favorite dinner of the year."

"No problem. Everything's under control." Annie tried a smile. Her mouth wasn't working right.

Mickey kicked his shorts onto his sweats and grabbed his robe from the closet. "Dammit. No matter how many times I tell Juanita to leave the fucking robe in the bathroom, she keeps putting it back in my closet. All my sweaters are getting mildewed."

"Mickey, she doesn't put a *damp* robe back in your closet, she washes and dries it and puts it away. You've been gone for four days. Why should I look at a moldy robe hanging over the shower for four days?" She sighed.

"Now who's turning into Aunt Bessie." He paused. "You okay?"

"You okay?" was the perfect family question. It was asked endlessly by wives of husbands, husbands of wives, parents of children, and children of parents. It held its own answer. It was the ultimate throwaway line in the complex internal wiring of the individual family, each of which operated, like DNA, in a singular and unique system; all polymorphous and nonreplicable. Everyone knew in a microsecond when someone was *not okay.* They knew. Whether or not they acknowledged it with the "You okay?" query, they knew. They always knew.

The answer to the question was most usually a lie. "I'm fine." Followed by a slightly relieved "Are you sure?" (the likelihood being that the not-okay feeling had been caused by them), followed by "Yes, I'm sure."

"Want to talk about it?"

Annie looked across at him. His robe was open and she could see his penis and the inside of his thighs. She thought about dropping down in front of him and sucking him off. She had always found his genitals peeking out of a half-open robe wonderfully erotic. Something about the teasing of it, the vulnerability and the power.

She rarely acted on her impulses anymore. Somehow she thought it would shock him. Their sex life had settled into an almost paternal form. Cozy and safe rather than lusty and dangerous. It had gotten, Annie thought, watching him, too cuddly. They picked one another's fleas like gorilla mates in the sunshine. It was almost as if too much passion between them was not quite right for a husband and wife of so many years. It seemed to threaten some part of their security with one another. How can my sweet, freckled little wifey suddenly fall on her knees and shove my cock down her throat? *Fuck me, baby. Tear me apart.* They had become more friends, pals, even adversarial comrades, than passionate sweethearts. They had grown too tender to inflict that kind of lechery on one another.

She had never thought of it that way before. Mickey saw her looking at him and tied his robe.

"How about that number of Ella's?" He avoided her eyes.

My looking at him like that disturbs him. It doesn't turn him on. Annie curled her feet under her.

"I'm very worried about her, but I can't push. I just hope she'll open up to me before she goes back Sunday."

Mickey nodded. "Don't worry, try to remember what twenty-two was like. She's got to go through all of this stuff. I never wanted her to go to law school in the first place, for many of the same reasons she described."

"I'm still hoping she'll come out here for a while and work in production. I think she'd be a fantastic P.A. You could help her."

"Sure, but you know how she feels about Hollywood. I'll try to talk to her about New York. There's a lot of stuff shooting back East now."

Mickey turned and headed for the bathroom.

"Mickey?"

"Yeah?"

"Are you having an affair?"

He whirled around, his robe opening again, his genitals showing their own outrage at the insinuation.

"Where did this come from?"

"Turquoise underwear in the Dannon's."

"I thought they were yours."

"Get serious. What did you want me to say? 'Gee, no, kids, ask your FATHER?'"

"I haven't even been here. I haven't used your car since last week!"

"The damn thing didn't have a date on it."

"Do you think that I would do that? In the back of your *car*? Is that what you think of me?"

She felt like a child. A naughty child. "No."

"Annie, I have never seen the fucking thing before in my life."

He turned and walked purposefully into the bathroom.

Annie didn't move. The light had shifted and she closed her eyes, feeling the warmth on her face. "You didn't answer my question," she said to no one in particular.

CHAPTER III

ELLA SAT ON THE ROCKS below the Santa Barbara Swim Club watching Toby chase one of the O'Brians' golden retrievers down the beach. Was it Sweet Pea or Snap Dragon? She could never tell. But if she couldn't even tell their kids apart, how could she be expected to know the dogs. The tide was coming in. Toby had better hurry or they'd both drown.

The O'Brians were so casual about stuff like that, leaving gates open and things. The total opposite of her family. In many ways she wished her family was more like the O'Brians, they were so cool. They smoked and turned on and drank whenever they felt like it and ate ham and donuts. They didn't seem to take anything really seriously. And their kids just got away with murder.

Maybe it wouldn't really be so cool if your parents behaved like that. It might be kind of scary, like no one was in charge. A happy medium wouldn't be bad. Ella hugged her knees tighter. The fog was coming in.

Toby had wrestled the dog to the sand and had it by the collar. Good. She wanted to talk to him before they went home.

Toby gave her the thumbs-up sign and she waved at him. He was grinning that Toby grin, she could tell even this far away.

Her brother had the most irresistible smile; his mouth went up and down at the same time and his right eyebrow sort of arched. Love for her brother flooded her, bringing tears to her eyes again. She was so hard on him, but he drove her *so* crazy. It was like somehow she felt responsible for him, as if she were his mother, not just the bossy older sister. She was on his case all the time, really overprotective. She felt that way about her mom, too. Why did she feel it was her job to take care of them all?

If she hadn't been so intent on saving everyone, she would have left the dumb underwear on the floor. If anything, she had made whatever it was worse. Why couldn't she just leave things be?

She shivered, pulling her sweater down over her knees and hugging them tighter. She looked out into the water at the oil rigs rising like sea monsters on the horizon.

God, I hate this place. Maybe that's why she was so much more intense about Toby and her mom. Maybe she felt guilty because she had gotten to stay in New York for college and they had all been exiled out here.

Poor Toby got nailed. She remembered his face when she said good-bye to him that first summer and they both realized, though they certainly had not known how to express it, that they were really separating. She would never come back in quite the same way again. She was going home and leaving him to some surfer-brained rich-kids' prep school. *Toby.* The teen king of the West Village! How could he possibly relate to this new peer group?

And her poor mother, surrounded by all those middle-aged women in Lycra biking shorts and riding clothes. She had been so happy when her mom met Molly. At least she wasn't one of the Hollywood Wives or some exercise flippo who never stood still. At least she had a sense of humor about it all.

A wave hit, splashing water onto her legs. The beach was disappearing fast. She jumped up and climbed over the rocks onto the path above the beach. Toby was running; his clothes were soaked and he was half carrying, half dragging the dog. She could not understand the allure of this place. Even the stupid beach. It was only usable for like five hours a day. On the Jersey shore or in the Hamptons, you could walk for hours and hours.

The Montecito beach was just a little curve. With oil rigs right out where you could see them! Oil rigs that spilled over and ruined everything, killed fish and birds and polluted the beach. So that was the big-deal beach, and just across the street from the ocean practically were the railroad tracks! And right next to the train was the freeway! A truly Future-World freeway with cars and trucks flying by twenty-four hours a day. Oil drilling, trains zooming, cars shooting by. This was what L.A. people thought was a great getaway. What a joke.

Anyone from the East Coast would just think the whole thing was hilarious. Like when she brought her roommate, Gwennie, here.

Montecito, Ella was convinced, was the total emperor's-new-clothes town. Not to even mention those women who rode their *horses* into the village! A *horse* pulling in next to a Ferrari so some spandex-head could pick up her Valium prescription at the pharmacy. She worried about her mother being here. She did feel that somehow she had abandoned her and Toby by staying in New York. And now this panty situation. She could never tell her mother what she had planned to tell her. Not now, not if something really weird was going on with her parents. Anger at her dad flushed her. What's he doing? Why didn't he even tease her mother or anything if the stupid pants were hers? Something's not right or I wouldn't be this freaked out.

Toby handed the dog up to her. He was soaking wet and gasping for breath. "Take him, quick! I'm dead. The damn dog weighs at least six hundred pounds. Hold his collar or he'll take off again!"

Ella grabbed the panting, wet animal. "Now *I'm* all wet!"

"A little oil-based water is great for the complexion." Toby crawled up beside her, trying to catch his breath. "Boy, that was scary. Did you see the way that tide came in? Like all of a sudden, we're at Mont-Saint-Michel."

Ella tried to stand up, holding on to the dog's collar. He shook himself, trying to dry off, splashing salty water all over them. "Come on, Tob, let's get back. Mom may want us and I need to talk to you about something."

Toby had never needed much of anything from the world. He was a loner like his mother and completely self-contained. Long ago, when Ella had sobbed to him about a fight with her best friend, he had put his five-year-old arm around her eight-year-old shoulder and said, "Don't feel bad. I've never had any friends and I'm okay." The only friend he had ever really needed or wanted was his sister.

Or it had been, until California. When she left, he had time to examine how much easier his life was without her. She took his love and devotion largely for granted and most of the time, Toby had to admit, she treated him like dirt. Then the rules had changed. It was extremely confusing for them both. So the sound of those old familiar words, "I need to talk to you," on his first trip home since starting college, broke through his defenses. He would have followed her, at that moment, anywhere.

When Annie returned to the kitchen, Juanita was basting and Ida Mae and Joe were playing gin rummy and listening to one of the Blond shows.

She was not at all in the proper June Cleaver spirit for this holiday. Was this the beginning of the end? Would she lose her enthusiasm for family life? Annie always looked at her life as if it were only a matter of time before her number was called. Today she stood on ground zero. Her mother's ticket had been punched twenty-four years ago. Was that why she was feeling so paranoid and weepy and generally pissed off and depressed?

She wanted to do what Mickey was doing. Lie down in a quiet room knowing that down below *others* were seeing to the machine that kept life moving. It was *her* birthday. Someone else should be doing this. She flushed, as if they could all see inside her head.

Let's not start the self-pity, dearie. You got yourself into this. All you can do now is show grace under pressure.

Juanita closed the oven. "This is the most fontostic turkey of all your Thanksgivings."

Annie picked up her list, trying to compose herself. "Where were you for so long? The kids said you were walking Portia. Portia can hardly make it across the kitchen."

"I take her next door. Mrs. O'Brian's friend, the goddess from the Greece, was having a ceremony. Mrs. O'Brian say she thought it would help me with my man."

Annie would have to talk to Molly. All she needed was for Juanita to turn into a cult follower. "You mean her friend Samantha?"

Juanita put down the basting syringe and wiped the counter.

"Yup. Only they don't say her that, they say her the Delphi article."

"Oracle."

"That's the one. I never seen nothing like this, Mrs. W. Out in Mrs. O'Brian's green room . . ."

"Greenhouse."

"Greenhouse. But it's not a house, it's only one room. My English is correct. So, okay. The article, she is standing up on a stool and there are many people there. Fancy people. I saw some people from Hollywood that have come here for parties, people with jewels. And she is talking to them in this beautiful voice, like an angel she talks. She is great big giant woman, with very large bosoms and long, long hair, looks like the color of that honey Mr. W brings from his health-food store. No one is talking or moving or nothing. Like my cousin Lupe the Witch, like she put a spell on everybody."

"Well, what was she saying?"

"I dunno. I was very far in the back and everybody was too big for me to see much. Something like, 'We have God's will in our lungs. . . .'"

Annie put down her list. "Lungs?"

"Maybe not lungs, just sounds like that. Something about the Holy Spirit in our bodies. She was holding her legs and throwing her head back like Ava Gardener. God in our lungs."

"Loins?"

"That's the one. What is this 'loins'? Not English."

Annie's father put down his cards. "Ah, loins! One of my favorite words. There are actually two definitions, Juanita, my dear. The loins are the parts of a man's or quadruped's body on either side of the spinal column, such as in culinary matters, a loin of veal, which is meat from this part of the anatomy. But my favorite use of the word is literary; 'loins,' which describes the area of the genitals known for strength and power. In some of your romance novels, you will see the word used in connection with 'quivering' and such. A lovely, sensual word. I'm sorry I missed this performance. She sounds like a fascinating creature."

Juanita listened politely, having no idea what he was talking about. "She not a creature, Mr. Joe. She a great big lady."

Annie felt jealous. Her father was paying more attention to Juanita and this invisible bombshell than he had paid to her in years. *He never even wished me happy birthday,* she thought, the truth striking her like an open hand.

"Come on, Joe, it's your turn to deal. *Afternoon L.A.* is starting; they got Jessica Hahn, Roxanne Pulitzer, and Rita Jenrette — three of your all-time faves. Yesterday they had James Dean look-alikes. Hard to believe he's been dead forty years. He's ageless."

Annie opened the refrigerator and checked the stuffing. "He's ageless because he died at twenty-six. That's a big price to pay for ageless."

Her father turned back to the television, not interested in any conversation in which he did not have center stage.

Juanita opened the dishwasher. "I don't get it. I think James Dean is making sausages. I just see the guy on TV. How he dead for forty years?"

Annie winked at Ida. Juanita in her innocence had just defined fame, a relative concept at best. "Same name, different cowboy."

Juanita stood up on her tiptoes, trying to put the cups away in the tall cupboards. "I am relieved to hear that. Jimmy Dean has a face very much like my new boyfriend. I got afraid again about the curse."

The back door opened and Annie's sister-in-law, Loretta, walked in.

"What curse?" Loretta asked, tossing her purse on the counter.

"Perfect timing as usual," Annie said, and crossed to kiss her unexpected arrival.

If Loretta Janetti Miller had been married to anyone other than Annie's brother, they would most likely have become great friends. Annie liked Loretta. She liked her solid Italian pessimism and she even liked that she was a shrink; it was cheaper and less of a commitment to talk to Loretta than to one of the others. At least she *knew* Loretta.

She trusted her. Not that Loretta didn't have her touchy-feely side — she could glaze over into psychobabble with the best of them — but it was not basically her nature. It came from being in a highly competitive profession in a town where there were probably more shrinks than swimming pools. But there was that elephant in the living room. She was married to Martin. If Loretta was so great, what was she doing with her brother? She didn't want to look at it that way, but she did.

Loretta had wandered into Martin's office in search of a mole removal and found love. Loretta liked to boast that Martin had saved the mole and preserved it in formaldehyde. A claim that Annie had not the slightest interest in challenging.

Loretta moved in to greet Ida Mae and Joe, the curse conversation thankfully sidestepped in the process. Annie checked her watch. It was only three o'clock. Loretta wasn't supposed to be there for hours. She was early and she was alone. Annie rarely saw her alone. The reason for this, Annie felt, was their awareness of the temptation to talk about their marriages. A giant no-no in interfamily relationships.

It wasn't until they came west that Annie had really spent any time with either of them. Martin had gone to Los Angeles for medical school and stayed. They had lost track. Annie was no longer sure why, despite her sarcasm about her brother. Lately, with her birthday approaching, she had found that she missed him. He was the only one on earth who could remotely understand how she felt. How many people are there in your life that watch someone die with you? Let alone a mother.

"Let's face it, I'm a cartoon character," Jessica Hahn was saying to one of the Blondes. "I know what the press thinks about me, but I'm having a ball. I know my Higher Power and the positive force will take care of me."

Rita Jenrette jumped in. "You're so right, Jessica. After what we've been through, you die or you grow. I've come from the depths and made something of my life, and I will not interfere with my karma again for anyone."

Roxanne Pulitzer patted Rita's arm. "You are so in touch. I know there is another life, and I don't want to cloud my karma either. I turn everything over to my Higher Power every day so that I will never repeat my past mistakes."

Annie brought the coffee pot and a plate of peanut-butter cookies over to the table and sat down next to Loretta. "Now how exactly do you think she *knows* there is another life?"

Loretta poured coffee and dunked her cookie deep into the cup. "Her Higher Power told her."

Annie's father stood up. "Wonderful legs, that Jenrette. Terrible taste in men; I knew her former husband from my days in Washington theater. But what a body."

Annie and Loretta stared at the screen, feeling competitive. Ida Mae picked up her coffee. "Your brain is in your boxers again, old man. We'll leave you girls alone; time for a little snooze before the party."

Loretta and Annie watched them go.

"I am torn by the nap idea. It means they'll be up all night. It's the same trade-off as when the kids were little. The respite of nap-time or the agony of a three-year-old just getting going at midnight."

Loretta grinned at her, grabbing for another cookie. "At least you only have today. We're taking them back with us tomorrow and they're staying until *Tuesday.* They never get to see Bentley, so I couldn't say no, but I'm tired already."

"Working hard?" Annie took a bite. Peanut butter was her favorite. She liked to press a piece against the roof of her mouth and let her tongue soften it, the way she had done as a child. Usually she tried to buy things that didn't tempt her, but Thanksgiving was permission.

Loretta munched. "I'm working hard trying to stay in business! Between the recession and the shrink-bashing epidemic in press and cinema, my practice looks like an old jacket the moths have fallen in love with. I lost three patients from *Basic Instinct,* two patients from *Raising Cain,* one patient from *Final Analysis* — I guess believing that Richard Gere was a shrink was too far a stretch. And that head-job at Harvard, the woman doctor who was accused of causing a student's suicide? Margaret Bean-Bag or something — three thousand pages of evidence, with tidbits from her notes like 'Say I'm your mom and I love you and you love me; say it ten times. . . .' I lost three, maybe as many as six patients — sometimes it's hard to tell. The capper was, of course, Woody and Mia.

"If it weren't for the producers who made all of those lousy movies, most of which bombed, and who are now anxiety-ridden and/or unemployed, I'd be like Lucy in *Peanuts,* with my little advice stand on the sidewalk. And now I'm also in competition with the New Agers: Marianne Williamson, J. Z. Knight, and don't get me started on the Scientologists. They've practically taken over Hollywood. They control as much talent as C.A.A."

Annie munched on her second cookie. "Gee, you're so far down you're even cheering me up."

"I will never admit I said this, but I'm more and more convinced that all people really care about in the end is their weight and their hair."

Annie put her head down on the table and rolled it back and forth.

"Oh, God, higher or lower power, upper or lower case, don't let her be right, please, pretty please."

Loretta poured more coffee. "I'm burned, Annie. This slump actually comes at a perfect time. I'm so sick of listening to everyone's shit. The world is really very simple. Everyone is being pushed by and having to perform for someone above them. Check it out. The president, he has to answer to the people. Heads of corporations have to answer to their stockholders; everyone under that level has numerous people above them squeezing and pushing. We spend all our working lives being squeezed or squeezing and that alone, without all of the endless personal problems, is enough to make the world crazy."

Loretta burst into tears, shutting her slanted, almost Oriental, brown eyes.

Annie did not quite know what to do. She reached out for Loretta's hands but they were threaded together as if she were praying.

"Martin and I are getting a divorce," Loretta said, opening her eyes as if the confession had surprised her.

Annie waited. Loretta was tough, not one to accept empty platitudes or facile comfort. "Is this good or not so good?"

"It's necessary."

Loretta laughed, seeing how unsettled Annie was. "Annie, you are such a trip. You should see your face. In your face lies the real difference between the Jews and the Italians. Both of us cry and scream and yell at each other and make a morality play out of everything from a bad haircut to cancer, but the Italians don't take any of it very seriously. We enjoy the turmoil. The Jews take every bit to heart. That's why you never have any fun. I'm sorry, honey, I didn't mean to shock you."

"No, no. Don't be ridiculous. I mean of course you *shocked* me. You two never even fight!" Annie swallowed. "Can you tell me why?"

Loretta blew her nose. "Pimples," she said. "It's basically pimples."

"Yours or his?"

> "According to Dr. Joyce Brothers, people who become very successful, whether men or women, may have higher levels of testosterone —"

Annie leaned over and switched off the set.

Loretta yawned. "Very funny. You know exactly what I mean. Look, this is tricky. I really agonized over coming up here and talking to you about it. No one else knows yet. Martin's your brother, and I don't want to compromise you, turn you into a quisling or anything, but honest to God, Annie, I just don't know who else would understand. I mean I'm not blind. It's clear you have your own problems with Martin.

"How would you like to spend night after night with a man who tells you about lancing pus-filled boils and infected cysts at dinner? He's just gotten worse and worse. His life keeps getting smaller and darker. And there is no way to tease him about any of it. He takes himself so seriously. I don't know what's happening to him, but I really feel that if I don't leave, he'll take me and Bentley down with him. I mean, can you imagine naming a kid Bentley? You don't *know* what that did to me. I have never called him that. I call him Bennie like you do, and it makes Martin furious."

Annie nodded. "I hope this doesn't sound judgmental, but Martin has always been somewhat pretentious and remote. What attracted you to him in the first place?"

Loretta licked crumbs off her full red lips. "Look, when I met Martin he was just out of medical school. He was alone in a strange city and he was sweet and smart and filled with zeal. You don't see that part of him, Annie, you're so filled up with all the sibling shit. All those games your mother ran on you two, playing favorites and pampering Martin. He was a good balance for me. He calmed me down and I cheered him up. You take a chance. Also, we had fantastic sex. I mean your brother really gets into a body. It figures doesn't it? I mean a guy who wouldn't throw up squeezing yellow grease out of some teenager's back must be pretty earthy.

"Who knows? You're ready to commit, you meet someone who isn't an overtly raving lunatic, HIV-positive, or a professional ass-grabber, you do it. Not many of us found true love at age six like you two."

Annie winced. "What makes you think that my mother played us off like that? Did Martin say that?"

"Sure. Remember, he did go through Gestalt therapy when we first got married; that was one of my requirements. But he's always been more aware of that stuff than you were. I say this as a friend, Annie, and you know I've said it before — having Mickey protected you from a lot of stuff the rest of us went through, but it also kept parts of you from growing up. Sooner or later, the subpoena is served. Maybe when we split you and Martin can work on this, though he's really shut down now. My saying I want out is like your mother dying all over again. He's pretty freaked. I'm just worried about Bennie."

Annie was standing on another minefield. Only this one had nothing to do with her husband or her children. This one was of her own making. Cluster grenades planted by her unconscious long ago, covered over so carefully and tidily that she had completely forgotten that the ground on which she now stood was anything other than a pretty, green field.

"I've had this feeling all week, this strange disconnected feeling, as if I was looking at my life like Emily in *Our Town,* as if I'd just come back from the dead and was watching everyone in an entirely new way, but really seeing myself too. I've outlived my mother as of today."

Loretta leaned over and kissed her. "Says it all, baby. You know that's part of my decision, too. I look at my parents and the older patients I have and they've had all this time to expand, and most of them, as far as I can tell, do the opposite. They contract. They *sink* to the occasion. Well, I want to end my life as a big-hearted, robust old lady, reeking of love and self-awareness. I want a more honest life. That's really what leaving Martin is about. I *am* getting smaller. Since we start out small and grow up, we should damn well keep growing *up* until the end! We should die bigger, not littler, than when we arrived!"

They sat for a moment, both absorbing Loretta's passion. Annie reached over and wiped Loretta's tears away. "Maybe I am a quisling," she said softly, "but you go, Loretta. Run as fast as you can."

Juanita came in, breaking their connection. "My turkey needs more juicing."

Annie jumped. "Oh, God, it's after four. I've got to get ready and wake Mickey up. Will you be okay here?"

"Hunky dory. Can I help?"

"There's a bag of fresh shrimp that you could wash and set up on a platter with cocktail sauce. Juanita knows which one."

"Never fear. I do great shrimp. Oh, I brought the wild rice stuffing. It's in my car."

"Wonderful. If Toby appears, would you ask him to light the fireplaces?"

Loretta laughed. “A Walt Disney Holiday. I love your quaint side.”

Annie shuddered. “Don’t ever use that word in my presence.”

Loretta followed Juanita to the refrigerator. “Annie, I forgot to give you your present.”

She was already gone.

Juanita pulled the bag of shrimp out and handed it to Loretta. “Mrs. W never think presents. On my birthday, I wanna hundred presents. I cry if one of my cousins forget about me. Mrs. W don’t know how to be like that. She always giving the things.”

Loretta poured the plump pink crustaceans into a colander. “I think, Juanita dear, that is about to change.”

CHAPTER IV

JACKIE WILSKI swung his fire-engine red Mercedes 600 onto the Pacific Coast Highway and turned up his Michael Feinstein tape.

We sit in a bar and talk till two,
about life and love like old friends do,
and tell each other what we've been through. . . .

Right on, Feinstein. The only thing he didn't have was the old friend.

Jackie had been approaching the drive up to Annie and Mickey's with a decidedly ambivalent set of emotions. He loved hitting the road in his incredible car, putting the top down and zooming. The car was a symbol of everything he'd worked for; it was his Fuck-you car and his I-did-it-my-way car and his eat-your-heart-out car.

He always took the long way, winding up the Pacific Coast Highway, sailing around the curves cut into the mountains, whizzing past Oxnard and Ventura, the ocean on his left, the hills on his right, bombing into Santa Barbara County. It was as close to nature as he had been in years. It made him feel free and confident.

So that part was great. What waited for him once he arrived was maybe not so great; like his mother and Annie's father. All his mother ever saw was Mickey. Mickey was A STAR. Big fucking deal. *He* had the power! *He* was the guy who made or broke the Mickeys. He was the man with the estate in Bel Air, the ski lodge in Aspen, and five shows on network. It meant diddly shit to his mother. In fact, it made it worse. Ida Mae Socialist-from-Hell Wilski had contempt for his entire lifestyle. And Joe, with his theater la de da, his phony intellectual bullshit: "Where are the Molières? Where are the young

Millers and Odetses? This is not the theater I knew." What a load. A load usually aimed directly at him, a tabloid king, beneath contempt.

What the fuck was so majestic about what his brother did? We're talking crime drama here. Mickey was no longer the promising young stage actor leaping around in his tights in some elitist Shakespeare in the Park production. He was a Made Man, TV owned his soul and his ass. Mickey was the one showing up like hired help, and for a psycho nerd like Stan Stein. At least he created his shows. What did Mickey create? A character who stole every Brando mannerism that wasn't nailed down, threw in a little Peter Falk, and said lines like, "Yo, Lieutenant, I found Ricco with a meat hook where the sun don't shine."

Jackie let the music smooth out his rage. It never got any better. Ten years of analysis and it still hurt that much. He kept having a fantasy, ever since he heard that *War Zone* might be going down for the count. The show would be canceled; Mickey wouldn't get another series and would end up working for him, hosting one of his shows. Maybe he would even create a show just for Mickey, just to even the score. *Bulimia Dateline,* interviews with bingers and pukers from all walks of life. Or some phobia show, *Phobia USA.* Mickey could do man-in-the-street kinds of pieces, visit agoraphobics in their kitchens, hand-washers in their bathrooms, take a panic-attack sufferer up to the top of the Empire State Building.

Christ. Was he still this angry?

Why did he still care so much what they thought? To his family he was a living, breathing punch line. Of course the third divorce was not going to help.

Okay. If he was going to be honest and not just jerk himself off, he had made some fairly serious mistakes. He had copped out by staying with the tabloid format. He had made enough money and contacts to take some creative risks, put his name on something with more substance. Mickey had even talked to him about doing a project together. But he was too scared. If he tried and failed it would be far worse than never having risked it at all. If he failed, he proved them right.

Plus Sandy and the other broads. He chose with his prick and he got exactly what such a choice deserves. How can an organ that has no brain, no vision, and only comes out in a frenzy and mainly in the dark make life decisions for a person? Good question. But one that a forty-one-year-old man should not be answering for the *third* time. His wives had taken the word "shallow" to a higher shoal. Why couldn't he learn his lesson?

The fact that Sandy wanted to move to San Francisco should have warned him. He hated fucking San Francisco. Everybody that lived in San Francisco looked like they made sixty-five grand a year. It didn't matter whether they made two million or twenty-five thou — they all had that smug, WASPy, J. Crew look and that pseudosophisticated preppy attitude. The land of the Energy Impaired. Not like L.A. or New York, where your neurons crackle. "Anything, baby, San Fran, sure — I'll commute." Sonofabitch. He must have been demented. Maybe he needed a separate shrink just for his prick. Why couldn't he be attracted to nice, sane, intelligent women? The only woman like that he had ever wanted was Annie, and all he had ever been to her was the creepo younger brother of THE STAR.

Maybe that's why he dove into the bimbo pool every time. Unrequited love for his brother's wife. Or maybe he just wanted her because she belonged to Mickey.

His head hurt. He wanted to get on top of this stuff before he got up there. The third divorce had hit him harder than he wanted to admit. He did feel like a failure. Natty little guy, always overdone. Hair too slick, couldn't ever quite get the clothes right no matter how fucking much money he spent. Not like Mickey. Mickey was no giant, though he was taller, bigger scale; but he had that look. He put on a baggy sweatshirt and some Levi's and he looked chic and elegant. Jackie couldn't ever get the thing right even if he did the exact same thing as Mickey. If he wore the same suit, on him it looked contrived.

Maybe that was the big blonde thing. That was something Mickey didn't have. But it only backfired, because it was something

Mickey didn't want, and, in the end, he didn't want either. It only made them feel sorry for him.

When he was in the eighth grade he had fallen in love with his first big blonde. She was a head taller than he was and a good thirty pounds heavier. He asked her to go to the movies, and she turned her wide, vacant, cow eyes on him and said, "I can't go around with a boy whose wrists are smaller than mine."

He had never gotten over it. They didn't say that now. Now the big blondes lined up for a chance to go out with him. Whoop de do. Where did that come from? *Whoop de do?* Every once in a while Jackie said something that came straight from his mother's mouth. A friend was going in for an operation and Jackie had said, "You mean you're going *under the knife?*" What an archaic, horrible thing to say! Pure Ida Mae. She still looked at surgery like she was watching the Life of Pasteur or something, like they threw you on a table, held you down, and slit you open. *Lollapalooza.* That had come out of his mouth at a screening at Michael Eisner's house no less. It was like being inhabited by his mother. Or "He's really a people person." He didn't even know what the fuck that meant. What would *he* be? An ant person?

His mother. Jackie rubbed his temple. He had just spent three sessions with Dr. Rhinehart dealing with his mother's first birthday present to him since childhood. A large box had arrived at his Hollywood office the day before his birthday. Ida Mae *never* remembered his birthday until a week or two after, when he would get a defensive phone call that usually started something like "Don't start. I've been working with my HIV volunteer group. I've seen sickness and suffering beyond anything anyone in Los Angeles could imagine. So I forgot your birthday. People are hanging by a thread back here."

Yeah, Mom, HIV doesn't cross the West Village state line. All of a sudden on his forty-first birthday this big gift-wrapped box arrives. His secretary and two of his producers were there. "From my mother. You know how mothers are." He was actually *showing off* that he had gotten a present from his own fucking mother! He found a scissors and managed to cut through the ten layers of masking tape. Everyone was watching him, getting into the spirit of the thing. Inside the box were piles of his old worn-out shoes and mangy sweaters that still had his camp name tags sewn into them. Little boys' shoes with huge holes in the bottoms. Shoes that had probably been stored in some closet for thirty years.

At the bottom of the box was a note. "Jackie. Thought you might want these. Happy Birthday, Ida Mae."

From the looks on the faces of his staff, he might as well have pulled fucking Alien Three out of the box! What could such a gesture mean exactly?

Rhinehart, the cop-out, wouldn't hazard a guess. But he was having his doubts about him anyway. Ten years, and he was still this stuck in this shit?

Resisting the process, Rhinehart called it. He had elevated his shrink to deity status and maybe it was time to reevaluate. Ten years with the guy and all that blind trust, and he was still fucked totally up. What about that idiot he and Sandy had met in Maui last year? Some psychiatrist from Seattle running around in his bikini trunks wearing a T-shirt that said, THE RECESSION GETTING YOU DOWN? TRY PROZAC. Imagine finding *that* out about your doctor! Jesus, the way his mind worked. What a peculiar selection of thoughts to be gathered in his head today.

Michael Feinstein finished and he flipped off the CD player. He was already through Ventura and he hadn't worked anything out.

Where was he? The family. He would be calm. He would not brag like he usually did, trying to impress them, but he wouldn't hide under a fucking rock either! He was proud of his new show. But if no one mentioned it, or mentioned it and made fun of it, he would laugh lightly, his Fuck-you-fool-I-drive-a-one-hundred-and-twenty-five-thousand-dollar-plus-tax-and-telephone-in-a-recession-car laugh and shrug his shoulders. "Well, to each his own," he would say politely.

He would talk to the kids. They loved his shows. He would talk to Juanita, who not only made him feel tall, but knew all of his shows by heart. He would talk to Loretta, who laughed at his jokes.

He had always liked Loretta. When Martin first started seeing her, Jackie had thought that Loretta was as close to a girl like Annie as he was likely to get. If only she had been a big blond bimbo, he would have fallen in love. That was it. He had to stop with the packaging. What he got was the human version of his mother's birthday present. A dynamite package with a bunch of musty junk inside.

Jackie slowed down. He was at the Montecito exit. So okay. He knew how to do this. And in a pinch he would do what Rhinehart had told him to do. "If it gets uncomfortable or you start to lose your observer, excuse yourself and go to the bathroom. Breathe deeply and re-center yourself. Break the old cord." He was all right. *I can handle it,* he said to himself, swinging his statement car off the freeway and heading toward the wound.

"Aunt Annie?" Bentley stood in the doorway peeking into her room. Annie was in the bathroom putting on her lipstick.

"Bennie! Come on in and give your old aunt a great big fat smooch!"

Bennie smiled, revealing a gap where his two front teeth had been the last time she had seen him. Flashes in her heart. Ella tripping on the steps, losing her front teeth. Toby and his tooth fairy obsession, little child-sweet pillows, quarters slipped under in the middle of the night.

Her nephew ran to her, his wonderful pointy ears revealed by his too-short haircut.

She loved her nephew's ears the most. There was something so impish and perky about them, the way they just came to little red points. Spocky ears. She loved Toby's ears too, but his were more playful. Flappy. Luckily, he had grown into them. They didn't stick out, they just had these long, velvety lobes. She loved to play with Toby's earlobes. He knew as a tiny boy that he had this ear power over her. "They're closed today," he would say. "Come back tomorrow."

She didn't feel the urge to play with Bennie's ears. They were too rigid. She was afraid she might break them. The other best thing about Bennie was that he loved to dance. He was totally enthralled with all forms of movement and completely unselfconscious about it. Loretta secretly took him to ballet even though Martin loathed the dance idea. Once, she had overheard Loretta defending Bennie's dancing — "Joy, Martin, it's about joy." Martin had just walked away. Poor Martin; joy was not a concept he understood.

Bennie threw himself into her arms, hugging tight. She held him, stroking his soft fine hair. Seven years old and about to step off the edge of the family precipice. She didn't know if Bennie knew anything, but from the force of the hug, Annie's guess was, he knew, somewhere.

"Quite a greeting from my main nephew."

Bennie held tight.

"Did you see Toby and Ella?"

He nodded, still holding on.

"You should have Toby take you to the beach before the sun goes down."

Bennie loosened himself so that he could look up at her.

"He's all dressed already."

"Well, maybe in the morning before you go home."

"I can't go between the hours of nine and two."

"The sun?"

Bennie nodded. "It's no fun anyway, because he makes me put on this gross lotion junk that's supposed to filter out all the bad rays and everything, but it's really thick and kind of orange. It makes me look like a pumpkin."

Annie laughed. She could see poor Bennie with his orange face, empty tooth sockets, and pointy ears. He would look like a pumpkin. "Well, you come back up on Halloween and we'll all go. You'll be right in style."

Bennie laughed his funny, wheezy little laugh. Bennie had asthma, which made his dancing all the more touching.

Annie led him out of the bathroom and into her bedroom. "Gotta put on my shoes, champ, it's time to start the show. Is everyone here?"

Bennie pirouetted across the room and flung himself onto her bed. "Uh-huh. Uncle Jackie gave me a ride in his car. Too radical. Mommy sent me up to ask you if she should put the shrimp out now."

"Oh, boy. I'm so late! Tell her yes, and would you ask Uncle Mickey to start taking drink orders. Are your grandparents down?"

Bennie bounced up and down on Mickey's unmade side. "Yep. Grandpa Joe has been making cocktails for quite a while. Everyone's already laughing too loud."

Annie stepped into her new black suede mules and went over to him. A small child playing on a big bed was too irresistible to pass up. She sat down beside him, gently pushing him back onto the pillows. "Uh-oh, I see the tickle monster coming; no way to stop him, he's out of control!"

She held him with her arm and tickled his skinny ribs gently with all her fingers. Bennie squirmed in glee. "No, no, no! Stop! Auntie! Stop it, please!"

"Say the magic word or the tickle monster will tickle you to death."

"I don't know it."

"All *good* little boys know it. Hee, hee, hee."

Toby. Little boy on another bed. Tiny Ella shrieking with pleasure. "Stop, Mommy! Make the tickle monster stop! . . ."

"Bentley?" They stopped mid-tickle, co-conspirators caught in the act. Her brother stood in the doorway.

"Hi, Martin. We were just fighting off the old tickle monster for a minute. How are you?"

"Just fine. Bentley, your mother sent you up to ask your aunt a question, not to roll around on her bed. We've been waiting for you to return with an answer. That is not how you accept responsibility. You wanted to be the one to go, you accepted a task; it is your duty to complete your task."

Bennie sat up, holding on to Annie's arm. Annie resisted the urge to knock her brother to the ground and unleash the full power of the tickle monster on him, preferably while Bennie held several pillows over his head. *He talks to him like he's reading it out of a book,* Annie thought.

She leaned down and kissed Bennie's forehead.

"Come on, pal. Let's go get 'em."

They stood up. Martin crossed his arms over his chest. He was so tall and bony. Maybe he'd been left on their doorstep. No one in her family looked remotely like her brother. He did not make way for them. "I believe you have something to say, young man."

Bennie looked up at him, holding on to Annie's arm. "I'm sorry, Father."

Martin relaxed. The drill sergeant after inspection. "Okay. Now run along. You still have your message to deliver."

"Aye, aye, sir." Bennie saluted for her benefit, Annie was sure. A kid with irony would always make out just fine. Irony was the weapon of choice against pomposity.

She went over and kissed her brother. His face felt cold and dry. He smelled of witch hazel. It was so like her brother to use witch hazel as an aftershave.

"Good to see you, Martin." He didn't kiss her back. She let him go. She was so uncomfortable alone with him. Her own brother.

He walked into her room and sat down in her chair by the window. "I suppose she told you."

"Yes. I'm so sorry, Martin." So far it was turning into quite a birthday.

His face looked drawn and pale. She did not know what to say.

"I don't suppose you're surprised."

"Why do you say that? I was stunned."

"I say it because I'm quite sure you never understood how anyone could be married to me, especially not someone as unlike me as Loretta."

Annie sighed. She could feel his desolation. She searched her heart for her compassion. She could only find her empathy for Martin in her childhood memories. The little brother that she loved and resented. Her frail, lonely, bookworm brother who never fit in. It had been her mission to be his mentor, keeping him from the outer limits of social ostracism: "No, Martin, you cannot wear green pants and a red shirt. It's too creepy. Wear the jeans I faded for you and the Shetland sweater. . . ." "Martin, you never wear dress-up shoes with chinos. Wear the penny loafers."

She had seen the same pattern repeat itself with Toby and Ella. Firstborn big sisters, little mothers to their brothers.

He had seemed so lost to her when he was little. A nervous, allergic, twitchy kid with horn-rimmed glasses and no social skills. She loved her little brother and had tried, as best she could, to nurture him and help him in the ways of other children.

It wasn't until he was in his twenties that her little brother had disappeared entirely and the present Martin had been born. It had always seemed to Annie that the change had come overnight. All of a sudden he was an ascot-wearing asshole. Stiff, humorless, and supercilious. The Doctor, who was always on call. He shut her out, slamming the door to their past between them. She no longer knew how to talk to him.

"Is there anything I can do?"

Martin laughed, a cold, bitter edge to the sound. "Don't tell Ida Mae and Pop. Let me do it my way."

"No problem on that one. I always leave the night-bombing to the special forces." She paused, watching his face. He managed a smile at her. He looked so forlorn. In that small, tense smile she saw her brother again.

"I outlived mother today." Tears shot forth, falling like raindrops on a puddle, the emotion coming up behind and pushing her down. She knew it was because he was there.

"I know," Martin said and raised his long narrow body from her puffy white chair. He walked over and put his arms around her. "Good for you, Annie. Good for you."

Traffic statistics show that more people travel on Thanksgiving than on any other day of the year. Thanksgiving is America's only egalitarian holiday. It is open to every race, creed, and color, hawk and pacifist, zealot and atheist alike, the ultimate family-value photo op.

People do not like to be alone on this day. To be alone on Thanksgiving is an American fear.

Relatives who despise one another bring cranberry muffins and big phony smiles to each other's tables. Thanksgiving means The Family, the American Dream in action, Barbara and George and all the Bushies posing by the fire, neat and shiny and complete with cute little grandkids and fluffy pups.

No one wants to be alone on Thanksgiving. The Wilders had never even considered such a possibility. This was the first Thanksgiving, Annie thought, as she stood in the kitchen putting the finishing pat on the meal, that the idea of the end had occurred to her.

She heard her family laughing and interrupting one another in the next room and imagined a year in the future, with silence. Martin and Loretta off in different directions, Jackie somewhere with God only knows who; her kids making other plans. Ida Mae and Joe would grow too old, and she and Mickey might even be heading for their own untrussing.

Everything changes, everything ends. Juanita held the roasting pan and Annie lifted the turkey onto the platter. It looked so wonderful. Crisp and golden brown and hearty. Nothing like its raw, naked, vulnerable self of just hours ago. Obscene, really, spreading it open and cramming things up inside it with a spoon.

"Juanita, how's the gravy doing?" Annie looked over her shoulder.

"Fontostic. I just zap it in the micro for a minute and we're ready to rock and roll."

Annie laughed. "Toby's home for two days and he's already influencing your vocabulary."

"Gotta keep on keeping on, Mrs. W. Don't want to be an out-of-it."

Ella came in. "Oh, my God, Mom, Grandpa Joe is telling the most embarrassing jokes. You would die."

Annie finished taking the stuffing out of the cavity, repairing the rape. "I can hear everything."

"What can I do now?"

"Just help us carry things in. Put it all on the sideboard. As soon as Daddy carves, everyone can take their plates and serve themselves."

Ella laughed. "Remember last year? No one wanted anything the same way? Remember Uncle Martin asking if you could take the butter out of the green beans?"

"Well, that's why this year it's buffet. Let's go, troops."

Annie picked up the turkey. Juanita strutted behind, gravy in hand. They began, the women marching back and forth, servant girls at the bacchanal, bringing bowls of vegetables and stuffings, potatoes and biscuits. The anticipation at the table rose, senses teased by the sight and smell of platters overfilled with bounty. Annie stood by the door watching Mickey carve, thinking of Thanksgiving in Somalia. She gazed across the table, her eyes moving from person to person. She had made a promise to herself. Tonight it was Elmer's. She would remove herself from the room and try to see everyone more objectively. It felt important for her to do this tonight; the day had been much too upsetting.

Her father was telling a joke. "So, the young Hasidic man goes to his rabbi for counseling on the eve of his wedding. They talk a while and the rabbi says, 'Is there anything else, my son?' 'Yes,' the young man says shyly, 'what about sex, rabbi? Is it pleasure or is it work?' Well, the rabbi is caught off guard. No one has ever asked such a question before. He ponders. The young man waits nervously. Finally the rabbi smiles. 'It's pleasure. Because . . . if it was work, my wife would have the maid do it.'"

Everyone laughed, even Bennie, who most likely had no idea why it was funny.

"Dinner is served!" Mickey, flushed with Merlot and success, turned to the table. "Let's not have any pushing and shoving now, form an orderly single line, and my assistant here will stamp your vouchers."

Ida Mae was first. Ida Mae was always first. "Mickey, sweetheart, give a big piece of skin to your momma."

Mickey piled his mother's plate with all her favorites. Skin and wings and legs, the proletariat portions of the turkey. White meat was for capitalists. No wild rice stuffing and asparagus for Ida Mae. A few green beans and some peas. Mickey leaned over and kissed her cheek.

Annie waited until everyone was served. She really liked to be last. Juanita made her dainty little plate and slid in next to Toby. Juanita really hated eating with them. She would gobble up her dinner and disappear, waiting until later in the kitchen to enjoy herself. Juanita knew exactly where every boundary line was drawn. Her class geography was good enough for Persian Gulf maneuvers.

Annie filled her plate and sat down at the opposite end of the table from Mickey. Usually she sat in the middle and let her father sit at the head. She just didn't feel like it today; paying him back for forgetting her birthday, or maybe just not willing to surrender her rightful place. She watched them eat. Jackie with his quick-stabbing thrusts, as if he were attacking his plate. Ella with her perfect manners, back so straight, one hand always in her lap, her mouth primly closed while chewing. Toby all elbows and wrists, spilling, dropping, stuffing things into his face, the baby always expecting to be left out, the platter empty before it reached him. Annie smiled. *Remember, Tob, all those years when you spilled your drink at every meal? Every time, your eyes brimming, never understanding why it happened. I'm sorry I got impatient when you did it. I'm so sorry I wasn't kinder about it. I wish I could go back just for a minute and do it better. . . .*

"Jackie, tell the story about your friend in Tokyo."

Annie saw Jackie's face when Mickey addressed him. The look of what, gratitude? Was that possible? He was grateful that Mickey had singled him out? Empathy for her brother-in-law swept through her. She felt guilty for giving him such a bad time about his shows. Who was she to judge? Writing about some converted dairy-barn inn run by a bunch of narcissistic old biddies was certainly no more noble than what Jackie did.

Jackie put down his fork. "I have a buddy, he's putting together this humungous coproduction deal with the Japanese, and he goes over there and it's the whole drill. Wining and dining and meetings that go on for eighteen hours, and finally he's got the agreement almost signed and the big kahuna invites him for one of their mother-of-all-dinners at his private club. So my friend and his partner are at this banquet table and everyone's feeling no pain and all of a sudden the big boss, who never says a fucking word — whoops! sorry kids — anyway, the guy probably speaks English as well as Margaret Thatcher but he will never talk. He leans over and whispers something to his translator —"

Bennie leaned forward. "What's a translator?"

"Someone who listens in one language and repeats what he hears in another. Where was I?"

Annie saw tension in Jackie's face. He needs this laugh, she thought, knowing she would give it to him no matter what.

"Okay. So, the big kahuna whispers to his translator, and the flunky stands up and everyone stops talking, like a lid slammed shut, the way they do when the CEO moves an eyelid, and the translator says to my friend, 'Mr. Hamayoshi would like you to sing.'

"'Sing?' My friend is like flipping his lid! I mean the guy is a *producer,* not Ezio Pinza. No one has ever asked this guy to sing! This guy doesn't even sing in the fucking shower. So he says to his translator, 'Please tell Mr. Hamayoshi I am honored by his request, but I cannot sing. I have no talent for singing.'

"Well, this goes on back and forth like Asian Ping-Pong.

"The chairman is starting to drum his fingers on the table and all the Japanese Brooks Brothers clones are really looking frightened. 'Mr. Hamayoshi says that you must sing,' the translator says for the sixth or seventh time.

"Well, now my friend is looking at his partner and his partner is giving him the heavy eyebrow action, like they're saying sayonara to a hundred million big ones. So my friend thinks, talk about singing for your supper. He's panic-stricken, but he stands up, and he can see all the salarymen breathing for the first time in an hour, and the boss lifts his four-hundred-dollar glass of cognac.

"Now, the only song that my friend knows the words to on a good day is, 'Oh, the mailman is a person in my neighborhood . . . da da da. . . . It's the people that you meet, when you're walking down the street, it's the people that you meet each day!'"

"Sesame Street!" Bennie clapped his hands, pleased to be in the know.

"You got it. The guy used to give his kid breakfast, and he watched *Sesame Street* with him. So he lets it fly. He figures What the hell. He does three choruses and a big finish.

"Silence. Dead fucking — sorry — silence. No one claps. Nothing. They all sit there. The chairman turns to the man next to him and starts talking. The salarymen take their cue, they start talking to one another, and my friend is standing there like the Universal Schmuck.

"Next morning his partner picks him up for the final meeting and my friend says to him, 'What was that about last night?'

"His partner is dying. The guy is wetting his pants, he's laughing so hard. Finally he says, 'I ran into one of Hamayoshi's guys who speaks English this morning. He said that Hamayoshi's translator screwed up, he didn't want you to *sing*. He asked something about golf. Your *swing* . . ."

Laughter rose up all around, surrounding Jackie. Mickey was banging on the table; even her brother had his face in his hands, as if being seen laughing right out loud was too personal. Her father, who rarely listened to, let alone laughed at, anyone else's jokes, was laughing his café-society laugh.

Jackie's small handsome face was flushed with success. He had taken a big risk and he had triumphed. He blew his brother a kiss, guilt sweeping him. His brother had no idea how angry and jealous he was. His brother had stepped aside and turned the single spot on him. As if he had known, without Jackie saying a word to him, that it was what he so desperately needed from them. It was his brother's way of saying that his divorce was okay, that whatever Jackie did was okay.

Annie blew him a kiss. The symbolic Elmer's sealing her mouth was proving to be incredibly interesting. This was the first dinner table that Annie remembered being at in her entire life when she was not doing the lion's share of the talking. Granted, it was not nearly as much fun, if she did say so herself, but it was extremely enlightening.

She glanced at them all from far away, an aquarium tourist before the big tank.

Mickey was telling Loretta some set anecdote. She watched him putting on his actor-in-real-life persona. Actors were quite amazing. There were so many costumes in their closets. It had been years before Annie had really figured out that there was an entire Mickey persona that was reserved for real life, but was a creation, another character. She called it "Mickey Live" because it had that dimension. Someone who seemed to be real but wasn't quite. Not real the way he was on Saturday mornings in their kitchen. It was more Mickey *acting* real, the way he did in interviews. She saw her friend Lina doing this same thing all the time. Every actor or actress she knew had their fake-real personality. Their "on" real. Some of them played wonderful mother and nature-lover; some, sensitive man of the people, or man's man, "I'm-not-like-other-actors-I-think-all-of-this-dressing-up-and-wearing-funny-clothes-is-ridiculous." Mickey's was more "Hey, I'm just Mick the Stick — a really cool New York kid."

Loretta was eating it up. Loretta always turned it on for Mickey. It was quite provocative watching people that you were close to as if they were fish in a pond, unaware of your piercing gaze. Mickey was oblivious to her scrutiny. He looked good. *He's the bride.* A shot of new information. All the attention goes to him. He's the one with the power health drinks and the collagen creams. He gets the facials, takes the megavitamins, goes on fad diets. He has the three-way mirror in his closet. He has the personal trainer, the state-of-the-art gym equipment. He wears the hair conditioning caps and plucks his eyebrows. I eat more than he does, drink more than he does, and exercise less. He's the peacock. His clothes cost more, his car is fancier. How did this happen? I *know* how it started. He earns his living on his physical being — he's a public person like my father was, only higher profile. Am I becoming my mother?

Annie stuffed a hunk of white meat into her mouth. No one seemed to notice that she was not presiding.

It has always been Mickey first. Was that true? She chewed, trying to test the idea. No one would describe her as a wilting violet. Was that the phrase? What a funny saying. How did sayings like that start? *Wilting violet.* Well, she wasn't one. First of all, she talked too much. Second, she was not shy — insecure, certainly, but not shy. She had style, she wore designer clothes and makeup, she did not walk six steps behind him carrying his key light, for chrissakes. And she certainly spoke her mind.

But maybe that was all part of the deal, that didn't threaten THE STAR. What if all of that was really just a pat on the head, a few flakes in the tank. What was she saying? Was it true? Here she was, thinking that she was as independent and feisty as anyone, and in fact, she was just a goldfish who thought she was a golden carp, given just enough nourishment to keep her from noticing that her growth had been curtailed.

Anger hit her. She was not going to ruin her Thanksgiving birthday dinner. She heard her own sweetly nauseating voice, "Oh, it's my present. I love to cook Thanksgiving for my family. . . . No, really, I never feel deprived." Bullshit. She suddenly realized that she felt damn deprived. They had all grown to expect such grand, selfless gestures from her. That was *her* fault. (That *was* her mother.)

The kids were teasing Jackie about his show. Looking at them made her feel better. They looked enough alike to be twins. Olive skin, big dark eyes, thick wavy brown hair, just like Mickey. The only thing she could see in either of them of her genes was hidden under Toby's overgrown locks. He had her father's ears. Inside, of course, was another matter. They certainly were hers there. Sometimes she saw so much of herself in Toby it scared her. She wanted them to be different from her. Why was that? Did different mean better? Or did it mean she wouldn't have to look at herself so clearly.

She took a long sip of wine, her sea-green eyes strolling down the tank.

Annie observed her father across the table. Flashes in her mind, the week before her mother died. She was in her room, reading; she had been to Jones Beach with Mickey and Martin. Martin had said something that upset her and she had stormed off down the beach. What was it? They had come home, she had taken a shower, and she was lying on her bed, reading. *Emma,* she was reading Jane Austen's *Emma,* and her mother. . . . The phone rang and she heard her mother say to someone, "I know what you're doing. You stay away from him." She went to the door and her mother was standing, looking down at the phone as if waiting for a kettle to boil. She was crying.

"Mommy, what's wrong?" Annie had asked. She remembered calling her "Mommy," and her mother had raised her hands over her face as if to wipe out the hurt or wipe out Annie's question. "Nothing. Nothing," she said, and went back to the kitchen.

Her father was laughing at his own jokes, a man filled with himself. What had Martin said that day? "Don't be such a dope, Annie; Pop has other women. Everyone knows it. I'm still a kid and I know it. You don't want anything to interfere with your perfect family fantasy. Why do you think you cling to Mickey the way you do. Because no one's paying any attention to you."

That's what Martin had said, and she had taken off.

She looked at her brother, his white face was stretched into a polite smile. His eyes watching her father were tight and cold. *He hates him.*

The Truths were tiptoeing across her consciousness, rushing to get through before the door was closed. "Okay, guys," the Truths whispered to one another, "she hasn't seen us yet, let's go for it. Single file, stay low, don't make a sound, this is our chance."

She had never spent any time alone with her brother after that day at the beach. Her mother died and she got married, shutting the door tight against insight.

My father was cheating on my mother. That's why he was never home. She was always focused on him; that's why she seems such a blur to me. He paid more attention to me than to her. She must have resented that, she must have resented me. That's why Martin got all of her attention. He was a little boy. I was Daddy's girl so she closed me out. He made her unhappy. He made her brain explode. Is that true?

She watched him showing off. My father is a weak, selfish person. He can be charming and funny, but he is not a nice man. *Turquoise streaked behind the Truths, frantically racing toward safety at the awareness section of her brain.*

Is Mickey like my father and I never saw it? Oh, God.

Annie stood up and reached for her glass. "Let's have a toast to Pop and Ida Mae for making this journey to be with us. To many more family Thanksgivings!"

Mickey stood and faced her across the long laden table. "And to Annie our angel — Happy birthday, honey." Everyone joined in the toast.

Molly, Billy, and Samantha wandered in, one of the Pats trailing behind. Billy held a bottle of Dom Perignon in each hand.

"Time for our Thanksgiving birthday toast," Molly giggled. "We have escaped from our silly ol' party and come to crash yours. This is my friend Samantha, the reincarnation of the Delphic oracle, at your service."

Mickey went to greet them. Molly wrapped her arms around his neck, giving him a very neighborly kiss. Molly was drunk.

Annie sat back down with her Elmer's smile in place. Flashes inside her head. Molly fucking Mickey in the backseat of her car. A strip of turquoise. Molly was introducing Samantha to Mickey. She looked at Mickey looking at Samantha. Molly had not exaggerated. Samantha The Oracle was one of those voluptuous, professionally seductive women for whom sexuality or at least the public aroma of sexuality was as much a part of her personality as a sense of humor or a hearty laugh.

Samantha was a curl-tosser, and now she was tossing them at Mickey. Annie saw Mickey fucking Samantha in the backseat of her car. Molly had one arm around Mickey and the other draped casually around Samantha. Annie saw Mickey fucking Samantha *and* Molly in the backseat of her car. Billy opened the champagne and Juanita ran in with fresh glasses. Mickey gave Juanita a little pat on the shoulder. *When I get to Mickey fucking Juanita in the back of my car I am going to blow my head off.*

Molly was heading toward her with swaying Samantha in tow. No. I do not want to meet this Devil from Delphi. I want to knock her to the ground and pummel her with my freckled fists. I want to throw her out of my house. I want to . . . I want to *be* her. Searing, lashing envy pierced her. It was like falling on a spike. *If I was a woman like that I would have power. I would never be afraid of being left.*

Jackie had jumped up from his seat and was hot on Samantha's trail. From across the table she saw her father rise, on the pretext, it seemed to her, of getting a glass of champagne, which she knew he never drank. He smoothed his goatee, taking a glass and moving in alongside Jackie; peacocks on parade, ready to spread their feathers for this Southern goddess. A goddess, Annie could see, well aware of the stir she was causing.

Loretta came back from the bathroom and surveyed the scene with her internal zoom lens. Samantha would have to be even more threatening to Loretta. Another guruess in the aquaculture. Martin had not moved, but he was watching Samantha with that narrow-eyed intensity usually saved for mole scanning. Loretta whispered something to Mickey, who was, to his credit, talking to Billy and Toby. Annie saw Mickey and Loretta fucking in the back of her car. The car was now much too crowded. Some of them would have to get out or she would never be able to drive off in a jealous huff.

Toby was leaning in, listening to Billy and Mickey. Loretta, clearly not liking the conversation, settled in next to Bennie, reverting to Motherhood in a pinch. Billy, Mickey, and her Toby were smirking. They all turned and looked at Samantha, who was holding court surrounded by Jackie, her father, and now Martin. Loretta tried to hug

Bennie, who slid off his chair, eager to join the males in their preening before the new female.

Annie moved fast, heading for the kitchen before Molly could corner her. She did not want to meet the Oracle. She had always prided herself on being able to handle any social situation with poise and wit. She had met many famous people, sat next to senators and Pulitzer-prize winners at dinner and had never faltered. Tonight on her very own birthday, in her very own house, she was faltering. Stumbling against the aquarium windows someone had moved into the middle of her dining room. Crash. Glass and water everywhere, shards of emotion and truth, great big jagged chunks and thousands of microscopic fragments embedded in her skin, painful when she touched them but invisible to the naked eye. She stood in the wreckage, a stranded aquanaut not knowing what to do or how to save the sea creatures.

CHAPTER V

"MICKEY, ARE YOU ASLEEP?" Annie's clock said one A.M.

"Almost. Why?"

"Nothing. Never mind."

"Come on, tell me."

"It's nothing. I mean . . . I just thought . . . you're leaving early. I won't see you till Friday and you know . . ."

"The F word?"

"It's been almost two weeks."

"Is that a reason?"

"I just think we should. It's important."

"I thought *should* was a New Age no-no."

"Stop it. Don't shift like that."

"Do you *want* to?"

"Do you?"

"I asked you first."

"Look, I'm as tired as you are. This was not exactly a laid-back weekend, but we need to reconnect. We've hardly spoken since you came home. Once we start I'll want to."

"You don't have to do that much to start."

"Thanks. That's romantic! You make it sound like I'm asking you to take out the garbage or fix the porch light."

"I'm sorry, angel. I'm a bundle of nerves. We should hear about the show this week. My head has been elsewhere."

"How about the porno? That always speeds things up. I'll get it."

"The tape broke, remember? It's five years old."

"Why won't you get a new one? You can't expect *me* to go in and buy one."

"At least if you do it, I won't end up in the *Enquirer*. 'TV star leads secret life as pervert.'"

"I'm going to ask Molly if she has one of those catalogues. You can order them by mail. Vibrators, anything."

"Yeah, but then you turn up on every freako mailing list in the universe. Do we want the mailman to see piles of plain brown wrappers and Nightgames catalogues?"

"Mickey, you're not *that* famous."

"Come here. Just come into my arms for a minute. I could use a hug. You feel so soft. What's that smell?"

"Lemon. Jackie gave me lots of lemon bath oils and things for my birthday."

"Jackie would love to get you into a tub of lemon oil."

"Jackie? That's perverse. I'm hardly his type."

"The others are just a smoke screen. It's you he wants. I should know, I'm his brother. I've watched him moping around you since he was in diapers."

"Well, judging from the way he was following the Delphi Article around all weekend, I'd say he's gotten over it."

"Hmmm. You feel good. Touch me for a minute, maybe we'll get lucky."

"I see. It's going to be the Samantha fantasy. I'm surprised she wasn't gang-raped on our dining-room table. You could have all taken turns. First my father, then Bennie —"

"Annie, this conversation is not helping."

"Sorry. Okay. Let's concentrate. I really think I need the release."

"MMMMM. That's good. Where's the Vaseline?"

"Your side."

"I only see baby oil."

"That's okay, too. Put some on my nipples. Then I'll do you."

"Shit, Annie! You're spilling it all over the sheet!"

"Sorry. I've got my eyes closed."

"Oh. Honey. That feels good. Just keep doing that. Long slow strokes, not too fast. That's good. Let me get you. Put your leg over me. Comfortable?"

"Umm. That's nice. Not so hard. Good."

"UMMMMMMMMMM."

"Can you get my nipple at the same time?"

"Yeah, just move your shoulder. Okay?"

"Yes. Oh, that feels so good."

"Rub my balls for a minute. Yes. Oh, yes. Are you close?"

"Yes. Let's just do it this way. I don't have my diaphragm in."

"Good. Oh, do it. Do it to me. Ohhhh."

"Oh — yes — a little faster."

"Good. That's so good — just like that."

"Oh — oh — I'm ready. Are you?"

"Yeah — faster now. Yes. Yes!"

"Oh — I'm coming now. Now!"

"AHHHH."

"Oh, my God, Mickey, I feel so, so out of touch with myself, my physical self. I don't even know what I really need. I mean like sex. I always think that if I'm irritable or anxious or whatever, it's psychological or PMS or premenopause, when most of the time I probably only need to make love with you, reconnect like that and just let go."

"I know. My schedule doesn't help. We get so out of sync."

"Also, out of practice. Can you reach the Kleenex?"

"Yeah, here."

"It's all over the place. Must be a month's worth."

"It's on the blanket, too."

"I'll get a towel. I don't want to shock Juanita."

"With all of her steroid cases? Nothing could shock her."

"You know what I think? I think she's a virgin. I think she makes it all up."

"Now who's perverse."

"Want a wet towel?"

"Maybe I'll just jump in the shower. I'm up now."

"Is it a compliment that you didn't fall instantly asleep like you usually do or is it an insult?"

"Christ, Annie, you can find a weed in any rose garden. What kind of question is that?"

"A wife kind."

"It's a setup. There is no correct answer. I'm dead no matter what I say. I'm taking a shower."

"Throw this Kleenex away, will you?"

"Maybe we should burn it, in case Juanita figures out what's on it."

"Flush it."

"Annie, that was a joke."

"I know, but it's not a bad idea, anyway."

"Want me to turn on the TV?"

"Nope. I'm really sleepy now. That was good. I was right, we needed that. I'm going to just drift off."

"Does that mean it wasn't very good or the best you've ever had?"

"Touché. I'm sorry. 'Night, honey."

"'Night, angel."

The Monday after Thanksgiving Annie sat at a back table in Maisy's, working on her second cappuccino and trying to concentrate on the *New York Times.* Quiet is what she had wanted. Quiet is what she had.

Everyone was gone, leaving behind, Annie thought, too many long, scraggly loose ends. She had never broken through to Ella. She just knew something was going on with her, but Ella had shut her out. That was one of the worst damn things about having them grow up. You could no longer manipulate, cajole, or take away allowances or ice-cream cones as a way of forcing them to tell you things.

She could hardly send a twenty-two-year-old woman to her room. "So, you want to grow up and have your own life, keep secrets from your mother, well, I'll show you." Rats. No child-care book went up this high. Toby seemed fine, at least until Saturday. After Saturday, he was a little weirded-out too. Maybe Ella had told Toby what she wouldn't tell her and that was why. Oh, God! She was not going to do this to herself. They were all back dealing with their own lives, not dwelling on her every vocal intonation and mood. Let them all go, Annie girl. She had to shut it off.

She scanned the front page, the coffee hitting her nervous system like the first dip on the Ferris wheel, taking her up and down simultaneously.

An El Al cargo plane had crashed into a low-income apartment complex in Amsterdam, tearing a chasm six apartments wide and ten floors deep and turning the surrounding area into an inferno.

Annie swallowed, foam and hot strong caffeine sliding down her throat. That was what life was really all about. There you were sitting down to a quiet family meal in the only semisafe place on earth, the privacy of your own home, maybe worrying about your kid's math grades or the dental work you can't afford and *swack,* a 747 crashes through your window, falling from the sky where heaven is supposed to be and taking all the dreams.

Saying good-bye once again to her children and sending Mickey back to the trenches — life in the end was mainly about hope and loss. One followed by the other over and over. But, of course, you had to be alive to even go through it. One 747 in your dining room can ruin your entire hope-and-loss philosophy.

Annie looked at her watch. She was going to Ojai to pick up her birthday present, but she was early. Merry Oates and Jessica Sanders strolled in wearing their tennis uniforms. They were two of what Annie called her "benefit friends," women who only invited her and Mickey to events that required a contribution (usually sizable) but never invited them socially. It had taken her a while to figure this group out, because they had been so friendly at first. She had invited them and their Hollywood husbands for drinks or Sunday barbecues. They would always come and have a grand old time. But after a while she realized that the only time she heard from them was when they were hawking one of their endless charities or politically correct causes. She would get an invitation, to buy a table at ten thousand dollars, or a seat at — the seat prices would run the gamut from a thousand or so to three hundred or so, with all the things that you were included or not included in based on what contribution you made. Why didn't they just put decals on everyone's forehead to show who the spenders were?

They would send the invitation with a perky little handwritten note scrawled in the corner: "Dear Annie and Michael, this is going to be such fun, please join us! Much love, . . ." They never went to any of them. But this did not stop the onslaught.

Between events, they might as well have fallen into the San Andreas fault. She never invited them anymore, but they didn't seem to notice.

They had seen her. Merry Oates waved and headed over. *Christmas is coming, benefits galore.*

"Hi, Annie. We were just talking about you."

"You were?"

"Yes, we saw your article in *Travel West* about that eighteenth-century inn in Monterey and we're going! It sounded just to die. We have this incredible fund-raiser Thursday in East L.A. and then the four of us are taking off for your inn. Are you coming Thursday?"

Annie laughed. "Sorry to say, I don't think I saw this invitation. East L.A. I would have remembered."

"It's such a good cause. A group of us have restored one of the original immigrant complexes. It's really the Los Angeles equivalent of a tenement, and we have turned it into a museum to preserve the struggle of our forefathers who arrived here and fought to forge a life. We're busing everyone in from the Bel Air Hotel, then back there for dinner and dancing."

Annie gaped at her incredulously. "You mean people are going to get all dressed-up and be *bused* into the *riot zone* to look at a building that everyone including our forefathers fought hand over fist to get out of and *then* go dancing?"

Merry Oates's smile, in a way not visible to the untrained eye, narrowed. Her eyes shut down. Just a tiny blip on the social radar screen.

Annie needed her Elmer's, but the damage had been done. She remembered what Loretta had said in her kitchen. *I want to lead an honest life.* She had never let her social-graces mask slip like this before. Something deep inside her felt different. Braver. Angrier. Lighter.

"Well, not everyone sees it like that, dear. Oh, Jessica has our goodies. Have a nice holiday. Love to Michael."

She was gone. Her legs, veined and flabby in spite of, Annie knew, countless tennis games and aerobics classes, moving stiffly away from the holder of the naughty pin so perilously close to her hot air balloon.

Annie felt sick to her stomach. Five years old and shut out of the hopscotch game. Why did I do that? What's the point? She picked up her bagel and took a bite, hoping to settle her nerves.

A tall, heavily built older man in jogging clothes was pushing a wheelchair across the room. In the chair was a deeply tanned, emaciated woman in shorts, her legs sticklike and akimbo in the chair. Her face was twisted, whether the result of a stroke or extreme discomfort, Annie couldn't tell. People in the room ignored them, trying not to stare.

This was not a Maisy's-type couple. Maisy's was the meeting spot of Montecito, the only place of its kind, with its giant cups of coffee and nouvelle California cuisine, hip and health conscious, and filled with the hip and health conscious trotting in from exercise class, riding class, tennis lessons, therapy sessions, yoga workshops; throwing their Italian totes over the backs of their high-tech chairs, greeting one another with bright, bonded smiles; sunshine people living sunshine lives. The couple did not fit. They intruded on the California-dream life. If there is no weather change, then time does not pass; if time does not pass then we will not be touched by the sickness and old age brush.

The man wheeled the woman over to the table next to Annie. She cowered in her chair, her mottled, birdlike arms tucked between her legs.

The man left her and went to the counter, returning with their order. He stood over her slamming down plates of designer food. The woman averted her eyes as if the very sight of the cheerful grub was a reminder of her condition.

The man, who Annie assumed was her husband, sat down and began to eat ravenously. Cutting and salting and chewing fiercely.

"Eat!" Annie heard him say to his wife, as if she were a French poodle.

The woman shook her head back and forth.

Annie took a deep calming breath.

A picture of herself and Mickey thirty years from now slid into view. One of them sick, crippled, senile. Was it possible that they could end up like that? How would Mickey be if she was ill, shriveled, powerless? Was there enough love to survive whatever life had in store? Everyone believes there is, but whoever really knows?

Generic marriage, as hard as it is, is a veritable cupcake compared to the added assaults of sickness and impairment. Annie picked up her purse and paper, her concentration scattered by the despair next to her, and headed out into the late November sun to claim her present and remove herself from the poor bullied woman and her own terror at such a fate.

She had always coveted one of Ivy Clare's pots. It was the perfect birthday gift, even if she ended up smashing Mickey over the head with it. She had hoped the drive up to Ojai would give her some time to think things through, but the scene at Maisy's had unnerved her. Her head ached, pulsing from too much emotion and speculation.

Having all those people around all weekend had forced her to hold so many thoughts and feelings inside that now she was not quite sure where they had gone or how to retrieve them.

She flipped on the radio looking for distraction, trying to remove the woman in the wheelchair from her mind.

> "Good morning. This is Health Hotline. A new report just in from Indiana University says that a drop in estrogen levels in middle-aged women leads to an overproduction of bone scavenger cells, which carve pits and craters throughout the skeleton. Another report just in from the National Institutes of Health, part of the first wave of research focusing on women's health problems, brings more bad news. Women's longer lives have a downside, more disability and disease. Women in nursing homes outnumber men three to one. Nine in ten

women over seventy-five have osteoporosis, and throughout life, women are sicker than men. They have fifty bouts of flu for every thirty-seven men have and thirty-one colds for every twenty-one for men. Women are bedridden thirty-five percent more days than men and are fifteen times more likely to have autoimmune thyroid disease and nine times more likely to have lupus, anemia, constipation, gallstones, arthritis, and bronchitis. Half the women, but only thirty-one percent of men, die within a year of a heart attack, and women comprise the fastest-growing group of AIDS patients —"

Annie turned off the radio. There was an overlook ahead on her right and she pulled over. She sat for a moment, looking out over the valley to the ocean. Then she screamed. One very long, very loud scream. She shut her eyes and folded her hands daintily in her lap as if waiting to be served afternoon tea, and she screamed. She screamed until her poor sticky brain hurt. She screamed away all the daily bombardment of fear. Fear about everything she ate, thought, did or did not do, fear that rushed toward her from everywhere. Newspapers, television programs, books, magazines.

Control through fear. We were all victims of the exploitation of our fear by the media, medical profession, recovery movements, bosses, everyone. No one entered her life anymore without their fear agenda. Buy this toaster, your old one reeks radioactivity; for just a small sum we will check your water for lead, your walls for asbestos, your lawn for radon. Buy Retin A or wrinkle. Buy Cellulite Gel or pucker. Buy vitamins or die. Catalogues were filled with products that had never existed before the fear crusades. Air purifiers, sunproof shirts, soap for washing vegetables.

All she had wanted was a little Tony Bennett.

The screaming relaxed her. "There's nothing like a good scream," her mother-in-law always said. She took a deep breath and switched on the ignition. She was late. She had never been to an artist's house before and she wasn't quite sure what to expect. She moved back onto the road, fumbling in the glove compartment for a tape, something with no unsolicited negative information attached to it. Stan Getz. Good.

An image of her skeleton, whittled away with pits and craters, flashed by. Maybe she *was* really right. Their mothers did have it easier. Ignorance may well have been bliss. We weren't even healthier! Our corpses would just have better leg muscles. Annie shook the thought away. No more death today, no more fear today, no more . . . turquoise underwear.

She was there. A long driveway with a hand-painted sign, CLARE, marked the entrance. Entering involved a left turn, but the road was quiet and she did it. Completing a left turn, even an easy, intersectionless one, always made her feel enormous self-satisfaction. She felt stronger. She visualized the holes in her skeleton closing up.

She moved the Range Rover slowly up a long unpaved driveway overgrown with weeds. All the brush and trees looked dry and neglected. Everything was hotter and dryer in Ojai, even without the years of drought they had suffered, but there was something else here; the property had the look of land that no one cared much about. A projection, Annie thought, but probably true.

In the distance at the top of the hill stood a rambling, wood-framed house. The parking area was down below and she pulled up against a tree, set her parking brake, and got out. Her neck was stiff and she rotated her head a few times and stretched her spine. She looked at her watch. Twenty minutes late. She pushed her glasses up on top of her hair and climbed the uneven brick steps to the house.

It was so quiet. So unlike her house, which always had various noises, voices, all sorts of humming household sounds; Portia, Juanita talking to her sister, her typewriter tapping, Mickey's NordicTrack whushing. This house felt different. Somber, isolated, and without good cheer.

There was no bell. A small note was pinned to the door: "I'm working. Don't knock. Enter quietly."

Certain things were very hard for Annie. Calling anyone before ten in the morning or after nine at night (her father's rule), walking into a stranger's house without waiting to be invited. She turned the knob as cautiously as a cat burglar and tiptoed in. Inside, the house was nicer. It was woodsy and rustic, with a skylight crowning a large open living area and a crackling fire in a fieldstone fireplace. Annie moved a few steps farther into the room and put on her glasses. The back wall was glass and she could see down into a studio where a tall dark woman wearing surgical clothes was totally concentrated on her work. She was kneading a large clay breast with her fingers, forming an aureola from the wet gray earth.

She had seen Ivy Clare's work in magazines and wealthy collectors' homes for years, but to be here actually watching her do it was exciting. Breast pots: all sizes and shapes, massive four-breast urns and tiny, delicate, single-bosom jugs, some starkly simple and others glazed with wild colors and designs; angry, proud bosoms. Annie loved their power.

"Hello."

Annie stepped back, startled. A tall, husky man was standing behind her. He was wearing paint-splattered jeans and he was smoking a cigarette.

His face was finely boned but weathered and framed by shaggy black and white hair, and he had the bluest eyes Annie had ever seen outside a Gerber's label. Beside him was a large black dog.

"I'm so sorry. The sign said to come in. I hope I'm not intruding. I'm here to choose one of Miss Clare's pots. It's a present. My, uh, birthday." Annie felt funny.

She kept her head down, looking at the dog. She did not feel capable of making eye contact with this man.

"I know. I've been expecting you. I'm terribly sorry, but you were a bit late and she's started now and we can't stop her until she's finished. She's just on that one nipple now, so it may not be so long."

Annie blushed at the way he said the word. He must be British, she thought. "Oh, that's all right. I don't mind watching for a while."

"Would you like something to drink?"

"Nothing, thanks." The dog looked up at him and he kneeled down, murmuring something to it and stroking its head, the smoke from his cigarette floating out into the air. The fire snapped. They were silent, watching the tall woman in the green scrub suit create a nipple out of mud.

The funny feeling inside of Annie moved. Her heart was beating too fast. Something was happening to her that she could not control. What had her sister-in-law told her? That she was so overcontrolled, she was out of control. She had thought that was absurd, out of control was not a concept that had ever had any meaning to her. Even "madly in love" had no meaning. When she saw Lina and some of her friends losing their minds over some idiot who humiliated them, cheated on them, abused them in some way, it dumbfounded her. She simply did not understand it. Her love affair with Mickey had never involved that kind of risk. It had always been there and it had always been safe. Not that during their courtship they hadn't broken up now and then and had their other flirtations, but it never felt serious; underneath she had always known that he loved her and they would be together. There were no surprises in their behavior toward one another. It was dependable. Annie believed that if she hadn't found Mickey she would never have had the courage to fall in love the way the rest of the world did. As a grown-up, with a complete stranger. How unnerving a thought that was.

What was happening to her? Her nipples were so hard they pushed against her bra. The warm pressure of arousal moved down her belly and soaked her panties. Passion. She was consumed with passion. Her body did not belong to a forty-five-year-old woman with a bumpy uterus. She felt as fertile and lush as a teenage virgin.

The dog, as if sensing her need or sniffing her lust, left his master and came to her, nuzzling her leg, pushing her skirt against her thighs. She reached down and held out her open palm. The dog began licking it, and the feeling electrified her. She moaned, turning her head too fast. Her glasses fell, crashing to the stone floor and cracking across the bridge. The man crossed to her and picked them up. Her hand trembled. He tried to meet her eyes but she looked down at the dog.

"I can fix them if you like."

She nodded. Squinting out toward Ivy Clare, who had finished the nipple and moved on to something else.

"She's going to be a while now, I'm afraid."

He was standing beside her, close enough for her to smell the woody, nicotine fragrance of him.

A voice that she realized must be hers but seemed to have nothing to do with her, a ventriloquist's trick, a lower, throatier voice than her own, floated down from somewhere over the top of her head. "I think that if you don't kiss me in the next five minutes I will simply cease to exist."

He turned toward her and she looked at him now, into those baby-food eyes. He motioned toward the front door and moved in front of her. The dog pushed between them, wanting to be included, and followed them out of the door and down the hill to her car.

He threw his cigarette onto the dirt and crushed it with his boot. Annie moved toward him, everything slightly out of focus. With her glasses on she would never have dared. He reached for her hands and pulled her to him. His hands were hard and rough. He was a big man. She was a small woman. Mickey was a normal-size man and they fit. She had never been held by a big man before. The scale of him was intoxicating.

"My name's Annie Wilder," she said in that voice.

"Oliver Taylor," he said, pulling her tight against him.

She felt his erection through her skirt. She was so wet, the insides of her thighs were dripping. "I have never . . . I only . . . my husband . . . I mean, I'm safe. . . ."

"Me, too," he said, and he kissed her.

He could have been Jack the Ripper.

She came the first time from that kiss. She had never been kissed like that. It was the opposite of the Kiss of Death — it was a kiss to bring *back* the dead. To resurrect the frightened, possibly betrayed, empty-nested, career-conflicted, motherless, overcontrolled Annie Wilder from the living dead. They could not end the kiss.

It felt as if to separate would be physically unbearable. They ravished one another with their kiss.

When he touched her breasts she came again, tears streaming down her red, freckled cheeks. "My God. My God." They both groaned against one another, as if saying the words for the first time. Annie saw the turquoise glide across her mind. Turquoise, and pitted skeletons, ha, ha, ha. She was alive. Oh, God, she was *alive.* She *was* a virgin. *Jesus. Jesus.* They moaned together. Two aliens seeing their first sunrise. Experiencing something for the first time; feeling something for the first time. After all the years of sex, they had found something new. A new feeling. How was that possible this far through life? A fresh feeling. *Jesus. Jesus.* The dog stood quietly and watched the two people create an explosion in their hearts.

They held on to one another for what seemed like a long time, still unable to let go. The dog barked. Annie pulled away.

Oliver reached for his cigarettes. She saw his hand tremble. "It's okay, just a squirrel. Cigarette?"

"No, thanks." Annie had never smoked, even before it was social anathema. She watched him light it and inhale. She loved that he smoked. It made him more mysterious, dangerous maybe. More *out of control?* Besides, he wasn't her concern. She wasn't his wife, having to pick and pull at his bad habits to ensure her own security.

He laughed. "I didn't think so."

"Shouldn't we, I mean won't she, aren't you afraid . . ."

He faced her with those eyes. "I don't live here. Ivy is not my woman. She's my client and my friend. I'm a dealer. I handle her work in England. I've been here on a business trip, but I go back tomorrow. I'm fifty years old and I've been divorced for a year, during which I have basically been too depressed to be very active sexually. I did not cheat on my wife and she, well, she channeled that energy elsewhere." He threw his cigarette down and took her face in his hands.

"Annie Wilder — I'm going to ask you to do something completely crazy, but please don't just discard it. Something has happened to us — something important that we must pay attention to. I have to go back to England, so there's no time for us now, but we must have some time. So please listen to me. I want you to meet me on the steps of the Victoria and Albert Museum at ten A.M. on January tenth. I know it sounds absurd and I know this will scare you and it will scare me, but I think we must do this. I fell in love with you the moment I saw you, before you turned around, and that is what you responded to. It came from me, first. If you don't show up, I know I'll never see you again."

Annie tried to talk, "I can't —"

"Shh. Don't say anything. Please, don't decide yet. Now I must kiss you once more, right this second, or I will never be able to resume my life."

CHAPTER VI

MICKEY THREADED HIS WAY through the noontime traffic. Thousands of cars filled with tense, frustrated people, inching along, desperate to speed forward on their way to a job they probably hated. Maybe they were all being controlled by the giant Job God, sitting up above the San Diego Freeway creating obstacles to prevent his hapless minions from getting where they really didn't want to go in the first place. He checked the dash clock. Eleven forty-five. Rats. He had to be back on the set by one-fifteen. He was really pushing it.

Today was his biggest scene for the week. Lina Allen was coming in to do a guest shot as his ex-wife. He needed all of his focus on that, not just because Lina was the world's biggest scene thief, but because he had a monologue. A close-up of him talking about their marriage. Christ, what a day for it!

It would have been easier with someone who wasn't a friend, too, though she was more Annie's friend than his. They had both known Lina since NYU, but she had always made him nervous. He never quite trusted her.

He didn't get it with her and Annie, either. She wasn't really Annie's type. She ran around with the Hollywood Wives and entertainment executives who were into all of that holistic-crystal-power bullshit that Annie hated. A pack of frustrated, emaciated women with that moon-eyed stare like B-sci-fi actors, babbling endlessly about the purity of their bodies while smearing their faces with collagen, stuffing their chests with silicone, slitting their faces open — *and* they were living in Los Angeles!

Mickey swung into the right lane and turned off onto Wilshire Boulevard. His throat tightened. *I can't believe I'm doing this, talking to a stranger about my problems! Worse, my brother's shrink!*

It had gotten so bad since Sunday, he felt as if he was going to simply explode. There did not seem to be any way to hold all of the panic inside himself. He never talked to anyone but Annie about anything really personal. But this was hardly something he could talk to his wife about.

At least his brother he could trust. Jackie had really been great. He didn't ask him any questions, he called Rhinehart and set it up. Rhinehart said he would see him once or twice and then refer him to someone else. That made sense; it wouldn't be ethical for Jackie's shrink to treat him, not that he was going to talk about Jackie. He only *wished* he was going in with the garden-variety childhood crab-grass to kill. Besides, he was only prepared to go a couple of times. He hoped that would be enough.

Mickey swung his Porsche into the parking lot behind Rhinehart's office. He put on his Dodgers cap and shades and checked himself in the mirror. He was being ridiculous. This was L.A. for chrissakes! They could practically hand out the Oscars at the Santa Monica AA meeting, so why was he paranoid about going to see a shrink? Almost everyone he had ever known was seeing or had seen one.

Whatever Mickey had expected, Dr. Rhinehart was not it. Mickey thought all shrinks had beards. He shook his hand, trying to adjust his Monty-Clift-in-*Freud* idea of a shrink to the reality of this round, shiny-faced man with an egg-bald head and bright pink cheeks. He looked more like the Pillsbury Dough Boy than Sigmund Freud.

Rhinehart motioned him to sit in one of the chairs near his desk. Mickey relaxed a little. He took off his Ray-Bans, leaving his hat on for protection. He always felt less vulnerable with his cap on.

The doctor slid a pair of rimless glasses onto his melon head. Mickey cleared his throat, waiting for his cue.

"What seems to be the problem?" the doctor asked impassively.

"Well, I, the thing is . . . I'm not sure how to start this. . . . You know how actors are without their lines. I . . . am, I . . . am . . . having an *affair.* Jesus! I don't believe I said it! I actually said it out loud!

Oh, boy . . . I'm cheating on my wife. God . . . how weird that sounds!

"I'm sitting here and I'm thinking I'll start by telling you a little about myself and I'm thinking, I'll tell you how I've been married since I was six years old and I'm ninety now. I know that sounds insane. But that's really how I feel. My wife and I, we weren't even childhood sweethearts, we were *toddler* sweethearts. We've been together since we were *six* years old. She just had her forty-fifth birthday. I'm three months older and she told me that together we're ninety years old and I kind of blew it off. I guess it was just too damn scary, but she was right. It's like we're combined. We're like one of those pairs of Siamese twins in the freak show.

"I mean it's great, my marriage, my children, it's what's gotten me through, kept me stable in this impossible business, and I've never, I mean, I swear to God, I've never cheated on Annie before!

"Believe me there have been opportunities, but I always felt that would make me into just another one of the bums I work with all the time. It was like my marriage made me special, gave my work more dignity. I didn't even *want* to cheat most of the time. I mean, there were temptations. I mean I'm an actor not a proctologist. I see sexy, beautiful women every day and I see them at their absolute best, but none of them were like Annie. My wife is . . . she's unique. She has this way about her. She makes me laugh and she's straight, I mean she always tells me the truth. She's smart and she smells, she has this wonderful fresh smell, and all this red hair and freckles. She still looks like a kid and she has the best laugh; it seems to kind of trill, to roll up her throat or something. So, I never did before.

"But I met someone, she's not anything like my wife. I know that's part of it. She has this darkness, this ferocity about her. She's very quiet. There's an almost feline stillness in her. It fucking hypnotizes me.

"She is *nothing* like Annie. God! Annie is like, what you see is what you get, she's so transparent she's like tracing paper, and she never shuts up.

"This woman, I can't stop seeing her. Sexually I mean. I mean, with Annie, there are things that it just wouldn't be nice to do with her. I mean we were so young when we got married and I'd had a little experience, so had she, you know, when we broke up and were trying to make one another jealous and stuff, but she was . . . I mean I think I'm the only man she's ever slept with. Almost the same for me. Once or twice in college, but really like nothing. So we were kids and we loved one another and it was great. I mean we've always had great sex together, but I mean I wouldn't have wanted to scare her with some weird request. . . . Don't get me wrong, I'm not saying I have some bizarre preferences; but she got pregnant pretty fast and then she was the mother of my children on top of it and so . . . I mean we . . . we're no prudes or anything. I mean we watch porno and we certainly aren't uptight about oral sex and stuff, but I mean we've been at it for decades now and it sort of settles in.

"I mean I don't really feel like I could come in, throw her down, and screw her in the ass all of a sudden. I mean, I could hurt her! But this woman, she'll do anything. *She's* the one who suggests the stuff! She has this thing where she starts licking me, starts on my feet and then really slowly, like in slow motion, she just licks her way up my body. It's amazing! So slow, she just tongues me into insanity. I mean the thing is, if Annie did it, I'd probably just start laughing. I wouldn't even *want* her to. I'd probably say something like, 'Hey, speed it up, kid, there's a Lakers game on at eleven.' Oh, boy! I know how crazy this sounds!

"I feel like I've never been free in my entire life. I'm ninety fucking years old and I've been married for eighty-four years! This thing just happened. I mean it was like a forest fire. One little ash and all the redwoods are gone. That's how I feel. I mean it's what I'm afraid of. My family tree, so to speak, we'll all be caught in this and burned to a crisp.

"See, I stay in L.A. four or five days when I'm filming, so I have more freedom than most married men. It made this too easy in a way. It wasn't like I had to go home to Annie every night and look her in the eye with some other woman's smell in my nose. When I'm home, I'm home. At least till lately. Lately it's been, well, as I said, I'm a little out of control now.

"But I've been very discreet. *No one,* and I mean no one, knows. And she, well, she's alone. She's no one's wife or mother. She's not into families; part of the attraction I guess. She's tough and very independent. She's never been married, never lived with anyone. She's probably had a hundred lovers, men and women. Ha! I mean she is *nothing* like my wife!

"So then Thanksgiving comes and we're all in the kitchen and my daughter, Ella, she's twenty-two and she's still living back in New York, she pulls, by mistake, she was reaching for a Kleenex, and she pulls these turquoise *panties* out of her pocket. I mean, these panties land in her yogurt bowl and then this whole scene transpires.

"It turns out she found them in Annie's car and was hiding them, assuming that I had fucked someone in her mother's car! What irony! I mean, I was totally innocent! What unnerved me the most was that my daughter would believe that I was capable of doing such a thing, but at the same time, there was obviously some vibe she was picking up.

"So Annie says 'They're mine' and goes through this whole song and dance. But later, she asked me if I was having an affair. I couldn't believe it! The first time in my entire marriage and I'm going to be confronted for something that, okay, I *am* doing, but on evidence that is totally bogus!

"But I know now that her antenna is way up. And the normal kind of 'not tonight dear' stuff that couples do, well, now it's really loaded with suspicion. Which is not the greatest male aphrodisiac. I know my wife. She is not finished with this, and I'm just so confused. I mean I have enough pressure on the set every day without my personal life coming apart at the seams.

"I can't keep doing this. I have to stop seeing this woman! But then part of me, and I know it's infantile, but part of me is kicking and screaming saying, 'No! I don't want to stop! I've been such a good boy, I want my dessert. I want to eat the entire quart of Häagen-Dazs. I don't want to stop until I throw up!

"I know guys who cheat on their wives all the time. For years! One woman after another and they never get caught. Okay, maybe they don't have the kind of closeness that Annie and I have or at least that we had, but just once in my entire life I run out of bounds and I get tackled by a pair of undies that I don't know anything about? It pisses me off. I know how that sounds, but I just wanted a little more time.

"I was working up the nerve to ask Annie how she felt about me taking a trip alone. That's the truth. I wasn't going to take this woman. I wanted to get away and try to figure this all out. But now, she'd be suspicious.

"Honest to God, Doctor, if I don't, I'm going to blow it. I'm going to flick the ash and ruin my whole life. I just don't know how everything got so complicated. I've always kept my life as simple as sand. Keep the priorities straight. Your marriage, your kids, your work.

"Well, the kids are grown now. I mean my boy is still in college; we still have to be there for him in a major way. But the fact is that he's gone for at least nine months of the year. We're alone now. My wife's in a career crisis and I may be too, so the timing sucks. I guess that's how life goes, things happen, it's not our call. I don't know what to do, Doctor. I just don't know what I want anymore and I can't see through this."

Mickey blinked into the sun. He had completely lost track of time. He checked his watch. He had fifteen minutes to get back to the set. He swung open the car door and jammed the key into the ignition. *Come on, baby, get me there.* He accelerated out of the lot, deciding to take surface streets and avoid the slave trail he could still see in the distance. He would just have to push it and hope he didn't get stopped. His phone rang.

"Mickey?"

"Hi, Jackie."

"How'd it go?"

"Where are you, in the trunk?"

"I made the appointment, remember. If there's one thing I know, it's the forty-five-minute hour."

"We ran over. I am really late. I've got to go, I can't speed and talk to you."

"Are you okay?"

"I'm fine."

"You sure?"

"I'm sure. Jackie, thanks, it was really helpful. I feel much better, just getting some stuff out like that."

"Yeah, I know. He's a trip isn't he."

"Not at all what I expected. Actually, I couldn't really tell you much. I think he said three words. '*I* did Hamlet.'"

"Good. Got another call. Keep in touch."

"I will." Mickey put down the receiver and forced his attention back into the outer world. He had a scene to do. A marriage scene.

> "Why couldn't we give it another shot? I'm lost without you, baby. There's no one else for me, you know that."
>
> "Ah, come on, Jerico. I just scraped the last piece of your damn chewing gum off the furniture. Think I want to start that all over again? Buy a cat. They like to be ignored."

Mickey slumped down in his director's chair and closed his eyes. Lina Allen came around behind him and rubbed his shoulders.

"God, I am wiped today."

Lina laughed. "Working with me is always a drain."

Mickey grinned. "Trying to stay in the shot does take some extra energy."

"Very funny." Lina stopped rubbing and sat down beside him in Stan Stein's chair. "Think I'll catch some disease?"

"Naw. They delouse it every evening."

"How was Thanksgiving? I really missed being there. It's so *me*, to turn down an invitation from two of my closest friends to traipse after some asshole who, it turns out, thought I was *Donna Mills*."

"You're kidding."

"Could I make that up? I met this guy when I did the AIDS telethon. He's Mr. Big Deal Executive with some international advertising agency who was underwriting the program, and he's all over me like a skin disease. 'Come ski with me at my place in Vail.' So off I go. Not only does the guy turn out to be a lush, but he thinks I'm someone else. I mean, do I look like Donna Mills?"

Mickey sat up, scrutinizing her with mock intensity. "Maybe just a little around the roots."

"Ha, ha." Lina lit a cigarette. "Don't say a word. I'm stopping next week. It's this or gaining ten pounds, and I'm working steady for the first time in a year, so I can't pork up."

"Good for you. Anything I'd know?"

"A pilot for Disney that could be really big. Second lead in a *Movie of the Week* for USA; a dog-food commercial — no comment please — I do not play the dog. A guest shot on Seinfeld; a low-budget Italian television miniseries with two weeks in Rome, no less. It's better than the cosmetics department at Bergdorf's."

"Will you stop with that? Is that your ultimate failed-actress scenario? Where old starlets go to die? You just scare yourself."

Lina inhaled. "You can talk because you have never *been* to the cosmetics department at Bergdorf's. You have not seen the array of women who all look like Donna Mills ten years from now, selling purple lipstick to horrible old dames with no lips. I have. I'll die first."

"Lina, you have the first residual check you ever received. Leonard has made a fortune for you. You are never going to end up handing out face cream samples or whatever they do. You'll buy a villa in Tuscany and retire with some Italian stud and several happy little animals."

Lina stamped out her cigarette. "Oh, that reminds me, have you talked to Leonard lately?"

"No. Annie does Leonard. Why?"

"Nothing. I've been calling him for days and all I get is that Girl in the Ultrasuede Swing he's married to or her machine doing her Betty Boop impression. 'Hi, this is Bambi of Bambi and Leonard

Lewis. We're at large right now, but so thrilled you called. . . .' It gives one pause, to have a man married to that twat-brain handling your life savings."

"They probably went away for the holidays. They're big spa goers. I'm sure he'll be back mid-week."

"It makes me very nervous when I don't know where he is. It's like not knowing where my bankbook is. He always leaves a number or his office has one. No one's answering there either."

"Really?"

"I think I'll drop by this afternoon. I got a tip from the Vail prick about a great biotech stock and I want him to check it out."

"Wanna run the next scene before they come back?"

"Sure. Listen, tell Annie I'll call her tomorrow. I want to come up and see her new pot."

"She hasn't gotten it yet."

"That doesn't sound like our Annie. I thought she'd be at the door before the turkey was cold."

Mickey pulled himself up and stretched. Dr. Rhinehart's face appeared in his head. "She went, but the artist was working. She has to go back. I just hope she gets one with big tits."

Lina picked up her script. "Oh, you men are so predictable. Let's run it. This is the best scene I've had in months. Maybe they'll bring me in as a regular."

Mickey yawned. "Don't hold your breath. We may all be auditioning for *Hollywood Squares* by next week."

"Not what I hear. I think they're going to give you another thirteen weeks, minimum. The show has such powerful fans, it's like a cult following. They wouldn't dare pull you now. Besides, I don't think they have anything to fill the slot. Relax."

"Yeah. We're in such a rational, fair business. I must be paranoid to think such a thing. Let's do the 'you were never home' bit. I'm having trouble with the motivation."

"What motivation? He's a cop. He has no motivation."

"Everyone has motivation, Lina."

"Well, right now my motivation is elimination. I'm taking these diuretics my herbalist gave me, dropped five pounds in two days, but my bladder is like Hoover Dam. I'm going to pee, call Leonard's office once more, and I'm all yours."

"Best offer I've had since lunch." Mickey checked his watch. They should wrap by seven. *God. I'm not through with this yet. Not even close.*

Annie completed her left turn and pulled into Ivy Clare's driveway. Returning to the scene of the crime, she thought, slowly easing her large car up the narrow dirt road. It had taken her three days to get up the courage to come back for her pot. Oliver Taylor had found her flight "quite sweet." After all, it wasn't as if he were Ivy Clare's husband, or lover even, but still, it was possible that she might pick up some aura.

Annie blushed. Ivy Clare knew people they knew. She was in L.A. all the time, had even spoken to Mickey on the phone. What would she think of a woman so wanton she could come with a total stranger while waiting to pick up a birthday present from her husband?

She was overdoing it. Certainly Oliver wouldn't have told her, and unless *Candid Camera* had been hiding in the bushes, no one but the dog and the squirrels saw them. Still, she felt seriously self-conscious. How could she be sure that anything Oliver Taylor had told her was true?

He and Ivy might do things like this all the time: seduce innocent pot-buyers as part of some sicko sex game between the two of them. A total stranger tells her that he fell in love with the back of her and wants her to meet him on the steps of a British museum in the dead of winter to talk about spending eternity together or whatever? She'd seen herself in a three-way mirror. Hardly the stuff of romance novels.

Why was she doing this? Annie picked up her purse and got out of the car. Why did she have to destroy the most intensely magical experience of her entire life? It felt like a dream, the prince who comes in the night to awaken Sleeping Beauty, only when she opens her eyes, he's gone. At moments, it did feel like she had dreamed it, so completely out of place and out of character had the event been.

The truth was that she *did* believe him, every single word. She did. She had never been a fool. She had a skeptical nature underneath her basic good cheer, and she had always prided herself on her ability to see people clearly.

It was one place she trusted herself: her judgment of people. It seemed hard for her to believe that all of a sudden in the middle of her life she would completely lose her instincts.

She did believe him. But still . . .

She climbed the steps, remembering her last trip. It seemed like centuries ago. She had begun to compartmentalize her life into her own version of B.C. and A.D. Before Oliver and After Oliver. In barely more than minutes she had committed an act that changed who she was and the course of her inner, and possibly outer, life forever. She was no longer sure of anything.

There was another note pinned to the door: "Wilder, come around back to the studio."

Annie went back down the steps, relieved at not having to face that room again, the shadow of Oliver Taylor walking beside her.

I fell in love with you before you even turned around.

Molly always said that men know when your antenna is up. They sniff it out, like a swine after truffles. If your antenna is down you could be Michelle Pfeiffer and Kim Basinger rolled into one and they still look right through you. But when it's up, look out.

Had someone snuck into her body and raised her antenna without her knowing it? Basically she'd had the sex drive of a shrimp for the last two years. What had happened to her had been as great a shock as if stigmata had suddenly appeared on her palms.

Good guilt image, Annie. She stomped through the dry grass to the studio. The door was open and she could see Ivy Clare inside. Her hands were caked with clay, but she was not working. She was standing in front of the same pot she had been molding that Monday, drinking a glass of wine.

"Miss Clare?" Annie stopped in the doorway. The woman did not break her contact with the pot for what seemed to Annie, as far as manners went, an inappropriate amount of time.

Her broad, suntanned face finally lifted. "Mrs. Wilder?"

"Annie." Annie said, still standing in the doorway. She did not like this woman. I know this game. This is the female macho having-the-edge game. This is the Hollywood meeting-power-seating game. Suddenly I'm the seller and she's the buyer. The hell with you and your tit vats. Annie wished she could take her first name back.

Annie walked in, not waiting to be invited. She was different now. This was A.O. or A.A.O. Annie After Oliver. She was not going to take any shit.

"What pieces are available for me to choose from? I believe you made the arrangements with my husband."

Ivy Clare smiled, a slow, secret smile as if she were party to some private joke at Annie's expense. It was clear that she had not expected Annie to reclaim herself.

She sipped her wine, her wide gray eyes taking Annie in.

"There are three on the shelf by the window that are unpainted. There is a smaller one that is painted on the middle shelf. The rest are too expensive or promised to clients."

Annie was starting to truly dislike this woman. The "too expensive" line was so pointed and unnecessary. Now she didn't even want one of the damn things. As much as she tried to separate the work from the creator, once she knew something awful about an artist, writer, or actor, it was always harder for her to enjoy the work. By now she had met enough famous people for it to be a minor, though disturbing, aesthetic problem. She had wanted this woman to be like her pots. Bold, but not arrogant; warm, but not obsequious; and wise, but not manipulative. Right.

Annie walked over and viewed her choices. Ivy Clare was watching; Annie could feel her eyes — *Maybe she too will fall in love with my back*. She turned. It was hard for her to concentrate now. This woman was really pushing her buttons.

Ivy Clare stood with her arms folded, one large clay-caked hand holding her wine, her long legs crossed at the ankles. She was wearing a blue surgical suit today. Only a very confident woman would have a working wardrobe of operating-room attire, Annie thought.

It was becoming a point of honor not to be intimidated or patronized by this woman. "What about the one you're working on?"

Ivy Clare's eyebrows raised. Annie had reshuffled the deck.

Once Annie said it, she dug her mental heels in. That pot had meaning to her. This was her Oliver pot. Her Passion Pot. Her return from the land of the long-married vessel. This was *her* pot.

Ivy Clare glanced over at the pot on the table. "It's not dry yet or glazed. But, yes, it's available."

"Good. I want that one." The pot was narrow, with two breasts, one at either end, forming an oval. It was the most interesting one in the room.

"How long until it's ready?"

"A few days. You can call me on the weekend."

"I have a very busy schedule. Why don't *you* call *me* when it's done." Annie reached into her purse and pulled out one of her cards. She slipped it under her pot. "Well, it was interesting, *Ivy*," she said, stretching the short, silly name out. There was nothing she hated more than rudeness.

Ivy Clare nodded. She was still smiling, but Annie thought her eyes had changed — the way game players' eyes do when they have lost a round.

Annie turned on her toes and walked away. She threw her purse into the car and slumped over the steering wheel, exhausted from the strain of holding her own.

I need someone to talk to, she whispered to herself. Who can I talk to about this? She started the motor and backed away from the memories.

She only really talked to Mickey, hardly an appropriate choice. Who could she trust? Loretta would understand, but Loretta was family. It was too risky. Molly wouldn't judge her, but Molly would toss the whole thing off in her nothing-can-shock-me, la-de-da way; not at all what she needed. Lina had certainly been through enough torrid love affairs to give wise counsel, but Lina had loose lips and she was Mickey's friend, too. (For all she knew Lina might even be who Mickey was sleeping with, if in fact Mickey was sleeping with anyone.)

The thought that she had no one to confide in but her husband, and it was about them, made her feel terribly lonely. That was why people stayed married to begin with, to have one someone they could completely trust, someone to talk to about anything. Was that true, or was it another one of her illusions? It was certainly no longer true for her.

"We are honored today to have the fabulous Ivana Trump with us for Celebrity Close-Up. Welcome, Ivana. Always so good to see you."

"I adore to be here, dear."

"Ivana, you are a role model to so many women who admired your courage through your terrible ordeal. Can you tell us how your life is different now?"

"Well, my life is much more economized. More real without the frills of my marriage. I have learned to live simply. Now if I want to spend time in the south of France, I *rent* a villa, I don't *buy* it. If I want a cruise, I *lease* a yacht for a month, I don't have to *own* one. I take my kids home to Czechoslovakia more, and we do things very natural. I get them out of the limos and New York and we do something outside."

"Ivana, you are such a classy lady. We'll be back with novelist, businesswoman, and lecturer Ivana Trump after this."

"What a gal." Molly sipped her tea, waiting for Annie. One of the Pats was beside her, brushing Portia's brittle mane. Juanita was in the laundry room folding things.

Molly called in to her. "Juanita, can you hear this? Ivana Trump is telling us how frugal she's become. You should grab a look."

"I coming in a jif." Juanita stuck her head out, but Ivana had vanished.

Annie walked in carrying two large bags of groceries.

Molly went to help. "Having company?"

"Are you kidding? I haven't recovered from Thanksgiving yet. This is survival rations. I thought we'd have a quiet weekend just the two of us, but Mickey called before I went to Ojai and said he may not be home until Saturday night. Problems with next week's script, and he's got an interview with the Japanese about being the spokesman for some new car. So it may be just Weight Watcher's for me and Portia."

"Where's your pot?"

Annie unloaded her bags full of all the minutiae of daily life: mouthwash, Clorox, cotton balls, deodorant, paper towels, Kleenex, toilet paper, kitchen sponges, and squeeze-mop refills. Human life stopped without this array of secretion absorbers, a continual rinsing out, wiping-up or -off process.

"It won't be ready until the weekend. Will you go with me? I was going to take Mickey, but he probably won't be back. I don't want to go back there alone."

Molly giggled. This was her kind of conversation. "Are y'all talking vicious pets, spooky caretakers, or strange sounds emanating from attic rooms?"

"She's a bitch. I have more trouble with her type than the aforementioned assembly. I really didn't like her."

Molly picked up the diet frozen dinners and put them in Annie's freezer. "Well, what on earth did she do? I mean you were only there to pick up a gift, hardly a major confrontation."

"She didn't *do* anything. That's the point. She was just . . . I don't know. Haughty. Impertinent. She had an attitude that rubbed me the wrong way. I'd like your opinion."

"I'd love to. She sounds like my kind of gal. I adore those ice queens. The more aloof and difficult, the bigger the challenge. Half the women I know, I am the only woman friend they have. No one else on earth can tolerate them. Even Samantha, she has followers galore, but no friends."

Annie put the sponges under the sink and poured herself a cup of tea. "Samantha has no friends because you're the only woman contrary enough to let her near their man. Women like Samantha don't want women friends; they want their husbands."

"Now, now. You don't even know Samantha. She really isn't like that. I know she seems to be, but that's just part of her persona. I've seen her do it. It's like what they used to say about Marilyn Monroe; that when she'd walk into a room, she'd flick an internal switch and turn herself on, become Marilyn. Well, Samantha does that too; when she's not being the Oracle, she shuts it off. She's very nice and down to earth then. The rest is business."

"Is this the cult equivalent of the hooker with the heart of gold we're talking about? Does she also become short, bald, and flat-chested when the switch turns off?"

Molly put her feet up. "Lordy, Lordy. I hear the green-eyed monster a squeakin' and a squawkin'."

"I admit it. I was jealous. I have always wanted, just for a day, to be one of those women who sweep into a room and consume all the energy. A devastating woman."

Juanita backed into the room, her small, chubby arms filled with freshly ironed laundry.

"Mrs. W, Miss Lina is calling you. She say it's important but she's on the move and will call you back."

"Thanks, Juanita. Did Ella call?"

"No, ma'am. But someone from the Santa Barbara magazine. Want to talk to you about writing something. I write it all down. I go get it."

Juanita set the laundry on the butcher-block cooking island and waddled off to her room.

"That's me," Molly said, wiggling her toes. "Samantha's press people want a feature on her up here, and I called my friend over there and suggested they ask you to do the story."

"I haven't written about anything but Revolutionary War objects and wild-berry picking for a long time."

"Don't y'all think it's overdue?"

Annie looked at her friend. Maybe she *could* tell Molly.

Molly stood up. "Gotta get the boys." Annie smiled at the Pat sitting so quietly, brushing poor old Portia's stringy mane. At least she knew this was one of the girls.

Molly carried her cup over and set it down next to the laundry. She stood for a minute looking at the pile.

Molly's long slender fingers reached in and pulled something out. Something turquoise. "I have been searchin' high and low for these. What on earth are they doing in your laundry?"

Annie gasped. What did this mean? Mickey and Molly?

Molly saw her face. "What's wrong with you, girl? You look like you just swallowed a worm."

"They were on the backseat of my car. Ella found them. They have . . . I mean we have . . . Ella thought . . ."

Molly threw her head back, her high, lilting giggle filling the room. "Well, I can just imagine what y'all thought! It was me and *Billy,* trying to put a little spice back into our love life!"

They both looked at the Pat, who was still brushing obliviously.

"One night last week, we had a little too much Cabernet and I got the bright idea that we should retrace our steps, you know, go back to the courting days, when you had no place to go but the backseat. Y'all were asleep, all the lights were off, so we just climbed over the wall and snuck into the car. Mainly, I dragged Billy. He was so afraid that Mickey would hear us and think we were prowlers and come down and shoot us or something that nothing happened. I think the panties were the only thing that got off. But we did have a good laugh about it. Oh, Annie-pie! I am so sorry! Did you think it was Mickey and someone?"

Annie's mouth was wide open. Mickey was innocent! What had she done! Was that all the faith she had in a man who had cherished her for almost her entire life? What kind of horrible person was she?

"Are you all right?"

"Oh, my God, Molly, this is terrible." Annie burst into tears and put her head in her hands.

The Pat put down the brush and went over to Molly, folding herself against her mother as children do when grown-up emotions explode.

"I don't get it, darlin'. I'd think you'd be relieved."

Annie sat up, realizing that the Pat was upset. "I am. I'm sorry for the outburst. Molly, I can't explain now; maybe later, okay?"

Juanita huffed in with the message. "I forget. I put it by your bed."

Juanita handed the paper to Annie. Her canny Latin eyes taking in the scene. The Pat holding on to her mother, Molly holding the turquoise, Annie fighting back tears. Her cousin Lupe the Witch had been right. She had seen trouble for her Wilders in the tarot. She had seen it for months. Trouble in the fall, will get very bad, Lupe had said. *Dios mio.* She was afraid for her family.

"Mickey? Are you awake?"

"Yeah. I've got an early call. What are you doing up? It's not even five yet."

"Not up. I never went down. Couldn't sleep. I called and called but your phone was off."

"I crashed. I tried you before I went to bed but you didn't answer."

"Oh, maybe I went for a walk. I just needed to apologize. I feel like such a jerk."

"It's too early for Trivial Pursuit. Tell me what you're talking about? Apologize for what?"

"The underwear, I mean for accusing you like that. For not trusting you enough. It turns out they belong to *Molly!* Oh, Mickey, it was just like a scene from a French farce! Juanita waltzes in with the laundry and Molly slips the turquoise panties out of our pile and says, 'I've been looking all over for these.'

"Those two are so crazy! They snuck over here one night just before Thanksgiving and had sex, or at least tried to, in the back of my car! Molly thought it would rekindle some passion, some teenage romance kind of fantasy. Anyway, I just really needed to tell you how sorry I am. Please forgive me."

"It's okay, angel. I really did understand how it looked. I've seen as many movies as you have."

"When are you coming home?"

"Still looks like late Saturday."

"Maybe I'll come down and we'll have a romantic Friday-night dinner somewhere. I have some things to go over with Leonard anyway."

"Honey, not good. I'm shooting the car audition Friday night. I really won't be available. Let's wait till I can enjoy your company."

"All right. Let me know how it goes. I'm so sorry I doubted you. I love you, Mickey."

"It's okay, angel, try and get some sleep."

Annie put down the phone. Portia rolled over and looked up at her. They hardly ever let her sleep in their room anymore; the smell was just too unpleasant.

Annie slid off the bed and sunk down onto the polished floor next to her dog. Portia rolled over, dropping her head into Annie's lap.

They had no idea what kind of dog Portia really was. She was one of nature's mix-ups. Annie had found her, a whimpering, shivering puppy, on the steps of a tenement on Bleecker Street near her father's apartment.

It was love at first sight for Annie, and for Toby and Ella, who were little more than babies themselves. They had carried her home and set about making her a proper member of their family. It had taken two days for her skinny little body to stop trembling. Annie considered Portia to be her animal reincarnation. First, she was all red. Her bristly coat, even her eyes. A motherless mutt, abandoned and left to fate, found and saved by the love of the good guys. She was scared, but she was a survivor. Annie had named her Portia because to her the name meant strength, a feisty, high-minded fairness. "The quality of mercy is not strain'd, it droppeth as the gentle rain from heaven. . . ." No one would mess with anyone named Portia, was the way she saw it.

The vet said, "All I can tell you for sure is that she isn't a Chihuahua or a Doberman pinscher." She was red and she was theirs.

In the same way that she could barely remember her life before

Mickey or before her children, she could barely remember her world before Portia. She stroked her weary old companion, calming herself as well. "Hang on, Ports. I know you're tired, I know your legs ache and your teeth hurt, but hang on a little while longer. Don't leave me now."

The dog opened her watery red eyes and looked up at Annie. She stayed very still, watching her master. Tears streamed down Annie's face.

Portia pushed her stiff arthritic body up onto Annie's lap, licking her face with her clammy, cold tongue.

Annie winced in spite of herself. The dog's breath really was awful. Portia rolled over on her back, spreading herself open for Annie's approval. Poor Portia, still plying her waning feminine wares. "You old slut, you." Annie stroked her belly, the dog licking her lips and arching her spine in pleasure, so sure was she of her need being satisfied. Annie envied Portia's trust in her. She no longer felt worthy of it. What had she done?

The phone rang. Mickey, she thought, startling Portia and interrupting the frail animal's ecstasy.

"Mick?" Annie flopped back down on the bed. There was no way she could take back what she had done with Oliver Taylor. Not that, in many ways, she even wanted to, but it had fallen into her lap like a hot potato at a hoedown and now she had thrown it back onto the plate. It was over. Her marriage was not compromised and they would, or at least *she* would, be better for the experience. She would put the entire thing out of her mind. It was like a dream and she was now awake and back in charge.

"Annie. Are you actually up of your own free will?"

Annie looked at the clock. Five-twenty A.M. "Lina? I thought it was Mickey. I had one of those premenstrual nights. Even a pill didn't help. Why in the hell would you call me at the crack of dawn?"

"Are you sitting down? Well, lie down. *Tie* yourself down."

"Lina, what is it? You sound awful. Are you drunk?"

"Drunk? Hell no, I'm not drunk. I wish I were drunk, that would be simple to fix! Oh, God. Annie, something terrible has happened, beyond terrible. Disastrous."

Annie curled her legs up under her, the way she had always done as a child when she felt bad news coming. It was the opposite of the flight response. It was her way of forcing herself not to flee. She literally sat on her legs, to keep herself from running away. "Tell me!"

"Leonard's gone."

She let her breath out. No one was dead. "What do you mean, *gone?*"

"I mean gone as in flown the coop; as in disappeared without a trace; as in so long, suckers."

"How do you know he isn't just on one of those getaway weekends Bambi drags him on."

"*Bambi's* the one who told me! I've been calling him for days. I went by his office after Mickey and I finished shooting yesterday, and his secretary stonewalled me. The place was in chaos, and there were a couple of pasty guys in black suits going through the files. No one would tell me anything! So I went over to their house and banged on the door until Bambi staggered out, looking like her namesake after the forest fire, and she was so stoned on lithium or Thorazine or something, she just poured it out.

"She woke up last Wednesday, just before Thanksgiving, and he was gone! He'd packed two Vuitton suitcases, cleared out all his files and the discs and papers in his personal safe, left her a note telling her not to say anything to anyone, that he would contact her at the appropriate time, and that was that. He's gone."

Annie took several deep breaths. One of them had to remain clearheaded. "Okay. So this is obviously not great news. But there are dozens of people that handle Leonard's accounts. It may be a little confusing for all of us for a few days; obviously he's had some sort of burnout or breakdown. He'll be back eventually and until then our money is in safe investments. We'll go over there together. I'll ask Jackie to help us, he's so good at that stuff. We'll hire our own accountant and take charge of it."

Bitter, cackling laughter against Annie's ear. "Oh, mother of God, Annie Wilder! You wonderful camp counselor, you! You need me to spell it out? Leonard has not had some midlife fit and wandered off to smoke peyote and learn the ways of the tribal peoples for a while. Leonard has *left*. Leonard has left with ALL OF OUR MONEY! All of it! When I say Leonard is *gone,* I am speaking symbolically for *IT* is gone. What the fuck do I care where *Leonard* is? Leonard could be on the next Mars mission for all I care. *He's got all our money!* All of *my* money and all of *your* money. He's got all of *everyone's* money! Leonard has just let fly the biggest raspberry in the history of Hollywood. He has vanished and he has taken everything we have with him!"

Now it was Annie's turn. Her legs had fallen asleep beneath her, trapping her in this unbearable place. *God is punishing me for outliving my mother and necking with a strange man.* "All of our money!" Annie felt her throat close. She could barely form her words.

"Every last cent."

"Even the stocks?"

"If there ever *were* any stocks. At the moment it looks like half the things he told us we had, we never had. Probably some fat Cayman Island banker had it in an account in the name of Mr. Leonard Lewis himself."

Annie unfurled her numb, throbbing legs and stood up, sending Portia creeping for the stairs and the steady good cheer of Juanita. "I'll be there as soon as I can. . . . We have to . . . Lina, we have to find him! The money has to be somewhere!"

Lina was sobbing now. "God, Annie. I'm really scared. I don't have anyone. All I had was that security to keep me from absolute terror. He took all I had to show for thirty years of hard work! I'm going to kill him."

"First, we have to *find* him. Lina, honey, do me a favor. Call Mickey — maybe he hasn't left yet, and call Jackie and have him meet us at your house. It'll be okay. It's got to be okay."

"Sure it does," Lina said and set down the phone.

Annie pulled off her nightgown and stomped into the bathroom, her legs still tingling. Hope and loss, she had said. This was the way life worked. The very second you started to get complacent, there was that 747 at the kitchen window. Her hands were shaking so hard, she could barely turn on the shower.

When Lina Allen called, Jackie Wilski was being ravished. Of all his Big Blondes, he had never come close to this. This was the mold-breaker. The biggest and the best. This one was a goddess, sent from the hills of Greece, reborn from the ashes of Athena and Aphrodite — sent to find *him*.

Samantha the Oracle straddled him, floating up and down, bouncing in slow motion, her long, honeyed hair billowing as if some invisible wind machine were hidden in his closet. Her enormous honey-dew breasts thwacking against her ribs. Giddyup. She galloped. *Tharumph, tharumph,* the sound of her sliding up and down on his ravished prick. The prick, who had now completely taken over his life — had his own credit cards, travel schedule, and list of demands. Whatever you say, *Sir. Tharumph.*

The divorce papers weren't even dry yet. *Sir* didn't give a shit. Samantha needed a place to stay in L.A. while she set about taking over Marianne Williamson's flock. No problem, *Sir* said. Jackie's got a dynamite guesthouse and a spare Mercedes you can use, doll.

It was worth it, he kept telling himself. She was fantastic. Maybe this is what he needed to cure himself forever. The Big Bang to blow him out of the black hole into a new galaxy. Maybe that was why he had found her at his brother's house no less!

She wailed, "Sex is god! God is love! Sex is God's love! I have the power of God's love in my cunt! I have the power of the universe in my pussy! I am the light! I am the hope!"

Jackie got a little nervous when she started this, and a bit anxious that she would lose control and crush him beneath her. *Sir* had no such anxieties. *Sir* thought the entire performance was incredible.

"I'll put you on my new show. I'll *give* you a show! We'll do Aimee Semple McPherson for the nineties. I'll get Armani to dress you. Yahooo!" *Sir* was busting the bronco.

"Jackie? It's Lina Allen. Did I wake you?"

"No. No. I'm up."

"People always say that. No one ever admits to being asleep even if you call them at three A.M."

Samantha was done. She rose, her legs pinning his thighs together, rising above him. If wings grew out of her shoulder blades now, he would not be surprised. *Sir* had collapsed in a heap on his dress side, an oozy, disheveled mess, waiting for his Goddess to clean him up, kiss him good night, and tuck him in.

"Do you often call people at three A.M. to see if they'll pretend to be awake?"

"The occasion has arisen. You sound funny. I'm sorry if I woke you, really. Something terrible has happened and Annie asked me to call you."

"My brother? Is it my brother?"

Jackie pulled himself up, causing Samantha to lose her balance and fall back down on the bed, not liking at all the fall from her pedestal, no wavering of attention too small to be overlooked.

"No. No. Mickey's fine. I mean I'm sure he's fine. He's shooting and I can't reach him, but it's not that, it's Leonard Lewis. He's disappeared with all their money. All my money too and most of the people you know. Annie's on her way down and she thought maybe you could help us. I'm going crazy, Jackie. I don't know what to do first. Can you come over and meet with us?"

"Sure. Of course. I've got to make a couple of calls. I'll be there in an hour." Jackie hung up, avoiding her hypnotic gaze. He had promised to introduce her to his P.R. people. Samantha turned the full force of her ancient eyes on him. She stretched her tawny goddess arms up over her head, bringing her breasts together in playmate cleavage.

"I do not believe in the alteration of order. If you allow yourself to be sidetracked by circumstance, you lose your way. When a course is set, then you must command your course and not be tossed about by the needs of others. The waters are filled with karma pirates just waiting to pull you off course."

Sir was finding this extremely interesting. He had regained his shape and was thinking of offering her some strawberries and champagne or maybe speaking Italian, but Jackie wasn't listening. "Hey, Samantha. Save it for the masses. You are looking at ten years of psychoanalysis here. My family's in trouble. I'm out of here. I'll call you later. Have Edgar make you some breakfast."

Samantha stood up, flinging her hair back. "It's your shipwreck, dear man. I am only the observer."

> "A ninety-year-old woman in New Jersey is undergoing treatment for rabies after being attacked by a raccoon that climbed down her chimney. She is the second ninety-year-old woman in New Jersey this week to be attacked by a rabid raccoon entering through a chimney."

Annie careened off the San Diego Freeway into her first left turn of the day. *Well, at least I have forty-five more years before I have to add "fear of attack by raccoon serial killer" to my worry list.*

She checked her watch. She had made it from Montecito to Los Angeles in record time, but from the look of the surface traffic, it would take her almost as long to get from the off-ramp to Lina's as it had from her house to there. She regretted now that she hadn't had a car phone put in. It seemed such an extravagance, but in an emergency, like trying to reach your husband to tell him that all of your money on earth is gone, it would be worth it.

She swallowed hard, trying to push down the lump of panic that had lodged in her throat. *Everything they had.* Dear God. Was this part of their marital test? To see how strong their bond was? Was it time for Annie (Job) Wilder to get hers?

Why had she thought that the tit for tat with her mother would be played out on an exact birth schedule? For all she knew God might be following the Hebrew calendar or the Chinese or who only knows what.

The worst moment of the morning had been admitting the real truth — if God had given her one of his famous double-edged sword trade-offs, and she could have chosen between Mickey being unfaithful or Leonard Lewis stealing their life's savings, she was not so sure that she would not have chosen adultery over abject poverty. She *was* a horrible person!

She had always felt that the money was what had saved their marriage. Not that it was any big fortune or anything, but she had seen so many couples, with professions far more secure than actors and writers, absolutely destroyed by money trouble. It sapped love, it built resentment and rage.

Money was what everyone fought about. Too much of it poisoned things one way or created the kind of ennui that the O'Brians had, or made it too easy to just leave, and not enough of it ruptured energy and joy and turned lovers into haters, each blaming the other and measuring themselves against the perceived failure. During all the early years of their marriage, with two kids and endless responsibilities, money had been what they fought about too, though it was rarely that overt. It never came out honestly or directly, but in petty battles and subtle criticisms.

She had never really believed in her own ability to make grown-up money. She married Mickey before she had ever had anything but a summer job. What she made was *cute* money, monopoly money compared to what his potential was. Her potential had never been much of an issue for either of them. She thought they were just old-fashioned and out of touch, except that she had talked to so many women, young, medium, and older, from high-powered careerists to secretaries, and they all felt basically the same way. No matter what they did or how much they made, they still had the fantasy that some man was supposed to find them and make more than they made, or at least take the burden off their shoulders.

Having some money in the bank had taken the pressure off the rest of their relationship and their lives. It was as if for the first time in their marriage they had let out their breath. They had been fortunate enough to have the dice roll their way, and they had prided themselves on not going crazy and spending it all. It was their serenity and their children's security. *Everything they had.*

Annie felt the panic push deeper against her throat. Okay. Mickey still had a job. She could keep doing the B&B stories. They had a certificate of deposit put aside to cover Toby's college and they could always sell the house in California and move back into their brownstone when the tenant's lease was up. Their mortgage wasn't large. They would lose money on the Montecito house, if they could sell it at all, considering the sorry state of the market. Well, they would have to sell it or rent it.

God. She was accelerating again! Stop it! You must stay in the present. You will do whatever has to be done. It's only money, it's not health or one of the children. Your husband is not betraying you. This is not the end of the world. Every time you turn on the news you hear about people going through things far more horrible than this, so don't be such a spoiled baby. Count your blessings. Everything happens for a reason. Maybe this is what you and Mickey need to pull you away from this hedonistic easy life. Maybe you're supposed to find a higher calling, work with the hearing impaired or Alzheimer's patients, lead a quieter, simpler life. You'll be a better person for this.

Everything we have.

Annie flipped the channels. She was driving herself crazy.

> "One of the great contributions of Scientology was the discovery that emotions can be plotted on a scale in an exact ascending or descending sequence. A four is the highest, enthusiasm. The individual is happy, vital, and successful and responding to life's challenges with energy and enthusiasm. The tone scale moves down from there to conservatism, boredom, antagonism, pain, anger, covert hostility, fear, and down to grief, apathy, and 0, which is body death. Where are you on this scale?"

Annie felt a scream coming on. The world had gone mad. Everyone wanted a quick fix. Now we had an emotional tone scale.

She pulled off Sunset Boulevard at Barrington and into the driveway of Lina's condo. Poor Lina. Think about her with no family at all. She had worked so hard, penny-pinching, saving all her life. Annie used to tease her in college that she was preparing for her old age and she hadn't even started her life yet. Lina had no backup. Every middle-aged single woman that she knew carried the weight of this terror within them. What a despicable thing for Leonard to do to Lina!

Annie rang the bell, waiting for Lina to buzz her in. The door opened and she could see Lina and Jackie at the top of the stairs, coffee cups in hand, waiting for her.

Tears streamed down Lina's face. "Bambi Lewis tried to commit suicide. We can't see her again for at least forty-eight hours."

Annie's mother instinct took over, the lioness hearing the scratch at her den. Her friend was suffering and her family's future was at stake.

"The hell we can't. What hospital is she at?"

"St. John's," Jackie said. "Psychiatric."

"Come on, we'll figure something out."

"Martin? It's Annie."

"Annie, are you okay? My nurse said it was an emergency."

"Well, it is. But we're all okay. Listen, something's happened. It's kind of hard to go into on the phone. Leonard Lewis, our business manager, well, he's disappeared with all of our money and the reason I'm calling is, I'm at St. John's with Lina Allen and Jackie. We've been here trying to see Leonard's wife. She tried to kill herself, or so they say. I think she's just trying to avoid everyone. We thought maybe she might remember something if we got to her before there's too much pressure, but they've been giving us the runaround all day and the feds have padlocked his office. So it occurred to me that since you're on the staff here you might be able to get us in. We're desperate, Martin, or I wouldn't ask."

Martin sighed. "When you say it's an emergency you mean it. The difficulty is, Annie, that I'm associated with the dermatology department, not the psychiatric unit."

"Come on, Martin. I mean every time Ella's skin broke out in high school, it was borderline neuropsych. You have patients with melanoma and all kinds of horrible diseases. You must know someone up there."

"Loretta does." His voice dropped. "I moved out last night, but I'll call her."

"Oh, Martin, I'm so ashamed! I've been so preoccupied with our stuff. I'm so sorry, I didn't even call to see how it went with Pop and Ida Mae."

"Not so bad; I think they're both too self-absorbed at this point to pay much attention. Is there anything else I can do to help?"

"Just a call to someone who can get us in to see her. There are cops guarding her door. I mean, the man is an embezzler! A criminal! Can you believe that your paranoid, worry-about-everything sister could have been so stupid?"

"You know what they say, 'The bigger they are. . . .'"

"Yeah, right. Wait until I tell Mickey."

"He doesn't know?"

"I just found out early this morning. He's been shooting all day. I've left ten messages, but he hasn't called, or if he has, he hasn't been able to get through."

"Annie, I've got a patient, but I'll call Loretta."

It was after eight that evening before they were escorted in to see Bambi Lewis. By that point they were all so exhausted, they could hardly remember why they had wanted to do it in the first place. A detective from the LAPD and an FBI agent were positioned on either side of the room, and Bambi Lewis was propped up against her pillows, her false eyelashes batting and her pink-orange hair teased up into its usual peaks and swirls, confirming Annie's feeling about the seriousness of her "overdose."

None of Leonard's clients had ever quite figured out the Bambi/Leonard axis, but that was true of so many marriages.

Leonard was fastidious, methodical, and professorial, the kind of man who wore a suit and tie at home on Saturday afternoon. Leonard read Proust on airplanes.

Bambi, the gossips said, had been a call girl. She was silly, but she was shrewd, and she was not oblivious to the reaction she elicited. She must have known that Leonard's clients and their wives made fun of her, but she never changed her overblown, showgirl style. In a way, Annie liked that about Bambi, thumbing her nose at all the pretensions of Tinseltown.

Leonard, as far as anyone could tell, adored her. How Bambi really felt was more obscure. She was a totally attentive and adoring public wife. The one personal thing that Annie ever remembered Leonard Lewis saying about her was that Bambi was always waiting at his shower door with a fresh towel. That had given her pause.

"Bambi? Can you hear me?" They had decided to let Jackie talk to her. Bambi responded far better to male attention.

Bambi Lewis opened her eyes, a little too easily for Annie's taste.

"Jackie, hi. So nice of you to come."

"Look, Bambi, I know this is a terrible time for you, but unfortunately, there are a lot of innocent people going through it with you. I know you talked to Lina, but we thought maybe there was some detail you overlooked. Please try. If we can find Leonard, we can find out where the money is. You're much too pretty to be suffering here like this. How about I give you a top spot on *Under the Covers.* You know how I am for damsel-in-distress stories."

Little round tears fell from Bambi's thickly lined eyes. "My poor Lennie. He never would have done this if I had been a better wife."

While this was intriguing, Annie was getting impatient. She started to move forward but Jackie held up his hand, stopping her.

"What do you mean, honey?"

"I did something terrible, Jackie. I was unfaithful to him. Just one little slip, but he must have found out."

"Why would your sleeping with someone make him run off with all of his clients' money? Come on, Bambi. We haven't seen any books yet, but this is no wake-up-in-the-morning-and-strip-the-bank-accounts deal. He had to have planned this for years."

Bambi pouted. "Well, it's what I think. I don't know anything about his business, it's the only thing I can think of."

Ask her who she was sleeping with. Annie was beaming a question into Jackie's brain. One slip and Leonard goes nuts and becomes L.A.'s most wanted. *What* had she done? All she had was one slip —

actually only a *half* slip. Maybe *she* had set the entire nightmare in motion.

"Bambi, I'm not prying, but it may be important. Who were you sleeping with?"

"Promise you won't tell anyone."

"I promise."

Annie and Lina rolled their eyes.

"Stan Stein."

"No shit. Mr. Perfect Marriage. Well, well."

"I just thought, well, maybe he got so mad he took Stanny's money, and then it just sort of escalated."

"If you were going to take a guess at where he'd go — I mean you two have been everywhere, you know how he thinks — where would it be?"

Bambi laid her head back and closed her eyes, the wet lashes sticking together. "I couldn't say. I dragged him around but he never really liked to be anywhere but home working." Bambi opened her eyes, causing lanes of black mascara to run down her cheeks. "Jackie? What's going to happen to me? Will they take my house and all my jewelry and stuff?"

"I don't know, kid, that's a long way down the road."

Lina put her head in her hands.

"Jackie, find him, please. You're smart. You can do it."

"We're all going to try, honey. Get some rest."

They turned and walked out. They had mostly wasted a day, and they all knew that it was only the first of many.

Annie drove fast, for Annie. She executed three left turns without holding her breath. She had to see Mickey. He was still not answering and no one seemed to know where the Japanese audition was shooting. She would go to the apartment and wait for him. She'd take a hot bath, have a glass of wine, and try to relax, but she needed her husband. This was their drama and it could not be played as a one-man show.

She didn't have the code for his parking garage so she parked on the street, a reckless enough act in the days and nights of the car-theft rampage. She pulled her box of documents from the back and lugged everything into the building. She took the elevator to the top floor and almost ran down the plushly carpeted hall to his door.

She had not been there in weeks. It felt strange coming into her husband's apartment like that. She had never felt as if it belonged to both of them, though that was certainly the way they had approached it. The show paid for it, which was a very nice perk, and they had originally thought that Annie would spend half of her time down there once Toby left for college. But somehow it had never taken hold that way.

When the show was on hiatus, Mickey never stayed there. It had the look of a place that people stayed in, rather than lived in. It made Annie uncomfortable; she felt slightly illicit, and oddly enough some of the best sex they had had in years occurred there, probably for precisely that reason. It was almost like going to a motel; it was not the house of their marriage.

Annie set down the box and fumbled in her purse for the key.

She opened the door and slid the box in with her foot, kicking off her shoes and throwing her coat and bag on the couch.

She closed the door, moving slowly through the darkness, forgetting where the light switch was. She groped her way across the room, steadying herself on chairs and tables, until she found the wall. She tried the switch. Nothing. She could see better now. There was another switch at the end of the hall by the bedroom. She let go of the wall and walked toward it.

The door to the bedroom was open and she hit the switch, flooding the hall with light as she entered the room. A bath. A pee and a bath, then I'll pour some wine and open some tuna fish. Oh, Mickey, please come home, I need you so badly.

Something was wrong. The bed. People were in her husband's bed. The light behind her cast strange shadows over the couple. She saw a pair of hands clutching a man's back. A pair of female hands.

Large, big-boned female hands. Something about the hands. She switched on the light. The nails were gray. Dirty. Street people had broken into her husband's apartment.

She backed up, fear flooding her. Her heart was pounding so hard she could barely breathe.

The police. I need the police. The woman's hands released. It wasn't dirt. Something else. The man jumped up, grabbing a towel from the bedpost. She saw Mickey's face, the light slashing across it. He was sweating, sweating from the effort exerted over this woman with dirty nails. *He never sweats with me,* she thought, her body fighting her over this picture, this truth.

She knew the hands even before she saw the face. The woman in the bed had crossed them calmly over her flat, boyish chest. Ivy Clare's hands.

Who had the last laugh now?

Annie drove. She drove fast. Annie never drove on freeways at night. She drove. She did not stop for gas, though she never drove with less than three quarters of a tank. She did not stop to relieve her aching bladder, though she always did before she took even a short car ride. Her only concession to her usual behavior was fastening her seat belt.

She listened to talk radio and she drove. She did not think, she just drove, stories pouring out of unhappy people's faceless, mouthless souls, companions in despair inside her urban cowboy car. A Range Rover for a couple from New York City who had thought, until five years ago, that Sun Valley was in Colorado.

Voices surrounded her, people like herself. People with problems in their lives. Problems with work, with men, with women, with money, with sex, with stress. I want, I need, I hurt, I can't, I won't, I should. People on the radio looking for the light at the end of one tunnel or another.

She did not stop until she saw the sign. CLARE. She hit her left turn so fast, the top-heavy car skidded. Annie held on, swerving into the driveway and parking behind the shrubbery. She unlatched her seat belt, pushing open her door simultaneously, and scrambled out, a plane crash survivor heading for the chute.

She pulled down her jeans, squatting in the dark, and let the hot urine flow, her eyes stinging with tears of release. She wiped herself with an old Kleenex and put it back in her pocket. She would leave no trace.

The moon was bright and she followed its light on the path down the narrow formless driveway, up the stairs, and around to the studio. She put on her driving gloves. She tried the knob. Open. This enraged her. Only a woman as arrogant as Ivy Clare would waltz off to Los Angeles and leave her work unprotected.

Annie switched on the lights. Her pot was still on its pedestal, her card still sticking out from under its left breast. Outrage.

She turned away and walked over to the shelves housing the other work. Her choices remained the same. Three on the top and the small painted one on the middle. She picked up the first, the "not-too-expensive-or-promised-to-a-client" pot and let it drop. The floor was cement and the sound of the clay smashing filled her head. It had a grand, full, cracking, crashing sound that was truly satisfying. She picked up the second one and held it higher, enhancing the sensation. The third bounced like a beach ball before it broke, and then the little painted single tit. Splat. She ground the glazed pottery deeper into the cement, stomping on the pieces with her cowboy boots, Annie Oakley replacing Little Orphan.

She turned, lightheaded from exhaustion, emotion, and lack of food. She crossed to the pedestal and picked up her breast pot, one hand fondling each mammary, and threw it against the wall. She backed up slowly toward the door and surveyed her work. Messy, but fulfilling. She slipped her card back into her pocket and walked over to the closet at the back of the studio. She was in luck: there was a broom and a dust bin and a pack of garbage bags. Annie carried them into the studio and began to sweep. She swept with great control and total concentration. She swept up every last shard and bit of clay dust, carefully checking the bin and the broom after each load.

When she was finished, there was no trace of the damage. It would be impossible to prove that any pots but the ones remaining had ever been in the room. Annie cleaned the broom and the dust bin and put them back in their exact location. She carried the garbage bag out, shutting the light and the door behind her.

She retraced her steps, sifting the dirt with her hand as she went, removing her footprints. She walked on the weedy grass all the way to the road where her car was hidden behind the bushes, throwing the bag in the backseat and easing herself in — heading off without her lights. There was not a car, a house light, or a soul in sight. Only the moon was watching.

Way to go, Annie, the man in the moon said, and she smiled up at him. In spite of everything, she gave him a smile.

PART II

FOR RICHER OR POORER

CHAPTER VII

"HEY, WHAT'S THE RUSH, pretty momma!"

Ella Wilder tightened her grip on her backpack and moved fast, eyes straight ahead, step brisk and steady, the de rigueur New York City walk. She really hated working nights. The three black kids were dressed alike in harem-style pants, bulky leather jackets, and boat-size sneakers. How truly dumb and how truly sad that they thought they looked so cool. Anger and compassion juggled up and down in her mind.

She didn't want to feel menaced and prejudiced about them, but she did, even though she would never admit it to her parents, or certainly her grandmother (who loved guys like that, the scarier and more obnoxious, the better). Ida Mae saw every crazy addict, knife-wielding maniac, and mugger as an innocent victim of an elitist capitalist society.

Ella had always thought that people were supposed to get more conservative as they got older, but her grandmother kept getting more and more radical. Now that there was no more cold war, no more communist bloc, and a Democrat was back in the White House, Ida Mae had shifted her allegiance to the domestic social agenda. It scared Ella out of her wits, the places her grandmother went, and the people she spent her time with and let into her apartment. It made her and Toby feel weird. After all, they were supposed to be the rebellious younger generation. She was always calling to check on her grandmother, rather than the other way around, and her grandfather, Mr. New York At Night, with his marble-mouth voice and phony friends — if she didn't stop by to see him, she would never hear from him at all. And the women he ran around with! All of those horrible old society widows with the heavy pearls and thick white powder on their faces. "The Editorial We's," her mother called them, because they said things like, "What perfume are *we* loving this season?"

It really upset her to have negative thoughts about her grandfather. When she was a kid and a teenager even, she had never looked at her family, or her grandparents for sure, with that kind of objectivity. Even when she and Toby ragged on their parents and criticized them all the time, the way all kids do, underneath they never really believed it. They really believed that their family was the best. God knows, she had spent enough time in other kids' houses! She had never come across a family she would have traded for, not ever, and she knew Toby felt the same way, though they certainly never told their parents that.

The thought made her feel sad, now that she was a grown-up herself, or maybe it was because of her mom's birthday and all of that talk about having outlived her own mother.

The very thought of something happening to her mother was so terrifying, she couldn't even think it for a second. But she was more and more aware now that people died every day. People her age, too. She had already been to two funerals for kids she had gone to school with. One of her best friends from high school had died of lupus, and then her friend from NYU had been stabbed to death in the lobby of her apartment building right across the street from the campus.

Ella wondered if life had always been this scary, or the world was just getting worse. She felt bad that she had left without saying something really loving to her mother. She was going to be more sensitive from now on.

Ella reached into her pocket and took out her keys. She never carried them in her purse anymore. Now she went out as if she were heading into a village in Herzegovina, keys at the ready in one pocket, and her pocket siren all set in the other. She stopped at her building and looked behind her. The boys had not followed her. She jammed her key in, pulled the door forward, and backed into the lobby. She would never admit it to her family, but she felt like she was living in a war zone, just like her dad's show. Her parents had such a romanticized view of New York — they didn't understand how much it had changed in the five years they had been gone. She hadn't either, until she had lived there alone as an adult. Well, it wouldn't be long now.

She took a deep breath, preparing for the six flights ahead of her. A sixth floor walk-up *and* a roommate and she could still hardly pay her rent. Okay, so night manager at a trendy diner was not a particularly high-paying job, but she was making more than most of her friends, even the older ones with master's degrees and stuff. Everyone was waitressing or bartending or doing grunt secretarial work. It was like Dickens. Venal employers picking off the smart, well-educated, and jobless post-yuppie college grads for slave wages.

She opened her door and turned on the light. Gwennie was staying at her mother's in Rye for a few days and she was alone. Heaven, absolute heaven. As much as she liked Gwennie, sharing a studio with another person wore on the nerves. They had both grown up with their own rooms, much nicer rooms than the fleabag they now shared.

Is that what life had in store for her? Instead of working her way up, she would continually be comparing the bleakness of her own accomplishments and surroundings with her childhood?

She threw her coat and purse on the couch and kicked off her shoes. She was really tired. It always took her forever to readjust from California to New York time, no matter how short her visit. She couldn't fall asleep at night and she couldn't wake up in the morning. At least she was working nights (though she had not told her family, who would have completely freaked out).

Ella closed her eyes, enjoying the quiet. The city was so noisy and the diner was like the city with the volume turned all the way up. What was it with New York restaurants? They blasted the music so that everyone had to scream over it. Kids were supposed to like loud music, and the diner catered to a pseudo-hip young crowd, but she always got complaints about how hard it was to have a conversation in there. Of course, the restaurants without loud music always seemed empty even when they were full, so maybe her boss knew something.

Ella yawned. She really was wiped. So much to think about and she couldn't put it off any longer. By Christmas when they went to Club Med she had to tell her family. And that meant that by Christmas she had to make her decision. She couldn't tell them if she wasn't clear herself. She would just blow it like the law school debacle. Of course, they were all tied up together; she did know that.

Ella flipped on the TV and padded across to the bathroom. She turned on the light and looked at herself in the mirror. Someone she worked with had told her she looked just like her dad. It had pissed her off, because she never told anyone who her father was, so that meant her boss or someone must have found out, and they were gossiping about her.

Did she? She did. So did Toby. She could look at her dad and see Toby as a taller version thirty years from now. Hopefully, Toby would keep more of his hair, though she was really mean, teasing him about it. With the yellow fluorescent light beating down on her, she saw dark shadows under her eyes, and her dad had those too. They always got worse when he was tired. She had to catch up on her sleep.

Ella bent over the tub and turned on the water, which trickled out in its usual passive stream. It took forever to fill the damn tub, but she just had to take advantage of having the apartment to herself and that meant a long hot bath. When Gwennie was home there was never enough hot water to go around.

Ella pulled off her clothes. All alone, she could prance around nude. Her mother never walked around naked; she always said it made her nervous. She liked to be "like a finger in a very cozy glove." Ella did too.

The apartment was chilly and she tied her flannel robe tight and shoved her bare feet into her big fuzzy bunny slippers. So like her mother to send a grown woman a pair of huge gray rabbits posing as slippers, with pink eyes and long floppy ears. She really loved those slippers. They made her feel that she was still part of a family, even if she didn't live with them anymore.

She swallowed hard — the thought made her feel like crying again. She had been averaging at least one good cry a day for weeks now. She flopped across the room to the kitchenette and put on the kettle. A nice cup of hot herb tea would help her sleep. She opened the fridge and picked up the container of yogurt. Rotten. She felt like crying again. All the things about growing up no one ever prepared you for. That wasn't really fair, since no matter what her mother had said to her, she just tuned out.

She was the one now who did all of that stuff her mother and Juanita did. If she didn't shop, she didn't eat. If she didn't haul her laundry down six flights and over to the Ying's Laundromat, she wore filthy clothes. Sometimes she wanted to go home so badly and curl up and be a little girl again and have her parents take care of everything, it hurt like a physical pain inside her. A tight, hot feeling under her breastbone.

The truth was that she had never really thought much about her life after reaching twenty-one. She had thought a lot about that goal, associating it with total freedom. Somehow it had always seemed so far away and so unachievable. Now it was almost two years behind her and she was still wandering around trying to figure out what had hit her. Adulthood was not all it was cracked up to be. So far it meant being poor, tired, confused, and exhausted most of the time.

Ella poured her tea and padded back to the bathroom to check on her tub. The water was trickling out, steady but almost in slow motion. She wandered back into the main room. She was starving but trying not to think about it. How truly stupid of her not to take a sandwich home from the diner.

She sat down in front of the television, sipping her tea. The hot fluid glided down her throat, calming her.

What was she seeing? Two men, one in his sixties at least, one younger, and a heavy-legged girl were sitting on the floor of a talk-show set wearing diapers and bonnets. Could this be true? She picked up the *TV Guide* to see if it was a *Saturday Night Live* rerun. No, it was a cable channel. The guide said "New talk-show host Don Davis interviews adults with infancy fixation."

Ella was transfixed. The older man was telling Don the host that he was the father of two grown children who thought he was a great dad. The younger man, who was now sucking on a bottle and rocking back and forth, was saying that he was a truck driver. The woman, who had spread her legs apart and straight out in front of her like only very little girls do, was yelling about equal rights and discrimination against people like themselves. "We don't hurt anyone. If we want to wear diapers and act like babies in the privacy of our own homes, it's no one's business."

At this moment they were joined by a tough-looking woman in a nurse's uniform. The Don man introduced her as an "infancy surrogate" who was hired to play with them, bathe them, and change them. Some woman in a badly fitted purple suit and horn-rimmed glasses came on to give the psychiatric interpretation, which all the "kids" rejected.

"We're happy like this. We're perfectly normal and we don't want to change." This made the studio audience very upset and Don, who had a big fake smile and hard glinty eyes, went around with the mike while they vilified the people and called them unkind names and laughed and snickered. None of this seemed to bother the guests. The nurse woman was now cradling the head of the truck driver in her lap. The therapist was shaking her head back and forth in strong disapproval.

"I can't stand this!" Ella had to call someone. Not someone, she had to call her parents. It was still early enough in California. This was too much to deal with alone. She only hoped it wasn't one of her uncle's shows.

Ella reached for the phone and dialed. She owed them a call anyway and the rates were so much lower after midnight. The phone rang and rang but the machine didn't go on. That was weird; where would her mother be? She was almost always home on weeknights when her dad was away. Oh, stupid! It was Friday night. They always went out on a date. But her mother never forgot the machine. She counted ten rings before Juanita's voice.

"Wilder home. How may I help you?"

"Juanita, it's Ella."

"Oh, hi! I was thinking it could be you or your momma."

"My mother? Isn't she out with my dad."

"Oh, no, no. Things got changed. Your poppa had to stay in L.A. and your momma, she was out of here at the creak of dawn this morning. Something came up and she go down there. I haven't heard nothing from no one. I think she's gonna stay down there. You know your momma don't like to drive at night, 'cause her eyes aren't so good in the dark."

Ella laughed. "My mother doesn't drive, she does the Heimlich maneuver with the steering wheel."

"What's this Highlick thing. I don't know that word."

"It's when someone's choking to death, and you wrap your arms around them and push the food up."

"I like this. I should learn this. Your parents are always talking too much while they eating."

"Will you tell them I called? It's nothing important."

"Why you don't try your poppa's apartment in L.A.? They are probably there by now."

"Okay, I will. You'd better put on the machine. I guess Mom forgot."

"Yep. She was outta here like the *diablito* was after her."

"That's so peculiar. What could have possibly happened? You don't think my dad is sick or anything?"

"No, no. She would have told me something like that. Don't get worried now. She just said business problems. It's cool."

"Business problems? Okay. I'll try them in L.A. Thanks, Juanita."

"Everything okay with you? It's late there for calling."

"Oh, yes. I'm fine. I was watching something totally bizarre on television and I thought they'd get a kick out of it, no big deal."

"Okey dokey. I tell your momma, just in case you miss her."

"Thanks, Juanita. Good night."

"*Vaya con Dios* and all that jazz, Ella, my baby."

Ella picked up her tea. The people in diapers had gone and a promo for another show was on. "Join us tomorrow night on *Killers at Large* when we go after The Red Menace, a serial killer stalking redheaded women in the Midwest. Tune in for a journey into terror."

Ella pushed the mute. Oh, my God, Mom would freak over that one. She missed her mother so much lately. She had always assumed that falling in love would make you forget about things like your family, but everything had just intensified. What was happening to her?

She put down her cup and shuffled back to the bathroom. The tub was filled enough to cover her. She dumped a capful of herb oil into the water and lowered herself slowly. God, she loved hot baths, another thing she shared with her mother. She reached for a rubber band, tied her hair up, and settled herself down in the small tub.

Better that she didn't try to call her parents in L.A. now. She'd wait until Sunday when she could call cheap again. They always told her to call collect, but she just didn't feel right doing it, it was so collegy. Let Toby make the collect calls.

That's what she'd do. She'd call Tob. He was always up till some ridiculous hour. Her brother was doing things she had done just a few years ago, and they all seemed so juvenile. She felt so old. That must be what growing up is, continuously looking back at yourself and thinking jeez, what a dork.

Ella picked up the soap and rubbed under her arms. She raised herself on one hand and soaped her body, lathering up between her legs and into her rectum. Can't be too clean, her mother always said.

Touching herself made her think of Willy again. Oh, God, she missed him. She had never imagined that she could feel anything like the way she felt when he made love to her. What was she going to do? Was she just copping out and running away from herself?

Her mother had fallen in love so early and had gotten married so young; she had always felt bad for her, not having had more adventures before she settled down. She had always said that she would never do anything like what her mother had done. What was wrong with her? She was almost too old not to have any idea what she wanted to do with her life.

Ella stood up and reached for a towel. They were all dirty. She had totally forgotten to drop the laundry off. She shivered, all the positive effects of the bath dissolving. She stepped out and pulled on her robe. She hated to put on a robe when she was wet. Her dad never used a towel. How gross, being wet and soggy in your robe. Toby did it too; it was just the way men were, too lazy to dry off first.

She leaned over, wiping her feet with the hem of her robe before slipping them back into her rabbits. A stab of loneliness hit her. A prickly needle of it. She needed to talk to someone in her family.

She stomped across the room to the phone. A Dracula movie was on and it made her think of her uncle Martin — that's what her mother called him when she thought they weren't listening. He did look like Dracula.

She flopped back down on the couch. That had been a shocker, her aunt Loretta and her uncle splitting at practically the same time as their uncle Jackie. What was going on? Some divorce virus? She had thought that the nineties were supposed to be this chilling-out decade. No one had sex anymore, no one trusted anyone physically. She couldn't believe she had trusted Willy, and he had a certificate and everything. People were supposed to be staying married these days and her entire family was coming apart!

Not to mention the still-unresolved issue (as far as she was concerned) of the slut panties. She was now absolutely convinced that her mother had lied. Those were not her mother's, no way. What if they split up, too? No. She would not think about that. Enough was enough for one night.

She pushed the memory dial. The phone rang. Come on, Tob, be home.

"'Lo?"

"Toby?"

"Who wants to know."

"This is the Click modeling agency in Manhattan. Two of our top models, Claudia Schiffer and Elle Macpherson, have seen your picture and are too shy to call themselves. They want your body, boy."

"Tell them I'll get back to them when the line thins out."

"You are such a retard, Toby."

"Is that what you woke me up to tell me? I'm not crazed and

burnt-out enough by the competition and workload, my own sister has to make a special call at one-thirty in the morning to insult me."

"I was lonely."

"Small wonder, if this is the way you treat your friends."

"How are you?"

"As well as can be expected with three papers due by next Wednesday. I have this medieval art history class and I swear to God, we looked at four thousand slides of the crucifixion today for this test on Monday and they all looked the same to me. Otherwise I'm fine. How about you?"

"Up and down. I was watching this cable show with these three people in diapers —"

"I saw it. Actually, it rocked me to sleep."

"Could you believe that? What if you were one of that guy's kids and you tuned in and saw your father like that. Can you imagine Dad?"

"Now that you mention it, yes. That streak of goo-goo has reared its head now and then."

"Toby, be serious."

"Then I'd have to totally wake up, and then I will never get back to sleep."

"Have you talked to Mom today?"

"Nope, not since I got back. Why?"

"I don't know. Something seems funny. I called and Juanita answered and said Mom was in L.A., that she had gotten a call before dawn this morning and taken off and not called in since. Don't you think that's strange?"

"Maybe something happened with the series, or Dad's sick."

"She told Juanita it was a 'business problem.' Maybe you're right, but they've been half expecting the ax for weeks. What could she possibly do by racing down there at dawn? It doesn't make sense."

"Did you call Dad's apartment?"

"No. I called you instead. I don't know. I just didn't feel like getting into a whole big deal tonight. But then I got worried."

"Ell, if anything was wrong, they'd call us. It's probably nothing.

Maybe it was one of her mercy missions, with all of the stuff going on with the rest of the family."

"Yeah. You're probably right."

"So, you haven't talked to them yet."

"No. I don't want to do it over the phone. I'm going to wait till Club Med at Christmas."

"Oh, grand. Do me a favor, save it until the last day so you don't ruin everyone's vacation."

"Thanks, Mr. Moral Support."

"Hey, I'm on your side but that doesn't mean that I'm happy about this, either. This is really serious stuff."

"I know. I know, believe me. It's never out of my brain for a second. Why don't you come into the city next weekend and we'll hang out?"

"Okay, if I can stay at Grandpa's. I'm not going to do another three-on-a-match number with you and Gwennie. I felt like I had been trapped in the girls' locker room. Besides, she snores."

"I don't blame you. Want me to call him for you?"

"That'd be great. This is really a nightmare; I never understood what you meant about college until now. My skin's breaking out for the first time in my life. I'm turning into Mr. Zit Chin."

"I know, Tob. It's really tough. The first year is the worst. You'll figure it all out. You'll be fine. Honest."

"On that positive note, I will return to my diaper dreams."

Toby hung up. Ella put down the phone and fell back on the couch. She closed her eyes. She should get up and take off her damp robe and get into bed. She hadn't brushed her teeth or put Chap Stick or moisturizer on or anything. She couldn't move. She'd just doze off for a few minutes and then get up, turn off the TV, and go to bed properly, just like her mother.

Toby put his hands behind his head and stared up at the shadows the streetlight was casting on his ceiling. He was wide awake. If there was one thing he had never had trouble with in his entire life before he went to college, it was sleeping. Staying awake had been his problem; now he was Mr. Insomnia. Of course sharing a room the size of a coat closet with a half-life who blew his nose into his pillowcase didn't help much. Thank God the geek lived in Newport and went home weekends.

Why couldn't he even tell Ella the truth about how he was feeling? He felt as if he were trapped inside someone else's personality. Keeping it light, always going for the joke, when the real Toby Wilder was banging on the walls begging to be heard.

He went home for Thanksgiving and acted like Joe College. He'd kept hoping that maybe his dad would see through the bravado and take him out or something; man-to-son stuff.

Usually they would shoot some hoops or throw the ball around on the beach, but his dad barely even asked him about school. The whole weekend had been really strange. They were The Wilders, but not the *real* Wilders. Everyone seemed off to him, sort of self-absorbed. That had scared him as much as what he was dealing with at school. His family was his backup; it was his place to get away from the world.

What was wrong? Of course, he had never opened up, so why should they. What would he tell them anyway? That he hated college, that they were wasting their money and his time. Most of this would come as no surprise to his parents. He had, after all, always hated school. He could remember all the way back to preschool when he would hold on to the bedpost and his mother would have to pry his fingers loose to get him to go. It had always taken two people to get him up for school. His mother called getting him up and out of the house her Jewish penance.

It wasn't that he was lazy, well, okay, he also was pretty lazy, but it was mainly because he hated school. He hated anything that involved big people telling little people what to do; and, later on, older people telling younger people what to do.

Why couldn't he tell them the truth? He didn't belong at Brown. He wanted to act and write screenplays and direct. He was frustrated and bored. Why hadn't he had the courage to choose another kind of school? An arts school even?

Maybe because they had all been so overcome that he had been accepted at a hot school like Brown. What a shocker. He had never been a good student. He was always the class clown and the first one out the door at recess. The only part of school he had ever liked besides drama and creative writing was sports.

His dad always said that he had never met a ball he didn't like, and it was true. Maybe he should have pursued baseball or tennis more zealously. Well, it was too late now, though all his trophies had sure helped him with admissions, and he did give good interviews, even he had to admit that, and the school in California, gush-brained wallet-suckers to the last, had written pretty overwhelming letters about him. Who knows, but when they accepted him and his parents were so overcome, like it was Harvard or something, he just went along with them.

Now he was stuck. He didn't belong here, he hated authority, and he hated traditional education. He didn't learn that way; he had to learn things for himself. That was just the way he was. Just because someone was the teacher didn't mean he was right or smarter or anything. So okay. He had an attitude problem, but he was also right. Even his literature classes were a drag, because he had already read most of the books on his own.

His modern-lit professor had never gotten over *Catcher in the Rye*. The only good class moment he had had since he'd been there was when he had said that he believed if *Catcher* was published today, it would have a small polite reception as a coming of age novel but that unless Holden's stepmother had molested him or his father had gone to jail for investment fraud or he had AIDS, no one would pay any attention to it. "Art is mainly timing," he had said, which was maybe not even true, but it sure made Professor Butt-head crazy.

Why couldn't he just keep his mouth shut? He was just like his mother that way. Only she never mouthed off in public like that. She was not the type to tell the traffic cop who had pulled her over for speeding that he was an ape-brained idiot. He should pay more attention to how his parents dealt with other people.

And now on top of everything else, Ella was going to drop a

plutonium-filled Christmas cake on their holiday table. Every time he thought about her, he felt like crying.

Toby rolled over onto his stomach, burying his head in his pillow. He had to get some sleep or he would never be able to get up at six and study. Study! How he hated that word. If he ever had kids he would never send them to school. He would whisk them away to some remote island and teach them himself.

The worst thing about being a teenager was that no one ever let you alone for a second. Sometimes he felt like a bacteria being scrutinized by grant-seeking scientists. The only good thing about college was being away from his parents' laser patrol. Sleep, Wilder. Turn it off and sleep.

CHAPTER VIII

LORETTA MILLER was couple-counseling. She was finding it extremely uncomfortable to be posing as a serene and knowledgeable marital adviser when her own husband had just moved into a studio apartment.

"So we finished our lo mein and the waitress brought the little bowl with the fortune cookies, and I was pouring some more tea for us, and when I looked down, he had eaten my fortune cookie! He'd just broken it in half, read the fortune, and eaten it! I couldn't believe it."

"I can't believe it, either. I mean, have we sunk so low we're fighting about fortune cookies? God, can't you see how childish you sound?"

"It's not childish. It's not about the fortune cookie! It's that you have so little regard for me that you would just take it. How insensitive and disrespectful. You know I always love to read my fortune! I would never take your cookie like that. Have I ever once, in all our years together, ever taken your fortune cookie? I felt violated, and then you just made fun of me —"

"I can't do this anymore. I've had it! It's always something that I'm doing to hurt you. Nothing I do is good enough! Nothing is ever right. I can't say or do anything without some reaction from you! I feel like I'm living in a prisoner of war camp!"

"It's just because you never hear me. I harp on things because I can't connect with you. I feel invisible, as if I was just a tiny little speck of dirt on your sleeve and at any moment you might just flick me off."

Loretta's light went on. She looked at her clock. This was her only session for the morning and she wasn't expecting anyone.

The couple turned to her with the patient's nuance detector, so sensitive it was triggered by the slightest blip.

Focus, Loretta. "Let's try something. Adam, switch places with Gina."

"You mean physically?"

"Yes. Change seats."

The couple stood up, awkward partners at the freshman mixer.

"Okay. Let's go back to the restaurant, only I want you to change parts. Gina is tearing open the cookies and Adam is pouring the tea. Don't say anything for a minute; just try to walk in one another's shoes."

Loretta watched them. Why had she never tried this with Martin?

"Okay, Adam. What are you feeling?"

"Look, I agreed to come here, but I never agreed to play patty-cake or do any of that dumb psychodrama stuff."

"I understand how you feel about that. But you two are not empathizing with one another. Coming here doesn't do anything. There's no magic about coming here. Going to the opera doesn't make you Pavarotti, does it? Well, going to a therapist doesn't make your marriage work. *You* make your marriage work." *Easy, Loretta, a little arch for eight* A.M.

Marital counseling was the hardest part of her work. Nothing ever prepared her for the power of emotion generated between two lawfully wedded people with years of denied feelings cohabiting under the surface, beneath the "controllable problems." *Who* was in her waiting room?

"Okay, let's stop now, but please think about trying this again next time. I really think it can be very helpful."

She opened the door and followed them out. Her sister-in-law was slumped down in one of the vinyl chairs. Annie did not slump. She remembered the call from Martin, something about getting Annie in to see a patient at St. John's; too late for them, too late for changing chairs and switching fortune cookies.

"Annie, what are you doing here? You look like you've been up all night."

"I have. Do you have some time? I need to talk to someone."

"You're in luck; I had two cancellations. Come on in. I'm all yours."

Annie threw herself down on Loretta's couch and kicked off her boots.

"Want some coffee?"

"I'd love some." Annie curled her legs under her. She needed a bath. "Were those patients?"

Loretta set down the coffee and curled up next to her on the couch. "Yep."

"Married?"

"The Mr. and Mrs. Bridge of the boomer generation."

"She looks like Hillary Clinton."

"Everyone looks like Hillary Clinton."

Loretta waited. She had seen her sister-in-law happy and sad and angry and anxious and frustrated and tired. But she had never seen her like this. She was different; something had been added to the mix of her character, something slightly flinty, but in a way more at peace. Some of the little Miss Muffet was gone. She could see it in the way Annie slumped into her waiting-room chair and flopped down onto the couch. Annie had become more Annie. This Annie seemed bolder and more relaxed with the idea of being herself.

"I know this is a bad time for me to dump this on you, Loretta. I didn't realize that Martin . . . that the two of you were that close to really splitting up! Maybe I just blocked it, but I was really shocked when he said he had actually moved out. Please forgive me for not calling you. I have no excuse. I've just been, I don't know, sort of moonwalking or something ever since the week before my birthday —"

Loretta put down her cup. "Annie! Just tell me!"

Annie crumbled, sobs cracking her defenses. "Mickey's having an affair with the potter, the one whose work he gave me for my birthday! Talk about tit for tat!

"You see, it started with this pair of turquoise underpants Ella found in the back of my car. I said they were mine, but they weren't, and I started to be suspicious that maybe Mickey had, you know, slept with someone in my car and I asked him and he denied it, but sort of elusive. Looking back, he really only denied knowing anything about the panties, which turned out to belong to Molly, so I . . . no, that comes later. . . .

"I went to pick up the pot and there was this man there. An Englishman named Oliver Taylor, and something happened to me, Loretta. I swear never in my entire life has anything like this ever happened! I lost control. I was completely swept away with passion for this man!

"And this man said that he loved me, that he had fallen in love with me before he . . . before I had even turned around, and he wants me to meet him in London at the beginning of January!

"Anyway, later I found out about the panties being Molly's and I was just . . . I mean, the guilt! I had done this wanton thing and my husband was innocent. And then Lina called to tell me that Leonard Lewis had disappeared with all of our money and so I raced down here yesterday and spent the day on that, which is enough of a nightmare all by itself. And then I went to the apartment because I couldn't track Mickey down and I was so tired and upset about our savings and everything and he was . . . he was there with her! It was like *Knots Landing,* I swear to God. I walked into his bedroom and they were doing it, right in front of me. Mickey and this awful woman!

"And the worst part was that he was dripping with sweat! I mean he was putting all of this energy into it, really giving it to her. Oh, God, it was so painful. I just raced out of there. I drove all the way back to Ojai. I went to her house and I broke her pots. You can never, ever tell this, because I could go to jail, but I just had to. I had to do something — I couldn't just be a good girl or I would have gone crazy, and driven back and blown them away or myself or something."

Loretta ran her hands through her short frizzy hair, rubbing at her scalp as if a bug had crawled into it.

Annie's eyes were so wide she could hardly see. "It's that bad?"

Loretta reached over and patted her arm. "Oh, honey, no. I'm sorry. I'm just trying to catch my breath. The last time I saw you my life was crumbling, and as usual everyone traipses up to the Wilders, who're always doing fine. You two were like Shangri-La in a way, I mean having a life like yours was what we all aspired to. You were making it all work. So, I am a little overwhelmed here. . . ."

"But *I* thought we were, too! Maybe that's what was wrong! I was complacent and smug and God's punishing me."

"Annie, don't start with the 'God is punishing me' shit. That's the result of not enough therapy, my girl. Believe me, if there is a God, he, she, or it is much too busy with other stuff to be planning vendettas against nice little redheaded girls, so drop that nonsense."

Annie sighed. "You're right. I'll cut it out. Besides, there's nothing like finding your husband in the throes with another woman to snap you right out of unnecessary guilt."

Loretta picked up her coffee. She was already exhausted and her day had barely begun. "Honey, I spend most of my life sitting here listening to couples tell me things, alone and together, that make your story look like animation material for Disney. You cannot believe how most people lead their lives! Clueless, they stagger around in their own movies, absolutely clueless.

"Life is basically one big mess, and if we're intelligent and moral, we spend most of our time trying to clean it up, make some order and patterning out of it, so that we can cope and learn and grow.

Loretta sipped her coffee. "One June several years ago when Bennie was just a baby, Martin and I took a trip across the California desert to Joshua Tree park. We stopped for gas at this funky old station and next to it, like a mirage, was this cactus farm.

"I was wandering around this cactus oasis in this paralyzing heat, when this old woman appeared carrying a watering can. She was quite fat and all covered up in long dark clothes and as she got closer, I realized that she was blind, totally blind. She said hello to me, even though I hadn't moved or spoken, and I just stood there, transfixed, watching her caring for these incredibly vicious cactuses.

"Finally, I couldn't stand it any longer and I asked her, 'Isn't it dangerous for you to work here without sight? Don't you get pricked?' 'Oh, yes,' she said, 'all the time.' 'But shouldn't you be in a safer place?' I asked. And this fat blind old woman put down her can and stood up straight as a stick and looked right into my soul and smiled at me. 'And where would a safe place be, dear?'

"Annie, no one knows how to do life. We're all making it up as we go along. Some people are just better improvisers than others. There is no safe place. We are all blind in the cactus patch."

"That's what I mean, Loretta. I thought we had it covered. I have always been so worried about everything that I made the safest, strongest, snuggest little nest I could, and then spent the last twenty years or so just flying back and forth, bringing in supplies, stocking up for the winter. And lo and behold, some buzzard just picked the whole damn thing up and made off with it."

"Me too, kiddo. You know what I really think about marriage with my clinical hat on? Marriage is about the civilizing and ritualizing of erotic passion into a livable form. A controlled violence. Uncontrolled emotion destroys marriage; even moderate jealousy, competition, and obsession wreaks havoc. The irony is, so does control, because the daily chipping away at passion that goes with taming a relationship takes another kind of toll. It's almost a no-winner contest and then add to this basic dilemma created by the form of marriage, all the problems and stresses that are piled on top, and it's astonishing that anyone stays the course.

"And then there's aging. Women are basically long-distance runners and men are sprinters. They burn out before we do. Every time I see a couple where the man has left or wants to leave for a much younger woman, it's because their race is done. They can't keep up with all of these stunning, smart, just-hitting-their-stride-at-fifty equals. It really isn't because they're trying to hang on to their youth, though that's what it looks like, and in a few cases it's true, but more often it's because younger seems simpler. They don't have to prove anything. They have seniority and can sit back while their baby bride huffs her way around the track for thirty years or so, by which time they've checked out.

"A woman you've grown up with, and grown older with, is far more demanding and challenging than someone who hasn't figured herself, let alone you, out yet. A woman's life is all about losing things. In marriage we lose our self-esteem because we lose our autonomy. We get softer and scareder and our edges dull, and things are always being taken away from us. Our virginity, our breasts, our ovaries, our children, our youth. What life forgets, gravity gets. Marriage gives us a foundation, but we never factor in for mildew and dry rot."

Annie shuddered. "I know this may sound a little Pollyannaish, especially at the moment, but even though marriage may be a flawed and difficult form, it has been the guiding force of life as we know it since Adam and Eve. There is something to be said for building a life with someone, raising a family, creating a home out of a commitment between two people, working and building and struggling together. It is a haven, and it does give direction and purpose to people's lives. Look at all the divorced and single people we know — do you think it's better for them, especially nowadays?"

"I know. I'd rather be married than out in the rain forest without an umbrella too, but all I'm saying is we should acknowledge how hard it is. You know what I think keeps people married more than anything else?"

"What?"

"Farting. I'm serious. Do you realize how long it takes before you're comfortable enough with someone to fart in front of them! Just think about starting over dating and having to hold all of that air inside you for years! Martin is the only man I've ever farted in front of. God, I am really going to miss that."

Annie uncrossed her legs; her feet were asleep. "You're right. I can't even imagine it! Oh, God, Loretta! What am I going to do?"

Loretta stood up and walked around behind Annie. She bent over and hugged her. "Right now you're going to go to my house, take a hot bath, and get some sleep. Bennie has dance class after school, so no one will be there all day. You can't even begin to think when you're this exhausted. I'll be home by six and we can talk some more. You are going to have to separate out the problems. You need to get centered a little bit before you deal with Mickey. Come on, take my key and go."

Annie pushed her tingling feet back into her boots. She realized that she had not slept in two days. It was quite fascinating how any physical need totally overrode any emotional agenda. All she could think of suddenly was sleep. She stood up, almost swaying with fatigue, and followed Loretta to the door. "I don't know what I would have done if you hadn't been here."

"You'd have done just fine." Loretta put her hands on Annie's shoulders and looked at her. "Listen, kid. I am not in any shape to be of much help to you right now. We're going to have to sort of stagger through this together; you lead one song, I'll lead the next."

"Okay." Annie leaned over and kissed her. "Except the samba. I always have to lead in the samba."

"Frankly, Annie, I don't think we'll make it past the box step."

Annie wandered around the quiet, sunny rooms of her sister-in-law's modern hillside house. She had eaten Loretta's leftovers, bathed in Loretta's tub, and was wrapped in one of Loretta's robes. What a strange feeling to be so close to another woman's life. She tried to remember if she had ever been all alone in anyone else's house before. No memory came.

She went to the sliding glass doors, pulled them open, and stepped out onto the deck. She had never understood their house, not that it wasn't nice. It was a lovely design, filled with glass and light, but what she didn't understand was her brother living in a house that was so exposed, way up in Beverly Glen. So much sun! There wasn't even an awning on the porch. Of course, she had never quite fathomed canyon houses anyway. Too many dark winding roads, not to mention the earthquake terror.

She took a couple of long deep breaths and executed one of her yoga sun postures. The blood went to her head. She felt dizzy. She bent over again and touched her toes and slowly straightened up. Time for sleep. She went inside, locking the doors behind her. It was so silent up there, so isolated. Not much of a neighborhood for Bennie. Who did he play with?

This house felt like Martin, not Loretta. Loretta was from Philadelphia. She grew up in a neighborhood with row houses and crazy Italian relatives running in and out. How could she stand it with no one nearby?

And now she was really alone up there, with all of those scary possibilities — earthquakes, forest fires, wild animals. Wasn't the Manson murder somewhere around there? What about the Hillside Strangler? *Stop it, Annie.*

She had enough real things to be afraid of now. Maybe that would turn out to be positive; it would decelerate all of her endless assortment of projected terrors.

Annie went into the kitchen and poured a glass of water and carried it back to the room next to Bennie's. She stopped at the door to her nephew's room. Pictures of Nureyev, Baryshnikov, and Gregory Hines were pinned on his bulletin board. She walked in and opened his closet, sniffing the little boy odors. His room smelled just like Toby's old room. Sort of sweet and sweaty and filled with scents of licorice and dirty socks.

In a box at the back of his closet were his ballet slippers and his tap shoes. She had taken him to class a few times, when she had been in town and Loretta was working. She had been uneasy about it, as if she were betraying her brother, but it wasn't as if Bennie collected shrunken heads or something. Although that would have been okay with her, too. He just wanted to dance! What she had not prepared for was that he would be good — not just good, gifted. She sat in the back, wanting to leap up and dance with him. He was working on a piece that he had choreographed himself for his school recital. She was amazed at his poise and assurance. He pranced around, a five-year-old prodigy, working out his steps.

"My diagonals are off," he said. He had worked out a routine to a

Willie Nelson song, and when he ran it through she held her breath. He moved with such grace and strength and joy and pure energy, unafraid and completely without self-consciousness. She envied him. No one will break his spirit, she thought, wondering if someone had broken hers. Why was her childhood so unclear?

She closed the door and left Bennie's private place. Maybe she would try to talk to her brother. Maybe if he went and watched Bennie, he would change his mind.

Annie pulled down the covers and slipped between the cool, fresh sheets. Bliss. She would sleep, and then she would try to think clearly.

Actually, she was amazed that she was as calm now as she was. She would have thought that she would be totally hysterical and unable to function at all. Well, maybe betrayal was like grief, the feelings washed over you in waves, ebbing and flowing.

Her body felt as if it were sinking, pulled down into the bed by the force of her fatigue. Her mind slipped away from her into half-conscious pre-sleep, and Mickey's face, dripping with sweat and shock, loomed in, testing her. Ivy Clare's hands folded like a mummy over her broad, flat chest . . . a mummy in the British Museum . . . Oliver Taylor waiting on the steps . . . steps — Bennie flew by in his tap shoes. Her aunt Bessie waltzed her around the room. Aunt Bessie always said, "Do the next thing." What did she mean? Something about when you're confused and have lost your way, do whatever appears next. What was next?

"Follow the money," Bennie said, and time-stepped with her aunt. Where was that from? She reappeared, running after her aunt, who turned into Molly, who turned into Samantha leering at her, holding her enormous breasts in her hands. Mickey danced in wearing tango clothes, reaching out for Samantha's breasts with black-gloved hands. *Follow the money.* Richard Nixon leapt into the dream, pushing Mickey away and tangoing Samantha off. Watergate. Robert Redford came up behind her, pushing his penis against her buttocks. "I loved you before you ever turned around." Aunt Bessie was screaming somewhere, "Don't turn around! Follow the money!" "Deep Throat," Robert said. "Deep Throat said 'Follow the money.'"

Annie rolled over, curling her legs up tight against her belly. The dream was leading her. That's what she would do. Let Mickey go for now. First things first. She had no control over her marriage. She would find Leonard Lewis. "Good girl," Aunt Bessie said, and tangoed away with Redford.

CHAPTER IX

THE DELPHIC ORACLE touched the drain of Jackie Wilski's black tile pool, feeling the pressure push against the bones in her ears and the sides of her ribs. She surfaced, air exploding from her mouth, her ears ringing. She would have to resume her training, now that she had a proper pool. Everyone she had stayed with in Montecito and L.A. so far was too cheap to heat their pools in November. If there was one thing she loathed it was cold water, so anti-life-force.

Jackie's pool was perfect, warm enough to enter without shivering but not so hot that she couldn't dive and swim. It would do just fine. She rolled onto her back and floated, feeling the late fall sun on her naked body, her hair billowing around her. Yes, this would do. Even Edgar the houseman was a gem. The sort of wonderfully muscle-macho chauffeur, cook, and bodyguard combo people in Hollywood were so fond of these days. She knew exactly how to handle the type. She would be remote and seductive, playing ever so slightly on his weaknesses and superstitions and balancing his desire to fuck her with the fear of her power. It made for an attentive and pliable servant every time.

Servant-casing was one of her primary skills. She had learned by trial and error that females were hell. They were on to her in a Metairie minute, and the same went for niggers and faggots. The faggots adored her at first, part of their drag rapture, wanting to be her and all, but it wore off the minute they realized that *her* power was threatening *their* power. Manipulative little cocksuckers they were, the house homos, but the niggers were the worst. She wasn't Southern for nothing. They were so infuriatingly slave-patient; it was in their genes, that kind of stoic control. I can wait, they told her with their eyes.

Edgar was ideal and so was Jackie Wilski. The truth was she was tired and broke and needed a man to take care of her; take care of her in her own way, which was somewhat different from the classic sense.

She was building a following, but all the money went right back out in P.R. and advertising and travel and clothes and renting the halls. She was still paying for the printing of her books and recording of her cassettes. She was caught in that small business trap; she needed an underwriter with power and money and connections, and she had found him on Thanksgiving Day in California.

He met all of her criteria. The man controlled tabloid television! He was small, therefore easier to physically intimidate. Small men always were, though they tried mighty hard to cover the fact up.

He was terribly insecure and competitive with his brother and needed a lot of reassurance — she was the world champion male ego booster — and he had an obsession with giant gentile women. Only the others had been dumb cunts with tits, and she was far more than his equal. He was rich and he knew most anyone she needed him to know. He could give her a show! That was more than J. Z. Knight or the Williamson bitch had.

He could provide a nice plump cushion on which she could rest her fine but weary ass for a while. Maybe a nice long while, long enough for a quiet wedding and a great big square-cut solitaire. Long enough to become a household word and garner significant alimony points. Quite a spell, possibly.

The fact was, she liked the little guy. She liked to fuck him and she liked to talk to him. Her momma had always told her that if she found some ol' boy that she liked to talk to *and* sleep with, snatch him quick because it didn't get any better than that. She had never doubted that her momma was right.

The Oracle swam to the side of the pool and dunked her head back, pulling her heavy, honey hair off her face. Heaven was a warm pool and a rich man in the sunshine, just like in her vision. That *was* the joke of it all. She wasn't a fraud! An opportunist, of course, and a pretty wicked gal, but she was also the real McCoy. She had the gift;

she had the sight, and she had seen her immediate future in New Orleans, having café au lait at Brennan's. A small, handsome man with a big fancy red car holding a television set. The set was on and it said, "California is the future." She was never wrong.

She strode across the pool, pulling against the water with her long, strong legs. She climbed the steps slowly, a Venus in the afternoon light, always on stage, the way good goddesses must be.

She slipped her robe on and stretched her arms high up over her head, arching her back. The only flea in the gumbo so far was this family emergency that had pulled him away from her much too fast for her taste, and she had been giving him her best ride, too. That was one trouble with the Jewish boys: they were big on family responsibility. Well, she would handle it today. She needed more information about his family, and hopefully dear ol' Molly would come through with that.

Up the stairs she went, taking each one slow, a priestess approaching her shrine. She heard voices from the house. Jackie must be home. Good. She always looked her most ravishing fresh from a pool. She strode across the marble terrace, feeling the warm stone under her feet. She did like this place. It even looked like a Greek temple. She could hold retreats right here, until he built her one of her own.

He was standing in the hall talking to someone. She felt the aura of something dark. She could not see the other person. She slipped in the French doors off the sunroom and silently made her way closer. The other person was a man. "I'm losing my mind," he said. He was crying. Jackie had his arm around him, trying to lead him into the study. They moved slightly and she saw the side of the other man's face under his baseball cap. Jackie's brother, the TV star. She walked faster, it was important to reach Jackie before his brother took hold.

"She never went home. She just vanished."

"Mickey, get a grip. She didn't vanish. She probably went to a friend's or a hotel. Come on in and sit. You need a drink."

"Jackie."

The men turned. Samantha stood in the center of the white marble hall, water glistening on her forehead, her flowing white caftan clinging to her moist body, the sun behind haloing her and making the cloth transparent.

Mickey flinched as if he'd been suddenly awakened. She focused her attention on Jackie. "Am I interrupting?"

Mickey put his sunglasses on and looked away from her. This was not a good sign. Jackie, however, was doing just fine, staring at her as if he were the toast and she were the cinnamon butter.

"Samantha, hi! You remember my brother, Mickey."

"Of course. Nice to see you again. I just had the most magical swim. I thank you for being a man of generous and sensuous heart and keeping the water warm. What a lovely treat at the end of a difficult day."

He was blushing. She smiled at him, turning the full force of her charm on High. She was nothing if not seductive. She channeled silently. *Don't listen to him. I am your future. He will try to pull us apart because he is jealous. Remember this when he speaks. Remember that I will be waiting for you.*

"Listen, honey, we have some things to discuss. Why don't you ask Edgar to give you a massage. He's the all-time best. We'll go to Spago later and show you off."

"Lovely idea." She turned, moving fast down the hall, her gown flowing behind her. Jackie watched her go.

Mickey watched his brother watching the latest mistake. Jackie had learned nothing! Only now he was in no position to give lectures on the value of committed relationships. He was no longer anyone to talk.

Jackie came to. "What? What are you staring at?"

Mickey looked away. "Nothing. It's none of my business."

Jackie moved in front of him, leading him down the long marble hall to his office. "Come on, let's have a belt." Mickey followed, unaccustomed to the shifting of roles. It had always been his little brother who came to him.

Jackie's Italian loafers clicked down the hall. Mickey smiled at the way his brother walked. The same cocky, clipped little Chaplin walk he'd had since he was a tiny little boy. Jackie closed the door behind them and motioned for Mickey to sit on the enormous black leather sofa. Mickey sat. He could barely remember ever being in this room. He usually saw Jackie at his office or met him in glitzy restaurants. None of his wives had ever entertained for him. If he saw his brother socially it was always up at their house. "The Haven," Jackie had called it once.

His brother was making drinks at an elaborate wet bar that Mickey had no memory of ever seeing before. It had gold faucets and that rare green marble that cost a fortune and a mirror behind the glasses and special lighting. All the bottles were the fanciest brands, and down below was a refrigerator for wine with a glass front and what looked like temperature controls.

Much ado about nothing, Mickey thought. The bar made him feel bad for his brother. He knew Jackie thought that he never said much about his toys because he was jealous, but he wasn't. He had just never understood the desire for all that crap. His tastes were just much simpler; not that he and Annie didn't like their nice house and their nice cars and being able to travel and have Juanita and all, but that was enough.

Neither of them wanted yachts or jewels or houses all over the place or Italian marble wet bars in rooms where maybe you poured a drink once a month. Even Jackie's cars, the Rolls and the 600, he didn't even like to be a *passenger* in them, it was so Reaganesque and embarrassing. Maybe he was his mother's son after all. But then, who was Jackie?

Mickey looked around the room. On every spare inch of wall, which seemed to be covered in some kind of watered silk, were ornately framed photographs of Jackie with famous people. Madonna (the Zsa Zsa Gabor of the twenty-first century, Jackie called her), Michael Jackson, the Clintons. It was a star-fucker's trophy room. The only people who seemed to be missing were the Queen of England and Roseanne.

In the very center was a whole series of pictures of him, Annie, and the kids, an entire series all across the middle of the wall. Mickey swallowed the lump in his throat. God, he loved the little putz. What a sweet thing to do, putting them right up there with the great and near great. A family tribute by the lonely uncle with no children of his own, no woman who loved him for himself. God, he wanted that for his brother. He wanted him to know how it felt to be really loved by a woman, not just used. Jackie thought his pecker was his heart; someone needed to give him an anatomy lesson.

Jackie strutted toward him holding two tall crystal glasses filled with ice and lemon and bubbles.

"Stoli and tonic, not a usual November drink, but somehow appropriate."

"Thanks." Mickey savored it. Saturday was the only day he let himself drink anything when he was shooting. Thank God, tomorrow was Sunday. He was wrecked. How was he going to pull off next week?

Jackie sat down beside him, crossing his slender ankles and putting his small feet up on the Regency hope chest that served as the coffee table. "Talk to me."

Mickey put down his drink. He hadn't eaten since last night and the booze had gone right to his head. He felt woozy and nauseated. "Most of it I told you on the phone. I just . . . I can't believe this is happening! You know that I have never done anything like this before in my entire life, and now Annie will never even believe that this was the only time. Oh, Christ, what a mess."

"But it wasn't the only time. I mean, it was hardly a one-night stand, Mick. You've been at it for months."

"I know. But still, it's not like a pattern or anything, not like I was one of those fuck-and-run guys we all know so well."

"You know, there are two theories on this. Some women think it's more of a betrayal if it's a lot of one-nighters and a pattern of running around and lying, and some women find it much worse if the guy has really fallen for someone. So it's a trade-off — is it better to fuck a hundred different women once or one woman a hundred times. You can bet that for Annie column A and column B are equally not okay."

"Oh, believe me I know that. But the horrible part, I mean the very worst part was having her come in like that! Jesus, Jackie, I can't tell you, having her see me screwing someone else — the look on her face! As long as I live I will never forget the look on her face — like I had just shoved a dagger into her. She might as well have walked in and found me murdering someone."

Jackie squeezed his lemon, sucking the tart citrus off his small, manicured fingers. "She'd have preferred walking in on you murdering someone, probably by a factor of fifty. Wouldn't you rather find her killing someone than fucking someone?"

"Are there any other choices?"

Jackie laughed. He knew the hard part was still ahead.

"What the hell was she doing there, anyway? It makes no sense! I'd just talked to her and told her not to come down because I was working. Do you think she was stalking me? That she had it all planned? But that doesn't make any sense, because she had this big box of papers and banking shit with her. She left the stuff right in the middle of the floor! She would hardly lug all of her documents with her to stake out a love nest."

"Mickey, I didn't want to tell you this on the phone. I've got more bad news for you. I was with Annie all day yesterday. She came down because Lina called her right after she talked to you. Leonard Lewis has flown the coop; he's vanished with all your money. That's why Annie was here. She must have called you twenty times, but you were nowhere. She was hardly spying on you. Why didn't you pick up your fucking messages?"

He stopped. He wanted to be supportive, not side with Annie. "Sorry, Mick. I didn't mean that to come out so harsh. It was just a really upsetting day and it just seems now, knowing the rest of it, such a waste."

Mickey tried to pick up his drink, but his hand was shaking. The fear he had felt in his kitchen making the Thanksgiving stuffing was back, moving into his stomach and up across his chest. "Oh, no. Oh, no! Poor Annie. She must have been . . . Oh, Christ! What a stupid asshole! I deserve this. You know why? I'll tell you why. I'll tell you the worst thing I have ever told anyone in my entire life, and then you can throw me the hell out of here.

"When Annie ran out? I fucked Ivy again. Fucked her harder. I couldn't get enough, like an addict. I could not stop. I fucked her until I passed out. Nothing could stop me, not even Annie's face, Annie standing there." Mickey covered his eyes with his hands, his body shaking.

Jackie lowered his legs and turned toward his brother. Now they were on his playing field.

"Hey, Mick. I know about this stuff. I've ruined my entire life with this stuff. I'm not judging you. At least you don't get married every time your prick shifts into auto pilot. You just know about my wives, you don't know how many other roller coasters I've been on with the bimbettes.

"I had this one that, in my insanity, I took to Ma's for Rosh Hashanah. 'Someone told me that I'm supposed to say something to you that sounds like, Dwight Yoakam,' she says. Ma and I look at one another. 'Dwight Yoakam? The country-western singer?' 'Yeah,' she says, 'Dwight Yoakam.' Ma gives her *the stare*. 'You mean Good Yuntuf, dear?'"

Mickey sat up; his eyes were red and running tears. "Get serious."

"My point is, I know about losing your balance over a broad. That's all I've ever done. No one can understand it until it happens to them. But this is not your pattern or character. This is your one-time insanity, and that doesn't mean it isn't terrifying and consuming, but it will pass, it will end. And you will never do it again; that you can trust me on.

"At the moment you've got four separate issues. Your show and whether or not it's going to be renewed, which of course takes the pressure off the other three issues, which are your marriage, your mistress, and your money. Two peanut M&Ms and two plain. I think I can help you with Leonard Lewis, and I would be honored if you would let me try, for my own reasons. The other three no one can help you with."

Mickey wiped the tears away with the back of his hand. He

reached for his glass. His hand had steadied. He was terribly thirsty. He drank the rest of the drink down. Jackie picked up their glasses and returned to the bar.

Mickey watched him. He felt lost again, as if their roles had suddenly switched. His brother was way ahead of him in this race. He didn't quite know how to handle it.

"So how do you get over something like this? I mean, if I can't just stop cold turkey. What do I do? I can hardly ask Annie to bear with me while I fuck my heart out for a year or so. She may not listen anyway, but if she will, what do I do?"

"You're not going to like it."

Jackie brought fresh drinks and set them down, standing over his brother, bigger for once. "You've got to ride it out, like a fever; go with it until it breaks. Shack up with her, take her to Hawaii or somewhere; lock yourself in a suite and lose control. One morning you'll wake up and she'll say 'Dwight Yoakam' and you'll be free. All of a sudden, it's like the clouds part and you look at the woman and you can't fucking believe you ever saw anything in her. But that's the only way to cure it, and it takes as long as it takes."

"Jesus, Jackie! Are you nuts? I have a job to do! If I lose the job we're bankrupt! I hardly have the luxury of flying off into the sunset to commit adultery in style until my dick falls off or Ivy starts looking like the Bride of Frankenstein. Besides, she's not like your airheads. She's brilliant and sharp as cut glass. She's got me by the head more than the balls. It's a head lust, and very dark, too; almost as if I wanted to punish her, like I don't have to care about her or be kind and loving. I don't understand it, but it's not about fucking."

Jackie pointed to the ceiling. "I've got one of my own upstairs at this very minute. Yes it is, Mick. It *is* about fucking. Don't confuse the issues. I know this shit. That's just denial. It's how you stay out of control. 'I can't understand it — it's more than I can cope with — it must be really deep and complicated'— it's about *fucking,* stupid. Write that on your shaving mirror, and don't forget it or you will really mess up your life."

Mickey watched him. He had never seen his brother like this.

This must be the way he was with his staff. He felt like a fool. He had done what parents do: stop seeing after their kids grow up — never letting them become who they are in the present, always seeing the ghost of their childselves. He had done that with his brother.

"I hear you. I just don't . . . what do I do first?"

"Go home, get some sleep. I'll try to find Annie. We can't do much about the money situation until Monday, but I think I'll make a couple of house calls tomorrow. First on the list, your boss. If you want to come, call me at ten."

"Stan Stein?"

"Yep. Leonard's got his money too, and it seems he was poking Leonard's wife."

Mickey laughed. "Bambi and Stan Stein? Forget about it!"

"She told me and Annie herself."

Hearing his wife's name hurt. It felt as if she were already moving away into her own life, going places and doing things that he was not part of. He stood up. His brother reached out and put his smaller arms around him, almost standing on his toes to do it. He wanted to talk to him about that woman upstairs. He was afraid for him. This one seemed much more threatening than all the others. But it wouldn't come out right now. It would sound as if he were trying to regain the upper hand.

"Thanks, bro."

Jackie let him go. "Mick, about money. You know I'll give you whatever you need. Don't sweat that part."

"Yeah, shack-up money. I don't think that's a great idea, but I appreciate the offer. I'm going to have to find another way to handle this."

"Maybe we can find one together."

Mickey put his arm around Jackie and they strolled out, down the long, empty hallway.

When Gerta, Stan Stein's parrot-faced German wife, ushered Jackie and Mickey into his office, he was on the phone. This was not unusual. No one who had ever worked for or socialized with Stan Stein had ever seen him doing anything but talking on the phone, eating, smoking cigars, or giving speeches. At the moment he was conducting all of those activities.

He motioned for them to sit, his cigar ash flying off onto his desk, which was filled with Sunday-brunch fare, several kinds of smoked fish, bagels, cream cheese, pickles, and onions. Everything about Stan Stein was bigger than life, beginning with his size. He was a massive, basketball-player-tall man with a huge, rock-hard gut and long skinny arms and legs, giving him, Annie always said, the appearance of an enormous Jewish Singing Raisin.

He would have been almost a caricature of a Hollywood mogul if it hadn't been for his voice. He was a French Jew, with a high nasal pitch to his heavily accented speech that sounded to the uninitiated ear as if he had either just inhaled a gallon of helium or someone was holding his nose.

"Murry, Maurice, *mon cher,* you are not seeing ze big picture, *n'est-ce pas*? Follow me, *bébé*. I want to do this show, very noir, very *négatif*, but in a positive way. I like this beautiful girl–ugly man concept. It worked for *Beauty and the Beast,* no? Women go wild for these ugly guys. Look at all the fashion models and the rock stars. That is what I want. Who is that one married to the Stone? He is the most ugly man alive and she is an angel. You see? It cooks.

"We play against type, but we don't make them like all of these other shows, down-to-earth, regular guys — we make them giants. Famous people and we work in all the teets and ass, fashion and music. It will go through ze fucking roof!

"Think about Woody Allen. I have never met a single woman, not even my maid, who has no teeth and is seexty years old, who would sleep with Woody Allen if someone had a pistol to her head, but there he is with intelligent, beautiful women fighting over him! Is true, no? Think of Woody, the nerdy, neurotic little pervert! Think of the Phantom of ze Opera.

"What? So beeg fucking deal, so she didn't love the phantom, do not be so literal! I want you to make magic for me. Now go and write this. I want a marriage between an ugly-faced rock star and a gorgeous fashion model. We go behind the scenes for a real look at unreal life. I am in love with this. Go!"

Mickey did not dare look at his brother. He felt like the character in *A Chorus Line,* reminding himself in Stan Stein's presence that he needed the job. It wasn't that he didn't like him, though maybe he didn't; it was that he always felt like a kid auditioning when he was with him.

Stein hung up the phone and reached out with one of his huge hairy arms and daintily picked up a mound of whitefish between his thumb and forefinger. He threw his large bearded head back and gobbled the fish, a barracuda taking the luscious bait, smacking his heavy pink lips. *"Magnifique!"*

He licked his fingers. "So, my *bébés,* what is up?"

Jackie sat forward. "Stan, you know what is up. Leonard Lewis is up. He's got all of Mickey's money and from what we heard, most of yours, too. We are trying to get a hold on this. You know how slow the feds are. If we wait for them, the trail will be ice age."

Stan gave them his big Buddha smile. He sat down at his desk, his enormous paisley silk robe fanning out around him. "How do you know this, about me and Leonard?"

Mickey watched Jackie. He was learning something else about his brother. If he wasn't intimidated by Stan Stein, he probably wasn't intimidated by anyone. Would he risk Bambi? It could make Stein mad. Stein mad was not a pretty sight, as anyone on *War Zone* could attest.

Jackie looked behind him. The door was closed, though Stein seemed to dominate his wife so completely, it might not have mattered if she was sitting on his lap.

Mickey and Annie always convulsed over the idea of Stan and Gerta doing it. "She must be on top, impaled like knockwurst on a stick," was what they had decided.

"Bambi Lewis," Jackie said without hesitation. Mickey held his breath.

Stein lifted a hunk of smoked salmon and repeated his bait ritual — the Buddha smile, altered by his long purple tongue flicking a stray morsel of fish from his upper lip.

"Ah, Bambi. Delightful. Such a, how you say, fuzzy girl. So pink and soft, like a piece of cotton candy. Poor little thing. She is okay?"

"No. She's in the hospital. She tried to kill herself, though from what I saw, I don't think it was a very serious effort."

"Ah. So *dramatique*. That is what I like about her. She has some of that younger Signoret thing about her, not the looks so much — she is much more flamboyant, more Bardot — but the tough-life quality. The bus stop persona. I so like women like that. I have never liked girls. I have never liked virgins of any kind. I only like historic houses, classic cars, Trumpy yachts, antique furniture, old clothes, and with women, I like a woman with, how you say, some mileage on her. Old buildings and old broads!"

"I hope you don't use that in your seduction pitch."

"Ha. Good, Jackie *bébé*. Very good."

Stan Stein picked up a gleaming Victorian silver knife and smeared a thick glob of cream cheese on a bagel. "I so love all of this American Jew food. You know we have nothing like this in Paris. I miss it so much when I go home, I have it flown in from New York."

Stein slipped a hunk of bagel into his mouth and chewed cheerfully. "I am thinking of opening a real *authentique* New York deli in Saint-Germain. Not that there are so many French Jews left in Paris, but because it is unique. It gives me a way to rub their pointy Gallic noses in their anti-Semitic shit.

"Do you ever think about why we know the names of the Nazis who murdered and destroyed, but no one knows the name of the general who refused the order to burn Paris? Imagine a world without Paris? This bothers me. Do you ever go to the Cluny Musée and look at the headless bodies and bodyless heads from Notre Dame? Did you know that before Napoleon, they were going to break up Notre Dame for scrap?

"The world reeks of barbarism; it is not just today. Always. Do you know about the Wannsee Conference? Do you know of this? It was the night at a lakeside villa in the suburbs of Berlin that Eichmann and his Nazi bureaucrats sat around after dinner with brandy and cigars and decided that eleven million Jews should 'fall away.' That was how he put it. 'Fall away.' I love this American lox and bagels because it is so happy about being Jewish. 'We have not fallen away,' the food says. Right?

"I married a German woman by design. I like to keep my enemies right by my side. I do not like to forget what is the truth. I look at my little German bride and I look out at my swimming pool and my greenhouse and I remember Wannsee. Hollywood is not Wannsee. Leonard Lewis is not Wannsee.

"You must understand that no French Jew or German Jew or any other European Jew who did not 'fall away' would ever be stupid enough to put their trust in anyone but themselves.

"Leonard Lewis I gave little bits to play with. It did not look like little bits to Leonard; I am sure that he thought he had a great deal of my money. That is what I let all of them think, but only I control my finances. So what Bambi told you is not true. It is true that we slept together, but the seduction came from her. I do not seek women or anyone else; never. I believe that Leonard found out, because the last meeting I had with him he was very rude, which is not his style. Do you want to know my theory?"

"Yes," Mickey said, a boy in synagogue before the great rabbi.

"I must ask you a question first. A very personal question."

"Go ahead."

"Did you have a piece of cotton candy yourself?"

Mickey flushed. Jackie squeezed his hand.

"No."

Stan Stein slammed his huge fist down on his desk, rattling the silver. "*Merde!* That destroys my theory."

Jackie stood up; being reverent made him edgy. "Okay, Stan, don't keep all the goodies to yourself. What theory?"

Stan Stein picked up a pickle, regaining his composure. "My theory is that Leonard took the money of all the clients who had fucked his wife."

Jackie paced back and forth before the mammoth Louis Quatorze desk. "Bambi said it was only you. One little slip."

Stein threw back his head. "Ha! I love this. This woman is fabulous! I hope she batted her great thick false eyes when she said this. The woman is worse than the Montmartre streetwalkers. She fucked everyone they knew! I know personally about everyone but two, Mickey and Lina Allen. I have had a private detective working on this since the moment he disappeared. No one steals from me."

Jackie turned and looked at Mickey.

Mickey stood up, too. "Maybe he *thought* she had slept with me. If you're right, it's a good place to start."

Jackie sat on the edge of his desk. "Can we talk to the detective?"

Stein let his sly frog eyes wander over Jackie; they were competitors of a kind. David and Goliath across a platter of smoked fish.

"Sure. Mickey's my friend. I look out for my people. I want this little shit caught. I'll call and say that it is okay. This is the best private dick in L.A., killer instinct." Stan Stein reached into his desk and pulled out a small pink business card.

Jackie reached over, his slender, hairless hand dwarfed by Stein's greasy paw.

"Thanks, Stan," Mickey said, and started toward the door. He needed some fresh air, the heaviness of the room, the man, and the conversation weighing him down.

"Mickey."

He turned. Stan Stein leaned forward; his bulgy eyes, Mickey thought, looked sad. "I was not going to tell the cast until Monday, but since you are here . . . they have given us the guillotine, *bébé*. We finish the last two episodes and we're history. I am very sorry, at a time like this, to tell you. I hope I have another show for you soon. I take care of my landsmen, no?"

Mickey tried to get a breath. The air wasn't here. He was not going to faint in front of Stan Stein. Jackie moved fast, taking him under the arm.

"It's definite?" Mickey managed to ask. The room was tilting slightly sideways.

Stein shrugged his giant shoulders. "You know me, Mickey. I don't let go until they break my fingers. I am working on better syndication, especially in the Orient, but you know how it is with revolving plot series, they are dead meat in reruns. Don't tell anyone else; let me do it. I may know something more on Monday."

Mickey nodded. He had to get out of there now. He realized something about Stan that he had never seen before. The reason he was so uncomfortable around him was that he wanted him to be his father. Especially today, he had wanted him to lunge across the room and lift him up in his gorilla arms and protect him, shield him from all the terror and hurt in his hyperventilating Hebrew heart.

"A Long Beach jury yesterday convicted an unemployed laborer of murdering his six-day-old son and feeding the infant to his pet German shepherd —"

Mickey hit the button, switching from the car radio to the compact disc player. The sight of a man feeding his baby son to his dog passed before him. He shook his head, trying to refill his kaleidoscope. Keep it simple, pal. You have really fucked up, but at least you are still in the neighborhood game, not in the major-evil league.

He turned onto San Vicente Boulevard and headed for the beach. He had no idea where to go or what to do. He had never had a Saturday in L.A. alone, though he had certainly been whining and moaning about how much he needed time by himself. Well, he had it now. He might even have it forever. Of course, all he wanted now that he had it was to be home in Montecito with his wife and kids, a clear conscience, and next week's script.

He tried to swallow. His throat felt like it was coated with sandpaper. *Canceled*. They were fucking canceled.

He parked his car at the end of the street and walked across to the pathway overlooking the Pacific Coast Highway and Santa Monica Beach, shielded from the possible stares of onlookers by his cap, shades, and neck scarf. It wouldn't be long before he'd start missing the unsolicited attention, if the experiences of his fellow former series stars were any indication.

Mickey leaned against the railing, looking down at the cars whizzing by on the highway below. He had no idea what anyone did in L.A. on a day off, unless it was summer and the beaches were open. He had never spent a free day there, and it was so unlike New York that he could not even fantasize about where people went or how they passed their time. I guess they work out and go to the movies and drive around. He really wasn't sure.

He sat down on a bench and looked up at the cloudless sky. An old couple, moving very slowly, stopped beside him. The old man was trying to help his wife sit down on the bench next to Mickey's. Her leg was in a brace and she was having difficulty finding a way to support her weight while she pushed herself back onto the seat. Her husband was not in much better shape than she was, but he was aiding her with delicacy and patience. Mickey stood up. "May I be of help?"

The old man turned his watery blue eyes toward him and smiled. "You're very kind."

Mickey walked over and took hold of the old woman's arms, bracing her with his weight.

The woman, her eyes more opaque, scanned Mickey's face, looking for signs of safety. She relaxed against him, letting him slide her gently down onto the bench. "Thank you so much," she said from far away.

Mickey let her go as carefully as if she were a newborn child, the way he had handled Toby and Ella all those years ago. "My pleasure," he said.

The husband patted his shoulder. "Bless you."

Mickey tipped his hat and returned to his bench. He had never really thought much about being old with Annie. Neither of them had ever talked about it except in a joking and offhand way. Maybe because they had each lost a parent so young, they had never seen a couple grow old together. Did he have some sixth sense that it wasn't meant to be? Or had they just taken it so for granted that it was not even an issue.

God help me. Tears splashing his cheeks. In twenty-four hours he had lost his wife and best friend (since they had always been the same person), all of his money, and his job. Just think what he could do with a whole weekend! Where the fuck was she! He could hardly call Juanita and ask her, since Annie was supposed to be with him. She wasn't at Jackie's or Lina's and no one had answered at Loretta and Martin's. It was hard enough calling around without raising suspicions. They were the couple that called one another ten times a day. How could he not know where his wife was for almost forty-eight hours?

If anyone found out what was going on, he would lose it. If no one knew, it was still fixable. What was he saying? Fixable in a real way or the perfect-marriage fantasy fixable, where his ego was obviously hung up big-time. What was more important for him to fix, the image or the reality?

Mickey tried for a deep breath. He felt so anxious, that every inhalation threatened to be his last. Was that it? He had lorded it over his brother and his friends because he had the great home life with the childhood sweetheart? Did he get off on the role so much that the heart of his real relationship could have been shriveling up, starved for fresh blood and oxygen, but as long as no one saw past the healthy-looking exteriors he hadn't been interested enough to cut the damn thing open and check the arteries? What did that mean? That he really didn't care about his wife or his marriage, but just about the form it gave his persona and his life?

What the hell was happening to him? Mickey stood up, bending forward to stretch his calf muscles. *I'll take a run up San Vicente and push through this haze.* The old couple on the next bench watched, their clouded blue eyes supplying what the sky left out. They smiled at him.

What could they be thinking? Do they envy me that my body still works the way I want it to? Do they feel old and ready to go or do they still feel like kids and hate every single second. Do they miss sex? Maybe they still have sex. Was that what Ivy was about? A death fuck or a death-defying fuck? I won't look back with regret at what I didn't do, was it that? Maybe if he went back and looked at how the whole damn thing started it would help. It was almost as if he had been sleepwalking for the last four months.

Mickey bent further down and touched his toes. He could see the couple still watching him. He needed to run. He straightened, taking a long, deep, much-needed breath and waved to the couple.

They waved back, turning to see him go.

Mickey crossed Ocean Avenue and headed up past his car. The center divider, the joggers' haven for the west side of Los Angeles, was so filled with afternoon exercisers that he could hardly set a pace. Where was he? Ivy Clare. His affair with Ivy Clare — a rhymed catastrophe.

Where did it start? Stan Stein's house last August, the party to open the new season. Annie wasn't there. Where was she? Rhode Island. She was with Toby, getting him started in school. He was alone, wandering around, already sick of the shoptalking schmooze and he'd just gotten there.

He saw the pot on Stan's terrace and he went outside to look at it. Annie loved the work, but he couldn't remember the artist's name. He put down his drink and touched it. It was hand-painted with bright pastel colors, and covered with tiny tits. It was irresistible. His fingers bumped along from nipple to nipple having a wonderful sensory trip. He even closed his eyes for a moment, yes, he must have, because the voice had startled him.

"Wonderful," the voice said. It was a deep, silky voice, an actress with serious training, he thought.

He turned around, embarrassed. The woman was standing with her arms crossed, holding a glass of wine in one of her large, square hands. Peasant hands, Mickey remembered thinking. He laughed, feeling invaded.

"Caught in the act," he said, or something equally stupid.

She looked at him, not smiling, which he found strange. She couldn't be an actress, she was nowhere near well-tended enough. Her hands looked dirty or something and her hair was almost wild, bushing out and sprinkled with gray. What was she wearing? It looked like operating room clothes. A surgeon who had taken a wrong turn at the Bel Air gate on the way to UCLA Medical Center?

She seemed to know what he was thinking, because she set down her glass and picked up the pot. "I love this one. I really hated to sell it."

"You're the artist," he said, feeling more relaxed.

"Yes. It was wonderful to see someone really connecting with the work. I rarely get to watch anyone like that. It was nice."

Mickey smiled. "Well, it's not that I'm any great expert or anything, but the subject matter does have its own tactile appeal."

"It's all I do," she said, her face stern.

"Yeah, I know. Stan talks about your work and we've seen your things several times, my wife and I. She's a great admirer of yours. Her birthday's coming up and I have been thinking of investigating pot possibilities."

"How nice, Michael."

"You know my name."

"Michael James Wilder of *War Zone*. I'm *your* admirer. I never miss an episode. I watch in my studio while I work."

"That's great. I never get to see anyone watching me, so we're even."

Now she smiled at him. It was a slow, wide smile, revealing perfect, bone white teeth. Actor's teeth, Mickey thought. The teeth were a nice surprise next to the hands, which were, now that he knew they were not dirty, extremely provocative. Strong, honest, female hands, not covered with some grotesque fake color or extended with pieces of plastic or wrapped with layers of glue and tape or whatever the hell crap all the women he knew put on them. He hated all of those phony hands. His wife was the only woman he knew who just had nice plain, clear-nailed fingers. But Annie's hands were small and freckled, not anything like this woman's — her hands could strangle a man. What a bizarre thought.

"I'm sorry, I'm terrible with names. I can't remember yours."

"Ivy Clare," she said, and picked up her wine.

"Right. Good screen name, I remember now."

"It was my grandmother's name. She came from Scotland and somehow her last name got lost at Ellis Island. I thought that made a nice symbol of all the things that have been taken away from women over the years, so when I started to show, I dropped my last name in tribute to her."

Mickey grinned. If she was going to turn into a bitter, man-blaming radical, it would be easier to make an exit. One way to find out fast was the injection of a little humor. "The pretension punch," Annie called it.

"Well, I changed my name too, but for far less noble reasons. Mick Wilski didn't seem as playbill-appealing as Michael James Wilder, and *my* grandmother claimed that they had chopped the entire first half of her name off at Ellis, which I guess I could have added back, except it never occurred to me."

"If my grandmother had bequeathed me some undesirable name, I'm quite sure I would have made the same choice. I'm Scotch-Irish, and we are nothing if not pragmatic about getting on with it."

"Well, I'm Polish-Jewish and we are nothing if not curious, so may I ask you a personal question?"

"That's a throwaway line. It can only be answered backward, after the question."

"Okay. Why are you wearing a scrub suit?"

She did not smile. He realized that she had beautiful eyes. Large and almost completely gray. He had never seen eyes that color before, except possibly on one of the O'Brian's Persian cats.

"I was in medical school, but still trying to take my potting and sculpture classes, and one day I raced to class from anatomy lab and I was still in my scrub suit. I was working with the clay and I kept seeing the body of this cadaver, a woman who had drowned. I kept thinking about her breasts. She had the most beautiful breasts, and there she was dead as dust, with these lovely, ripe breasts still so enticing, which was confirmed by the looks on the faces of my male colleagues.

"I started forming the clay as a breast, and the feeling of molding this exquisite life-shape with my hands totally took me over. I couldn't stop, and I missed my next class and my pathology lab, and when I was through, I had done my first breast pot and spent my last day in medical school. These are my good-luck clothes. I always wear them when I'm working."

"I see a great reliance on symbolic and superstitious iconography, good in an artist."

"Also in a Catholic. Come with me. I'll answer your question."

Mickey looked back at the party. He could see Stan Stein waving his unwieldy arms about, towering over his party like a giant Semitic elephant. He was in no hurry to return and it was too soon to leave.

Ivy Clare led him down the steps to the terrace and through the pruned and polished garden, past the Roman bath pool, across the tennis court to the back of the property, where the greenhouse and caretaker's cottage were.

The door to the greenhouse was open. She stopped in the doorway to wait for him and he realized, as he moved toward her, that she was taller than he was. She moved into the room and gestured to a makeshift table in the center, two sawhorses holding a mammoth slab of wood, created, it seemed, to hold the massive clay pot on top of it.

The center of the greenhouse had been converted into a studio. The pot was bare; no breasts had been cast or added and it looked de-sexed or amputated, waiting patiently for its missing pieces.

"I've been here working for several weeks. I needed to do this on the site, but it's going very slowly and Stan keeps having all of these parties and dinners, and though I hate to admit it, I get seduced. This world is so different from mine; I keep thinking of that nice big pool and I hear the laughter, and Stan, demon that he is, keeps phoning with offers of Montrachet and Norwegian salmon and things. It's terribly distracting."

Mickey laughed. "Well, come spend some time on the *War Zone* set, and you will find out that Stan doesn't treat all the people who work for him with such largesse; us, he would nail to the floor for eighteen hours at a stretch if he could get away with it. Count your blessings."

"I don't work for him, Michael. I'm just creating a piece of art for him. It's different."

He flushed. "Sorry. I didn't mean to relegate you to the lower classes. Call me Mickey; everyone does."

She put down her wine glass. "I loathe nicknames. Especially little-boy names. Mickey is the name of an impish five-year-old, not a mature and powerful artist."

Mickey sipped his drink. What was happening here? He felt off-balance. "Jesus. You are one heavy water-woman. Remind me never to take you to Disneyland."

She smiled, without her perfect teeth this time. "Were you thinking of inviting me to join you in a Magic Kingdom?"

He started moving back toward the door. "Only rhetorically. I hate the fucking place. Too much cute, even if he is my namesake."

"I've offended you," she said, shifting slightly toward him. She offered it as an observation without defense or apology.

"Yeah, a little." *I've wandered into a Humphrey Bogart movie.* "I'd better get back," Mickey said.

"Not yet." She moved toward him with her big woman's grace. "We're not through."

He waited, feeling helpless, hypnotized by her confidence. No one in his life had this kind of confidence, not even his mother. His mother was feisty and pushy, but she was always trying to prove something. Whatever made this woman tick worked on an entirely different clock from any he had seen, he thought, not knowing what to say.

She stopped before him and lifted her green cotton top up over her head, flinging it behind her onto the cement floor. She undid the tie to her formless pants and dropped them. She wore no underwear. Her body was tan and strong-looking. Her chest small-breasted, her stomach flat, her hips wide and feminine — a humping figure, his brother would say.

He had rooted, like one of Stan's precious orchid plants. He felt damp and weak with tension. She came up to him and lifted his baseball cap off his head, throwing it back where her clothes were.

He felt as naked as if she had stripped him bare. She covered his mouth, leaning down slightly to kiss him. Her lips were warm; her tongue slipped in between his teeth, breaking down each barrier as she passed it, poking through with its salty-sweet tip.

"Stay still," she whispered, withdrawing her mouth. She stood right up against him, looking into his eyes. He had never been so excruciatingly uncomfortable — or as excited. The excitement was perverse, because it was mixed with true fear, the blind man approaching the ledge, tapping his cane along the ground, hoping to feel the air before he stepped off.

She reached down with one of her remarkable hands and cupped his genitals. She did not try to undress him and she did not kiss him again. She simply kneaded his cock and his balls as if he were a freshly dampened lump of clay that she was forming into a new shape. She massaged him. He closed his eyes. It was too personal to share with a stranger.

"Open your eyes," she demanded, and he did. Her touch was perfect. It *was* the Magic Kingdom. She did not stop until he came, shooting off inside his party Versace's like a farm boy behind the barn. He had been insane from that moment on.

Mickey stopped running. He was dripping wet and he had absolutely no idea how far he had gone. He was panting. He wiped his face with his shirt and turned around. He had never felt this lonely. Nothing in his life had gone right from the day Ivy Clare did him in the greenhouse. She was the dark force he had been running from all his life; the shadow against the wall in his little boy's room.

He had never been as paranoid and fear-filled as his wife, but he had always felt that out there somewhere the shadow still waited. It must have been one of the things that had brought him and Annie together. They had built their castle and filled their moat, warding off the dangers.

Ivy Clare had crossed the moat with her left hand. It had been that easy. She had ruined his life, he now believed. But he also knew, limping down the dividing strip between the trendy cars coming and going on either side of him, that he was not ready to go back to their fortress, re-arm the ramparts, and forget about her.

He just couldn't. It would be a lie and his wife would know it. All he could say to Annie now was that he was sorry. That was the only thing he was absolutely sure was true.

Annie eased her Range Rover down the long gravel drive leading to her house, feeling like a recently released hostage returning home after years in captivity. It was impossible to believe that only two days had passed since her life had been abducted.

Everything looked different. She parked in front, checking ever so casually to see if Mickey's car was in the garage. Empty. Her stomach flopped. What was the fantasy? That he would be waiting outside, groveling in the gravel, a tormented slobbering wreck begging her for forgiveness? Absolutely.

She picked up her purse and walked to the kitchen door. She hoped Juanita was still at her sister's and she would have some time to herself. Her clothes were filthy and she was badly in need of a shampoo.

She opened the door. Portia saw her and slowly rose to her feet, too slowly for Annie's taste. She knelt down and her dog came to her, two mangy redheads crouching on a kitchen floor. "Hi, pal," she said, and buried her face in the stiff, graying fur.

Someone was knocking. She jumped, frightening Portia, who tried for a bark, which came out as a mournful honk instead.

Annie got up. Billy O'Brian was standing at the side door. The underside of good neighbors was that they were always there when you needed them, but also when you didn't.

Annie walked over and unlocked the door. "Hi, Billy," she said, trying not to sound like she felt.

Billy shuffled in, his hands in his pockets, as shy and hesitant as his wife was forthright.

"Sorry to barge in on Sunday morning."

Annie laughed. "Since when?"

"Molly barges in; I just follow quietly." Billy smiled, revealing the perfect gap between his front teeth.

"Oh, I get it. Good cop, bad cop. Want some coffee?"

"That'd be great."

Annie measured the coffee and filled the pot with water. Mickey always brought her coffee in bed on Sunday mornings. He had ever since they were newlyweds. He'd bring the coffee and sit beside her and they would talk about all the things they hadn't gotten around to during the week. No agenda or anything, just a good rambling married persons' kind of talk.

"We know what happened, Annie."

Annie's hand tightened on the pot. She poured the water through, not knowing what to say. What did they know? That she had smashed Ivy Clare's pots? that they were robbed? or that Mickey was having an affair? No way they could know that.

"What?" Annie pulled the switch and moved to the refrigerator.

"We know about Leonard Lewis. It's been on the news and in the papers, not to mention half the village. All the Hollywood weekenders seem to know someone who had money invested with him."

Annie turned around and rested against the counter.

"It's a nightmare, Billy. I don't know what we're going to do."

Billy cleared his throat. Annie realized that he was there for a reason. For all the time she spent with Molly, she was rarely alone with Billy. They had certainly spent enough rollicking dinners together and had the in-and-out-of-one-another's-house ease of buddies, but underneath all of the camaraderie, there was a void even between her and Molly. They talked and talked but what did they really reveal? She had never even seen Molly cry.

Mickey really was her one true friend. He was the only person she had ever let close enough to her. *Oh God. . . .*

"Listen, Annie, I don't want to butt in where I don't belong, but I'd really like to help. I'm a little rusty because I've been spending a lot more time on my golf game than my law practice, but when I put my heart in something, I'm a damn good lawyer. I worked for the D.A. in New Orleans and I clerked for the Attorney General. I've done a fair amount of white-collar-crime work, embezzlement and bank fraud. If I could donate my services to you guys, it would mean a lot to me."

Annie felt her lip trembling. "Billy, that is so sweet, but we couldn't ask you to do something like that for free. It isn't right, and at the moment I have no idea how we would pay you. I mean, Mickey's still working, but we're going to have to be very conservative now and I just don't think we can afford it."

Billy stood up and thrust his hands deeper into the pockets of his green corduroy pants. Annie always thought that Billy O'Brian looked like an L.L. Bean cover boy, his clothes a toney blend of outdoorsman and preppie hotshot.

"Annie, listen to me. This is hard to talk about. We've known one another quite a while now and we both, Molly and I, think of you and Mickey as our best friends, so I'm going to risk it. Let me do this. I *need* to do this.

"I'm drowning, Annie. I need to be helpful, useful to someone. Molly doesn't need me, and the legal world sure doesn't, but you guys do. You need a lawyer for this. Consider it a selfish act, then you won't feel funny about not paying me. It *is* a selfish act! I've got to get my self-respect back. I've thought about nothing else since I heard the news report. Please let me help."

Annie reached out and hugged him, patting his plaid-shirted back, as if he were one of the Pats. "Oh, Billy. Of course, of course. We'd be so grateful. I mean, I'm sure Mickey will be, too."

She released him and he stood beside her at the sink while she returned to the coffee preparation.

"I've already talked to Mickey. I called him as soon as I heard."

Annie poured coffee and carried the cups to the table. Billy followed behind with the milk and sugar. She tried to keep her voice steady. "Oh? When was this?"

Billy sat down and offered her the milk first, always the Southern gentleman. "Last night. I tried all day, but you guys didn't answer."

"Oh, right. Well, there was a lot going on."

"Mickey said that he and Jackie were going to see Stan Stein this morning to see what he knew."

Mickey knows. Annie felt dizzy, as if she had jumped up too fast; her equilibrium was thrown off by Billy's innocent information. Jackie must have told him. She felt sick to her stomach that something this personal, involving all their worldly goods, should be passed around by others and not shared by them together, not that she hadn't tried.

"The papers!"

Billy looked up. "What?"

"Oh, God, I left the papers at Mickey's apartment. They're the proof of everything. I wonder if he knows that!"

Billy looked at her oddly. She had revealed more in her outburst than she had intended.

"He took everything over to Jackie's office. Jackie's assistant is having photocopies done. It's all right."

Annie relaxed. Portia swayed over and rested her sour-smelling head on Annie's knee.

"Mickey's going to be filming until they break for Christmas, so it's really going to be you and me and Jackie."

Billy grinned, gratitude shining in his eyes. "No problem. Mickey said you've always handled the business decisions anyway."

Annie stroked Portia's face. "Yeah. Swell job I did, too. They should make me secretary of the budget at least."

"Hey, Annie, don't do that. This guy was a master. A lot of very sophisticated businessmen got taken for the same ride, so don't blame yourself."

"I should have kept everything in a box in the closet like Ida Mae told me to. It's all of this new-technology, twenty-first-century stuff. I really, truly, hate it. I can't even find ribbons for my typewriter anymore. Not cartridges, just plain old typewriter ribbons. I got too big for my Doctor Dentons, that's what I did. I should know myself better by this late date."

"I think we're going to find this guy and the money."

"Jackie's not so optimistic." They sipped their coffee. "Listen, Billy, now that you're offering your services as a selfish act, can I take advantage of the situation and ask you to help our friend Lina Allen? He's got her money too, and she's in worse shape than we are."

He grinned his irresistible gap-toothed grin. "I'd be delighted."

"You're a real pal. I'll call her machine and give her your number. I'm sure she has a better paper trail than we do; she's a fiend about finances."

"There, you see, and she got suckered too. It's not your fault."

Annie smiled. "Billy, I am the number-one world champion blame accepter of the entire universe. I've got a real talent for it."

Molly glided in surrounded by all the Pats dressed in Sunday finery. "Annie-pie, how could y'all just take off like that without so much as a good-bye note?"

Billy stood up. "Molly, you know why. Don't give Annie a bad time."

Molly's children moved with her as if attached by invisible cords. "Y'all look like you've slept in your clothes. What happened to you in that wretched town?"

"It's a long story," Annie said. She was glad to be back in her house, surrounded by her dear, crazy neighbors and her fading dog.

"Don't we look extraordinary compared to our usual Sunday attire? We are actually going to church for a change."

Billy moved his brood back toward the door. "Let's let Annie have some privacy. She's had a hard weekend."

Molly resisted; she was searching Annie's face for information. "Why don't y'all come over for dinner tonight. I'm frying chicken just the way you like it."

Annie sighed. If she was going to be alone, maybe she would. "Let me see how I feel after some serious napping." She paused. "Is the Delphic Article still there?"

Molly's eyes widened. "Haven't you heard? My Samantha is cohabiting with your little ol' brother-in-law. Lightning struck right in your dining room on Thanksgiving Day and she has been cavorting around his mansion just about ever since."

Annie slammed down her coffee cup. "I don't believe this! He never said a word."

The Pats swayed toward Billy, knowing they had lost their mother's attention. "Mama, we'll be late for church."

Molly giggled. "Since when is that something y'all care about. No, we won't; we're going. Annie-pie, I'll fill you in on the details tonight. Poor Samantha is quite smitten with him."

"Oh, spare me. Let's see how smitten with him she'd be if he wasn't a TV mogul and a millionaire, if he was Hank the handyman, for instance."

Molly gently steered her chicks forward. "Not fair, dear. Same could be said of any single one of our men. We are all the things we do, not just beans in a bag. . . . See y'all later."

They were gone. Annie and Billy stood side by side in the doorway, watching them go. Annie put her arm on his shoulder. "Billy, you're wrong about Molly. She does need you. She needs you very much."

"Annie? Annie, honey?" The voice came from far away. She was in the middle of a dance. She was doing the tango with her brother. Her mother whirled by in a bright red dress. "The tango is just a samba with danger," her mother said. Her brother twirled her out and in, dipping her all the way back to the floor. He leered down at her neck, fangs emerging from the sides of his mouth. "No!" she screamed, executing a flawless back flip into her mother's arms.

"Annie, wake up." The voice again; she was trying to reach it, but she was so sleepy. Her eyelids fluttered. Where was she? Loretta's? Someone was there on her bed. Her eyes opened.

Her husband was sitting beside her. His eyes were bloodshot, as if he were hungover or had been crying.

"What are you doing here? You have to be on the set at six tomorrow."

He covered her hand with his. "Annie, honey, something's happened."

"No shit."

Annie looked at him. He *had* been crying. Good.

He sighed. "No, I mean something else. Ida Mae got me when I came back from my run. She and Ella have been trying to reach you. I guess you haven't picked up your messages yet."

Annie pulled herself up. She felt disoriented. She didn't even remember falling asleep. She had come upstairs to wash her hair and that was about all she remembered. She must have lain down for a second and passed out.

"Ella? Is something wrong with Ella?"

"No. No, she's fine. It's your father."

"What happened?"

"He died, honey. Early this morning."

She looked at her husband, his shoulders heaving, tears flowing so freely, while she felt frozen, encased in a giant ice cube, pushing all emotion out of her freeze-dried heart.

"How? He was just here. He was fine."

Mickey wiped his eyes. "Heart."

Annie curled her legs under her, the ice woman seeking meltdown.

"Where? What happened?"

Mickey shook his head. His lips were quivering. His lips only quivered when he found something amusing.

"Mickey, your lips are quivering. Is this funny to you?"

Mickey shook his head. "It's not, really, but I just don't think I can say it."

The ice was beginning to thaw. "Mickey!"

"I'll write it down." He leaned over and grabbed a pen and notepad from the side of her bed. He scribbled something and handed the paper to her.

Her pulse was racing. She read it twice to herself before she could read it out loud.

"Cause of death, heart attack during sex with surrogate . . . sex therapist."

They looked at one another. His mouth was vibrating up and

down. Her ice creaked. She could feel the edge of hysterics way down between her neatly tucked and frozen toes. She held on.

"Apparently he'd been running around with some wealthy, much younger Southampton heiress, and in his rampaging narcissism, I guess he thought he'd, you know, fight gravity.

"The surrogate freaked, ran upstairs to Ma, and she went down and found him in really bad shape. She called the paramedics and they rushed him to Saint Vincent's, but it was too late."

"He was seventy-five years old! Was he completely insane? What would have made him do it?"

"Annie, your father was a vain man and a ladies' man, a really bad combination. He was always talking about face-lifts, eye tucks, penile implants, testosterone injections. He used makeup and eyebrow pencil and he's dyed his hair for thirty years. His whole life was sort of a theatrical illusion. It's not *that* out of character."

"Oh, my Lord. I cannot deal with this. This cannot be how I lose my father!" She felt the cold move up — stinging dry ice and fire inside her head.

Mickey reached for her hands. "Ida Mae was crazed. She said, 'Mick, the old fool did it this time. I'm upstairs taking care of my AIDS patient, a kid who's fighting for one extra month of life, and there's Joe Miller, throwing himself into the jaws of death so he can waltz around Southampton with a bunch of Jew-hating right-wingers! Serves him right!' Then she broke down and bawled like a baby. I've never heard her cry like that, and Ella couldn't even talk about it. She was horrified."

Annie sat up. She was melting now. She could feel the grief starting to move.

From the day her mother died, she had promised herself that she would never lose anyone that way again. She would be prepared. She would have made her peace and had her say. For years she had been trying to find a way to have a real talk with her father, an honest, looking-back talk, even a fight. Just when she was feeling strong enough to risk it they had moved to California, and from that time on her visits with him had served his need for polite distance much better than they had served her desire for honesty and closeness. They had never come near to her fantasy talk, and now he was gone.

Gone. Without warning or closure, and gone in this compromised, ridiculous way, without a shred of nobility or dignity. It was a clear message of how little she, Martin, or their children really meant to him. He had risked his life in pursuit of acceptance from a bunch of strangers, people who did not love or want him as he was, and that had been more important than anything else.

What kind of man would make that choice? Now she was left to wander around in an entire new maze of questions. Her mother and her father, gone forever. She, stumbling forward, trying to find her way, with no path in sight. She needed a guide, someone who had a map and compass. Someone who knew what the markings on the rocks meant and where the painted arrows were on the trees. Someone who had a vague idea of what was happening to her life. So far, the only one she could see was herself.

"I've booked you on the four-thirty flight from LAX. We've got to hurry, honey."

Annie nodded. Do the next thing, her aunt Bessie's voice kept reminding her lately. Well, what happens when the next thing keeps changing? She stood up, chipping away a shard of her numbness. "I'll be with you in ten minutes. Just throw my black suit and shoes and things in a suitcase, and a couple of sweaters."

He watched her. "I've already done it."

She sighed. He was the only husband she knew who would ever dare pack for his wife.

"Thanks," she said, as politely as if they had just met.

CHAPTER X

"I REALLY BELIEVE, darling, that everyone has five lives. In the first one you're dead at age six; or worse, you're very poor. Your wealth grows in each successive life until the last one, when you are the richest and most famous."

Annie threaded her way through the crowd at Ida Mae's, trying to find Ella and Toby. Except for her family, she hardly knew anyone at the after-funeral gathering. No one but the family had been at the burial, so coming back to a house full of strangers was disconcerting and invasive. Who were these people? There was something terribly sad about her father having an entirely formed and intact life without her, a life that she had no part of and, in fact, knew almost nothing about. It made her feel diminished, less than she was. She was invisible to these people. "I'm his daughter," she wanted to say to no one in particular.

The truth was, she had been shocked by how many friends her father still had. There were his old show-biz cronies from Tin Pan Alley and the Stage Deli as well as his society widows and their debutante daughters and the slightly threadbare fringes from the old guard cultural elite. This mixed with Ida Mae's lunatic fringe made for a unique mourning contingent.

She saw Ella and Toby moving down the hall toward Ida Mae's room. Mickey had already left for the airport; they had shot around him so that he could be there for the funeral. He was front and center for this episode, which, ironically enough, would turn out to be the last.

She was almost relieved that he was going, since neither of them was really ready for The Talk anyway. At least they had enough respect for one another not to just rush in and spout a lot of facile dialogue and end up lying and compromising their marriage even more. On the ride down to the airport they had talked about Leonard Lewis and their financial predicament, which had gotten much more serious with Mickey's news about the cancellation. Neither of them had mentioned Ivy Clare.

Ida Mae's ninety-year-old cousin, Max, grabbed her sleeve. "Annala, Annala. Let this be a lesson to you. Stay away from the doctors and you'll live as long as me. I never been sick in my life and I still go to work every single day. Your father went to doctors and just look what happened!"

"You're right, Max." Annie kept moving; one learned early in the relative game how to maneuver through without being corralled. If Cousin Max started on the medical profession, it was an all-day commitment.

She had no small talk in her. The whole idea of a party after a burial had always seemed grotesque to her. When her mother died, she had simply gone to her room and curled up on her bed until everyone had gone home. But now she was a grown-up and supposed to be able to handle such things.

They had lowered his casket into the ground right beside her mother and she had thought, I wonder if she wants him there. I wonder if she's forgiven him. His casket had been closed, and she kept trying to imagine what he looked like inside, all dressed up with his Turnbull and Asser ascot and matching handkerchief, a red rose in his lapel, his best navy gabardine suit, his goatee combed into place. She had almost asked them to take a photo, but that was not really an image she needed inside a head already too crowded with new information about people she loved.

Two young Upper East Side types, daughters of his widows for sure, were tossing their long frosted manes around and drinking straight scotch.

"Well, this is my very first funeral party. It really made me think about what I'm most afraid of. I mean, death is so remote, but not being able to buy couture and my health, I guess, are real fears."

What were these people doing there? Could they really have had relationships with her father? She was trapped on the Uptown side of the room, trying to make it to the other side, where she felt more grounded.

"She's just an eighteen-year-old girl, but she's like a middle-aged woman. I mean, her only claim to fame is that she had an affair with Prince Charles. Her family doesn't even have any money, not a dime more than fifteen million, and now she's going to NYU! I remember when no one worked; now they're all on Wall Street or working at Sotheby's. It really ruins them. They lose their cool so very fast."

Annie crossed the line, to the side of the apartment without little black dresses and velvet headbands. It felt as if she had planet-hopped from Mars to Jupiter.

"I'll tell ya what's gonna happen if Clinton blows it and the Conservatives return in '96. We're gonna have David Duke's America. They're gonna slice it up into fifths. Put all the Jews in one fifth — a region made up of comedians, movie producers, and lawyers; then one-fifth for the blacks — lots of singers, tap dancers, and basketballers; one-fifth the Irish — bar owners and cops; and then your Orientals — an entire region filled with grocers and nail-boutique owners."

"You forgot the Italians — singers and pizza-makers, right?"

"Right. Then each group will have to negotiate with the others in trade agreements, so the Orientals can have some sporting events and the Jews can get their nails done."

"I'm going to write an article about instruction manuals. You know how they explain things to you, like you were too dumb to breathe? I read this booklet that came with my toaster. It says, 'This is what to look for in a toaster: a range from light to dark; a lever to raise and lower the bread; should toast evenly on both sides.' Some schmuck gets paid to write this for the one idiot who buys a toaster and does not know this instinctively?"

"My favorites are the owner's manuals that come with new cars. I just bought a car, and I'm reading the booklet and it says, 'Number one — do not drive with the seat in a reclining position. Number two — liquids used in motor vehicle engines are poisonous and should not be consumed under any circumstances. Number three — each day check to see that there is enough fuel in the tank for the journey to be undertaken. Number four — when lowering the hood, look to see that fingers are clear of the linkage.'"

"See? Am I not onto something? Now, of course, there probably is one putz who's going to get in the car, lie down, chug a couple of shots of motor oil, slam the door on his fingers, and take off with an empty tank to buy himself a toaster! But for the rest of us, they never explain anything so anyone can understand it! It took me three months to figure out where my hood latch was."

"So who thinks this garbage up? Somewhere there are rooms full of madmen inventing products to ruin our lives, waste our time, and squander our money. All of a sudden I can't live without an umbrella that lights up on rainy nights or a fake rock to hide my spare key in. I'm going to write the article."

Annie pushed through to the hall. She liked this side of the room considerably better. She picked up a glass of seltzer and a macaroon and started down Ida Mae's hallway.

She stopped at the door to Mickey and Jackie's old room. The door was closed and she opened it quietly, not sure whether it was empty or if one of Ida Mae's strays was in residence. She opened the door.

Ida Mae, Toby, and Ella were sitting on Mickey's old bed. Jackie, Loretta, and Martin were sitting on Jackie's old bed. Annie felt like crying again. She had grown up in this room. Ida Mae's house was always much more fun than her own. She had turned from a child to a young woman bouncing up and down on their Dick Tracy bedspreads. The bedspreads, faded, remained.

"The A-list at last." Annie slipped out of her shoes and sat down in the old red, painted rocker she had claimed as her chair when she was six years old.

No one said anything. She had the uneasy feeling that she had interrupted something. A conversation about her and Mickey maybe?

Or was it just her prickly paranoia that always reared its barbed head when she was stressed out.

Who knew what? She was not very good at either lying or keeping secrets, and she was having trouble remembering what anyone had been told. Loretta and Jackie knew about Mickey's affair. Only Loretta knew about her and Oliver Taylor. Martin, Jackie, and Loretta were aware of Leonard Lewis and the money and the series being canceled. She hoped no one had told the kids or Ida Mae anything. Was that complicated enough or had she left something out?

Ella was staring at her. Annie winked at her daughter and stuck out her tongue and crossed her eyes.

Ella laughed. "Mom! You are too funny."

"Didn't I hammer it into your pointy little head that it's not polite to stare, especially at your mother."

"I wasn't staring, I was just thinking about something."

"Call the *Times,* we have a major breakthrough here." Toby grinned.

Jackie laughed. "Toby, I'm going to star you in a sitcom. No, better yet, I'll put you to work as a writer."

Loretta poked Jackie. "Say no, Toby, or you'll spend your gravy years trying to find maniacs and perverts so increasingly repulsive and shocking that not even the *Star* has uncovered them."

"Actually, I'd just have him keep looking for Elvis and Marilyn Monroe."

Ida Mae squeezed Toby's arm. "Find Jimmy Dean for me while you're at it, my darling boy."

Annie watched Ella. "Ella, you're still doing it. What's the fierce look for? Did I interrupt something private?"

She looked at Jackie and Loretta, trying to make her point.

Jackie shook his head. He looked tired, Annie thought.

"No, we were just trying to make sense of all this and get away from the groupies."

Ella pulled her legs up, crossing them under her the way Annie did. "I was just saying that I feel angry at Grandpa. I just can't help it. I feel like he was just a stranger and he never let us be close to him. He just shut us out, spending his time with all of those awful people. Some of those girls are my age. It's disgusting. I just don't know what to feel."

Toby put his arm around his sister. "I always thought that Grandpa really thought of us more as pets. You know, he liked us to run around and play and stuff when we were little, and he could sit at his desk and read and talk to his cronies on the phone, but he never was interested in really relating to us. So when we grew up and we needed something more, he just sort of let us go. I guess I never expected anything else, but Ella did."

Ella put her head on her brother's shoulder and cried.

Annie felt left out and hurt that they had all come together without her. She remembered her Elmer's. Don't say a word, kiddo.

Ida Mae pushed herself off the bed. She seemed thinner and older to Annie than she had just a week ago.

"I'd better get back before my gonifs stuff all the chopped liver into their pockets." She walked her Bette Davis walk toward the door, stopping before she opened it and turning to them. "Listen, kids, I know you think I'm just a crazy old pinko and a do-gooder, but let me tell you something. We've all been brainwashed about death and what we're supposed to feel and all that crap for centuries. Now with all these young people dropping faster than flies in India, I'm seeing it different.

"Joe Miller was my friend, forty years. But he was what he was. He cheated on his wife and he was a vain, selfish man.

"He wanted to be rich and famous and he wanted to be a matinee idol like Ronald Colman. Well, he never made it, so I guess as he saw the Grim Reaper coming closer, he wanted one last shot at lost youth. Was it a nice choice as far as character or values go? Nope. But he didn't do it to hurt nobody. He was proud of all of you and he loved you kids.

"It's just that there's love and there's love, and most of the time we don't get the kind we need from no one and we don't give it so good, either. People fail this family love test every day. So don't be too hard on him. Like the rest of us, he did the best he could — not the best possible, but his best."

They watched her go. They were all crying now. She had broken their futures down into the clearest, simplest terms. She had summed up Joe Miller's life and his passage out of it and taken the blame and anger from their shoulders.

He did the best he could. Annie put her head back against the small chair and closed her eyes, rocking back and forth.

What Ida Mae said was true, but what she could not figure out was how to decide what *was* the best you could do. Was that too harsh? Was the rule of thumb the best you could do under extraordinary circumstances? She would have to think about this. She wanted to be able to clarify it for her children — this was their first life loss.

She opened her eyes. Martin had left the room without a word. Loretta had her arm around Jackie, who was resting his head on her shoulder. Was Ida Mae really speaking to him? Annie thought that in some way Ida Mae had been making an apology to her youngest son, sensing that some of the anger directed at Joe would follow her into her grave, too.

Annie stood up. She needed to talk to her brother alone. It was a brand-new need. "I'll be back," she said, leaving the people she felt safest with behind.

Ella slipped her shoes on and nudged Toby. "Come on, we should go help Ida Mae." Toby got up reluctantly, knowing Ella had something else on her mind; years of experience in the job of younger brother made him quick to decipher his sister's hidden messages.

"Okay. I've got to get a six o'clock train back to Leavenworth."

Loretta laughed. "Do I detect some freshman discontent?"

Toby shrugged. "Yeah, just a sensitive-youth-coming-of-age story, no major trauma, one episode on a *Family Ties* rerun at best." He smiled at them. They were his favorite relatives. He was afraid they would ask more questions.

Jackie stood up and opened his arms to them. They were both taller and bigger, making the hug somewhat difficult. Jackie laughed.

"Jesus, don't think it isn't hard on the ego to have both your nephew *and* your niece stooping down to hug you. Stop this growing up bit, will you, please?"

Ella kissed the top of his head. "We'll come back before Toby leaves."

Jackie sat down in Annie's rocker and Loretta lay back down on his bed. She realized that she had never been alone in a room with him before.

"So?" Jackie looked at her, searching for signals.

"So, what?"

"Want to talk about what's going on?"

Loretta crossed her arms behind her head. She was aware of his eyes on her.

"Are you staring at my legs?"

"No."

"Yes, you are. You're making me nervous."

"I was not. I was staring at your feet. You have beautiful feet. I've never seen you without your shoes on before. I love feet. I'm a connoisseur."

Loretta crossed her ankles. "Gee, I'm impressed. I would have thought anything under a size ten would be of no interest to you what with all of those Bigfoot types you're so fond of."

"Touché."

They were quiet, trying to decide where to go next.

Jackie stopped rocking. "You know about Annie and Mickey, don't you?"

Loretta sat up, tucking her feet away from his eyes. "Yes, but I don't think anyone but us does. I know Ida Mae doesn't and the kids don't."

"Annie had planned to tell the kids about the money situation on their Christmas trip. Hopefully, the rest will be settled by then."

Loretta scratched her head. "You really think it's going to be that easy? A lot of damage has been done. Walking in on someone like that, Jackie, that really costs."

"Yeah, that was a bummer. But you're talking about Annie and

Mickey! I mean if they can't pull themselves back together, we're all doomed."

"I didn't say they couldn't, but Christmas is two weeks away! No chance. I don't know how they're going to pull off the family vacation. Those kids are human sonar screens. They will know something's wrong. In fact, they already do. Ella asked me if something was wrong, and don't forget she's the one who found those damn panties. It was her antenna that went up in the first place."

"Mickey saw my shrink. I'm hoping he'll go back and get a referral. This broad has really messed with his mind."

Loretta stretched her legs back out, wiggling her toes defiantly. "Look who's talking. You're boffing that Wonderwoman charlatan who's probably going to slip you some ancient Greek potion and take over your life. You're hardly one to be dispensing advice on obsessive love."

Jackie flushed. He was hurt and angry, though he didn't quite understand why. "Hey, Loretta, first, it is none of your fucking business who I'm boffing and second, it may just be that because I've taken that trip myself, I know more about how to help him than one of you hitchhikers."

Now *she* was hurt. Why had she said such an inappropriate thing to him?

"I'm sorry, Jackie. You're right. It's none of my business. I just, well, I called you a couple of times for Annie, and Samantha answered and her attitude was like it was already her house, and I got worried about you. I can't entirely take my therapist's hat off. It is one thing to go through some dark relationship stuff and learn and go on, but it is something else to keep repeating the pattern. I'm sure Rhinehart tells you that all the time."

Jackie frowned. "He and everyone else. She didn't tell me you called."

"I rest my case."

They were quiet again. Loretta had not had a conversation alone with a man who wasn't her patient or her husband in a very long time. She really liked talking to Jackie. She always had. He was so clear, you could see right through him like a newly washed window. She wondered what it would be like to kiss him. What the hell was the matter with her?

"So, what can we do?" She looked up at him. He was staring at her again and she wondered if he could read her mind.

"Not much as far as their marriage goes. I'm going to do my best to help find their money. Annie and I were supposed to go see this private detective that Stan Stein hired, but she's got to stay here for a while and take care of Joe's estate. Can you believe this happening on top of everything else?"

Loretta reached down for her shoes. "That's how it goes, Jackie, my dear one. Nothing much changes, we coast along in our various semizombie coping modes, and then, splat, the air conditioner drops from the thirty-fifth floor right on our little noggins. Everyone gets their turn. They're getting a superdeluxe unit all the way down from the penthouse. The trouble is, I've got one of my own going on."

"What do you mean?"

"I guess no one told you. Martin and I have split. I've already filed for divorce. So, unfortunately, this isn't coming at such a great time for me to be offering them much help."

Jackie shot up out of the rocker. He had no idea why this news was so unnerving.

"Christ, Loretta! I had no idea. I'm stunned."

Loretta's feet had swollen; it was hard to get into her pumps. "Why? I can't imagine you ever saw me and Martin as the couple of the year."

"Compared to my choices, everyone looked like the Nelsons. I guess I never thought about it. You were just married. How's Bennie doing?"

Loretta pushed her feet down into her pumps. "Actually, he's okay. Nothing's worse than living with all of that tension and fake politeness. Martin doesn't fight, you know. How many evenings of 'Would you ask your mother to pass the Parmesan' can any kid take? He's dancing every day. He's okay. He's having a recital next Friday."

Jackie stopped pacing and looked down at her feet.

"Your shoes are too tight."

Loretta blushed. "Now don't make some swollen-ankle comment and hurt my feelings. Too many hours sitting on planes does it every time."

"Can I go?"

She stood up and hobbled toward the door, needing to break the intimacy.

"Go where?"

"Bennie's recital."

She turned and looked at him.

"Sure," she said softly. "He'd really like that."

Dr. Martin Miller crossed Bleecker Street and headed toward Washington Square Park, thrusting his hands deep into the pockets of his high-school overcoat, rescued from his father's closet. It was colder than he had thought, or maybe California had weakened his tolerance. He realized that he didn't even own an overcoat any more. Funny how all the things you can't wait to get away from, like bundling up and being cold, are the things you miss. His eyes teared, the wind bruising his cheeks.

Nothing much had changed, except for the homeless on the streets now.

A haggard young man with several crusted red sores on his face was sitting in the doorway to a tenement building with a cardboard sign propped up on his lap: HAVE AIDS, NEED $15 MORE TO GO HOME TO FLORIDA. PLEASE HELP ME. Martin pulled a ten-dollar bill out of his pocket and dropped it into the man's Styrofoam cup. The man looked at it, but did not say thank you or acknowledge Martin in any way.

Rage flashed through him, cutting into his skin like the wind. He wanted to grab the man by the throat and shake him. How dare he not say thank you! How dare he ignore him as if he were nothing, as if he were invisible.

A heavy-breasted black woman grabbed his sleeve. "Don't give that phony nuttin'. He's been sittin' there all year. He ain't got AIDS, he paints those things on and by now he coulda been on the French Riviera, all the suckers like you throwin' bills at him. Go get your money back."

Martin shook his head and kept walking. Maybe that's what he should do, but causing a scene, unleashing his emotion, was just not the way he handled life.

Maybe Loretta was right, maybe that *was* the problem. He crossed the street in front of the NYU law school and headed into the park. He had no idea where he was going. He had simply felt overwhelmed and stifled in that apartment.

His loneliness throbbed inside him, pulsing against his heart like a drumbeat. His very worst fear had been realized. Everyone he cared about was gone.

He stopped at the Arch, where he had played almost every day as a child, and looked up. Had he really ever been anything but lonely? Maybe in the beginning with Loretta, but now he couldn't even be sure of that, only that when he made love to her he felt connected. But when it was over, it was even worse than before.

He turned and walked to a bench, the only one free of derelicts. Two policemen were huddled by the entrance drinking coffee, the steam rising from the paper cups. He envied them. They had a community, a group to identify with. How had he ended up doing face peels for frightened housewives?

A husky young man in a jogging suit and ski parka was throwing a ball to his little boy. The child was encased in a snow suit, giving him the appearance of a stuffed animal or a doll and making it extremely difficult for him to catch. The father, aware of his son's predicament but most likely under strict orders from his wife not to take the ridiculous thing off, was patiently guiding his child toward the ball.

Martin felt the loneliness twist up inside him, an aching, palpable sensation. Had his father ever taken him here to throw a ball around? No, not even close. Had his father ever taken him anywhere? They went to the theater constantly, but never alone. The theater was perfect because his father could show off for his friends — "There's Joe Miller and his wonderful family" — without having to talk to them or relate to his mother. The theater didn't really count.

The rage rushed at him again. His father had never cared about him. Martin didn't fit his idea of a sophisticated man; he didn't look right and he didn't have any patter.

The truth was that they could barely stand one another's company and had never had a serious talk or even a fight in Martin's entire life. He had no idea how to grieve for his father as a real person; the hurt felt more like the loss of hope, the hope of one day finding the link, making the connection.

The little boy ran for the ball and tripped, rolling over and over in his padded room of a suit. "That was a close one," he said, using a grown-up's lingo and brushing himself off. His father laughed, his face red with cold and love.

I have never been looked at like that, Martin thought, fearing he might cry.

Who was he to feel sorry for himself? He was doing the same damn thing to his own child, repeating the pattern of distance and disapproval that his father had shown him. Had *he* ever taken Bennie to the park and just stood around tossing a ball? No.

Loretta *was* right about him. He knew she was, but he had not known how to listen to her, let alone change. All his life he had felt as if he were disconnected from other people. He lingered on the outside of the playground, separated from the others by some invisible shield that he could not see and could not penetrate. He just didn't fit.

The only place he felt engaged was in his office. When he examined a patient, the exchange was one that he could understand. He knew what was expected of him and how to respond to their needs. It did not bring him joy, but it brought him peace of mind. It was only when he left his office that the loneliness and confusion surrounded him. It had cost him the only woman he had ever loved, and it had cost him his son, long before he had physically left.

The young father lifted his child up and kissed his flaming

cheeks. *I want someone to do that to me.* The absurdity of someone lifting a gangly, middle-aged six-foot-two-inch man up into the air for cheek kisses shocked him. Was he losing his mind?

Moving out of his house had not been difficult. He had simply packed a suitcase, taken his Beethoven tapes, his microscope, and his slide projector, and left. Being so alienated from everyone, it had seemed no more real to him than what he had been doing for years, wandering through his home life, an alien mimicking the customs and rituals of the strange creatures around him. He had become, by that night, totally disengaged from himself.

It was only when he arrived at his new home that the true nature of the loss had hit him.

His apartment was in a maze-like compound of trees and pools, barbecue areas, and racquetball courts, a vapid and depressing attempt to convince the newly abandoned that the single life was one long hot-tub soak.

Such complexes had come into fashion in the seventies, before the sexual plagues ended the fantasy, and now they seemed duplicitous, a sick joke played on the guileless. Lonely people like himself wandered around the paths between the buildings, carrying beer cans and cocktail glasses, looking for a party that had been over for ten years.

When he closed the door to his unit, disappearing into his exile, the space contrived to reach the lowest common denominator of human taste, not pleasing or offending any of the inmates, he knew he was lost.

They were the rooms of a person who had nothing to show for his life. Green shag carpeting and simulated wood cabinets. Mud-beige tile, off-white walls, a green-and-brown plaid sofa and chair, and a glass-topped coffee table with black Spanish-style iron legs. A mustard Formica dinette table with brown vinyl chairs; a print of Van Gogh's *Sunflowers* on the wall of the living room and a print of Monet's *Water Lilies* on the wall above the cheap double bed with the fake brass headboard in the bedroom.

Martin walked around, realizing that he was surrounded by

strangers, each living in a place identical to his, probably denying the despair of this enforced sameness by filling the blankness with potted plants and macramé pillows, bringing in stereo sets and color TVs, hanging pictures of relatives and pets on the walls. This, it seemed to Martin, would only make it worse. It would make it real, or permanent. He had gone into the small, cold bathroom and thrown up.

The happy father carried his son out of the park. Martin stood up. It was getting too cold to sit and the cops had gone. It was starting to get dark. He turned and headed back toward the entrance.

What was he going to do? He had to do something about himself. Maybe it was too late for his marriage and maybe he and Loretta were not right for one another, but he didn't want to lose his son. He did not want Bentley to bury him one day, hating him, filled with bitterness and anger, the way he had buried his father.

He had wanted Loretta because she was so unlike himself. He had hoped that she would bring him out of his cage, open him up and lead him across the impenetrable field, onto the playground with the others. But that is not what happened. Her connectedness only made him feel lonelier, more aberrant and unsure.

At least his father had brought some fun and life into their house. The trips to the theater and dinners at Sardi's were far more enjoyable than his insistence on perfect table manners and no entertainment without educational benefits. What was the matter with him, not letting his son dance? What had he proved? He had encased himself in plaster like some wretched car crash victim, and no gesture or movement held any chance of joy or spontaneity.

The wind picked up, blowing his outgrown coat away from his body. He shivered, tears of cold and anguish running down his cheeks. He needed someone to talk to. He had no friends, not even his own sister.

He had always been better alone than with people, more comfortable and relaxed. People meant danger, unkind remarks, all the teasing from his childhood. Nerd, cretin, Frankenstein's monster they called him in grade school; "geek" they called him in high school.

Annie was always fixing him up and trying to make it better, but it had never gotten any better, not until medical school.

Doctors were allowed to be solemn and quiet; it was even preferred. But he still never really felt safe until he was home alone in his room with his slides and his books. Now it was no longer working. Now, when he came home to his singles' cell and closed the door, he felt as if he would simply cease to exist. As if the distance between himself and the others had grown too vast to bear.

He turned down Sullivan Street and headed for Bleecker. Something felt wrong. He stopped and turned around. Two menacing figures, their faces hidden under ski masks, were moving up on either side of him. His stomach turned over and he could feel the fear. He started toward the doorway closest to him, reaching for the knob. Locked. They were on him. Something poked against his side through his coat.

"Give us the money, man, or we'll stick your motherfuckin' liver." It was the high-low voice of a teenager.

Martin was so frightened he felt as if he were strangling. "My pocket, in my pocket, I'll get it."

One of the boys grabbed his arms and pushed him against the wall. "Don't move, honky. We get it."

The other boy pulled up his coat and thrust his hand inside his pants, pulling out his wallet.

"Got it," he said, and the boy holding Martin knocked him across the head with something sharp, shoving him down, a big man cowering in terror and humiliation.

He covered his face with his hands, his fingers coated with blood. "Please, don't kill me!" He heard laughter. A foot slammed into his side, fists pummeled his back.

"Martin! My God! Martin!" A voice he knew. The boys stopped beating him and ran. "Your lucky day, motherfucker," they said, leaving him limp and quivering on the cold, filthy cement.

He could not stop crying. He felt as if his entire being had been cracked open, as if he had been shelled and laid out, a walnut on the autopsy table, no longer human or entitled to any kindness or dignity.

He tried to sit up.

"Someone call the police! Get an ambulance!"

He sobbed into his bloody hands. He did not want the police. He did not want an ambulance. Who was calling his name? He moved his fingers. A woman was running toward him, her red hair flying around her face.

His sister was here. His big sister was here, just as if they were still small. He pulled his knees up to his heaving chest. His sister had come. He was not all alone.

She had saved his life. He was still alive. He wanted to be alive, he realized, and the shuddering hysteria slowed.

Annie knelt beside him and cradled his head in her arms. "Oh, my God, Martin. Don't cry. I'm here. It's okay. You're going to be okay. I'm here."

"Annie, take me home, get me out of here." He pulled himself up, holding on to her shoulder.

"Martin, you need a doctor. We have to file a report."

"I *am* a doctor. I'm okay. I only had fifty bucks and a couple of credit cards. They'll never catch them, and I couldn't identify them. Please, just get me out of here."

Annie looked around. People were peeking out at them from apartment windows and shops but no one had come to help them. She found this unimaginable. She steadied him. Blood poured from a gash on his forehead.

"I'll stand up first, but I have to let you go for a minute."

He nodded and released her. "Do you have a Kleenex?"

She reached into her coat and pulled out a package, handing him the whole thing. "I think I have a Band-Aid in my purse."

He laughed, shock filling him with adrenaline. She held out her hands and he grabbed at them and pulled himself up.

"That's my sister, prepared for any possible emergency."

She put her arm around his waist. "I've got a pocket siren, too, but the cowards didn't give me a chance to use it."

He held the Kleenex over his eye. His side hurt, but his ribs felt all right, bruised but not cracked. People moved past them, their eyes darting sideways.

"They probably think I'm drunk," Martin said, trying to stand up straight.

"Naw, they probably think we're married and I just punched you out."

They were almost back. "Take me to Pop's; I don't want to go back upstairs."

"Okay." Annie pulled out her keys and opened the door. Looking at him was hard, her Dracula, now soaked in real blood. Her brother, who had always been so collected, sobbing like a broken child in the middle of the sidewalk. She helped him inside and they paused together in the hallway of their growing-up place, a house that now seemed far more full of death than life.

Martin let go of her and walked to his father's bedroom. Annie followed behind turning on lights. They half expected Joe Miller to saunter out, offering one of his overly urbane welcomes.

Martin turned on the bathroom light and looked at his face, his sister's reflected in the mirror behind him. He laughed.

"You look worse than I do." He ran the water, reaching for a clean towel. He had no idea what they had hit him with, but the cut was too shallow for a knife. He was lucky.

Annie watched him tending himself. "I thought they had killed you." She turned her face to the wall, her body shaking. "I thought they had stabbed you and you would die too and we'd never get to be close again and I'd never get to say how sorry I am."

He turned toward her, holding a piece of cotton soaked with peroxide to his head. "Annie, what do you have to be sorry about?" She was crying about him. He found this hard to believe.

"I've been so caught up in my own life, I just let you go. I stopped trying to understand why you were the way you were and I just judged you. I never saw your pain. I forgot about my little brother. I forgot how decent you were and how lonely you were. I let you down, Martin."

She took his arm and led him out of the bathroom and back into their father's bedroom. The bed was freshly made, as if he had just stepped out for a bite to eat.

"Lie down and I'll get you some aspirin." She wiped her tears, helping him off with his coat and shoes, loosening his tie, settling him down on her father's bed.

He had never been this tired. He could still taste the fear, pure, sour terror, on his tongue.

His entire adult construct revolved around being calm and in control, but he had collapsed under the aggression of his tormentors like some wobbly, will-less hysteric. It was his sister's courage that saved his life. She had just shot forward without thinking of her own safety. She had chased them off.

Annie held the aspirin and a large glass of water. He reached up. His hand was shaking.

"You're in shock," she said, tipping the glass for him.

He swallowed and lay back on the pillows. The room smelled of his father, lime aftershave and shoe polish and stale pipe tobacco. His head hurt, and he tried to focus his eyes in the twilight. There were photos in little frames on his dresser and night tables of his father with various women and prominent people, but none of him or his sister or their children.

Annie sat down beside him.

"Aren't there any pictures of us in here?" he asked, his voice sounding small and weak.

She blew her nose, shaking her head at the same time.

"No. I looked when I came down earlier to put our things away. Some baby pictures of the kids and a few old ones of us and mother in my old room. We were relegated."

"Annie, you don't have anything to be sorry for. I pushed you away; I pushed everyone away. I guess there was so much hurt and anger inside me that it was the only way I could keep functioning. Well, now I've blown it big-time, so I can afford the luxury of falling apart. I was too jealous of you to be any kind of a brother to you."

"Me? *You* were jealous of me?"

"Always. You weren't afraid. You just went out into the world every day and took your place in the lineup."

"*I* wasn't afraid! Are you kidding! I am the most fear-ridden person I know. I'm afraid of everything."

"No, you aren't, because you overcome it constantly. Really being afraid is being paralyzed by it. People who are really afraid don't keep walking into it every day; they dig trenches and hide from themselves. You proved my point tonight. You just ran forward and saved my life."

Annie blushed. "My God. I never even thought about it. I mean they could have had a gun or rushed me, too! I can't believe I didn't think about it!"

"Annie, you tried your best to be close to me. I got more of Mom's love and attention than you did, and I used that. I was jealous and I exploited your loss. I'm the one who's sorry."

Annie took his hand, stroking the long white fingers. The last time she had held his hand, hers was the same size.

"Look, Martin, I don't want to interfere with my new hero status, but I've been pretty much in my little cocoon as well. I pushed all of that information about Mother and about Pop right out of my head. It really wasn't until this Thanksgiving that I reconnected with the truth. I stayed away from you because you knew the truth. It was both of us. I'm a first-class blame accepter, as you well know, but I really do have some to accept here. My life has gotten pretty messed up too. I would say we are back in the nursery and the playing field is level. We can stop running away from one another now."

Martin could barely keep his eyes open, but he did not want to back away from this conversation by falling asleep. He had not had a conversation like this in his entire life.

"You mean the money?"

She watched his face. She knew if she did not tell him the whole truth, he would find out and the crater between them would reopen.

"The money, and Mickey's series has been canceled, and he's having an affair. A major affair."

He could not find the words again, not out of fear like in the doorway, but because he was so moved that she would confide such a vulnerable truth to him.

"Don't say anything. You have to get some rest. I don't want to talk about it; I can't, really. I just found out and then all this happened. I just wanted you to know."

She leaned over and kissed his forehead. "I'd better go back upstairs and explain what happened to us. I'll be down to check on you, and I'm staying in my old room, so I'm right here if you need me. You just sleep, Martin."

His eyes fluttered, exhaustion pulling him down. "It'll be all right, Annie. He loves you."

Annie stood up. "I'll call about your credit cards. Don't worry. You've been born again, bro."

He let go, the words echoing in his throbbing head. That was the way it felt.

"Where were you?" Ella stood in the doorway to her grandmother's apartment, her hands on her hips.

Annie hugged her. "That's supposed to be my line."

Ella followed her mother inside. "Mom, no kidding, we were really getting worried. Where's Uncle Martin?"

"Downstairs, asleep. I'll tell you all about it. I need a glass of wine, if Ida Mae has such a thing."

Toby came out of the kitchen holding an enormous slice of pepperoni pizza. "There's wine; Loretta brought some. We sent out for pizza; the vultures ate every single crumb of food. I never realized how those Park Avenue types could chow down. They were shoving all the old guys like Cousin Max out of the way trying to get to the chopped liver. 'Oh, pâté,' they said."

"Where are they?" Annie opened the refrigerator and took out the wine. God bless Loretta.

"Jackie took Loretta and Ida Mae out for dinner. We decided to wait for the police to call."

Annie carried her glass and the bottle into the disheveled and deserted living room. "You were almost right."

Toby and Ella followed her in.

"Want some wine?" Annie flung herself into Ida Mae's reading chair.

"Toby, get some glasses." Ella sat down on the worn suede couch. Annie looked around the apartment, relaxing for the first time. "Your grandmother has created her own unique interior design, the 'used bookstore motif.'"

The entire room was lined with wooden bookshelves, which covered windows and closet doors. The furniture was arranged as if visitors were there to browse and read, rather than converse. Chairs and tables were placed for easy access to the bookshelves, some chairs were even back to back. The dining-room table, which had been cleared, was usually filled with books and catalogues and piles of old magazines.

Toby loped in. "Anything else, memsahib?"

Annie put down her glass. "I thought you had a six o'clock train to catch."

He slumped down next to his sister. "I changed it. I'm getting the six-thirty tomorrow morning. I don't have class tomorrow until two. I didn't feel right leaving so soon."

"Ah, Tob, you old softie." Annie passed the wine to them. Toby looked down, hiding his crooked smile.

Ella poured. "He didn't go because you took off and we were worried about you."

"Ella, you're doing it again. You're stealing all of my Jewish-mother lines."

"Tell us what happened."

"I went out to find Uncle Martin and I walked around for a while, and then I was heading back up toward Washington Square, because I remembered he used to always play there, and I was coming up Sullivan and I saw these two thugs beating someone in this doorway and I realized that it was Martin. I started yelling, I guess — I don't really remember — and they ran away."

It is not easy to shock or silence any urban person under the age of twenty-five, but Toby and Ella sat open-mouthed.

"Uncle Martin was mugged?"

She nodded. "They took his wallet. Which reminds me I've got to call and report his credit cards missing. They hit him on the head with something. There was blood all over, and they were punching him and kicking him. I thought he was being killed. They had ski masks over their faces. It was terrible."

"Is he okay?" Toby sat up straight.

"He's in shock. He wouldn't let me call an ambulance or the police, and frankly, I don't blame him. People were watching and no one came out to help; no one even called nine-one-one. Can you believe that?"

Ella looked at Toby. "Yes," she said.

Annie sat back in her chair. "I've always felt so safe here. I know that sounds dumb, but I've always felt safer here than in California. But there isn't any place that's safe anymore. They're kidnapping suburban housewives right in broad daylight from supermarket parking lots; dragging people out of their cars at stoplights; shooting at families cruising down country lanes on Sunday afternoons; raping and murdering doctors in their own hospitals. I am so afraid for you kids, I don't even know what to tell you to do. If I could lock you in a room for the rest of your lives, I probably would."

Toby licked tomato sauce off his fingers. "Naw, we'd just die from radon leaking through the heating vents or get lead poisoning from the walls or something. We're cool; don't worry about us. We've got better street smarts than Uncle Martin. I mean, I love him and all, but he is not exactly a savvy kind of dude."

Annie sipped her wine, tears falling again. "Poor Martin."

Ella moved closer to her. "Mom, are you okay?"

Annie nodded. "I'm fine."

"Are you sure?"

"I'm sure."

They were silent. The family truth-meter ticking in the background. She had to tell them.

"I lied. I'm not fine. I don't mean just about Pop. I didn't want to tell you kids like this; I wanted your father to be here, too, but he couldn't stay. We've had something happen, something pretty awful. You know Leonard Lewis, the man who manages and invests all of our money? Well, he's disappeared, it seems, and taken it all with him, not just ours; we weren't singled out; he's taken all of his clients' money and he's gone. What makes it more serious is that Daddy's show has been canceled. So, my bunnies, our nice comfy Easter basket has been pilfered. I don't want you to worry, because we'll get through this. Billy's going to help us, and Uncle Jackie, and I'm sure Daddy will get some offers. And I'm going to start hustling my wares as soon as things settle down. I don't want to upset you two, but it just didn't seem right to not tell you. It's your lives, too."

Toby reached for Ella's hand, which was coiled into a fist at her side.

"I knew it. I knew something was wrong. I could just feel it. I tried to call you, and Juanita said you'd left at dawn to go to L.A. for 'business matters.' I just knew something had happened."

Toby swallowed. "If you can't pay my tuition, it's okay. I can come home — I mean here — and work for a while."

Ella laughed. "You only wish."

Annie looked at him. He had offered much too easily. "Tob, aren't you happy there?"

"I'm okay. I just meant I don't have to go to such an expensive school."

"Honey, it's not *that* bad, and besides, we have a special account for your college that was not turned over to Mr. Lewis, thank God, so don't even think like that."

Ella sipped her wine. "I don't want this to sound crass, but does that mean we're not going to Club Med for Christmas?"

Annie jerked back in her seat. She had completely wiped the vacation out of her mind. "Oh, God, kids, I spaced it! No, no. I mean we've already paid for it. Of course we're going. We all need it. I just forgot."

How would she and Mickey pull that off? It was only a couple of weeks away! She would probably be in New York until just before they left. Well, maybe it was better that way. They would be with the kids, and they would have some time alone at night to try and sort out their situation. Maybe it wouldn't be so bad after all.

"Mom?"

She had wandered off. "Yes, honey. I'm sorry, I'm just a little spaced tonight."

"You'd better call about the credit cards. Those creeps are probably already hitting some mall."

"Right." Annie stood up. "I want to check your uncle, too. Save me some pizza."

They sat side by side watching her go. Toby put his arm around Ella, feeling the way they had felt as tiny children, sneaking into one another's beds in the dark after their parents had gone, huddling together for comfort and protection against the night sounds. Sounds, it now was clear, that grown-up people heard all the time.

In the middle of the night of her father's burial, Annie wandered through the shadowed, airless rooms of his life. Her family slept around her like the night before Christmas, though visions dancing in their heads were most likely not sugarplums. Jackie above, alone with his mother — the mogul, back in his little-boy's bed; Loretta on the sofa next to Martin — the tangled strands of marriage pulling her back to her husband's need. And her children — tucked in tight in her brother's old room.

She wandered, the ghost of Christmas past taking a lateral stroll through her own memory. Little Orphan Annie, Little Orphan Annie, the thought whistled in her head, taunting her ever so slyly, testing her resolve.

She stopped at her father's desk and sat down, realizing that she had never done that before. It had been as sacred as a king's throne when she was a little girl and she sat now, waiting for him to saunter in and throw her out.

She opened his private drawers. Con-Ed receipts, business cards with vaguely familiar names on them, matchbooks from famous restaurants, playbills from new shows, notes from friends: "Do try to come to Clement's opening on Saturday — it should be divine."

The daily business of an old, but functional, man's life. What had she just read about old people alone? The men are much more mobile and independent and able to care for themselves than the women? What exquisite irony. All of those World War Two brides, spending their lives caring for their supposedly helpless husbands, only to end up the ones bedridden and dependent while the sprightly old farts were out playing croquet with the widow across the way.

I wonder why he never got married again. Now that she was her mother's age it seemed ludicrous that her father, who had been only a few years older, would have spent so many years alone. It was not that he hadn't had opportunities; maybe he loved her mother more than any of them had known. He almost never talked about her; but then, he almost never talked about anything very personal.

Maybe he had never recovered, or maybe he just felt guilty and staying single was his penance. She would never know now. She would never know anything more about him than she already knew. She had tried to talk to Ida Mae about their marriage, but she hadn't had much more information than Annie. "When your mother was alive," Ida Mae had said, "Joe and I hardly spoke. Your mother couldn't stand us, thought we were a bad influence on you. After she died, he never talked about her. I know he ran around on her, and when you kids were at school I would hear them fighting. But he didn't leave, Annala.

"No one ever knows what holds a marriage together or what busts it apart. My Moe and me had a great time, never fought, had one helluva sex life, worked together, shared all the same politics. The guy never strayed; too scared of me maybe, but loyal and true. When he died, I realized that I hadn't loved him for a long time; got over it like we had just spent a couple of Sunday afternoons together instead of thirty years.

"You live long enough, Annala, the truth don't hurt so bad. Your father, he was a Weak Willy; he never could face up to things. But they had their own kind of marriage. No two alike, every one is like a fingerprint."

Annie shuffled through his papers looking for something personal, something she could claim from her loss.

He had not even left a will. There were no bequests, no diary, no letter to his grandchildren. There was nothing.

"The typical pattern of a pathological narcissist," Loretta had said. "They truly believe that they will never cease. Their own existence is hyperreal to them; they cannot see over it."

The only thing it made easier was her job as executor. Executor of what? He didn't even own his apartment.

There was nothing for her to hold on to, to take forward with her as an heirloom or a family icon. She closed the drawers of his battered old desk. The desk was so like her father; from a distance it looked fancy and valuable, but up close it was a poorly made copy, a facade to impress those across the room.

She got up and floated barefoot across the parlor, through the dining room, unchanged since the day her mother stopped using it. The kitchen and dining room — her mother's rooms, left almost as a shrine to her memory. She saw her mother racing back and forth, bringing plates of food, her attention completely focused on the mundane duties before her. Annie could not remember her sitting with them, but only flying back and forth between her rooms.

She entered the kitchen, the cold linoleum chilling her bare feet. She opened the refrigerator. A box of cigars, a half-empty bottle of sweet red wine, a loaf of rye bread, a jar of pickled herring, and a half-eaten Hebrew National salami. Annie smiled. Poor Pop. He could put on his airs, wear his ascot, drink his goyish martinis with the curly little lemon peels, but at home alone in the kitchen, the Jew sprung forth. Pickled herring and Manischewitz, the comfort food of his roots.

Annie leaned against the sink and looked out the window. There was no one in front of her now; she was next in line. A spark of excitement shot through her. The most dreaded thought was the most tantalizing. *No one in front of her.*

Her life had been erased like one of those metallic drawing pads the kids used to have. You could draw and draw and squiggle and squiggle; draw a family and a house and a dog and a car and a smoking chimney and a picket fence and a mommy and daddy and kids and friends, and when there was no more room on the page you just pulled it up and the entire picture disappeared, leaving a clean slate to start all over again. There she was, with a brand-new page. There was a thrill about the possibility, even more potent than the fear of such freedom.

She poured a glass of water and followed the moon shadows down the hall to her room. The door to Martin's old room was ajar and she tiptoed in.

Her children slept, replicas of herself and her brother, ancestors to their presence, filling the room with memories. She moved closer, looking down at her son, sleeping on his back, his hands folded pharaoh-like across his chest, the funny cartoon smile on his face.

Oh, Toby, my baby boy. You aren't happy in your fancy school. I knew it, I just knew it. She wanted to hold him close and whisper in his ear, *Toby, Toby, flee on your donkey, flee this wicked place* — an Anne Sexton poem about an insane asylum? Same thing. Annie reached down and touched his hair. *You've always hated school. I wish I could wave a magic wand and have it all behind you.*

Ella turned over, rolling herself up tighter in her covers the way Mickey did. "I don't know yet," Ella said, talking in her sleep to someone inside her head.

Ella was avoiding her, the same way she was avoiding Ella. The flip side of being close to your daughter. They could not be together for long without talking about personal things; when Ella avoided her it was always because of this. *Ella-Bella, my beautiful princess, whatever it is, don't be afraid to tell me.*

She sighed. Nothing about being a parent ever got even the tiniest bit easier. It was like an endless crossword puzzle, with a perpetual array of new blank spaces demanding to be filled in. What was a four-letter word for motherhood? Loss, of course.

"Mommy?" Toby opened his eyes. He almost never called her that anymore. Her heart swelled. She moved across the room and sat beside him.

"Did I wake you?"

"Naw. My sleep schedule is totally screwed up."

"I can identify. I'd bring you some warm milk only there isn't any. How about a nice cup of hot pickled herring, think that might work?"

Toby grinned, closing his eyes again. "Don't make me laugh, I'll wake up too much."

"How about the old lullaby?"

"Remember every night you'd put Ella to bed first and I'd get upset because she'd always manipulate you into reading her an extra story, and by the time you'd get to me, you were out of patience?"

"I remember you *thought* that, but in fact it always took twice as long to get you to bed as Ella, what with the search for maniacs, and the pee-pee rituals, and the forty questions about death and God and why birds fly and all. That's why you only got one story. But you got all the best songs."

He yawned. "I'd take the lullaby, but promise you won't tell anyone."

She stroked his strong, tightly muscled arm. "I was never here." She waited, letting him relax away from her. "Lullaby, and good night, while the angels lie sleeping. Lullaby, and good night, I will see you when it's light."

This was all she had left of her parents, she thought, humming the chorus. They had taught her this song. Her mother had sung her to sleep with this song and she had sung her children to sleep with it. It was not much of a legacy, a fragment of a song, whose words she had mostly forgotten and whose origins were unknown, but it was, Annie thought as she lulled her man-child to sleep, better than nothing at all.

When his breathing slowed, she eased herself off the bed and out of the room, saying good-bye to this place. Tomorrow she would begin to dismantle what was left of her original family.

She would do it with her usual precision and orderliness. She would label the clothes for Ida Mae's charities and box the books for her father's cronies. She would pay the outstanding bills and donate the furniture to the Salvation Army. She would have the apartment cleaned and turn in the keys and sign the papers closing the bank accounts. And then she would go back to Montecito, where things were not so easily sorted out anymore. She would go home.

"Angel?"

"Hi, Mickey. Oh, my God! Hold on a minute!"

"Annie? What's going on?"

"You won't believe what just happened! I heard this noise. It sounded like it was raining, but the sky is absolutely clear. So I went to the front window, and this well-dressed Oriental man with a briefcase was peeing in Pop's doorway!"

"Have you had enough yet?"

"If Martin's mugging didn't do it, a little pee-pee isn't going to scare me off."

"Are you almost through?"

"I think so. A few more days. I can't believe I've been here a week already. I want to make sure Ida Mae is okay, too. She puts up quite a front, but I think she's going to be really lonely without him downstairs."

"She'll be fine, Annie."

"Okay, Mr. Reading-Between-The-Lines, so I'm stalling a little. It's been very comforting being here. Ella and I went by our house yesterday. We just stood across the street in front of the Fennelis' and reminisced. Remember the wedding reception we had for Martin and Loretta when the caterer didn't show up, and Ida Mae and I took everything edible in the freezer and microwaved this whole mass of leftovers while you ran around the house pumping champagne into everyone so they wouldn't notice what they were eating?"

"I remember steaming plates of burnt lox."

"Oh, God, that's right! How's the show going?"

"Fabulous. All we needed was to get canceled to do really good work. We've got the best script we've had in years. Everyone is at optimum energy. Stan's directing, and he's just cooking, taking all kinds of risks. We'll probably all get Emmy nominations — a perfect television ending."

"I talked to Juanita; she said you haven't been home."

"Didn't seem to be much point with you gone."

"There's always a point in going home. Besides, Juanita and Portia need their little pats, too."

"Come on, Annie, give me a break."

"Anything else new? I've sort of let real life go."

"Jackie and Billy O'Brian have been working on our Leonard Lewis dilemma. Billy's been over to see Bambi a couple of times. Jackie's going to take Samantha with him to see the private detective. She had some dream or vision, or whatever the fuck she has, about where the money is."

"Don't tell me this! There goes the last drop of his common sense! I don't want that New Age bimbo involved in our private business! Can't you talk to him?"

"I didn't want to hurt his feelings. He's putting so much time into this. Oh, some good news."

"Good news? I used to know what that term meant, but I can't quite remember."

"I got the Japanese car commercial. They want me to come over right after the first of the year, and Jackie's talked to his buddy — the one who sang because the translator messed up? He's got a couple of things lined up for me while I'm over there, so at least there will be some new income coming in. I thought maybe you'd come with me."

"Mickey, look. I know we're both just treading water now and that's okay, but sooner or later we're going to have to reach the side of the dock. Did you forget about Club Med?"

"No. . . . Annie, you're being so . . . I don't know what to say to you. . . . I know you don't want to talk about it yet and God knows I don't, but you're just being so great. . . ."

"Great? I'm not being great. I haven't had the luxury of losing it yet. Trust me, you will live to retract your compliment."

"I need to ask you something."

"Go for it."

"Did you, I mean that night, did you go back to Ojai to Ivy Clare's house and take some of her pots?"

"No."

"Annie, it's okay to tell me the truth. It just seemed so out of character, but she has no reason to make something like that up."

"I have no idea what you are talking about."

"She says certain pots, the ones she told you were available, are missing, just vanished. She thinks you did it."

"Well, gee whiz, I'd advise the poor dear to call the pot police immediately, and I will be on the lookout for any suspicious person lurking around with bulky objects hidden under their clothes. This could be the new urban crime, sort of post-carjacking, now we've got pot-napping! Where will it all end!"

"Annie."

"You want to start? Get ready to grab your compliment and head for the hills! After finding my husband panting and sweating over that *American Gladiators* reject, I hardly had the wherewithal to drive around the block let alone back and forth to Ojai. I was, in fact, at Loretta's, which she will swear to in a court of pottery law."

"I'm sorry. I never should have brought it up. I tried to calm her down. I just didn't want her to call the cops."

"How cozy, you two kids commiserating about your poor wife's possible criminal behavior. Is she staying there with you? Are you coming home to romantic dinners for two? Let me guess. Tandoori chicken, cooked in a *clay* oven, and snapper diavolo baked in a *clay* dish. Does she shape your oatmeal into cute little titties and stick in raisin nipples? — sort of a lecherous, lying, cheating bastard's happy face?"

"Annie, please —"

"I can't believe you would ask me that! You're not trying to protect *me,* you're trying to protect *her!* Tell her to go ahead and call the police! Tell her to bring in the marines and the United Nations peacekeeping force and the Israeli Defense team and the CIA! I hear the FBI has a tit-pot task force. Go for it. Have the party."

"Annie, it's okay. She's not going to call the police. She can't prove anything's missing. I never should have brought it up. I'm sorry. . . ."

"You're *sorry?* Well, love is never having to say you're sorry. Don't you read? You never do have to say you're sorry, because sorry doesn't mean a flea's fart to me. It would be like Hitler saying, 'I'm really sorry.' So don't worry about it, Mickey, just take your patronizing, bullshit compliment and go pump your biceps or something. I'll be home before we go to Club Med, but when exactly, I'm not sure."

"Annie, honey . . ."

Whatever Jackie Wilski expected Stan Stein's private detective to be like, a bespectacled matron with photos of her dogs and numerous grandchildren on her desk was not it. "Emily Smith," she said pleasantly. "Not what you expected, right folks?" Jackie and Samantha settled down in the chintz-covered matching armchairs before her tidy oak desk.

Samantha turned her charm laser on the woman. "I never expect anything. I'm a psychic."

The older woman smiled, revealing a museum-quality set of probably false teeth. "It works for me," she said crisply.

Samantha tightened. This was not what she had in mind, excluding the fact that she had lied. She always expected things to go her way. She had assumed they were meeting a man, a sort of rough-around-the-edges Mickey Spillane kind of man. She would have to rethink this situation.

Jackie was grinning at the powdery creature. "You're fantastic. Did anyone ever tell you you should be on television?"

"Oh, sure, all the time."

"No, I'm serious. I produce talk shows. I've gotta book you. You'd be great."

Samantha leaned forward. "Can we move on now, honey?" Jackie looked at her sharply.

Something was wrong. Ever since he had come back from that damn funeral in New York, she had been picking up odd vibrations from him. It wasn't her impulse that had changed; it was coming from him.

His damn family had been filling his mind with negative ideas about her. Usually it only took her a few minutes of intense concentration to bring him back to her, but this was different. She had strolled up from the pool naked in the twilight to greet him and he had not even embraced her. He had not wanted to take her upstairs that second and throw her down and ravish her. She had been so stunned, she had lost her energy for the rest of the evening. "I'm really beat," he had said and kissed her cheek. No man had ever said anything like that to her before.

The dowdy old creature's eyes were focused on her behind the bifocals.

"Certainly, Miss . . ."

"Cove. Samantha Cove."

"Cove. What a fine name. Very evocative."

"Yes. I like sea images. Water is the life force."

"Mmmm." Emily Smith smoothed her skirt.

Jackie leaned forward. "Okay. Let's not take up too much of Mrs. Smith's time. I guess you know why we're here. I'm trying to help my brother and his wife find Leonard Lewis, and since you're working on the same case for Stan Stein, he was generous enough to give us your card. Have you found out anything?"

Mrs. Smith leaned down and primly pulled a file out of a box next to her desk. "Not as much as I'd hoped."

She set the folder down in front of them. "He bought a ticket for San Francisco on November twenty-second. We don't even know for sure if he used the ticket himself, but someone did. My guess is he picked up a false passport in San Francisco, because the trail ends there. He stayed at the Saint Francis Hotel overnight, under the name of Jake Jerico, and paid in cash. The bellman remembers that he had two expensive suitcases and a briefcase and that he seemed nervous. I'm following up with my documents gentleman. If he got a fake passport in the Bay area, I'll know very soon."

"Jake Jerico is the name of my brother's character on *War Zone*."

"Mmm-hmm. I found that to be an interesting detail, myself. Almost as if he was sending some sort of signal."

Samantha shifted in her seat. She was not used to being pushed into the background, not to mention losing center stage to a woman like this.

"May I see the folder?"

The detective looked at Jackie, who nodded, regretting that he had not listened to Mickey and left Samantha at home. Somewhere over the skies between New York and L.A. he had come to, the spell had been broken. He had gotten off the plane and it was gone. But not just about Samantha; he felt as if it were broken for good. He had passed at least a dozen gorgeous blondes in the last week and *Sir* had not even tipped his cap.

Samantha took the file and held it against her formidable chest. She did not open it or look at any of the papers or ask a single question. She had made the gesture to grandstand, but she was really getting a signal. Her hands were fire-hot on the folder. She closed her eyes tighter, throwing back her head. Her breathing was shallow. Mrs. Smith and Jackie watched her.

"What is it?"

"Shh," she hissed. "Don't talk."

Colors flashed before her face. She was the priestess now, at home on her temple mount. "I see someone, pink and orange. A pink and orange woman. He wanted to punish her. He doesn't have the money. He ran away. He ran away because he was afraid, not because he stole the money."

Mrs. Smith leaned forward, threading her pale, veiny fingers together. "Do you see who has the money?"

"No. Only a woman, all pink and orange."

"That's his wife, Bambi."

Samantha shuddered and put down the file. "She's not telling the truth."

Jackie looked at the detective, who was nodding her small gray, permed head up and down. "I have been having the same hunches myself."

Samantha opened her eyes and very slowly handed back the file. She so loved having the tide turn her way.

"I'm glad to be of help, for Jackie's sake."

She turned her high-beam smile at him, but he wasn't looking at her. He was looking at the little granny.

"That makes sense. Stan said he thought Leonard was getting even because Bambi had affairs with all his clients."

Samantha stood up, furious at his insouciance.

"I have to go. I have a group to lead in an hour."

"Me too. I've got a recital to go to."

Samantha whirled around. "You're not coming with me?"

"Sorry, hon. I promised my surrogate nephew. I'll drop you at the house."

Mrs. Smith stood up politely. "You'll let me know if you see something else, Miss Cove?"

Samantha smiled. "I won't see anything else, Mrs. Smith."

Annie squinted into the piercing California sunshine, trying to refocus her eyesight and her perception. Ten days — may as well have been ten years. She felt the way she had as a child going back to school after being out sick: lost, vulnerable, and out of sync.

She looked at her watch, blinking to focus her day-blind eyes. Was New York really that much darker, or had it just been a gloomy week? Her flight was early and Molly was late. She pushed her suitcase forward, closer to the curb. Molly was always late.

She yawned, and the thought of her beautiful house and her nice clean, sweet-smelling king-size bed flitted in and out of her mind. Now that she was this close, she could hardly wait. Ten days in the house of death, dark and cold and waiting to be discarded, had made her appreciate how lucky she really was.

She took off her coat and threw it on top of her luggage. She had so much to do before they left for Mexico, if, for that matter, they were still going. She had not talked to Mickey since their phone fight.

She was convinced that Ivy Clare was staying at his apartment with him. Anger flooded her, making her even hotter than the unseasonable weather. Would he just leap out of bed with her and zoom back to Montecito, throw a bathing suit or two in a bag, and off they would go, the Wandering Wilders on another Christmas adventure? She now understood with new empathy the sordid cases she so easily dismissed on television and in the tabloids, where women wracked by jealous rage committed infantile and horrific acts of retribution. Smashing pots may have just been the beginning; maybe smashing heads was next. *Stop it, Annie. You are not going to turn into one of those bitter victims. Grow up.*

Yeah, sure. Grow up for what? To find out that maybe I've spent almost my entire life with a liar and a cheat? Maybe my entire marriage has been one of those fifties sci-fi concoctions — I Married a Monster from Outer Space. Maybe the real Mickey will turn up, having worked his way out of his handcuffs and crawled down from the alien spaceship where the impostor has kept him stashed all these many years. Fifties sci-fi always had a happy ending.

Molly's bright green Volvo station wagon screeched to a halt, ending her reverie. She picked up her bag and coat and flung everything into Molly's already cluttered backseat.

"Sorry, sweet-pie, the traffic was epic."

Annie slid in beside her and reached over for a hug.

"It's okay. I needed the reentry time. It feels like I've been gone forever."

"It's always like that coming back from home; something about regressing into the previous self. Just wreaks havoc with time frames."

Molly swung the car onto Sepulveda and headed toward the beach. "I thought we'd stay off the freeway for a bit; it's too brutal up there."

Annie snapped her seat belt together. "Fine with me. I am seriously looking forward to my own bed and a long hot bath, but everything else waiting for me I am in no hurry to face."

Molly looked over at her. "Anything new about Leonard Lewis?"

Annie laughed. "I was about to ask you that. I turned it over to

Jackie and Billy while I was away and I haven't heard a word. Somehow, in this case I didn't think that no news was good news."

"Billy won't tell me anything. He's treating it just like a real case with a real client, and I am left out in the cotton field and not liking it one little bit."

"Great. That's the last thing I want, for this to cause problems for you two. He really wanted to help, Molly. I think he needs to be contributing something."

Molly giggled, but Annie thought it had a sarcastic tone, not her usual glee. "Oh, he's contributing something all right, but what and to whom I have not yet figured out."

"What does that mean?"

"It means my darling Billy-boy has strayed into another pasture."

Annie kicked off her shoes. "I don't believe it."

"It's true. I can feel it. It's all because of this damn case. I'm not blaming you, Annie, but it's turned his head all around. All of a sudden he's the crusading lawyer, dashing to the rescue of his desperate friends. The phone is ringing and he's running down to L.A. every other day and just so full of himself, being needed by all of these damsels in distress. Sooner or later he'd have to succumb to one hussy or the other."

"What hussies are involved in *our* money troubles?"

"I've narrowed it down to two. Your friend the actress, or the wronged wife."

"Lina and Bambi?"

"Sounds like a hillbilly singing team, don't it now."

"Molly, how do you know that? Maybe it's just that he's changing that's threatening you. It doesn't mean that he's having an affair."

"Oh, really? And this is the happily married expert speaking?"

Annie curled her left leg under her. It didn't seem right not telling Molly, when she was confiding in her. At this rate of sharing, she'd have to run an open editorial in *Variety* before the year was over.

"Molly, Mickey's having an affair. A real one, no speculation involved. I walked in on him and saw with my own shortsighted little peepers. You must swear that you will not tell anyone, not even Billy."

Molly swerved, almost sideswiping a cement truck.

"Oh, my Lord!"

"Careful! Maybe we shouldn't have this conversation while we're moving. This is more of a flatland, table-and-chair conversation."

Molly turned onto Ocean Avenue heading north. "Too late now, we've gone too far. So that's why you've been so distant. Is that why you stayed in L.A.?"

"Yes. He's screwing that horrible woman who makes the breast pots, if you can imagine it."

"Ivy Clare! No wonder she was so rude to you."

"I don't think that had anything to do with it. I think she would have behaved exactly the same if she had never met Mickey. Maybe even worse."

"What are you going to do?"

"I'm going to Club Med for Christmas with my children. He will either appear and go with us or he won't. What happens after that is anyone's guess."

"Annie-pie, is this a new you? I would never have imagined that you could handle something like this so well. I'm falling completely to rack and ruin and I'm not even sure. What happened to you?"

"Lots of things have been happening, but don't be fooled by how I sound. This is today. You should have heard me on the phone with Mickey three nights ago. Besides, none of it feels real yet. I think I'm still in a daze, so don't be too impressed. I haven't gotten close to what the betrayal feels like yet; I'm still coasting on my outrage. Also, a dead father thrown in adds some distraction."

"I'm not so sure about that. I've heard a lot of ladies' laments in my day and no one has ever sounded as grounded as you do. I hardly even recognize myself. I feel like the reverse of Samson and Delilah, as if Billy's cut off my hair and I've lost all of my grit and strength and self-confidence. I was in the village yesterday and I saw those awful women you call the 'benefit friends' at Maisy's and I thought they were laughing at me, at my clothes, and I had to bite my lip to keep from bawling all over my tuna salad. If my Billy leaves me, I'll curl up and die, Annie-pie. I will."

"Molly! Get a grip. You're the one who's always skipping about, tossing off adultery bon mots like daisy petals, making fun of traditional marriage. Was that all a lie?"

"I didn't think so. But Billy never cheated on me before. I felt so safe and in control of him."

Annie stretched her legs out. "When Billy came to ask me about helping, he was pleading, Molly. He said he had to do something to get his dignity back. He said that you didn't need him, but we did. I told him that you did need him very much, but he didn't hear it. That's what this is about, Molly, that bravado of yours. We *all* believed it. You must talk to Billy and tell him how you really feel. You have to stop trying to have the upper hand all the time."

"I don't know how not to. I've always had the upper hand. I can't even bear the *thought* of being vulnerable to some man. I've always used my money to keep Billy under my thumb. I did encourage him to cut back on his practice, I know I did that. I made my little nest so finely feathered, he stopped wanting to spread his wings anymore. But it's just not in my nature to turn into one of those eye-batters — 'Whatever you want, husband, dear.' Look at all those sappy political wives, what they put up with, smiling and gazing at those deceiving honkers like little plastic chicks. I'm afraid I may be one of those awful women who need all their ducks in a row."

"Molly, you are grossly underrating yourself. If that was really true, you wouldn't be able to see it so clearly. Billy is not a duck — he's a man. You may find that if you start treating him like one, some of your other marital problems will improve also."

"You mean sex?"

"Quack, quack."

"Annie-pie, you are so different! I swear if I didn't know better I'd think it was you having the affair. You know one of the thoughts in my head since Billy's been acting so strange? I keep thinking that I wish it was us that lost all of our money. If we had to start over together with nothing, we could work as a team, but as it is I'm much too spoiled and too lazy to throw out everything we've acquired and start over."

"Why don't you ask Billy what he wants to do with his life? Maybe the answer will help you both find a better way to be together. . . . Talk to him."

"I will. But first I've got to find out if he's doing it, and who to. I've been down here since yesterday following him around, but he's been with Jackie the entire time. I spent the night there with Billy, and my pal Samantha was very off her stride. I think Jackie's getting ready to deplane."

"No kidding. That's fantastic!"

"I asked her about Billy, but she had no vibrations. I've always thought that she was the strongest, most independent woman that I have ever known, and there she is moping around after your brother-in-law like he was Tom Cruise or someone."

"My brother-in-law is a lot more appealing than Tom Cruise, who looks like a chipmunk and is a Scientologist to boot."

"Shall I seek a better example?"

"Molly, all that talk about you and Billy and Samantha, was that just talk?"

Molly accelerated onto the Pacific Coast Highway.

"I'm all talk, Annie-pie, it's what I do instead of having a real life. When the children go, I'll most likely retreat into my little nest and finish off whatever worms are left, and when they're all gone I'll just close my eyes and go to sleep."

"Molly, stop it. You're making me really nervous. I don't like the way you sound one bit. Is Billy home now?"

"Should be."

"I want you to promise me that you'll stop this nonsense about following him around, and you'll talk to him, tonight. Don't make my mistake. Deal with it."

"What mistake did you make? You never held Mickey back; you always put his work first. You did everything they always told us we were supposed to do — have a career, but be supportive and don't ignore your responsibilities to your man and your children. What mistake did you make?"

"Too much familiarity, I guess. I wasn't independent enough. I wasn't a challenge anymore. I mean, I have *always* been there. It's not just about him, either. I mean I think I have been feeling the same way too, yearning for romance, for some fresh energy to restart my engine before it just rusts and falls apart.

"I don't just mean sex — I mean that jolt of fresh emotion. Being with someone who knows nothing about you and is seeing every one of your card tricks for the first time. I've never had that and neither has Mickey, except when he's performing, which is certainly more than I've had. It *is* about what I want too! I don't even know anymore. I'm officially an orphan now and everything in my life is up for grabs, and I'm not sure that Mickey and I are supposed to go on together, as terrifying as that is to face."

"I can't even think about that."

"Don't, Molly, just tell your husband that you need him and you're jealous. I have a feeling you won't have to think further than that."

It was getting dark when they pulled into Annie's driveway. The lights were on in welcome and Juanita was standing in the kitchen doorway. Mickey's car was gone, though his last day of filming had been the day before. Annie swallowed. "Want to come in and have a cup of tea?"

Molly undid her seat belt. "If I can splash some bourbon in it."

"You're on." They walked arm in arm to the door, leaving the bags in the car.

Juanita ran out. "Oh, Mrs. W! It's so good that you're home. Come on, quick!"

Molly and Annie exchanged looks.

"Portia," Annie whispered, breaking into a run.

The dog lay on her side on the floor by the stove, where she had spent so many peaceful nights while Annie cooked and talked to her, as if she had gone back there to wait for Annie.

"She sick, Mrs. W. I called the vet. I was gonna get a cab to take me."

Molly came in carrying a blanket. "Wrap her in this."

Annie knelt beside the dog and kissed her, whispering into her good ear. "I'm here, baby. It's going to be okay. I'm not going to leave you again."

The dog whimpered when she slid the blanket under her swollen stomach.

"Juanita, will you call Mr. O'Brian and tell him where we went. I'll call you from the vet's. Don't worry."

Tears glistened on the tiny woman's smooth, caramel cheeks. "She gonna leave us, Mrs. W. My old friend gonna go to Jesus." Juanita trotted out, her tiny feet crunching across the gravel, and opened the car door. Three women, doing what they knew how to do best, taking care of someone other than themselves.

It was cold in the waiting room, the bare rubber floor and the stiff plastic seats, immune to pet accidents, held no heat. The dim light from one yellow ceiling fixture cast harsh shadows on the sterile, empty walls. Molly had gone to get coffee and Annie waited for the verdict.

A young girl came in carrying a lumpy ball of fur, with a muddy, wagging tail sticking up between her arms. She carried the mutt over to the reception desk.

"Some old geezer just threw this puppy out of a car window into the middle of the street."

The nurse shook her head. "You think you've heard everything."

The girl held the shaking creature tight against her. "I just read about a woman who put her baby in a frying pan filled with boiling oil. Fried the kid like a potato. Grossed me out, even though I've always thought people were nicer to dogs than they were to each other."

The nurse handed her a form. "Lots of sickos out there. We had a bulldog in here last week been used in a porno movie."

Please, Annie chanted silently, shivering in her plastic chair, *please don't take her now.*

It was hard to even remember her life before Portia. Portia as a puppy, an abandoned whelp like the trembling pup in the teenager's arms. Portia was as much a part of their family life as Juanita. The unconditional love of her children had been lost at adolescence, and the love of her husband was of an entirely different strain, but Portia had never flagged, never looked at her with anything other than total acceptance, and she had gotten used to it and taken her for granted, and now it was probably too late to make it up to her. She had let her dog down.

The teenager sat down near the door, trying to hold the puppy and fill out the form.

"Do you want me to hold him for you?" Annie smiled at her.

"Thanks." The girl looked up. She reminded Annie of Ella when she was that age.

She walked across the room and took the shivering cur from his savior, walking him round and round the room the way a new mother walks a cranky infant. All her babies were gone now.

The door opened and a portly, bald man wearing a raincoat and carrying a swollen cocker spaniel in his arms ran in. "She's ready," he said happily to the nurse, handing the bloated mother-to-be across the counter.

Annie and the girl watched him. He took off his coat, rubbing his hands together in glee. "My dog's having pups. First time. Don't know how she managed it; I never let her out alone. Maybe it's an Immaculate Conception."

Annie sat down, holding the puppy against her stomach, warming them both.

"That's wonderful," she said, thinking of the cycle of events: one dog abused, one dying, and one bursting with health and life, round and round, everyone's turn on the carousel.

"What're you in for?" he asked, smiling broadly.

Annie looked up at him, thinking he had a nice face.

"My dog's very old and I don't know . . ."

The man looked at her lap. "Looks like a puppy to me."

"Oh, this isn't my dog, I'm just helping."

The girl handed the form back to the nurse and came to reclaim her prize, smiling now, excited by her good deed and her new friend.

Annie handed him back, feeling the cold, damp spot where he had been, now an absence, something missing in her life. She crossed her arms over her lap, trying to re-create the warm full feeling of holding the pup against her, feeling its frightened heart beating against her womb.

"Mrs. Wilder." The vet stood in the doorway, his face grim.

Please, no. Annie stood up and followed him in. She could hear the cheerful sounds of the birthing at the end of the hall.

Portia lay on the cold metal table like a large, discarded rag doll, her body limp, her chest heaving in a labored effort to breathe, her weak, drippy eyes watching Annie.

The vet looked tired, Annie thought. He was so young, she always had trouble believing he was a real doctor for animals or anyone. "It's time, Annie," he said quietly.

She felt sick to her stomach. "Are you sure?"

The young vet ran his hand along Portia's back.

"Yes. She's had a massive stroke. Her stomach's terribly distended. I'd say congestive heart failure too. She's lost most of her sight and she's suffering."

Annie nodded, biting down hard on her lower lip. She was having trouble controlling her emotions.

"What do we do?"

"You say good-bye and then you hold her, unless you don't want to, and I'll give her a shot. She'll go very fast and without any pain."

"Okay."

The vet walked out. "Call me when you're ready."

"How about next leap year," she said, her voice shaking.

She lifted the dog into her arms and carried her to the vet's chair and sat, rocking her and kissing her mangy red face. Portia's eyes followed her. She did not believe that she couldn't see. Her tears fell in fat wet circles on the dog's neck.

"I don't know what to say, kiddo. I never got to say good-bye to someone I loved before." The thought slammed into her. It was true. She had never said good-bye to her mother or her father. She held

Portia closer, burying her face in her fur. She could feel her heartbeat, the opposite of the rescued puppy, so slow that every beat seemed to take all of the animal's will.

"You're my best friend, and I've been honored to live such a wonderful part of my life with you in it. You know how much we all love you and we will never, ever, stop missing you. Maybe you'll keep an eye on us from wherever you go. Don't be afraid. It's going to be all right; somewhere peaceful and wonderful is waiting for you.

"I'll never forget you . . . never, ever. I love you, old friend." She wrapped her arms around her dog, covering Portia's body with her own. It was almost more than she could bear. Emotion convulsed her, shredding her control. She could not stop crying. She could not let her dog go.

Was it possible, she thought, hovering over her dying pet, that she could feel more pain at the loss of her dog than the loss of her father? Or was the grief spasm an accumulation of every loss.

She wept for them all, images poking in and out of her head. Her mother on the kitchen floor, her father telling his jokes at Thanksgiving, Portia in her Santa Claus suit. She saw them all whizzing around inside her head, soaring off above her over the rainbow, carrying their new secrets far away.

The vet stood in the doorway. "Okay?"

She lifted her shattered face, Portia's eyes still on her. "Okay."

Molly was alone in the room when Annie came out. She handed her a container of coffee. "Want to sit a minute?"

Annie shook her head, taking the coffee. "No. Let's go."

Molly followed her out, opening the car door as if Annie were impaired. She got in and sat in the dark, sipping the stinging brew.

Molly slammed her door and fumbled in her purse for the keys. "Damn stupid of me in downtown Santa Barbara at night. I should have locked the doors." She extracted the keys and turned on the engine.

Something fizzed inside Annie's head.

"Molly, how tired are you?"

"I'm beyond tired. I had three cups of fast-food coffee. I'm adrenalinized. Why?"

"Could you drive me to Ojai?"

Molly giggled. "Is this some sort of Jewish mourning ritual?"

"Actually, you're not far off."

"It would be my pleasure."

They drove without talking, until it was time for Annie to give directions. Up the mountain road they went to the plain wooden sign marked CLARE. Molly turned off her lights and they coasted as silent as a rowboat down the well-worn driveway.

Mickey's car was parked where her car had parked not so long ago.

"We can go home now," Annie said.

CHAPTER XI

VACATION, from the Latin word *vacatio,* meaning freedom, exemption from, intermission; a time of respite. The most loaded and evocative of words. A word to make people smile, sigh, long, hope. The mantra sentence of contemporary life: "I need a vacation."

There are as many varieties as there are potential vacationers, and the choices, given the burgeoning state of the travel industry, are endless. One can trek in Nepal, raft in Colorado, hike the Grand Canyon, or ski in Vermont. There are barge trips on the Seine, castle tours of Scotland, opera jaunts in Italy. The options are as vast as the imagination and the budget.

If the anticipation rarely matches the reality, and the actual experiences of exhaustion, disorientation, and anxiety fight for equal time with the pleasures of the journey, it is of no matter. It may well be in the end that the magic of the word, the promise of the adventure, is the real vacation. Everyone needs something to look forward to.

For families, where the interests of a group of large and less-large people traveling together have to be somewhat balanced, the resort vacation has been historically ideal, and emanating from this perennially popular notion, taking the family vacation to the level of conceptual art in the guise of packaged travel, came Club Med.

Almost everyone wants to go to Club Med at some time in their lives, either to meet people during the swinging singles weeks or to take a snarly, school-and-job-depleted family on a sojourn that almost guarantees no disasters. Chartered flights, egalitarian room and food plans, free beer with meals, and all the water sports, tennis, and Ping-Pong tournaments, aerobics, and snorkel cruises that anyone but a triathlete could hope for.

It was in this spirit that the Wilders sent in their money some nine months before their actual Club Med experience was to occur. None of them had ever been anyplace remotely like it. Because of Mickey's paranoia about being recognized, they had booked their own air tickets, so the shock of the true difference between the "Club Med philosophy" and a regular resort did not hit until the battered van that transported them from the airport screeched into the palm-lined driveway.

The Wilders had not arrived at this balmy-breezed, oleander-scented intermezzo in the best mental shape for dealing with the instant smack of awareness that this was not what they had expected. The sight that greeted them was not featured in the seductively luminous, high-gloss brochures.

Eight hundred or so pasty, sweaty, Gap-dressed tourists, in various stages of jet lag and frustration, were lined up in the parking lot, surrounded by a Samsonite and Le Sport battlement of luggage, more suitcases than any of them had ever seen in one place, including Macy's luggage department.

The refugees from urban America were identified by stickem tags on their shirts branding them by charter load — Dallas, Cincinnati, Atlanta — as if they were all convention delegates or entrants in some macabre version of the Miss America contest. They huddled before a group of robotically bouncy young men and women, mostly of the white, American-mall variety, and all dressed alike in unisex short-and-shirt outfits flaunting the Club Med insignia. They were all tan and they were all smiling, which was the main way you could spot them in the swollen mass of humanity. Around their young golden necks were whistles.

Annie, who had been as eager to go to this place as to Bosnia, but had succumbed to years of the kids' pleading, came up beside Mickey. They had barely spoken in the three days between her arrival home and their departure, but they were allies now in what looked to be the beginning of a survival struggle.

"They're wearing whistles around their necks. Oh, my God."

Mickey put his arm around her. "Forget the whistles, look at the eyes. We're talking *Stepford III*."

"They've all got clipboards, Mickey. It's like YMCA camp. They're going to make a thousand people stand here while they check us off and assign our cabins. I'm going to end up sharing a bunk with Susie Needleman again, and I'm going to run away."

A very tall young man with bloated biceps, shoulder-length blond hair, and what appeared to be several rows of pure white teeth stepped forward with a megaphone.

"Hi, guys! Welcome to Club Med. How many of you have partied with us before?"

Scores of hands went up, horrifying Annie.

"Mickey, It's some kind of cult."

"Groovy! We apologize for the jam-up, but as you G.M.'s know, Christmas is the ultimate party. We're gonna take good care of you if you'll just be patient. We'll have you all checked in in no time, and then the good times will roll! Our fantastic G.O.'s will be passing among you in a moment with your wristbands, but before that, for those of you who are here for the first time, let me explain a few of the rules. First, my name is Thor Grossberg and I run the sports program. What do we say?"

Hundreds of the arrivees shouted, "Hi, Thor!"

Annie leaned against Mickey. "*Thor* Grossberg? The only Norwegian Jew in captivity. I'm going home."

Ella came up. "What's a G.M. and a G.O.?"

Annie shrugged. "I haven't a clue. Some cult anagram. Why don't you raise your hand and ask *Thor*."

"Mother!"

"He seems like such a nice boy, and Jewish, too."

Toby came up. "This girl just told me that G.M.'s are Genteel Members and G.O.'s are Genteel Organizers."

Annie grimaced. "Gen*tile* or Gen*teel?*"

"Like in French, meaning nice, polite, like that."

"What a relief." Annie wiped sweat from her forehead.

"Okay, now let's talk about the beads. For you first-timers, no money is accepted anywhere in the club. You can buy beads at the service desk, and they are used for drinks and extras. They come in different colors and lengths, but make sure you buy enough each day, because once the desk closes at night, if you want to party and you've run out of beads, it's, like, a bummer!"

Annie turned to Mickey. "A new worry. Bead anxiety. Maybe we should stockpile, like Russian housewives. This sounds like it could be serious. Maybe we could sell our surplus at a profit to desperate, beadless Gentiles late at night."

"Shh, Mom. Listen."

"Okay, once you have your wristbands and your room numbers, the G.O.'s will help you locate your luggage and drive you up to your rooms. They will answer all your questions about restaurants and reservations and tell you where to sign up for tonight's activities. Just remember, we are here to make your vacation the party of a lifetime. All right!"

Annie put her chin on Toby's shoulder. "I think Thor has spent one too many days on roller blades; his gears aren't catching."

"Mom, don't be so cynical. Get in the spirit."

"Oh, Toby, not you, too! Am I to be lost in space here, with my own family turning into a bunch of pod people?"

Toby gave her his glazed, horror-movie stare. "Why, Mrs. Wilder, I don't know what you mean."

A short brunette with a mass of Farrah-Fawcett fluffed hair appeared. "Hi, guys! I'm Tanya, your G.O. Can I have your names, please."

"Wilder," Annie said. "There are four of us."

The girl tossed her hair back and forth several times while scanning her clipboard. "Annie, Mickey, Toby, and Ella?"

"Exactly right."

Toby nudged her. Annie tried a smile.

"Great! Okay." She reached into a bag tied to her waist and pulled out four plastic bands. "Are you all together?"

Toby and Ella moved forward. Mickey had retreated behind his baseball cap and glasses, at once pleased and upset that no one seemed to have any idea who he was.

"Yes," Annie said. In public she was used to being the family spokesperson, shielding The Star from unnecessary exposure.

"Great! Okay, these are your ID bands. I'm gonna seal them on to your wrists and you are not to take them off until you leave. If you lose your band, you must report it immediately, and if you're not wearing it you, like, can't eat, and security will stop you on the beach. It's real important that you're wearing it at all times. Do you want the left wrist or the right?"

The G.O. creature held out the bands, extracting a metal device from her pocket that looked like a staple gun. As far as Annie was concerned, she might as well have been brandishing a tattoo needle at Auschwitz.

"Wait a minute. Are you telling me that I have to wear a band on my wrist for an entire week?"

Toby and Ella stiffened, shooting one another the frenzied look of young, hip people whose uncool parents were about to compromise their social standing.

The girl's vacant, see-through smile cemented. They had obviously been trained for difficult adjusters.

"It's really no big deal. It's just like when you're admitted to a hospital." If she had chosen the wrong thing to say on purpose, she could have done no better.

"Yes. I see that. Just like a hospital, a prison, or . . . a concentration camp. There is absolutely no way, Tana —"

"Tanya."

"— Whatever — that I am going to wear a wristband."

The girl's smile remained untouched. "Some guys wear it on their ankle. I can do that."

"I have a better idea —"

"Annie!" Mickey came forward. "It's okay, miss, just give them to us. We'll take care of it."

The girl looked ever so slightly confused. "I'm supposed to seal them. You can't *eat* without them."

Mickey held out his hand. "Don't worry, I'll take full responsibility."

The girl turned to Toby and Ella. "How 'bout you guys?"

Annie put her hands on her hips. Would they dare?

Toby blushed. "It's okay, just let my dad have them." Annie smiled. United they would stand, united they would fall. The first victims of starvation at any Club Med in the world.

The girl handed Mickey the bands. "Well, do you guys have, like, luggage?"

All bets were apparently now off. If they refused wristbands, maybe they were so unbalanced as to appear with only the clothes on their backs.

"Yes, right over there." Mickey led the creature to their pile.

Toby went with him, leaving Ella with her mother.

"Mom, if we're here we're going to have to relax and enjoy it, or the entire vacation is going to be a nightmare."

"Okay. I'll try. I'm sorry, I didn't mean to embarrass you, but can you believe this?"

Ella leaned over and kissed her. "I guess it's sort of more of a place for normal families."

"Normal! It's Buchenwald for yuppies."

A pretty blonde with large, floppy breasts marched by, talking into a walkie-talkie. "We have Michelle and Linda Olson, but no beds, and we can't find the Schneider family or the guy from Vancouver who wasn't with a group, and the Portillo family from Mexico City has the Gueverro's luggage."

A middle-aged woman with bright orange hair and the leathery, too-tan skin of the pleasure-seeker stormed up to the floppy blonde, costumed in cutoffs, a Daisy Mae blouse, and fourteen pounds of turquoise jewelry displayed on her neck, ears, waist, and wrists. "Where do I sign up for the karaoke singing? I missed it last night and I am not going to be left out again tonight."

The blonde turned on the same Tanya and Thor smile. "No problem. In the main reception in one hour."

"My daughter and I want to do 'Some Enchanted Evening.'"

"Great!"

Ella pinched Annie. "Mom, I think I'm starting to veer toward your point of view."

"Well, don't rule Thor out. I've always wanted a Jewish Viking for a son-in-law."

Because Club Med was designed to accommodate single adults traveling alone, the double room that Annie and Mickey finally arrived at, identical to the one their children were occupying across the passageway, was perfect for their current situation.

There were two entrances and two separate double-bedded areas that could be sealed off for complete privacy by sliding a mirrored set of doors together. There were two doors to the bathroom and separate sink and cabinet sectors, with only the discreetly hidden toilet and shower to be shared. Annie closed the sliding door between their rooms and collapsed onto the bed.

The hacienda-style bungalows were all the same except for locations, which were color-coded yet extremely difficult to tell apart. The most distinctive feature of their purple section was that it was at the very top of the hill — equal to climbing to the roof of a nineteen-story building, their cheerful golf-cart driver was eager to point out.

The other couple in their cart was making their fifteenth visit to Club Med. "We just love it," the hatchet-jawed husband from Montreal had offered, scratching the crotch of his green-and-purple-flowered jogging pants. "You can meet up to fifty new people a day here if you're lucky."

"Yippee," Annie had moaned, ready to fling herself out of the cart and take her chances with the cliff-angled incline. *I never even talk to the person sitting next to me on an airplane.*

Mickey knocked on her door. "Come in." They had never before slept in twin beds, let alone with a door between them. She kept her eyes closed.

"I thought I'd go down and check things out, maybe take a swim. Want to come?"

She shook her head. "They'd have to use a forklift to get me back up that hill."

"Annie, they have carts that take you up and down; you don't have to walk."

"I do too. It's a matter of pride. I'll wait until dinner. I'm totally wiped out. Maybe the kids will go."

"They're already down there. I'll sign us up for dinner."

"Great. Ask which restaurant is the least popular."

Mickey laughed. "You're on." He stood in the doorway, watching her. She put her arm over her eyes. They had not been alone together in such an immediate and intimate way for weeks.

"Want me to rub your back? That always puts you to sleep."

"No, thanks," she said, wishing he would go away.

He sighed, wanting to hold her. He wanted to throw himself into her arms and sob out his confusion. The distance was unbearable, to be so alone with the person closest to you in your life. To have lost the ease of that closeness was the loneliest feeling he had ever had. "Okay. I'll try not to wake you when I come up."

She turned onto her side, curling her legs up against her belly. "Buy beads," she said, drifting off.

He laughed, standing a moment longer, not wanting to go without her, needing, as always, her protection, her endless running of interference between him and the outside world, the world of ordinary mortals.

He closed the door and left her, pausing for a moment on their terrace. The view was spectacular; even Annie had had to admit that. He heard a loud honking noise below him coming from somewhere close by. Mickey leaned over the edge of his balcony and looked down. A naked, beer-bellied man wearing a straw hat was standing by the railing blowing into a large shell. He turned back toward where his wife was resting. *Annie would love this.* It was always his first thought whenever he saw anything funny or beautiful or new. *Annie would love this.*

God-fucking-dammit. He put on his sunglasses and headed for the stairways, a mass of routes that he hoped all led to the beach. The place was like a small town, filled with carts whizzing pleasure-seekers back and forth, dressed in sports costumes designed to attract strangers of like interests. Golfers in golf attire, tennis players in tennis garb, scuba divers in rolled-down wet suits, jocks in spandex with Day-Glo footwear — social codes without words. He took the stairs fast, trying to break through his fatigue.

An overexercised middle-aged woman wearing a shocking-pink cat suit and an enormous black gaucho hat, a huge emerald ring, and full stage makeup came running up the stairs toward him, a Walkman attached to her tiny waist, and matching pink weights encircling her wrists and ankles. *"Buenos dias,"* she said, offering him a grotesquely seductive smile.

"Hello," Mickey said without stopping, visions of an aging singles world filled with encounters such as this making his heart twitch with fear. He increased his pace, his breath coming too fast in the intense heat. Jesus, she was jogging *up,* with weights no less, and he was hardly making it down! A pretty young girl intersected him from a side path, followed by a pale blond kid wearing what looked like the entire J. Crew summer catalogue. "Hi," the kid said to the girl, "we took water aerobics together this morning."

"Je ne parle pas anglais." She shrugged, not slowing down.

"Oh . . . sure. Uh . . . *sí, sí, señorita."*

Mickey smiled, thinking of Toby and grateful to have a son with better social, not to mention language, skills. He'll need everything he can lay his hands on, Mickey thought, feeling the fear of the future coat him like the sweat moistening his skin. What was going to happen to them?

Two heavily muscled jocks tossing a volleyball back and forth came from behind, passing him on the steep staircase. "I don't know, man, we're talking about one wild bitch. She made me these crab cakes with some special Mideastern spices and shit in them — turned me into a fucking satyr. I was so hot, I was hissing like a teakettle. I've been begging her for the recipe for like six months. If she doesn't give in soon, I'm going to break into her fucking house and steal the stuff."

Man talk. Mickey had never been part of that kind of male macho chatter. Even when he played a role where he used dialogue like that, he felt uncomfortable. It always felt dirty and like a betrayal of Annie. The conversation with Dr. Rhinehart about Ivy Clare was the only time in his entire life he had ever talked in a sexually explicit way to anyone, even his brother. It was a locker-room bonding that he had never had anything in common with. Maybe that was his mistake. If he had had someone to talk like that with, maybe the power of his obsession with Ivy Clare would not have taken control of him. Women would be reduced to objects of conquest, not mythical, magically powerful sirens.

He was down. He stood at the last bank of stairs and looked out at the beaches below him. The sight was overwhelming. Everywhere the eye reached, people were in the act of pleasure, splashing in blue tile pools, laughing and shouting in various languages. A trio of half-moon bays bustled with boats, snorkelers, and jet-skiers. Groups of elegant Mexican families settled like royalty, the women painted and bejeweled, every hair in place, covered with long, gauzy gowns as if they intended to segue straight from the sand to a ball at the Camino Real. Hypnotically bland voices droned announcements from loudspeakers, a party-animal version of Big Brother. "Hey, all hearty G.M.'s, water polo, side pool in fifteen. Be there!"

Mickey took off his cap and fanned his face. How would they ever survive a week of this? He sat down on the top step, trying to get his bearings. Several well-tended, privileged-looking families were arranged on the grassy knoll to his right. Mickey recognized one of the men; he was an agent at ICM. Perfect.

The men were smoking cigars and playing cards in one group and their wives, who looked interchangeable, as if they had been chosen from some tony West Los Angeles bride-pool twenty years previously, were sunbathing and talking in another group.

"The best egg rolls are from that little joint in Culver City. I know egg rolls. Sung Lee doesn't hold a candle to this place; now for moo shu, you're right, but never egg rolls."

"Their Peking duck is too greasy, gives me the worst heartburn."

"You can't eat Peking duck in L.A., only in New York, at that place on Mott Street Joe Heller used to hang out at. I've told you that maybe a thousand times."

Mickey pulled his cap down and stood up, turning away from the group. The last thing he needed was to be recognized by someone who traveled in packs and could spend endless hours lying around talking about Chinese food.

He missed his wife, another outsider, with whom he had always shared social absurdity. Neither of them had ever fit into that banal, social coziness, the couple connections that served as marriage enhancers. They had always felt that couples who needed other couples around them all the time were couples who did not want to be alone together.

Now, without his wife, he envied their ease. The woozy, schmoozy camaraderie of grown-up people with things in common, relaxed with others like themselves. Neither he nor Annie had ever felt that there were any others like themselves and had always preferred friendships that were unique and special. But now he envied them their sameness.

He took off his shoes and picked up a towel from a stand. A big blond boy about Toby's age came toward him.

"Hi. I'm Chris. Sorry, but these towels are only for the jet-skiers. You've got to go into the fitness center and sign out for your towels."

Mickey blinked at him, frustration rising like bile in his throat. "What?"

"New today, right? Sorry, man, you've gotta go back up the stairs to the fitness center and check out your towels for the week. Don't lose them; there's a humungous towel fee."

Mickey's voice sounded strange, as if he were choking on something. "I have to use the same towel for a week?"

"No, dude, if you don't mind standing in line you can have a fresh one every day, but most folks, hey, they just hang 'em and dry 'em, too much hassle."

Mickey stared at the boy-man. It was almost as if he had wandered into some *Quantum Leap* episode. He could not find common ground with anyone.

The kid looked at him. "You look familiar. Ever been here before?"

"No." Mickey turned away. He no longer had any ego investment in being recognized; he wanted nothing more than to remain invisible for the entire vacation. Where were the kids? He needed contact with someone who loved him.

"Hey, I dig it. You're Jerico. High cool! We've got Fabio here this week, the guy who poses for all the romance-novel covers. Two celebs the same week, far out!"

"No, I'm not —"

"Hey, don't freak. We never, like, gossip about the G.M.'s. We get too many VIPs here. But, like, we work six-month shifts and we don't have TV or newspapers, so anyone from the fame game is, like, connection. Here, man, take the towel. Just bring it back when you're done. Our secret, okay? What you want to do in the a.m. is get down there like at eight when the Step class is going. That way, no line. Dig?"

"You have to *stand in line* to get a towel?"

"Hey, man. That's the Meddie way. Stand in line, meet the person in front of you, behind you; it's a social opportunity is how we see it."

Mickey took the towel. "Thanks for the tip," he said, in the same strangled voice. He walked down the beach looking for his children. He had not seen so many people on one beach since he was a kid at Coney Island with his parents.

Maybe he was wrong. Maybe somehow this privacy-violating and depersonalizing place was exactly what they needed. He and Annie were no longer an island in such streams, they were now a part of the flotsam from many shores, cast adrift in a world run by people who could live pleasantly for six months at a time without reading a newspaper.

What was the Club Med ad line — "Leave the world behind"? What did that really involve, anyway? Well, there was certainly nothing and no one here but one another to connect them to what they were running away from. Maybe all of this was part of a sort of marital time-out: "We are calling a time-out, sports fans. Mickey and Annie Wilder are taking ten at opposite ends of the field to rethink the game plan and catch their breath after a helluva third quarter — twenty-three, count 'em, years on the field!"

Mickey dove into the water, letting the salty coolness clear his confusion. This phantasmagoria of international trendies might be perfect. Because the truth was that as much as he missed his wife and longed for their closeness, the two weeks that he had been given, the joker's gift of a dead father-in-law providing him with time to sink to the bottom as his brother had advised, fuck that woman out of his system, had not broken the spell. He was not cured, he was not back, and sometime before this week was over his wife would slide open the doors between them and make him admit this terrible truth to her sun-kissed face.

If religion is the opiate of the masses, then adaptability is the Xanax of the American middle class. What is unmanageable, frustrating, and disorienting on arrival becomes an effortless part of daily ritual by day five.

Once the Wilders found their personal paths through the Med maze, they discovered, to their mutual amazement, that they were actually having a good time. They now had their towel-procuring, bead-buying, chaise-finding routines down to a science and knew the best restaurant and the seating areas that gave them privacy. Annie was taking dance classes and swimming every body of water on the grounds. She had her book bag and her spot under a tree at the far end of the prettiest beach, where, it seemed, no one else wanted to sit. They were all having a wonderful time people-watching at this voyeur's paradise, and their endless eavesdropping filled their meal conversations with enough humor and small talk to mute the underlying issues.

Toby and Ella had taken up with a pair of Iranian brothers from Great Neck, Long Island ("Beverly Hills with snow," Annie called it) who, though cocky and spoiled, were veritable walking textbooks of Club Med information, and had even taught Mickey and the kids the Club Med song and dance, which was performed by the entire populace at the conclusion of each night's entertainment.

Mickey was working out and had accepted a tennis invitation from the ICM agent, which had turned into daily games with enough show-biz small talk to make him feel as if his career was still viable.

It was a perfect place to avoid one another without the slightest awkwardness. The kids hanging out on the beach, Annie in the shade with her hat and her books, Mickey trying everything, wind surfing, snorkeling, jet skis, even deep-sea fishing.

In the evenings the G.O.'s madly lip-synced the entire production of *Grease,* the Michael Jackson video, and several scaled down versions of Broadway shows. There was disco dancing and parlor games, and by the time they staggered, usually one at a time, back up the nineteen flights to their room, everyone was too satiated and exhausted from the strains and stresses of recreation and pleasure-seeking to deal with anything but an aspirin and a shower.

But, as with all avoidance, sooner or later the subpoena is served, the phone is answered, and the faint click turns the tiny, ticking bomb from petard to plastique. It may well be that this inevitable explosion is the price avoiders pay for delaying facing up to the reality of their situations.

There was no particular order to the explosions, and they began separately, each family member starting out the day aware that the vacation was coming to an end and that certain agendas were still piled neatly in their folders, waiting for the meeting to be called. But no one knew the agendas of the others, or that Toby, who really had no agenda but his unhappiness at school, would wander into the main reception area after his water polo game to have his swollen finger looked at by the Club physician.

At his mother's urging he had come in from the sun and taken a number and hunkered down in the waiting room with his last week's copy of *Sports Illustrated.* When he heard the page, he didn't react. There were no phones in the rooms, or anywhere in the resort but at the main clubhouse. A great deal of explanation had been given to them the first day about receiving or making phone calls, but none of them had paid much attention. After all, they had come here to get away from all the junk at home.

When he heard his father's name being called, his first thought was that it was his uncle Jackie calling to tell them he had found Leonard Lewis. There was no possible way to reach his father in time and so he jumped up, holding his throbbing finger against his chest.

The brunette with the Farrah Fawcett hair from their first day was working the desk and she told him where to go and how to receive the call. He ran across the lobby, flinging open the door to the phone booth and punching the code she had given him into the phone.

The connection was full of static and it was hard to hear.

"Hello?" he said, too loudly, as if compensating for the distance between callers.

"I couldn't help it, don't be angry with me, baby. It feels like you've been gone forever! I just needed to hear your voice. I did something new, in your honor. I threw my first penis pot. I'm calling it the Big Prick. It looks just like yours, Michael. I can even suck it. Why didn't you call me? You promised!"

Toby could feel his heart flapping against his ribs as if he were being pursued, chased by some fearsome thing.

Maybe it was a mistake. He shivered, his damp swimsuit chilling him. "Who is this?"

"Michael?" The woman hesitated. "Excuse me, is this Michael Wilder on the line?"

Toby felt dizzy. He took a deep breath. He was not going to fucking faint. He had to think.

"Just teasing," he said, keeping his voice low. He sounded enough like his father on the phone now to get away with it.

"You scared me for a minute. Calling in there is quite an experience. I hope you're surviving the dreadful place. It must be America at its cultural worst."

"Yeah. Where are you?"

"Well, I didn't go to Santa Fe. I worked right through Christmas. Saint Clare in Ojai. I toasted myself with that fabulous Chardonnay you gave me, but it's not the same as licking it off your big, hard cock."

The words came at him like punches, body blows, curling him up in the booth, his heart slamming against his chest. *She was talking about his father.*

"Sorry. It's a bad connection. I've gotta go."

He slammed down the receiver and rested his head against the side of the booth. He felt himself slipping away. *Please don't let me faint.* Sobs shook him. *Oh, God, everything's going to end now.*

What he and Ella had been sniffing out, like their poor dead dog looking endlessly for invisible bones, were the secrets of their parents' life. They had felt something; Ella first, but after his grandfather died, he had felt it too; his mother was different and they were different together. Something was missing, something had changed.

Hearing about the series being canceled and the money missing had actually been a relief, because that did not threaten his family, his protection on the earth. One husky obscene voice, murmuring in his ear, had ripped his childhood out from under him.

When they came together for their last dinner, they all could feel the shift. The ease was gone. The end-of-trip letdown, they murmured, feeling the tension.

Toby was silent, the pain in his face attributed to his sprained and bandaged finger. As far as Ella knew, it was she and she alone who was about to toss the grenade. She had waited as long as she could and she had to tell them tonight. She was taking a different flight, back to New York rather than to California with Toby and her parents.

"Are we up for one more night of dessert debauchery?" Annie said, trying to keep up her chirpy patter, but wearing down under the weight of the other moods.

Ella put down her fork. "Before dessert, I've got to talk to you both about something really important."

Annie and Mickey met eyes, the parental bonding outmaneuvering their estrangement. "Sure, honey." Annie smiled at her. "Is it about law school?"

Ella shook her head. "Mom, don't lead it, okay? Just let me get it out. I've met someone."

Another Mickey-Annie look. Mickey lifted a curl off his daughter's face. "Great!"

"His name is Willy Watts and he's the most wonderful person I've ever known. I met him at the diner and we just . . . it was like in a movie. . . . We just fell totally in love."

Toby, who knew what was coming, leaned back in his chair and closed his eyes.

"What does he do?" Annie said, wanting to kick herself immediately for the obvious mother question.

"He's a wine and food writer and he owns his own restaurant. He's traveled everywhere and he knows so much. I've never been with anyone like him."

Toby tapped his good fingers on the table; this was just about unbearable. He knew it was not going well, even without the fact that he might beat his father's face in before Ella got to the punch line.

"What's the name of his restaurant?" Mickey asked, trying to keep the concern out of his voice.

"It's so neat. It's just like his name, 'Willy Watts.' It's a huge success."

Annie and Mickey looked at her. Annie shrugged. "I've never heard of it. Where is it?"

Ella took a long, deep breath. "In Australia."

Silence. Toby increased his tapping. Annie sipped her wine,

which she somehow knew was not a good choice for one approaching the end of a very short pier. "*Australia?* As in north is south, day is night, Sydney Opera House, and 'Put another shrimp on the barbie'?"

"It's in a fancy suburb near Melbourne. I know that this is a big surprise to you. I don't know why I didn't tell you about him. It was like it was so precious and special and personal that I just couldn't tell anyone. I've always told you guys everything, but I've never been in love before and somehow I just couldn't. I was going to tell you Thanksgiving, but it was all too chaotic, and then after Grandpa died and the money and all, I just didn't want to upset you."

Mickey's jaw was so tight his teeth ached. "Why would your falling in love upset us?"

"Not that part." Ella looked straight into her mother's eyes. "Willy's asked me to marry him. I've turned over the lease on my apartment to Gwennie's cousin and I'm moving to Melbourne in March to be with him. I was hoping that he would be able to come back here and meet you all before I went, but he's so busy right now. He's really going to try to come to California with me in the summer so we can all spend some time together. He'd really like to come sooner, but it's so far away and it's really expensive to go back and forth."

Toby sighed and lowered his head. He was trying to keep from jumping up and smashing everything on the table.

"So far away," Annie said, as if talking in her sleep.

Mickey cleared his throat. "Ella, honey, it's not . . . please believe that it's not that we're not happy for you, but you're talking about running off to the other side of the planet to marry a man that you hardly know and that we've never even heard of before ten minutes ago. You're still just a baby."

"Mom was younger than I am when she married you, she already had me at my age, and I *do* know him! We were together every single second, practically, for the entire three months he was in New York. I feel like he's my soul mate, like I've known him all of my life. Besides, he's older, he's thirty, and he's established. It's not like he was just some stranger who wandered in. My boss has known him for a long time. They studied together at the Cordon Bleu in Paris and he thinks he's a genius."

"Australia," Annie said again, the trance of disconnection lifting and dumping yet another unwanted truth onto her already full plate. "Ella! This is us you're talking to! We've never, even bicoastal, gone longer than two months apart in your entire life! We talk on the phone almost every day! You're talking about Australia! Our *winter* is their *summer*!

"You might as well be heading up the first moon colony in terms of how often we'll see you. Oh, God!" Annie's body was trembling; she put her face in her hands, grateful that they were at a table behind a palm tree, out of view of all those sparkling eyes. "Everything. I'm losing everything I love."

Ella burst into tears, slamming her fist on the table. "That's not fair! It isn't something that I'm doing to you. I'm suffering, too! Don't you think I know what I'm losing? My family has been my entire life! I've never even had a real boyfriend! It was always like, if I had you guys and Toby, I didn't even need anyone else. But I'm a grown woman now. If I don't let go of you, I'll end up like all of those retards around me, still living their parents' lives at thirty and never growing up!

"I didn't plan to fall in love with someone from Australia, Mom! I didn't plan on falling in love or getting married for years, but I have, and now it's all I think about, moving there and getting married to Willy and starting my own life and my own family."

Annie tried to stop crying. She was appalled at herself.

This was not how she wanted to let her daughter go. She felt as if she were standing on the roof of a flood-ravaged house, and she had climbed up as far as she could and still the water was licking at her heels. There was nowhere for her to go but into the current. Her father, her dog, her security, her marriage, and her daughter.

"Ella, sweetheart, please don't cry. I'm so sorry. I just . . . it's not been the best fall, honey, and it's just, you know how mothers are. I just never thought that when you got married or started a family I wouldn't, that we wouldn't, be part of it all."

Annie tried again. "This Willy Wonka . . ."

"*Watts,* Mother."

"Watts. Willy Watts. Gee, it sounds like some new high-tech lightbulb or something. Does he have a nice family?"

Ella wiped her eyes. "I think so. They're very close. He talks about them a lot. He has two sisters, and his father is a barrister and his mother is an artist. They sound like fun."

Mickey blew his nose into his napkin. "Does he know that you haven't told us any of this until now?"

"Yes. He kept telling me to. He wanted to come out and meet you before he went back, but I just couldn't deal with it then. I guess maybe it was too hard for me to accept what it meant. What leaving home really meant. If I told you, then it was real. It's not his fault; he's a very elegant person. It was me."

Mickey looked at Toby, who had closed his eyes again.

"What about you, Tob? Did you know?"

Toby nodded, not making contact. "Yeah, she told me Thanksgiving."

"What do you think about it all?"

Toby opened his eyes. Anger at his father snaked through his stomach, nauseating him. He was barely holding on.

"It's her life. It's her business."

Mickey looked at Annie. "What kind of a snotty answer is that?"

Toby shrugged. "Sorry. It just came out that way."

"Well, I can see that, but what's the attitude about?"

Toby hunched forward, avoiding his eyes. "No attitude."

Annie stopped crying. Something else was happening here.

"Toby, what's wrong?"

"Nothing. Can't I just be a little bummed out? Does everything have to be the fucking Spanish Inquisition? No wonder she wants to move to Australia; it's the only way she'll get any peace from the laser beams."

"Hey, that's enough. Don't you talk to your mother like that. Since when is loving you two and being concerned about you an invasion of your privacy? We give you kids more space and respect than any parents I know."

"Yeah, well, maybe that makes it easier for you, too."

Mickey's face was red with rage. "What's that supposed to mean? How dare you talk to me like that!"

Annie touched his arm. "Mickey, calm down."

Toby tried to stand up. He was so dizzy, he could hardly move. "I gotta get out of here."

Ella pulled him back down. "Toby, what's the matter with you? Are you sick?"

He nodded, bending his head down between his legs. Annie stood up, dipping her napkin in her ice water and coming around to place it on the back of his neck. "Honey, try to take some deep breaths." She knelt beside him, the way she used to when he was small and sick from all the junk no one could ever stop him from eating.

He could smell his mother's warm, fresh, lemony smell. No one ever smelled as good as his mother. He opened his eyes a little, trying to focus, and saw her small, freckled hand on his leg; something about that hand was too painful for him. He pushed back in his chair away from his mother, knocking the plastic party seat over. His father jumped up, crossing to him and grabbing him by his hurt hand. "Toby, what the fuck's the matter with you?"

"With me? Nothing's the matter with me, Mr. Perfect Family Man! Why don't you check the reception desk? See if they have any messages for you, Mr. Big Shot TV Star Asshole!"

Toby pushed him away and ran off, hitting the stairs and moving up, gagging on his own vomit, not feeling the embarrassment that would have, at any other time, mortified him down to the marrow of his almost-nineteen-year-old bones. His family was falling apart. His father had betrayed them and his sister was leaving him forever. He lurched up the stairs, a wounded creature whimpering in the moonlight.

Annie knew instantly that Toby knew the truth. Ella would know soon. They had lost the right to lecture their children on family loyalty or romance etiquette. Ella went after Toby, and Annie and Mickey took the cart up, sitting in silence on their last vacation night, maybe their last vacation night anywhere.

When Mickey was in bed, Annie slid open the door between them, standing in the shadows, quiet as the sky.

"I've met someone too, Mickey. I almost had sex with him the day I met him — even before I knew for sure that you were having an affair. He just overwhelmed me. He asked me to meet him in London and I'm going to do it. I suddenly realized when I saw Toby's face that the reason we haven't had the big scene is that there isn't one written.

"You have nothing to say to me, because you are still sleeping with this woman and are obviously not willing or able to stop. You've lied to me and you've cheated on me, but I don't really hate you for it or anything. I'm more scared and hurt than angry now. It probably had to happen sooner or later, and it happened to both of us at almost the same time.

"I mean, I'm not excusing you. My attraction to this man was hardly planned, and it certainly isn't the same as you sneaking around and betraying me. For a while I thought maybe my whole marriage had been a lie. You weren't who I thought you were; you've been out there all along catting around like the rest of the jerks; but I know in my heart that isn't true. I don't think that anymore, Mickey. But whatever made it happen, neither of us is ready to let all of this new information go. I think we've come to a crossroads and we have to take some wrong turns, maybe, before we either find our way back together or to the right road for us to walk alone.

"I don't care about anything right now except not hurting those kids any more than we already have. And we still have our financial situation and you have to go to Japan and all of that. We have to keep our wits about us."

He sat up in the dark, staring at her as if he had never seen her before. He had not heard one single word that she had said after, "I almost had sex with him the day I met him." Annie. *His* Annie and some strange man? He could not absorb this.

"Now there are no more secrets," she said, and slipped back between the walls.

Just before dawn Mickey came into her room, slipping in beside her, and she held him while he cried. They held on to one another and they cried together at the loss of one another and for the pain they had brought into the lives of the people they loved most. They held one another, knowing that it would not change or fix anything, that it would not heal or absolve. They merely gave comfort in the way that married people who have been through hard times and swell times together can give comfort. They were trying not to lose, along with everything else, the essence of their bond.

PART III

AS LONG AS YOU BOTH SHALL . . .

CHAPTER XII

LINA ALLEN tightened the paper sash on the disposable robe, wishing she had put on some lipstick. She sighed, leaning back on the table.

Why bother, since nothing would help, not with this lighting! For a good part of her career she had fervently believed that everything in life was timing. Now she just as fervently believed that everything in life, her life, anyway, was *lighting*.

She reached inside the horrible green paper and scratched. The itching was driving her crazy. It was bad enough to break out in hives, or whatever the disgusting things all over her body were, but now they were moving onto her face.

A tap on the door.

"Come in." She sat up, arranging the folds of her flimsy protection.

Martin Miller opened the door and stepped into the room, filling the small, aggressively bright space with his gawky presence.

"Miss Allen? I'm Dr. Miller."

"I think we met at Annie and Mickey's."

He looked into the folder, which held Lina's medical information, a safer view of her than the actual person. Forty-six years old, actress, single. No family history of asthma, diabetes, or hypertension. No mental illness, whooping cough, or fainting spells. Suffers from migraine headaches and low estrogen levels, for which Premarin is taken.

"Yes, I know. I didn't think you'd remember me." He smiled without looking at her and Lina could see a faint pinch of color touch his chalk white pallor.

"I didn't think you'd remember me, either, so we're even in the lack-of-self-esteem contest."

"Well, you know, we all look different in the real world."

Lina laughed. "What a relief. I thought you were going to say 'with our clothes on.'"

He refocused on her folder. He *was* blushing. He did have a certain shy sweetness about him, so unlike the kind of guys she usually met.

"I don't mean to start out with a complaint, doctor, but considering that most people come in here with something fairly unattractive growing out of them, a dimmer or two just for the initial meeting would be much more calming."

He put her folder down on his desk. "You're right, of course. Doctors do have a tendency to depersonalize. This is, after all, a physician's operating theater, not a piano bar, but factoring in the patient's comfort and self-consciousness is important. I apologize."

Lina felt like crying. Was she so vulnerable that having even her lighting concept validated could bring her to tears?

"That's very kind of you. I'm wrong to complain, but you know how actresses are: vain till the end. I've never even had the courage to see a male dermatologist before, didn't want any man to see me at anything but my best."

He sat down on his stool, bringing them closer together. "Anything better would be gilding the lily," he said.

Now *she* was blushing. "Don't kid a kidder, doc. I know how I look. I look like shit. I need my eyes done; I need a major peel *and* a face lift; I need lipo on my stomach, and its almost time for the minoxidil; even with the damn estrogen my hair's thinning out. But since our dear Leonard Lewis disappeared, I'm lucky to be paying my plant maintenance, so to speak. I mean I'm working pretty steady, but there's a big payment delay so the old cash flow is fairly slow, and I'm supposed to play in a celebrity tennis tournament this weekend in Palm Springs but I've broken out in these horrible, itchy, ugly things all over the place and I'm desperate."

"Lie back then and let's have a look. Desperate tennis-playing film stars are my specialty." He stood up and gently guided her back down onto the table, to the sound of sterile paper crackling.

"Hardly a film star," she mumbled, tears welling in her eyes. He was being so nice to her. She hadn't realized how lonely she was, how needy for someone to confide in. Annie had been away, and Leonard, to whom she had always gone as father confessor and ego-booster, was history.

She closed her eyes while he slipped his long, bony fingers into his sterile gloves and delicately opened her robe, inspecting her angry, throbbing bumps.

"What is it?" she asked, tears sliding down the sides of her face and onto the paper covering her resting place.

"Turn over," he said softly, and she did.

"How long have you had this?"

"Well, that's kind of hard to say. I had some right after I found out about my money being gone. I just put calamine on them and they went away. Then, a few days ago they just started popping out all over, but I was shooting a commercial so I just ignored them."

He stopped touching her and she felt deprived — his touch had been so comforting. She really was in trouble.

"Okay, you can get dressed now. When you're ready, come next door to my office and we'll talk." He picked up her folder and smiled at her. "The lighting's somewhat better in there."

She laughed without turning over. Thankful that he was allowing her to reclaim her dignity, such as it was.

She pulled her sweater over her head and stepped into her shoes, shaking out her hair and reaching for her makeup bag. Why had she revealed all of her flaws to this man, doctor or not? What was it that she wanted? She never talked about the things she was insecure about to anyone, not even to Annie. She was always too afraid someone would agree with her. Why did she trust him with all of that information?

Maybe it was that the unhappiness in his eyes reminded her of herself.

She pulled out her compact and looked in the small mirror. God, she really did look like shit, even without the three swollen, red lumps on her cheek. Maybe Jackie would loan her the money to get the plastic surgery done so she could extend her shelf life by a few more years anyway.

What was she saying? She had never in her entire life borrowed a dime from anyone, let alone a man! Well, this was somewhat different, more like a small-business tax credit for updating the office supply system, or a home improvement loan.

What if she ended up hawking Chia Pets on cable ads or like poor Dionne Warwick with her Psychic Friends Network ("All it takes to find happiness is a phone and an open mind"!). Oh, God, it was too depressing to think about.

She wasn't even a drug addict, or a recovering alcoholic, or an incest survivor. She couldn't even revive a faltering career by coming out with some bio-purge revealing bouts of chocolate-cheesecake gluttony or one-night stands with celebrities while under the influence of some noxious substance or other. Maybe she could make something up.

She powdered her face and reached into her bag for her lip-liner. Why was she doing this to herself? She was still working and the phone was still ringing and she had her pre-Leonard agent back, who was very hot at the moment. She had to get a grip. Now that Christmas and New Year's were over and Annie was back, she'd be better. They'd really dig into the Leonard search and she'd feel more in control.

Actually, even without her money disappearing, she never felt normal during the holidays. From Thanksgiving until New Year's Day, she was always a total wreck, but this year had been the worst; this year if there had been an ambulatory man in her life she would probably have tied him up, thrown him into the trunk of her car, driven to Las Vegas, and married the poor bastard. She had been alone too long; her survival skills were breaking down.

Every Christmas card she opened was like a red-hot ember on a freshly burned palm.

The worst were the ones that most reminded her of her country-club childhood and always featured a typed account of the sender's past year.

These people seemed to have no daily life, but simply segued from kayaking in Wyoming, to scuba diving in Mexico, stopping off here and there to marry off their children, attend law school graduations, pick up awards, and crew on yachts named after fish or sea shells.

The updates were always written in the third person as if a truly stupefied biographer, having run through every life that held any interest to the world, had been reduced to churning out annual holiday greetings from the American establishment. "It was a year of equine accomplishments. Muffy and Drew deftly managed large horses over wooden fences and both Buff and Harper wrangled written words into print!" Yahoo.

She really had no one left from her childhood that played any real part in her present life; they had been laid to rest with her parents long ago.

But the cards still found her, letting her know that that world still existed, like a parallel reality lived invisibly, almost in another dimension. This year, it had hurt. This year she had faltered, regretting her choices, stumbling over the sanctimonious smuggery of these other lives. She had fallen asleep Christmas Day with the pile of letters clutched against her chest, sobbing, beneath the Dalmaine, "I know this isn't real, their lives are not this safe." "On the sailing front, the *Sea Scape*'s crew held its twenty-fifth (gasp!) reunion, a landmark land-and-sea affair for our hearty band. . . ."

Her hand was shaking. She could not line her lips. She sighed, settling for a slash of pink, and left for the promise of better lighting.

She settled into the leather chair facing him, using all of her finishing-school poise. If there was one thing she knew how to do, it was sit down.

"Will I live?"

He smiled at her. "I certainly hope so. If not, it will have absolutely nothing to do with your skin condition." He reached for his prescription pad. "You diagnosed yourself. You have a rather robust case of hives, and since you said in your questionnaire that you aren't allergic to anything and haven't tried any new cosmetics or medications in the last month, I think it's safe to assume that the outbreak is psychogenic."

"My mind's doing it to my epidermis?"

"Correct. I'm going to give you some topical medicines to deal with the body part and something for the itching. Do you have a therapist or would you like me to prescribe something for your nerves? I'm not much of a Dr. Feel Good, but with something like this and especially since you have a public appearance coming up, it can be tremendously helpful."

"Yes, please, and is there anything cosmetically that I can put over the ones on my legs? My tennis skirt is fairly revealing."

He was blushing again. "Yes, as a matter of fact, I have something that was developed for burn patients. It's quite remarkable, miraculous, really."

He reached behind his desk and handed her a bottle. "You're very fair skinned. This should work nicely."

She took the bottle and the prescriptions. "Thanks," she said, feeling the tears pushing against her lashes again.

He looked at her, reaching for a Kleenex without comment.

"Miss Allen —"

"Lina, please."

"Lina. I don't want to be presumptuous, but I have some idea what you're going through and I know how much my sister cares about you, so, if you'd like, I can do a very safe and effective cosmetic peel on you. Really, you look fine, you have beautiful skin, but I know what you're up against out there. I'd be glad to donate my services."

She blew her nose, knowing that what was left of her face would crumble with it, but no longer caring. She tried to smile at him, but she was crying too hard.

He waited, awkward in his kindness, obviously not used to such open displays of anyone's emotions.

He stood up and left the room, returning with a cold cloth for her face. She had calmed down and she managed a shaky smile. "No one's been this nice to me in a very long time."

"That's too bad," he said, returning to his seat.

"Look, I'm not very good at accepting things, especially from men, even ones I know, but if you mean it, I will pay you as soon as we find Leonard Lewis."

"No. This is a gift. I don't like loans."

Lina folded the damp cloth neatly and placed it on his desk. She put the prescriptions in her purse, closing it primly. She uncrossed her legs and leaned forward.

"Well, then, if that's the deal, how about a trade? An all-expenses paid weekend in Palm Springs — the only string attached is that you might have to watch me play tennis."

Martin looked stunned. He opened his mouth, but nothing came out.

She laughed. "I see. No one's been very nice to you lately, either. I'll pick you up Friday evening about six-thirty."

Jackie raced into Rhinehart's office and flung himself into one of the chairs by his desk. He had stopped lying on the couch and started missing appointments.

"I know, I know. I'm sorry. I've got crises on every single one of my fucking shows; my co-hosts on *Under the Covers* are no longer speaking to one another and I spent the night in Edgar's room, hiding from Samantha. I asked her to move out yesterday and she went ballistic. I mean we're talking major meltdown. She chased me down the hall with my free weights! *Edgar* was afraid to deal with her. She tore around my house with a bottle of Jack Daniel's in her hand, screaming and ranting and raving, all night long. I almost called you twice. I almost called the police about ten times, but she finally wore herself out.

"Edgar carried her out while she was sleeping it off and we drove her to the Beverly Wilshire and checked her in. He had to fucking lug her up the service stairs! But *I* feel fantastic! I did it! I broke the spell! I'm cured, doc!

"It was like a miracle. It started at Bennie's recital. I'm sitting next to Loretta before the show and she's telling me a story and suddenly

I'm all choked up with these feelings, and I'm thinking, you poor pathetic little schmuck, you have never been out with a woman who was interesting enough to *talk* to, let alone *listen* to!

"Even Samantha, I mean, she wasn't a helium head, but she was so off the wall it was almost as boring, not to mention that the woman was incapable of any honest or direct exchange. Everything, including 'pass the salt,' had a secondary agenda.

"So I'm like practicing on Loretta. Because she's safe — I mean she's like family, but she's still a woman alone with me and I'm conversing. I mean here is this funny, smart, decent lady I can talk to, someone I can share with as an equal! Where have I fucking been all of my life! Unbelievable!

"We're kibitzing with one another, and I felt really comfortable with her, and pow! — I came to. I thought, *yes,* this is what I want — a real relationship.

"I don't even want to dwell on it and spoil how fantastic I feel, to be free of that bimbo shit.

"Is this possible? I mean, can it really just vanish like that? After all these years of repeating the pattern? Tell me I'm not headed for some major shoe-dropping here?"

Rhinehart laughed. Jackie took a breath. Rhinehart rarely even smiled at him, let alone laughed.

The doctor took off his glasses and placed them neatly before him on his desk. Jackie had never seen him without his wire-rims. It made him uneasy. It was too personal.

"The answer to your question is yes, though your perception that this is some sudden lightning bolt of change is not correct. It has been a long, painful, but steady climb to the peak of your problem.

"Many events in your life in the past months have accelerated your climb, but there is always the moment, if one is very, very fortunate, that the top is reached. Very much like birth and death; the gestation period goes on and on, the birthing process seems an eternity, and then, suddenly, there is the moment of birth, of arrival. And we go through it again with death. You may fall ill and suffer and wither away, but you are still alive, and alive until the moment you depart.

"The same is true with human change. Nothing appears to be changing, but small, seemingly insignificant bits and pieces of old thinking and neurotic patterns give way imperceptibly. Then resistance rushes forth, regression or what seems like regression appears; round and round it goes, but the road is always pushing you slowly upward, and if you don't give up, eventually you reach the top of the mountain.

"So, no, I am not as surprised as you are; I have seen this coming for some time now, and no, you don't have to be afraid that some giant clodhopper is going to fall on your head. Not that you won't have some backsliding, and of course there is still that entire other side of the mountain to climb down, all new and never before attempted. But it is *down.* It is healthier and happier and ultimately easier. I am very proud of you and I am very happy for you."

Jackie let his breath out and sank back in his chair. Rhinehart had never talked to him like this before. It was almost as if a favorite inanimate object had suddenly come to life, as if the toy soldiers in the *Nutcracker* or his beloved old stuffed panda had suddenly strolled over and struck up a conversation.

Rhinehart leaned forward a little and smiled at him again.

"Jackie, it is time for you to go. I have kept you here too long, but I'll admit something to you. You are my favorite patient. I have so enjoyed you. You are a fresh breath of air in here and I will miss you."

Jackie was frightened. "I was? You will?"

Rhinehart scratched his egg-smooth head. "Jackie, I would not be telling you this if it wasn't time for you to go, and go as a grown-up man. You have always put me a little bit up on a pedestal, and this is a better angle from which to view me from now on."

Rhinehart put his glasses back on and stood up.

Jackie took a deep breath, not quite ready to relinquish his chair.

Rhinehart waited, making room for Jackie to depart.

Jackie eased himself slowly up, noticing for the first time in ten years that he was slightly taller than his savior.

CHAPTER XIII

ANNIE FELL BACK against her pillows, blowing her nose so hard her ears finally popped. A raging upper-respiratory infection and a collapsed family unit were her souvenirs from their week at Club Med.

The only good thing about feeling this rotten was that it gave her an excuse for crawling under the covers and not dealing with any of it. She rubbed some Vicks onto her chest and picked up the paper. So much had happened since they'd been gone. Famous people had died, gotten married, been hired and fired all without her knowledge. She just hated to be out of touch.

They had even gone out and changed the names of the city zoos! Negative stereotyping or some politically correct animal-rights fanatics' mumbo-jumbo. She had really liked the name "zoo." Somehow it wouldn't be the same, taking the kids to the "Animal Wilderness Protected Species Enclave" or whatever they were going to call them now.

Not that she had zoo-age kids anymore. Maybe if she went to Australia to visit Ella when Ella had kids, she could take them to the zoo there. Maybe they were so far away that the name controversy wouldn't apply for quite a while. One could only hope.

Ella. Australia. She sneezed and reached for another Kleenex. Where did all the mucus come from? It seemed impossible that the human body could pump out such an inexhaustible supply. She felt like some small, self-contained manufacturing plant. Too bad there wasn't much demand for what she was producing.

She sighed, leaning back and closing her eyes again. It was no use. She was too light-headed to concentrate. The house was so quiet, not familiar to her at all. Juanita was still on vacation with her sister, Portia was gone forever, and Mickey was back in L.A. cleaning out the apartment and finishing up the last *War Zone* bits, or at least so he said. She was no longer trusting of anything.

The O'Brians had gone home to New Orleans for the holidays and were still away, and Toby had been like the Philly Flash, up and out every morning first thing, totally defensive and noncommittal about where he was going. He was taking advantage of her illness to log some major car time, which was fine with her, since he was also doing the marketing and running her errands.

He had not spoken one word to Mickey since that horrible last night in Mexico, and the tension between them was so unbearable, she was grateful that Mickey was now in L.A. and would be leaving for Japan in a day or so. Maybe then she could try to talk to Toby and help him sort things out.

She coughed, feeling the honking tightness in her chest. Great; the damn infection was moving down. She had to get better and start focusing on Leonard. She couldn't let Jackie and Lina and Billy carry the burden. If she could just get a few days' rest, she'd be fine.

She heard Toby's squeaking-sneaker steps in the hall. "Tob?"

Toby stopped at her door and pushed it open a crack.

Annie looked at the clock. It was only nine A.M. This new up-and-out Toby was unsettling. Usually when he was home on vacation you needed a police whistle to rouse him before noon.

He poked his head in, wearing her Mets cap backward, framing his suntanned face. "Hi. I didn't want to wake you up. How're you feeling?" He looked worried and sad. They weren't used to seeing her sick.

"I'm okay. Nothing a new nasal passage wouldn't fix. I feel like I've got the Alaskan Pipeline hooked up to my sinuses."

He laughed and moved a little into the room, unwilling to make the commitment of his entire body. "Want me to make you some breakfast before I go?"

She smiled at him. "Thanks, *Mom,* I'm fine."

He grinned, her favorite grin. "How's about tea with lemon and double honey like you always gave us."

"That would be great, if it's not too much trouble."

"Well, of course it is. It's a really serious imposition, but you *are* my only mother so I'll just have to deal with it. Be right back."

He was gone before she could ask him the obvious next question, which was where he was going, which was of course the reason he had left so quickly. It was obviously none of her business.

How does one talk to one's son about intercepting a phone call from one's father's mistress? Doctor Spock had not written on the subject and neither had anyone else to her knowledge. She sneezed again, her head feeling light and heavy at the same time. She was not going to cry, for her son's sake, not to mention her poor, overworked membranes.

She did not know how to help him through this and neither, it seemed, did Mickey, who was completely devastated by Toby and Ella's rejection. He had been their hero and he had compromised himself — possibly beyond all repair — with the three people he loved most on earth. She felt sorry for him, she truly did.

God, what a mess! She had never for a moment believed that it would come to this, that their children would be dragged into her and Mickey's problems! That was the most unbearable part of the entire thing as far as she was concerned.

Toby had another week of vacation and then he would be gone, and maybe nothing would be settled between any of them.

He kicked open the door and came forward, carrying a tray with an entire pot of tea and some toast with peanut butter and a rose from her garden in a little silver vase.

"Aw, Tob, you dog, you."

He put the tray down, daintily for him, and started for the door. "I'll be back later. Want me to pick up something for dinner?"

"Dinner? It's only nine A.M. Where are you going?"

"I've got some things to do and I'm going to hang at the courts and see if I can pick up a volleyball game, stuff like that. Do you need me for something? Want me to get you some medicine or anything?"

She smiled at him. She was *not* going to cry. "No, sweetheart. I'm okay. It just seemed like a long time to be out. Take some money from my purse and pick up Chinese or something, whatever you want for dinner; my appetite is nil. I'll see you tonight."

His grin slipped and she saw his unhappiness under it. She knew that he was trying to find a way to talk to her.

"Don't say it, okay?"

Annie laughed. "You know that I am bound by the mother's book of ethics to say it every single time."

"Okay, we'll say it together."

"Okay."

They looked at one another. "Drive carefully and fasten your seat belt."

"I love you, darling."

"I love you too, Momma."

He was gone. Her head felt as if it might just explode, shooting bad thoughts, fear, anger, dreams, memories, rage, mucus, and brain matter all over her pillows.

She poured her tea. Maybe tonight when he came home they would try to talk about it.

Toby fastened his seat belt and slipped his new UB40 tape into the cassette. He hated lying to his mother. He really hated it, but what choice did he have? He could hardly tell her that what he was doing every day was following his father around. His father had come back from L.A. last night and was at that whore's house in Ojai. He could hardly tell his mother that!

He was driving too fast. He released the pressure on the pedal; at least he could keep that promise to her. He hadn't figured out what he was going to do when he got to the witch's house, he was just sort of playing it by ear. If his dad wasn't there, he was going to confront her, tell her to stay away from him. He wasn't totally sure that he would be able to go through with it.

Everything was so messed up! How could this be happening to them? This was the kind of garbage he had watched all of his friends go through. He had probably always felt a little superior — "Not my family, we're different." Yeah, right.

He started up the hill leading to her house. His heart was beating too fast. He drove for a while, not quite remembering how far up it was. Could he have passed it?

CLARE. He checked his rearview mirror and hit the brake. He made his turn and parked behind the bushes at the far end of the driveway.

He got out, locking the car, and crept up the driveway as quietly as he could. His dad's car was nowhere to be seen. He went up the steps to the house, pausing before a handwritten note on the door: "I'm in the studio working. Do not disturb, unless a matter of utmost urgency."

As far as Toby was concerned, he qualified. He followed the only path around to the back of the house. He could see her or someone inside. He climbed the brick steps and knocked. He was really nervous now. He wished that he had spent more time figuring out what he wanted to say.

The door opened. A big, broad-faced woman with bushy hair stood before him. She was almost his height. She looked mean and kind of scary. *This* was the woman his dad was hurting his mother for? His beautiful, kind, lovely mother? It didn't seem possible. He didn't really know what he had envisioned, but she was totally not it. Maybe someone like Sharon Stone or something, some sex bomb who had fried his father's brain. He must really not know him at all — that was the only possible explanation.

"Yes?" the witch said, giving him a kind of snotty, appraising smile.

"I'm Toby Wilder. I'd like to talk to you," he said, surprised at how steady his voice sounded.

She stepped back and motioned him forward.

"Come in," she said, far too cool for his taste. He wanted to smash her face. "I'm in the middle of glazing a piece so I only have a few moments to waste."

Waste. That was what they were to her. Now he understood how people killed people. Of course he had thought he knew; he had certainly wanted to murder his sister often enough but that was different. Because at the same time he was furious at Ella he always knew he still loved her.

He followed the woman inside. She was wearing a scrub suit or something, like the ones they sold at the Army/Navy surplus in Providence, right along with camouflage outfits, Russian army coats, and Israeli desert boots. He had always thought that the kids who bought that stuff were dorky and insecure, and *she* was hardly a kid. His father had really lost it.

She picked up her paintbrush and went back to work as if he were just some delivery boy or something. She hadn't even asked him to sit down or if he wanted a cold drink or anything like his mother would have done. His mother even asked the kid who brought the pizza if he wanted a cup of coffee.

"You look like your father," she said, not even pretending to be innocent of why he might be standing in her studio like that.

"Yeah, I know." He crossed his arms over his chest, the way he had since he was a baby; his mother called it his pouting pose. "No touch me," he would say, and cross his little pudgy arms over his sleepers.

He waited, never having been in a situation like this. Somehow he thought that she should ask him the first question. She didn't, but nonchalantly dabbed patina on the stupid pot shaped like a big fat boob or something.

His anger was building. She was not only hideous, she was really a bitch. "What *is* that?" he said, hating himself for blinking first.

"One of my new single-breast pieces. It's for a museum show in Amsterdam."

"It's really stupid," he said, shocked at himself. His manners were usually pretty good.

She smiled, without stopping or looking at him. "Thanks," she said. "Now would you like to tell me why you're here so I can go on with my work?"

He paused. Somehow, even in his limited eighteen and a half

years of experience in dealing with people other than his family, he knew that she had the upper hand and nothing good could come of his plea. He had expected someone so different. He had expected someone who would be fairly freaked out at his arrival and would be nervous and contrite, or concerned for his poor hurt feelings or something. He didn't know what to do.

"I'm here to ask you to stay away from my father. You're hurting a lot of innocent people and it sure doesn't seem that it's any big deal to you, so why don't you just find another victim and leave our family alone."

She put down her paints and picked up a mug of coffee, taking several small sips. "I see. And why are you telling me this? Wouldn't it be more effective to tell it to him?"

He flushed. "I will. I just wanted to see what I was dealing with. Who you were and what the big attraction was."

She looked at him, her big fluorescent-gray eyes unwavering. He was not used to people who were this completely in control. No one in their lives was like this. Maybe that was what his father was hooked by. Maybe it was like being hypnotized by a great big jungle cat.

"And now that you have seen?"

He uncrossed his arms, drawing himself up as tall as he could. "Now that I have met you, I think he must be having some kind of midlife crisis or something. He couldn't possibly in his right mind choose you over my mother. He'll figure that out sooner or later, so why don't you just cut him loose now. It's obviously no big sweat for you, but it's destroying our family.

"We always had the closest family, and now everything's falling apart and my mother's just buried her father and her dog and my sister's moving away and all their money's gone and my dad's lost his job —" He stopped. He had not meant to reveal so much.

"Please," he said, no longer caring what she thought of his manhood. "Please let him go."

She put down her coffee and ran her hands through her wild, bristled hair. She yawned, as if his pain were too tiring to deal with. "Your father is a big boy. I'm not making him do anything he doesn't want to do. He's free to return to his Little Red Riding Hood any time he wants to."

Flames shot into his brain. He *could* kill her. "Don't you talk about my mother like that! Don't you dare!"

She picked up her paintbrush. "Well, I see where she gets it; you're just as crazy as she is. Please leave now and don't come back."

In one leap he was across to her, kicking over the table holding her coffee and paints. "I'll fucking kill you!"

"Toby!" A male voice coming from behind him. He turned. His father, wearing a robe Toby had never seen, was standing in the doorway, his face drained of all the Mexican sunshine.

Toby was trapped between them, a roped calf frantically looking for the hole in the ring. He turned back to Ivy.

"Take it back, what you said about my mother or I will, I'll fucking kill you!"

Mickey was on him now, holding his arms. "Stop it!"

He struggled, wrenching himself free and turning on his father, his fists up. "Don't fucking touch me!" He was crying, but his anger made him feel invincible. Mickey reached up to grab his wrists and Toby pushed him back as if he were a child or a puppy.

Mickey stared at him. It was the first time they had confronted the new reality of their relationship. Toby was now bigger and stronger than he was. If he wanted to, he could probably beat the crap out of his father. Such a possibility had never before consciously occurred to either of them, and from its truth there was no turning back.

It was the first footprint on the fresh trail of their changing relationship. A trail that threaded its way onward to the ultimate changing of the guard, when the scout, sometimes gently, sometimes violently, moved in front of the lieutenant.

The ease with which he had thwarted his father terrified him even more than it did Mickey, and he turned, stumbling over his own feet and running out the door.

His father did not follow him, which made him angrier and even more frightened. Every time he had been really upset from the day he was able to pull himself up and waddle across a room, his father had always come after him. It was the one thing he could count on, his father coming after him to calm him down, bring him back, cheer him up.

No one came. He had to do something to pay this hurt back, to even the score. He searched around for his father's car. He ran back to the house. Nothing. He started down the driveway, spotting an outbuilding off to the side, half hidden in the brush by a weedy stand of trees, overgrown and wild like the witch herself. It must be a garage.

He ran over and pulled up the door, revealing his father's Porsche. Of course he'd hide it! What if his mother came or some private eye she could have hired to follow him. If his dad was true to form, the keys would be in the glove compartment. Toby slid into the driver's seat and opened the latch. Keys. He slid in the ignition key and without stopping to consider the gravity of his act, he shifted into reverse and backed straight out, turning in the clearing and taking off, leaving his mother's car, locked and all alone at the bottom of the drive. Only it felt like he was leaving his whole family trapped inside the sorceress's house, like Hansel and Gretel, while the fire in her oven was being stoked into flames hot enough to burn them all to a crisp.

He screeched out of the driveway onto the road, downshifting and not caring that he was disobeying his mother's orders. He had to do something to help her. To help all of them. He had to do something to show the entire family how insane they all were right now.

L.A. He would go to L.A. That's where all the trouble started, that's where he would fix it. He would figure it all out on the drive. He didn't give a shit about anything else. Even if his father called the cops and said that he had stolen the car, and they picked him up and threw him in jail. It would be worth it; it already was.

Mickey walked back up the driveway into the studio. Ivy had cleaned up the mess and was sitting on her model's stool, sipping a fresh cup of coffee.

"He took the Porsche. He left Annie's car at the bottom of the driveway, but it's locked and he must have the keys. He's seen too many episodes of *War Zone.*" Mickey sighed. Everything in his entire body hurt in some strange, nonphysical way. It was almost as if his soul ached. He had never felt anything quite like it. "I've got to try and find him."

"Maybe you should just leave him alone for a while. He's no baby."

Mickey watched her, unnerved as always by her control. For some bizarre reason he thought of President Bush falling over at the state dinner in Japan, puking on the prime minister's lap, and then jumping back up and giving the okay sign and making a joke, and Barbara watching the whole thing so calmly and then staying to deliver his speech for him. He had joked with Annie about how Jewish people should probably never be president, because if such a thing happened, the wife would be screaming and running around yelling, "Get the paramedics! Who knows the best doctor in Tokyo?" and the guy would be lying there changing his will. Ivy was like the Bushes.

He rubbed the sides of his aching head. "What did you say to him that made him go off like that?"

She crossed her legs, sipping like one of those Barbie broads in some fucking Maxwell House commercial. "Nothing, really. He was fairly antagonistic and gave some teen manipulation speech to make me feel guilty. I just told him he was as crazy as his mother. In hindsight it was an unfortunate choice of words. Not having children, I tend to underestimate blind faith."

Snap. Mickey felt a shifting inside his chest. A springing sort of release that moved up into his head as if a slingshot had discharged, snapping the thong and bonging the ball right out through the center of his head. *Thwonk.* It was out.

He exhaled. "Dwight Yoakam," he said to himself.

He laughed, feeling a pressure exiting his being. "I just heard it, like Jackie said I would. Dwight Yoakam."

She put down her cup and stood up, throwing her hair back in the way she knew always excited him. "Hey, Michael baby, what are you on about?"

He turned his back on her and walked to the door. He had to get dressed and try to find his spare key. Sometimes he kept one in his toiletry kit. If not, he would have to call a locksmith and waste a lot more time.

"Michael!" There was alarm in her voice now. At least what would pass for alarm in someone like Ivy.

He turned and looked at her. It was unbelievable! It was exactly the way Jackie had described it. What had he ever seen in this woman? He had almost destroyed, maybe *had* destroyed his marriage, for this coldhearted head case?

"I said 'Dwight Yoakam.' It's the Wilski brothers' version of 'It's Over.' You don't belong in the same *century* with my wife. Look, Ivy, I'm sorry to sound so glib. Believe me, I don't feel that way. You have consumed me at the expense of everyone and everything else in my life. It's been so powerful . . . so dark. I've been out of control ever since that afternoon in Stan Stein's greenhouse. I couldn't stay away from you, but God knows, I didn't want to lose myself and my family. The thing is, I'm basically a nice man, and what I just saw without any romantic illusion about your mystery and magic is that you are not a nice person. In fact, you really are what you appear to be. A cold, calculating bitch. You hurt my son and it broke the spell. I'm going home."

He dressed quickly, finding the spare key in his bag, and headed back to Montecito, to see if Toby was there. After that, he had no plans. Actually, if he lost his family, he had no immediate life.

Bennie Miller leaned against the playground fence waiting for his mother. He hated Mondays. She was always late because she had a group, and he always had to wait, while the other after-schoolers chose teams and played basketball or softball or volleyball. The other second-graders didn't want him on their teams. He had hoped that private school would be different, but it wasn't, only a snootier version of the same thing he'd faced since nursery school.

He zipped up his jacket. It was cold and his chest felt a little wheezy. Where was she?

A black Porsche zoomed up, the horn honking. It looked just like his uncle Mickey's car. Bennie watched as it stopped almost in front of him and the driver jumped out.

"Yo, Bennie, how's my main man?"

Toby! What in the world was Toby doing at his school? He waved to him, running toward the gate. Toby met him at the other side by the security guard.

The guard stood up. "Where are you heading, Bennie?"

"It's my cousin, Toby!"

"That's nice, young man, but only your mother is authorized to pick you up today."

Toby put on his most charming, serious attitude. "Sir, my aunt has been unavoidably held up and I just happened to be at her office at the time and she authorized me to pick up my cousin. I have a note with her signature on it, if you're concerned."

The guard looked at Bennie, who was grinning his pumpkin grin and bouncing up and down. "Toby! Neato!"

"All right, just sign here, and put the exact time."

Toby signed, keeping his face impassive. The guard lifted the gate latch, releasing Bennie into the free world.

"Come on, kiddo, let's rock and roll."

Bennie raced after him, letting Toby open the heavy black door for him. Toby ran around and jumped in beside him. "Seat belt, cuz."

Bennie giggled. "This is so great! What were you doing at my mom's office? No one said anything to me."

"I lied. I wasn't at your mother's office. I just faked him out. I took a chance you'd be here. I remembered your mom saying that she had a group on Mondays and it was a bummer making you wait, because of the ball game factor —"

Bennie flushed. "She told you that?"

"Don't be a dork. Of course not, they don't call me Dumbo Ears for nothing. I eavesdropped on some phone call with your dad. She was trying to work out having him pick you up or something. Besides, you don't have to pretend for me; you're a dancer, not some net jock."

Bennie sighed. "But then, why are you here?"

"I'm kidnapping you."

Bennie started to laugh, but changed his mind.

"Give me a break, Toby."

Toby downshifted, stopping at the traffic light.

"I'm serious. Your mother is going to pull up there any minute and freak. Then she is going to yell at several school officials and then she is going to call my parents, which is the purpose of this whole event. We're making a statement."

Bennie's eyes were bulging out of his small, urchin's face. "We are?"

"Yep. We're going to bring them back to what is most important in their lives, namely us, so they will fix their marriages back up and stop acting like a bunch of infantile assholes."

Bennie stared at him. "You're serious."

"Completely. Want me to tie you up and lock you in the trunk?"

"Toby!"

"Just kidding. Look, I've already stolen my dad's car. They've probably got an APB out on me anyway. I'm a desperate man with nothing to lose."

"You have to take me to an abandoned building and hold me for ransom. I don't mind as long as there's no rats, and no coffin rooms like that little girl from Long Island."

Toby laughed. "Bennie, you are my kind of dude. I always knew you were one of the cool ones. Tell me the truth though, are you scared?"

"A little."

"Do you agree with me about our parents?"

"I agree about mine. I didn't know anything was wrong with yours."

"Well, there is. Plenty. They'll be where yours are in a day or two."

Bennie nodded. He felt so sad. "I'm really sorry, Toby. It's the pits."

"So are you in or should I just take you home?"

"In for what?"

"I have a plan. I thought that we'd cruise on over to Leonard Lewis's house and try to find something that the cops have missed. Maybe if a couple of kids can do something to show how much we care about our families, that will impress them. What do you think?"

"You mean like breaking and entering?"

"Sort of more like trespassing."

"Toby, if we go inside without being invited, we're breaking and entering. Don't you ever watch *Law and Order*?"

"Naw. It's on past my bedtime."

Bennie laughed. "Well, okay. I'm in. But if we get there and it looks too complicated, then I may change my mind."

"Deal."

Toby maneuvered the curves of the canyon, over from the valley side where Bennie's school was and down Sunset Boulevard to Holmby Hills, where the Lewises lived. Toby swung into the driveway. A plain, unmarked car was parked across the street, conspicuous in the quiet, fancy neighborhood.

"Look, over there. I bet it's the feds watching Mrs. Lewis."

Bennie swallowed. "The feds? Toby, I think I'm a little more scared than I thought."

A funny sound in Toby's ear, coming from beside him. Bennie was pulling on his sleeve. Toby looked over at his cousin. His face looked weird. The tips of his ears were bright red, but his face was almost bluish white, and choked wheezing sounds were coming from his chest.

"Bennie, what is it?"

"Asthma-attack-I-can't-breathe, Tob."

Toby climbed out of the car and ran around to Bennie's side. He lifted Bennie out and stumbled across the street. *The feds.* Toby swallowed his panic. He seemed to be moving in slow motion. . . . Help . . . they can call for help. . . .

"Annie?"

"Loretta? What's the matter, you sound upset."

"*You* sound like someone's holding your nose."

"That's exactly how I feel. What's going on?"

"Listen, I'm at the Cedars emergency room. Bennie's having a major asthma attack and Toby's here. Toby was with him when it happened. I knew you'd be worried and I think you and Mickey should come down and get him. Annie, the adrenaline isn't helping enough. I'm afraid they're going to have to do a tracheotomy. Oh, damn, I'm so scared."

"Mickey's here. We're on our way. Where's Martin?"

"I have no idea. I called his office and was informed that he had gone to Palm Springs for the weekend and was still not back."

"Palm Springs? My brother in an open desert with blazing sun? of his own free will?"

"All I know is what I was told. I asked them to beep him but I haven't heard yet."

"We'll be there as soon as we can. Thank God they're all right; we've been worried sick about Toby."

"You should have been. He kidnapped Bennie from his school."

"Oh, God! I'm so sorry. It's us. It's our fault."

"Not important. Believe me, he's learned some lessons here. It's okay, Annie. Just come."

"We're on our way."

They had talked all afternoon, from the moment Mickey came back from Ivy Clare's. She knew about Toby's visit and his vanishing with Mickey's car. She knew about "Dwight Yoakam" and that he was free of Ivy Clare's spell. He had cried and he had begged for her forgiveness. He had told her that he loved her and that he would die if he lost her. He told her how jealous he was of her almost-lover — how funny that word sounded to her — and that it was unbearable for him to think of her with someone else.

He had all sorts of ideas for restarting their life. They should sell everything and take off for a year and live in Mexico, or somewhere cheap, and maybe write a screenplay together. They should produce something with Jackie. They should go back to New York and the theater, and he would teach acting and she could try to write something serious.

They could go to Australia and travel for a while, and check out the film opportunities there and be near Ella during her resettlement. On and on he had talked, begging her to go to Tokyo with him, pleading for another chance.

It was everything she had hoped for. But all the loving, earnestly spoken, flattering words dropped around her like melting snowflakes, evaporating before they hit the ground. She could not connect with his emotion.

In the drawer next to her bed was a letter that had come for her that morning. It had no address, only a London postmark, and written inside in a large scrawl of red ink, "January 10th, 10:00 a.m." Her date with Mr. Destiny.

She couldn't believe that she could be in the place that she was, that she was not huddling in her husband's arms, running back to the shelter of his love, the cave of their marriage. But nothing was the same. They had both walked too far forward into the daylight.

When the call came from Loretta they were talked out. They slammed the lid on their dilemma, parents first, always parents first. It was a commitment that they had made together as husband and wife, but it was a deeper commitment than the one they had made to one another.

They were instantly aware of the difference, when one of their children was at risk. They drove to L.A. in total silence, without even turning on the radio, as if any diversion was a betrayal of their son and their nephew.

Toby was sitting alone at the end of the hall outside the pediatric intensive care unit. He was hunched forward in a plastic chair, his large, tan hands clasped together. Annie thought he was praying. He looked up, his face red and covered with tears.

Annie knelt in front of him, covering his hands with her own.

"It's all my fault. If he dies, I killed him!" He shuddered. She had not seen him cry like that since he was a little boy. She could not bear his pain.

Mickey sat down beside him. "Toby, it is not your fault! No matter what happens, it's not your fault. It's *my* fault! The whole thing is *my* fault. You were only trying to help your mother! No one blames you."

"Loretta does, I know she does!"

Annie pulled a tissue from her purse. "Why don't you ask her? But right now, why don't we all just try to be positive and stop projecting some morbid scenario. Bennie has been having asthma attacks since he was three years old. This is not the first time they've been through this, so let's not make it any harder for anyone."

Annie got up and sat on her son's other side. They flanked him, offering, with their presence, as much comfort as he was capable of absorbing. That was all that they could do. The powerlessness of parenthood always involved not being able to take any of the hurt away. You could never crawl inside them and feel it for them. You could never make their own struggle easier.

Annie kept her hand on Toby's. Mickey thought it was his fault, she thought it was her fault, and Toby thought it was *his* fault. Loretta probably thought it was her fault, and when Martin showed up he would think that it was his fault. Bennie probably thought it was his fault too, though why, she couldn't quite say, but no doubt he did. Was there anyone else?

Martin raced in. He was wearing a pink polo shirt and khaki shorts and he was *tan.* Her brother was *sun*tanned.

"I got here as soon as I could. Where are they?"

Toby pointed to the ICU. "In there."

"Any news?"

Annie shook her head. "We just got here. No one's come by."

He turned and moved down the hall, not pausing at the forbidding doors, body language that only a doctor would use.

Toby was sobbing again. Mickey was crying, too. She saw Bennie's little face, bouncing up and down on her bed at Thanksgiving. Sweet little pumpkin head.

Annie closed her eyes. She felt numb. She envied her son and husband their tears; she was holding on to her fear, wrapping it tight, holding all of her Mickey hurt and her Ella hurt and her Toby hurt and her Bennie fear like a badly dressed wound inside her, too tight to let the injury breathe.

Loretta appeared. They stood up, watching her but not moving, trying to brace themselves, prepare for her news. She stopped before them and smiled. "He's okay. The drugs and the oxygen finally did it. They didn't have to do a trach. He's doing fine."

The tourniquet broke and Annie burst into tears. Toby pushed through them and ran off down the hall. Mickey ran after him. Annie opened her arms, and Loretta collapsed against her shoulder. She held on to Annie. "So damn unfair. Why do they always have to pay for our junk."

"You'd better find someone much higher up the food chain than me if you really want an answer."

Loretta laughed. They held one another for a moment. Annie patted her back, the way mothers quiet children. The gentle tapping motion comforted her, too. What a wonderful thing patting was, Annie thought. Why didn't grown-ups do it to one another? Why didn't grown-ups do it to themselves?

Loretta let go and sat down in a chair. "I would pillage for a cigarette and a cup of coffee."

"Want me to go get some for you?"

Loretta shook her head. "No, not yet. Sit with me for a minute. Martin's in there now. I can go with you when Mickey and Toby get back. I want to talk to Toby first. I'm worried about him."

"He thinks you blame him."

"That's why I want to talk to him."

"Do you know why he did it?"

"No."

"Toby went to see Ivy Clare to try and appeal to her higher moral sense, of which there seems to be none. She insulted me, he went nuts, Mickey came in, they fought, and he took off in Mickey's car. I don't imagine his thinking was too linear. I guess he saw himself and

Bennie as two soldiers on the same side of a war. I'm so sorry, Loretta."

Loretta smiled at her. "Don't be sorry. As horrible as going through something like this is, I can't tell you what it's done for Bennie's self-esteem. You should see him. You should *hear* him. It's Toby and Bennie's Great Adventure. The fact that Toby singled him out and asked for his help . . . Toby gave Bennie an enormous gift today. Since we have a happy ending here, I've got to tell you it's been worth it."

Annie took her sister-in-law's hand and held it against her face. "Oh, Loretta, you are really something. Will you tell Toby?"

"That's what I'm waiting for."

Annie passed tissues. They blew their noses and wiped their eyes. Annie sniffed. "I think that I have cried more in the last month than in the entire last five years, and I've always been a fairly decent crier."

"Me, too."

They turned toward one another. Annie smiled.

"I know what you're going to say. I don't believe it, either."

Loretta sighed. "He's *tan.* He's motherfucking tan."

"He's tan *and* he's wearing shorts."

Loretta nodded. "No tie."

"His hair is parted on the side. No more Dracula peak."

Loretta folded her soggy Kleenex and put it in her pocket.

"I smell something female. Definitely female."

CHAPTER XIV

ANNIE SWUNG HER CAR into the supermarket lot, hitting the bump too fast and bouncing herself against the roof of the car. *Slow down, take it easy.* She had been whispering the same message to herself for days to little avail. She was leaving tomorrow and she had to pick up supplies for Juanita.

Leaving tomorrow. She swallowed her fear. It was almost dark and her headlights cast eerie shadows on the asphalt.

She would not get ahead of herself. She would stay in the present, as Loretta was always advising. Get groceries, go home, pack clothes, make sure Toby was ready to go back to school, reconfirm the tickets to New York and the ticket to London two days later. Call Ida Mae with flight times and have her call Ella. Make sure passport is packed. Anything else? Probably a whole lot of things.

She maneuvered into a space as close to the entrance as possible. She hated being in large, empty parking lots in the dark now. Too many scary things had happened to too many nice, normal women and innocent shoppers like herself in big, empty parking lots. She slipped her pocket siren into her purse and pulled the car forward.

A woman was standing next to her car waving at her. The woman was all bundled up in insulated-looking winter wear, her flat face half hidden by a cap and lots of gray, stringy hair. What did she want? Annie turned off the motor, but the woman kept motioning her forward. Annie pushed the window control.

The woman leaned her globous, smiling head into Annie's safe zone.

"Why are you waving at me?" Annie asked, surprised by the sharpness of her tone.

The intruder seemed not to notice. "I was directing you, dear, not waving at you. I was just helping you pull in further. You don't want to stick out and have someone hit your beautiful car, now."

Annie felt like rolling the window up and smashing her patronizing do-gooder face against the roof.

"Thank you very much but I've been parking for a long time." She rolled up the window and turned off the ignition. God, she was turning into a bitch. Where was that polite, always pleasant old Annie? She had lost her somewhere between L.A. and Montecito in the last two months. Frankly, except for fleeting moments of intense anxiety at the loss, she was absolutely thrilled that she was gone.

The woman did not move or open the door to her own car. She knocked on Annie's passenger window, smiling her fat-cheeked, infuriating smile. Annie couldn't believe it. She opened the door and climbed out of her car. "Now what seems to be the problem?"

The woman stood up on her toes and smirked at her over the top of the Range Rover. She had one of those cat-about-to-gobble-the-tweetie-bird looks, which made Annie even angrier.

"Well, I can't imagine that you'd want to go inside to market and leave your lights on. I thought you'd want to know. I bet you're a weekender. I can always tell. They're not used to thinking about things like pulling forward and switching off car lights. They have all that L.A. rush, rush, rush."

Annie ignored her, reaching back in and grabbing her purse. Yes, the lights were on, but they were on the timer and would soon switch off. She prayed for this. If this awful lady had the last word tonight she would probably ram her car or something even more horrible.

She locked her door and walked past the woman. The woman followed her. "Didn't you hear me, dear? I said your lights were on. No one wants a dead battery at night in the dead of winter."

Annie turned. "They're on a timer. Now please, just leave me alone."

The woman continued on. "I doubt it. I have a timer; no timer lasts that long. I'm just trying to be helpful. I was going to compliment you on what a beautiful car you have —"

Annie whirled around, rage engulfing her. "I said leave me the fuck alone! Don't say one more fucking word to me! Get out of my face! Go help someone else!"

The woman was still smiling. "I was just being considerate," she said. Annie stormed off, her heart pounding against her throat.

She couldn't believe what had just happened! She had told a chipper, well-meaning busybody to go fuck herself in a supermarket parking lot! And the best, or the worst part of it was, she had *liked* doing it.

Okay, Annie. Focus. Buy the stuff and get it over with. At least she was just shopping for Juanita, so it wouldn't take so long. She was a compulsive label reader, so marketing in the age of endless choices and ingredient variants often took her several hours. Juanita wasn't into nutrition awareness. Juanita wolfed down Kraft macaroni and cheese dinners and canned pork and beans and stacks of flour tortillas stuffed with butter and salt or sugar and mountains of Snickers bars. Juanita would outlive them all.

She paused at the health care section. Massengill. She took a deep breath. What was she doing? She never pumped that junk up her tunnel for Mickey, but for Mr. Destiny? It was all so premeditated now. Everything she did was a conscious grown-up decision, a deliberate walking into the den of adultery.

This added an entirely different dimension. No more swooning with desire and being semi–out of control, as she had been at Ivy Clare's. No more Barbara Cartland version in which the woman was not responsible for her behavior. For *this* round she was on the phone with British Airways, booking flights and hotels rooms, and casually dropping feminine hygiene products into her market basket. She picked up two and threw them into her cart and headed for the checkout counter.

There was a line, and she pulled out her *New York Times* and tried to concentrate. She had not had the luxury of sitting at Maisy's with a cappuccino and her papers for weeks.

An interview with Kelly Klein on her new swimming pool book. Well, that would be distracting. She scanned, looking for the personal parts, not the least bit interested in how or why she had done the book, which sold for $100 and was about as relevant to anyone's real life as the Hope diamond. "I did this book because my architect said there were no pool books, even though everyone needs one."

Everyone? What sort of fool would say something like that in print? Could her world possibly be that insulated? *Everyone?* As in 'on earth,' in the South Bronx, Somalia, Haitian boat refugees, the girl working at the checkout counter. Everyone?

She read on. "I have amazing clothes. I have an amazing closet . . . though sometimes I wish I was married to a plumber so I would have beautiful sinks and tubs. . . . I am Calvin's muse." (Isn't *he* supposed to say that?) "He designs everything for me. I happen to be very American, look very American." (Oh, have mercy. She means WASPy, and she doesn't even understand the difference?) "I love everything he does. . . . He's just the best guy in the world. I never felt threatened by his success and fame." (I would think not, since it's why you married him, dear thing. Can you be threatened by a silk pantsuit?) ". . . I'm so happy I can wear his clothes and look as beautiful in them as I do." Annie skipped through, feeling angry again. "What major disappointments have you had in your life?" the reporter asked.

Annie pushed her cart up. Okay, she was willing to give her another chance. The question had apparently invoked several minutes of pondering while Kelly licked cookie crumbs off her perfectly manicured fingers. Annie was incredulous. Had she ever known anyone who would hesitate even for a microsecond at such a question?

"When I don't win in a horse show. I like to win. . . . It's a very hard sport. It's all about appearance and performance, so you have to be as beautiful and perfect as possible. I love the way the horses and the people look all dressed up. I forget about everything else in my life, the tensions of New York." (Of course, all of that wardrobe anxiety!)

Annie tossed the paper into the cart. Absolutely astonishing! There really were people who thought like that, let alone lived like that. She wished her a huge ugly boil on her little American nose. Better yet, fat. Yes! A boil on her nose and Blimp City.

Annie took the red rubber separator, differentiating her products from the woman's before her, and began to unload her cart. She thought about Kelly Klein and her father. Would they have gotten along? Her father would have loved her. Tears filled her eyes. She missed the old fool, and she missed her mother. Suddenly, her mother was back in her life and her heart on a daily basis, as if she had only just died — the loss was that profound and that real. She had been waking up in the night sobbing for her mother. *I want my momma,* she heard herself saying.

Too much change was spinning her around; the past, the present, the future of herself revolving before her like a Ferris-wheel ride. Round and round she went, not quite able to pull all the new information together with who she had been or what she had lost.

If I could only talk to her one more time, just for a minute. If I could only tell him what I really felt. How much he hurt me and how much I loved him. Someone was running the wheel too fast, and she could not center her view, she could not tell where the ground was or if she was looking up or down.

I miss my mother. She wiped the tears away and tossed the Massengill and a box of SOS pads on the rubber counter. Good choice of companions, she thought, the douche and the SOS. Was that what she was doing? Was her choice not to run back to Mickey but to pursue her own midlife crisis a form of Morse code?

She had lost her safety net and when Mickey had swung back into view, her flying Wilski, ready to restitch it beneath her, what had she gone and done? She had untethered herself further. She was now in free fall, rocking back and forth in her little Ferris-wheel cage, free-falling without even knowing if she was upside down.

All she knew was that she had turned down Mickey's plea to go to Japan with him and he had gone, dejected but not feeling that he had much rope to work with. And she was going to settle her son back in school and try to give her daughter the permission she needed to go forth on her own journey, and offer Ida Mae whatever Ida Mae would allow. And then she was going to London to sit on the steps of the Victoria and Albert Museum for a few minutes to find out whether she was the biggest fool for love on record, and possibly figure out what she was going to do with the next stage of her life.

She opened the door to the kitchen, still expecting Portia to drag herself over to greet her. Molly was sitting at the kitchen table working on a crossword puzzle and listening to one of Jackie's shows. Juanita wobbled over and took the bag of groceries from her.

"Toby called, Mrs. W. He say he be home after dinner, he hangin' out with his friends, saying good-bye. He say for you to chill, he's all packed and he'll sleep on the plane."

"Okay. Juanita, there's a couple more bags in the car, will you get them?"

"No problema."

Annie laughed. Ever since Juanita had seen that Schwarzenegger film, that was her favorite expression. What was she going to do about Juanita? Leaving her all alone in that big house for weeks at a time, without even Portia to take care of, let alone keep her company. The thought of losing Juanita now was just too much. Juanita was part of them. Juanita held almost the entire history of their marriage and their children. How could she let her go?

Molly swayed over barefoot and threw her arms around Annie's neck. "I missed you, you little redheaded silly, you."

Annie felt guilty. So much had gone on since she had last seen Molly that she hadn't had the time to miss her back. "I would have missed you, too, if my life hadn't been a completely overwrought, crisis-ridden nightmare. When did you get back?"

"Last night real late. We all slept most of the day like a litter of puppies. Want to come over for dinner and fill us in on the happenings of the Wandering Wilders?"

"I'd love to, but I'm going away again tomorrow, and I've got to pack and tear several tufts of hair out, and all before morning."

Molly watched her. She picked up a cigarette and lit it.

"I know. Juanita said that y'all were off to New York, dropping Toby and spending a couple of days with Ida Mae and Ella, and then 'going far away on a kind of vacation.'"

Annie sighed. She walked to the sink, picking up the kettle on her way. "Want some tea?"

"Lovely." Molly blew smoke rings.

"Juanita gets too seduced by you, Molly-O. If you want information ask me, don't ask Juanita. Okay?"

Molly giggled. "Okay. Except y'all have been very withholding of late and you know I'm Miss Curiosity."

"Yeah, well, remember what happened to the cat."

Molly stubbed out her cigarette and wiggled her toes. "I tell y'all everything."

Annie thought that she looked hurt. She sat down next to her. "I'm sorry, Molly. This stuff is really hard for me and I'm truly frantic tonight. I'll give you the speeded-up version; the rest will have to wait until I get back."

Molly's face brightened. "Back from *where?*"

"London," Annie said, feeling her face heat up.

Molly pulled her knees against her chest and folded her long slender arms around them. "I see," she said, cocking her head sideways as if in preparation for information that it was vital for her to retain.

The kettle whistled. Annie got up and went to make the tea. Juanita came puffing in with the groceries.

Annie smiled at her. "What took so long?"

Juanita wouldn't look at her. "My boyfriend, he come by. I tell him, don't come to my Wilders, but he can't stay away from me. He is pushing my buttons all at once."

Annie looked at Molly. Was it possible that Juanita really did have a boyfriend?

"Juanita darlin', is this that Mr. Regis Schwarzenegger y'all was telling us about at Thanksgiving?"

Juanita covered her face with her little pudgy caramel hands and nodded her small dark head up and down. "Yep. Yep. Mrs. Molly, you tease me. That not his name. You know that."

"Well, it is a perfectly fine name, and it's the only frame of reference I have for the gentleman until you tell us his real name."

"What means this 'frame of reference'? I don't hear that before."

Annie handed Juanita and Molly cups of tea. Molly could tackle that one. She sat down again.

"Well, it's a little hard to explain. Let's just forget it."

"I'll look it up. His name is Pomfi Romero. He has his mother a Filipino and his father a Dominican. He's a god."

Annie laughed. Juanita might be making her own decision about the time to let go. "Juanita, the house is yours until I come back. I trust your judgment, so please feel free to have Mr. Romero come over and keep you company."

"That's very nice of you, Mrs. W, but I don't like a guy hangin' around while I'm at my work. I see him on weekends at my sister's. It's cool."

Juanita bustled back and forth, putting her groceries away. Annie watched her. She did not have to worry about Juanita. Juanita knew how to take care of herself.

"I gotta load to do for Toby to take." She picked up the laundry supplies and left them.

Annie turned back to Molly. "Okay, before I start, tell me about you and Billy. Did you ever talk to him?"

Molly stirred sugar into her tea. "I most certainly did. I did exactly what y'all told me, and guess what? You were right! He was absolutely overcome with emotion that I would be that upset and jealous and needy. So I reduced myself to a little puddle of gelatin and got my man back. I do believe that he never did anything." Molly lit another cigarette. "I gotta tell y'all though, it was real scary for me, being the control freak that I am.

"I have always just loathed and despised needy women, all those tormented lady poets, like Anne Sexton, who just keep disintegrating and falling down in globs of drink and self-pity, and some man is always coming to their rescue. I abhor women who manipulate people like that. Neediness is one of the great seducers of all recorded time and I just despise it in myself. I really had to do some major shifting to reach out like that, sobby and desperate and begging and all."

Annie smiled. "You were very brave. You know what to do to keep it from getting to that point again. You won't have to go down on your knees next time, just a little attention and some ego pats."

"All I need to do is picture my Billy with some floozie; that'll keep me on track."

Molly let go of her knees. "Enough about me now; time is short, so you'd better start at the beginning, meaning Club Med, and give me your very best synopsis of current events, or I will never be able to let you leave this room."

Annie leaned back. "Okay. This is probably good for me, since I haven't relived any of it out loud. Let's start with our last night in Mexico. . . ."

They leaned in toward one another, two women in a quiet kitchen.

CHAPTER XV

WHEN ELLA GOT TO THE RESTAURANT, covered with snow and out of breath from her subway walk, her mother was waiting. Her mother, sitting at the old family table in the back of her grandmother's favorite Village Italian, reading a book. She could not remember ever coming upon her mother in public without seeing her bent over a book.

Her mother looked up, sensing her presence, and waved. Ella gave her coat to the hostess and started toward her. She was always a little embarrassed by the way her mother watched her and Toby. Adoringly, with a little smile and a kind of softness in her face and around her eyes, which were usually so alert, and on guard, almost. What was that song? "The look of love is in your eyes"? Well, maybe it was written about lovers, but it was the way her mother watched them.

Her mother stood up and reached across to kiss her. "Hi, baby. Ummm. Cold cheeks. I love those frosty little cheeks."

"Hi, Momma," Ella said, and kissed her back. God, she was not going to cry in a restaurant. What was happening to her? If she didn't have at least one good cry a day now, she could hardly cope. Sometimes she didn't even know how much she missed her mother until she heard her voice or saw her face.

She let go and sat down, afraid that one more minute of her mother's loving embrace would dissolve her facade.

"I thought Toby and Ida Mae were coming." Ella took off her beret and shook out her long dark hair.

Annie sighed. "Well, Toby had to get back to school, though from my conversation with him on the plane, I'm not sure he should stay there. He's really unhappy. Anyway, he wanted to get back and I don't blame him. Ida Mae's house has been turned into a combination lending library and AIDS hospice."

Ella blew her nose. "Oh, I know. She's so busy, I have to make a date two weeks in advance to have breakfast with her. I think it's great, though, that she's so active."

"Well, you're right about that. She dumbfounds me. I'm convinced when I'm her age I'll be shuffling between the TV, the microwave, and the rocking chair, and happy to do so."

"Oh, Mom, stop it! You will not. You'll be just like you are now, only a little more wrinkled and cranky."

"Wrinkled and cranky. I hate this idea more and more. Something depressing to look forward to. I will never be wrinkled and cranky, or gray for that matter. I will keep my little red head right into the grave, but —"

"I read somewhere that hair dye can give you cancer."

"If that were true, then ninety-seven percent, maybe ninety-eight percent, of all the women on the civilized part of the planet would have it. I will not put that on my worry list, thank you ever so."

Ella laughed. "I'm sorry I interrupted you. So why won't you be wrinkled and cranky?"

"Oh. Right. I forget. Oh, don't forget about forgetting. You should have said wrinkled, cranky, and forgetful."

"You mean senile?"

"I prefer forgetful. Everything is a matter of degree."

"Okay, so why not, you know?"

"Because I will at some point overcome my terror and deliver myself to your uncle Martin, who will sear me with acid like a sirloin and peel me like a plump black grape, and I'm sure I will be popping Prozac or whatever the afraid-of-old-and-alone drug of the moment is. I'll be rocking away, watching *Murder, She Wrote* reruns, just as smooth and mellow as a pet rock."

"What makes you think you'll be all alone?"

Annie looked startled. "Oh, gee, I don't know. I guess I just associate old age with being alone. It's been my experience, from our families, you know."

Ella pushed her hair back. She felt like crying again. She had caught her mother off guard. She didn't know if what was happening between her parents was something she could talk to her about. Had Toby? He had been out there with them since the mayhem in Mexico. Poor Toby, the scourge of the youngest child, always having to be there for the bad stuff.

"Want some wine?"

She knew her mother was trying to change the subject. "Sure. I just got off; I traded shifts so I don't have to work tonight."

Her mother's eyes flashed. Shit, she had slipped.

"You've been working *nights?* You never told me that!"

Ella handed her mother her glass and waited while she poured her some wine, smiling at the baby portion. She still thought of her as a little girl at the seder table, getting a little sip in her glass to feel part of the grown-up ceremony.

"Well, are you surprised? You're freaking already! I didn't want to worry you."

"I'm a mother; your *job* is to worry me! Do you have the Mace I sent you? What about the pocket alarm? It apparently throws an enormously frightening noise for hundreds of feet."

"Mom, I have them both. I take them with me every night. I never take the subway home and my boss watches while I get a taxi. I'm fine. I don't like it either, but it pays better and anyway, it's not for long now."

She saw the sadness in her mother's face. Oh, damn, she didn't want to see it. Her mother reached for her hand and stroked it. She loved her mother's hands, they were so cute and friendly, all white with freckles all over them, and so warm and soft. She could remember the comforting way they felt on her forehead when she was little and sick with something.

Her mother looked up at her. "Can we talk about Australia?"

Ella stiffened. "I don't know. I mean I want to, but I just can't handle another Club Med. It's hard enough as it is."

Annie let her go. "I know, baby. I'm so sorry. It was just . . . it was such a shock, and the timing of everything. I let you down. I don't want you to leave feeling disconnected from us. What can I do that would help you?"

Ella sipped her wine. She had absolutely no idea how to answer her mother's question. "I honestly don't know. I guess if you and Daddy are okay, if I know you're all right . . . I guess that will help me more than anything. I mean, I know that's kind of selfish because it means I can go off and not feel guilty, like I'm abandoning everyone when so many awful things have been happening. But also, because then I won't worry about you guys all the time and I'll be able to start a new life there."

A new life there. The words hung between them across the small table in the noisy, smoky restaurant. She saw that look on her mother's face again. She knew now why it was so painful to see it, because it was the way she felt inside.

Annie poured more wine. "Look, Ella, I can't be phony with you. If you're old enough to make this decision and take charge of your life like this, you're old enough to hear the truth. Your father and I have been through a really tough time, and we have some maybe even tougher times ahead, both financially and personally, though he has broken off his relationship with that pot person and he seems to be genuinely and totally committed to saving our marriage and going forward from this.

"But now it's my turn. I've been married all my adult life, too, and I'm not so sure I can or even want to just wipe my tearstained hands on my little wifey apron and resume. I have some thinking to do myself, so I can't promise you the happy ending you want to take with you, nor can I pretend that I'm thrilled about you leaving us! It's just so far away and it's a man we've never even met! What kind of battery-brains would we be to just say, 'Great, honey'?"

Ella lowered her head. She couldn't handle this.

Her mother leaned toward her. "Ella, none of your head lowering. I know all of your childhood tricks. We have to talk about this. I'm going to London tomorrow and —"

"You are?" Ella felt frightened.

Her mother looked funny. "Yes, I am."

"In January? Alone? For what reason?"

Now it was Annie who wouldn't make eye contact.

"I need to get away by myself for a while. I wanted to be in Europe, but somewhere that they spoke English, and besides, there's all those quaint little inns to write about. We need to make some money."

All of that made sense, so why was her mother acting so evasive?

"May I finish? I'm going to be away for a while and your father is in Japan, and God knows you two didn't leave on the best of terms. At least Toby got a chance to express his anger and hurt. You may not really get to, if you're leaving the beginning of March. I am assuming, though, that you will come out and be with us before you go."

"Of course. And I told you, Willy's going to come, too."

"That's wonderful, honey. But the fact is that we don't have much time together to deal with all of this, and what I want you to know, really need you to understand, is that whatever happens with your father and me, or however much we miss you, that we are always there for you separately and together and so is Toby. I want you to pack that love and support in your carry-on and never forget it even for a second. I know that this is in many ways harder for you than for us, but it's your journey, Ella-Bella, and no one, mother or otherwise, has the right to mess with someone's journey. I bless your journey, darling. I hope it leads you to all the love and happiness you deserve. . . . I . . ." She stopped. She had nothing left to say.

Ella shuddered. She was really losing it now. At least her back was to the room and no one could see her.

Her mother let her cry, passing her a tissue. That was her mother all right, an endless supply of Kleenex just in case.

Annie sighed, blotting her own tears. "Lucky for us the service is as lousy as usual. We can have a complete catharsis before they even hand over a menu."

Ella wiped her face and looked up. "Thanks, Momma. What you said really helps. I don't want to be phony with you, but I need to feel that if I tell you I'm afraid, or have moments of doubt or whatever, you won't pounce on it and use it to manipulate me into not going. I've got to go now, even if it turns out to be a terrible mistake and I come back."

Her mother smiled at her. The sadness was still in her eyes, but she seemed more relaxed. "I know, sweetheart. So okay, tell me every single thing about your fella, your plans, everything. Paint me a picture, baby girl."

Ella laughed. Her mother hadn't said that to her in a hundred years. She always said it to her when she was little and wanted Ella to describe something she had done or somewhere she had gone without her. She inhaled, feeling a flood of relief. Now she could share this wonderful, scary thing called love with her mother.

Annie was early. She had not wanted to be early, and had planned the short walk from her hotel to the Victoria and Albert accordingly, or so she thought. But it was barely twenty of ten and far too cold to wait outside. Besides, it wasn't exactly an enticing image to meet one's dream lover crouched on a museum step, eyes watering and nose running from the freezing air. Far better that she should saunter out and find him there, waiting nervously. Oh, brother, she had watched *Casablanca* one time too many.

Annie wandered around the cavernous rooms closest to the street. No sense getting lost in the labyrinthine old vessel and missing him, either. She seemed to be in a quarry of carved marital crypts. Husbands and wives buried side by side and re-created in granite gravestone images.

She stopped in front of Sir Robert and Lady Elizabeth Something — the last name had worn away. They looked so serene. Marital accord, the hard way. Their hands were folded neatly across their chests. Poor Lady Elizabeth's nose and fingertips were gone, but Sir Robert was completely intact; was there symbolic meaning in this?

She wondered what, if anything, they might be saying to one another inside their stony tomb or up in heaven or wherever they were. How different would marriage be when you were both dead, and all the games, anxieties, power plays, sexual tension, health, child-rearing, and money worries were several hundred years behind you. Maybe you would no longer have anything to argue about, let alone talk about. . . . Why did she think like this?

What was that pop anthropology article she had read on the plane? Something about humans being genetically programmed to cheat on their mates? A divine thing for her to read, when just getting on the plane and into her crowded little bonus-mile freebie seat had almost finished her off! Maybe she just simply lacked the adultery gene. Maybe that's what it was.

The author claimed that the only reason women ever started looking for mates to begin with (pair bonding she called it) was that four million years ago women were forced out of the trees and onto the ground. And standing upright meant needing someone to help rear their young, which they now had to carry in their arms. Annie wondered if this would hold up in a California divorce hearing as an excuse for ending a relationship. "Well, Your Honor, once I didn't have to schlep the kid around anymore and my two arms were free again, well, I looked elsewhere."

The scientist also believed that adultery benefited both sexes in ancient times. Men made a lot of babies, which was good for posterity, and women, by slipping off to the nearest Iguana Inn for an hour or so, were rewarded with more food, protection, and firewood-hauling, and if a husband was eaten by a tiger, the wife had a nice backup; a-pair-and-a-spare sort of thing. Why did ancient women seem to have it worked out better than modern women?

Fifty percent of all couples cheat on one another, the scientist claimed. The thought made Annie sick to her stomach. Why? It should have been comforting — at least she wasn't doing something totally aberrant and unknown in her culture. Well, it didn't. It made her feel dirty and lonely. It wasn't a nice way to treat someone who loved and trusted you, even if *they* were doing it, too.

Almost every creature on earth seemed to comply. Even chickadees, who spent a lot of quality time building nests together, zoomed off to chirp up some other set of feathers as soon as they found an excuse to leave the nest. "Saw a fabulous twig set in town that would look just to die for in the parlor. I'll just fly back and see if it's still there." Yeah, right. Human nature was no better or worse than any other nature.

She walked back to the center hall and checked her watch. Still ten minutes to kill. She swallowed hard, feeling light-headed. She should have had something more than coffee and juice for breakfast. What if her nerves brought on an attack of hypoglycemia and she passed out in the lobby, and he was outside waiting, and someone called an ambulance and they took her out the side door to a hospital and he never even knew that she had shown up. God, how Deborah Kerr.

She sat down on a bench in the hall by the door. A small, chubby-cheeked boy and a slightly bigger girl were playing alone. He was driving a small tricycle round and round the atrium, under the watchful and not so approving gaze of the guard.

Annie watched them. The older child was giving the little boy tricycle riding instructions, which he was blithely ignoring. He pedaled over to Annie, his flushed face peeping out of his slicker.

"Hello," he said.

Annie smiled. They reminded her of Ella and Toby, but all small children reminded her of Ella and Toby.

"Hello. What a lovely tricycle."

"My daddy made it for me."

"How wonderful."

The girl marched over, her wellies squeaking on the cold stone floor. Her face was tight. She was out to right some terrible wrong.

"He did not, Tommy! That's a lie! He bought it in a store."

Annie watched the little boy struggle with his confusion, looking at Annie for enlightenment but quickly choosing for himself the only appropriate defense.

"No, he made it!" he said, still staring at Annie.

"He did not!" the girl said, also staring at Annie, judge before this tiny civil case. "It was mine, but I got too big, so Daddy gave it to him!"

Tommy, Annie thought, was experiencing his first major reality confrontation, his fantasy father image and his trike now basened by his sister's intrusion of fact, as older sisters were wont to do. Mickey had always called it "shedding a little dark on the situation."

Mickey. Oh, God help her. She looked at her watch. Five minutes past ten! She jumped up, startling the children.

"Well, it's a lovely trike, no matter where your father got it. How wonderful to have such a nice dad."

She walked past them to the door, wishing that she was back there all those years ago, picking on her baby brother going round and round the fountain in Washington Square, no thoughts besides instructing Martin on better tricycle skills clouding her head, no decisions to make, no loved ones to betray.

He was standing halfway up the staircase, waiting. He had cut his hair, and it made him look younger and more vulnerable. His face was pink from the wind and his hands were hidden in the pockets of his overcoat. He smiled at her, looking surprised.

She was so nervous she thought for sure that she would never make it down the steps but would trip and go rolling past him, all the way to the bottom and across the road, not stopping until she was back in Montecito in her own bed.

"Hello, Red," he said, so softly and so sweetly that she stopped, feeling the fear float out of her as if it were attached to some internal hydraulic pump that she had just pushed down on with all her might.

"Hello," she said, standing above him so that they were almost the same height.

He shook his head, looking at her with such tenderness that she could hardly stand. "I don't believe it."

"What?" she said, knowing the answer.

"You really came." He laughed and pulled his hands out of his pocket, reaching out for her.

She moved forward and he linked his arm through hers and led her down the steps.

"I don't believe it, either," she whispered.

At the bottom they paused, not having thought any further than the moment of rendezvous.

"So okay, what do we do now?" she said, looking up at him.

"Well, actually, I have given that question almost no consideration, since I did not really believe that you would turn up."

Annie laughed. "Well, you believed it enough to be standing there, unless you offer such invitations to scores of strange women, hoping one will be foolhardy enough to drop by."

His face darkened. She had hurt his feelings.

"You do know better than that."

She sighed, surrendering further. "Yes, I guess I do."

"Where are you staying?" He took her arm again.

"Just a few blocks away, at a B and B."

"Ah, a generation-X establishment."

She pointed in the direction of her hotel. "I'm sort of an expert. I've been writing about them for years."

"I see. Sounds very interesting."

They walked across Kensington High Street. "It's not. I hate the damn places; far too cute. But I make money at it, for the time being anyway. I would really like to try writing about something else."

They were quiet, absorbing the truth of their total strangeness. They had shared passion of extraordinary power, had actually fallen into a love haze, but they knew no more about one another than straphangers bumping together on their way to work.

"Here we are." Annie pointed to the gleaming, freshly painted and polished Georgian house before them.

He smiled. "Oh, yes, Number Twenty-one. I know this one — caters to smug sots with Greenpeace emblems and hideous bumper stickers with socially aware drivel like 'Furs are worn by beautiful animals and ugly people' stuck on the rumps of their Range Rovers."

Annie laughed. "You've nailed the clientele, but I take exception to the Range Rover."

He laughed. "Ah! Well, you are the exception, though it is not the car I would have chosen for you. Too bulky — no elegant curves." He turned her toward him, looking down into her eyes and holding the sides of her small, freckled face in his big, warm hands.

He leaned down and kissed the cold tip of her nose. "Annie," he said. "Hello, Annie."

It was as if she had never heard her name before. As if it were some magic password connecting her body to her shining female soul. She felt exactly as she had felt that day in Ivy Clare's living room, the dog brushing against her calf.

She closed her eyes. "Oh, God," she moaned, and he kissed her.

"Can we go inside before we both turn into bloody icicles?"

She nodded, unable to open her eyes or break the spell.

"Sure. But I don't think icicle is a real fear."

He laughed and took her hand in his, leading them up the steps to the polished red door, crossing the threshold into the unknown, two wayfarers setting off on an odyssey. For the first time in Annie Wilder's life, she was making things up as she went along.

He pulled her into the room and sat down on her chenille-covered sleigh bed. She locked the door behind her. The only sound was the ticking of the clock in the hallway.

"Are you hungry? Do you want some tea?"

"No," he said, watching her. "Take off your things," he ordered, his voice trembling slightly, taking the menace out of the command. "I must see you."

Annie blushed. "I can't unless you start, too. I guess I've read too many feminist-consciousness-raising books."

He smiled at her. "Okay, fair enough. Equality in all things." He stood up, taking off his coat and scarf first and piling them neatly on a chair. He slipped his sweater over his head and then his undershirt, adding them to the pile. He faced her and kicked off his shoes. His chest was well formed and covered with small, curly black hairs, and there was a slight paunch over his belt, which she found terribly erotic. He looked like a man, a real man, strong but not actor-pampered and Nautilus-inflated.

Annie threw her coat on top of his and pulled off her boots, glad that she had bathed before she went to meet him.

She unbuttoned her jacket and opened the zipper on her long

tight skirt. She had never done anything like this before. She stopped and went to the window, drawing the curtain and softening the light in the room.

"I want to really see you," he said.

"Oh, please, Oliver." It was the first time she had said his name out loud, a stranger's name, a new name in her life. "Give me a tiny break here. I'm a real-life middle-aged woman and my naked body has not been put on public display in a very long time. In fact, never."

He laughed. "Do you have anything to drink here, steady the nerves a bit?"

"On the dresser," she said. "I lifted some little bottles of sherry from the airplane."

He walked to the dresser and opened two, handing her one. They clicked their little bottles together.

He returned to his viewing stand near the foot of her bed. "I apologize. It wasn't very gallant of me not to bring champagne and flowers, but I really didn't believe that you would actually appear, and standing there like a true fop, with welcoming presents in my arms, was a bit too much of a risk."

She laughed. "I thought about it too and didn't, for exactly the same reason."

She put down her bottle, the sweet liquid calming and soothing her, moving down into her belly. She stepped out of her pantyhose and undid her bra.

He sighed. "Beautiful," he whispered. "Absolutely beautiful breasts. More beautiful than I could have dreamed of."

She swallowed, wishing that she had taken another sip of sherry, and pulled down her panties. His words reassured her. This was their enchanted cottage; they appeared to one another as perfect as their fantasy. How they might appear to the world outside held no reality or importance.

She crossed to him and he reached out for her, pulling her naked body to his brawny chest.

She felt his lips between her breasts, just above her solar plexus.

She held on to him. What had she read about the solar plexus being the place where we hold feelings? She felt herself opening from there, from the touch-point of his mouth, releasing all the anxiety and tension of her life; she was flooded with the sensation of opening; the pain of her losses poured out, cleansing her and giving her back her real power, her safety within herself.

His hands moved down her back, caressing her buttocks and the tops of her thighs, his mouth drifting back and forth across her breasts, sucking and licking and kissing her nipples and the soft underskin, tracing the line from her bra. She stepped back, leaving him leaning forward for her. "I want to feel you," she said, hardly recognizing her voice.

He stood up and unbuckled his pants, letting them drop, the sound of his coins and car keys thudding against the carpet. He pulled off his shorts and she saw him. A big, naked man, his penis hard for her. She had never seen any man but her husband fully naked before, except in the movies.

He walked toward her and turned her backward, cupping her breasts in his hands, and she felt his erection pressing against the top of her buttocks. Lovely. Unbearably lovely.

"You're circumcised," she whispered.

He buried his face against the back of her neck, tonguing her like a hungry kitten.

"Bloody right. Think you'd hooked up with some heathen?"

He turned her around, holding her away from him for a moment. "You're magnificent," he said, and he kissed her, pulling her closer and closer, leading her backward until he could lower himself onto the bed without letting her go. They could not let one another go. He rolled her gently onto her back and she opened her legs to meet him. "I must fuck you just for a moment, and then I want to kiss your lovely little red cunt and fill you with my fingers and suck all of your toes and everything else I can find, but I just must be inside your magical pussy first. Please let me."

"Yes," she said, and he slid himself inside her, and she came, feelings flowing now like milk and honey, like nectar and fine wine, just flowing, so easily, so quietly. She reached out and pulled him down on top of her, feeling his full weight against her as he fucked her, pulsing into her, releasing sensations that she had never experienced before.

"Oh, yes," she said. "Oh, yes."

Three mornings later, Annie sat up. "I think maybe we should go for a walk or something."

The room was dark. Pizza boxes and Chinese take-out cartons, empty beer cans, and fish and chips trays lined the dresser. They had not left the bed, let alone the room (except to sit in the hallway while the maid changed the linens, thinking, Annie wondered, God only knew what); otherwise, they had only rolled off to bathe and pay the food delivery boys.

Now she was awake and in need of exercise and fresh air. Sleeping Beauty nineties-style, the prince leaning over to bestow a kiss and staying to bang her brains out.

Oliver turned over, three days' growth of new beard making him look like a bushwhacker or mountain man.

"Do you think that's wise? What if we're overcome on the way? I'm not convinced that we're stable enough yet to take such an enormous risk. Intercourse on the streets of London is frowned on, rather."

Annie ran her fingers through her curls, massaging her scalp. "I think we'd better chance it. We have to, you know, sooner or later. We're going to have bedsores if we don't get up pretty soon. We'll just have to do our best."

He raised himself up on one arm and leaned over, burying his face against the top of her sleep-warm thigh.

"Maybe later," he said into her leg.

"Oliver, really, I'm serious. . . . I think I'm serious."

He lifted his head and smiled at her. "Well, if it means that much to you. You Americans and your health regimens. I have actually gone three whole days without a cigarette in deference to your wishes, so a bit of open air is probably not without its good points."

"Great. I'll just jump in the shower." She slid out of bed, feeling his eyes on her and still shy under the pressure of his gaze. "Don't ogle."

"I'm too shortsighted to ogle; you look rather like Venus rising from the sea, shell and all. Besides, it's every dirty old man's right to ogle."

"You're still too young to be a dirty old man. And I know, because my father was one of the world's champions." She disappeared into the bathroom.

He followed her, stopping at the door. "May I watch?"

Annie blushed. There were still limits.

"No, you may not. It takes me years and years before I can allow that."

"I see," he said, without leaving. "Well, I'll just have to wait then."

She avoided his eyes. She had no idea how to respond.

He waited, sensing her discomfort. "I have a better idea than a walk," he said, discharging the tension. "Why don't we push on and take a little holiday. Have you ever been to Scotland? We could just set off and see where we land."

Annie tightened her towel around her, still waiting for him to leave before beginning her ablutions.

"No, I never have. Is it, I mean, is it all right? Can you just leave like that?"

"Oh, yes. My gallery is basically on hiatus until the beginning of February. I've got the inventory blokes and the accountants in, the next show is pretty well planned, and my curator is one of those truly fantastic Irish Catholic spinsters who is capable of running Parliament, let alone my gallery."

"Well, then, I'd love to. But only if you close that door and let me alone."

He grinned at her. His smile reminded her of Toby. Was that a deviant thought?

"Fine. I'll make some calls. We'll have to stop by my house for some clothes and things. I'd like you to see it anyway before we're off."

He closed the door and Annie turned on the tub. Could all of this be real? Could this actually be her and not some Annie clone, walking and talking like her, but not really there?

At moments she felt as if she had passed through the looking glass and was now wandering around in her experience, partly involved and partly searching for the way back through the mirror.

Scotland, she thought. It felt as if she had been gone for years rather than four days. Her husband, her children, her daily life floated in and out of her head like holograms, pleasant or painful, slightly abstracted like film images of someone familiar, but no longer tightly connected to herself.

Two middle-aged lovers in a small English car whizzing down the west Scottish coast in the rain, listening to Ella Fitzgerald sing "Here's That Rainy Day." Soft Scottish rain dropping like love notes on their car. Two people enthralled with one another; ecstatic with the newness of one another, every personal detail heard for the very first time by the most besotted and captive of audiences.

"All the women in my family danced. I was actually even a dance minor in college."

"You were? Let's go dancing! I love to dance. My wife had three left feet. I've almost forgotten how."

"It comes right back."

"Do you like Latin dancing? Jorge Ben and that sort?"

"You know about Jorge Ben? I can't stand it! I'm mad for him! I put on his records at home and dance myself into oblivion."

"I should like to see that. I know a wee bit about you and oblivion."

Two people bewitched in a small hotel on a Scottish bay, the sea echoing outside, the crackly *tings* from a log fire lulling on the inside, moaning in harmony on a feather bed while on the radio Rosemary Clooney sings "You've got to take what little pleasures you can find, when you've got sweet Kentucky ham on your mind."

Fresh river trout and Kir Royales in sparkling crystal goblets in an almost empty dining room on the Isle of Skye; sharing their bliss in the winter evening candlelight with two stork-legged sisters who drank single malt scotch while they dined.

Four-poster beds in restored Scottish castles, the smell of winter roses inhaled during their sex, mingling with the fragrance of one another; bubble baths in claw-legged tubs, fluffy white robes waiting on shiny brass hooks.

High tea with clotted cream and scones so light and fresh they hopped into their mouths — mouths raw from kissing and talking. Endless talking, biographers of one another's histories, wanting all the information no longer of any interest to the familiar loved ones in their former lives.

Blood-rare black-Angus steaks and fresh asparagus, decanted claret in a Lord's guesthouse; the only other guests a pudding-cheeked pair of newlyweds who never made it down for breakfast, the only thing they all held in common.

"Do you know Mozart's *Magic Flute*?" Oliver washed the last bite of his steak down with a swallow of wine.

Annie shook her head. "I am an opera illiterate. I have never been able to sit through more than two acts of any opera, and I don't even feel bad anymore about admitting it."

"I have a friend, a brilliant musical scholar, who is convinced that opera is the one form of music that one must come to young, that the love is an acquired taste, so this was not a loaded question."

"Good. My father was in the theater and I grew up on Rodgers and Hammerstein and Jule Styne. We never quite made it to the Met."

"Who is Jule Styne?"

Annie laughed. "Well, honey, he ain't Mozart, but in certain circles it would be just as bad admitting you didn't know who he was as never having seen *The Magic Flute*."

"An entertainer?"

"A composer of Broadway shows. A very famous and gifted one."

"I see. I've just learned something new." He took her hand and kissed the center of her palm, making her shudder.

He winked at her. "Ah, another erogenous zone. You are fast becoming some bloody human mainframe; whatever I press instantly supplies more information."

Annie blushed. "Shall we segue back to Mozart so I can finish my dinner in peace?"

"Oh, yes. Well, *The Magic Flute* is a very dicey opera. Many people find it pretentious, allegorical mumbo jumbo accompanied by bursts of luscious music, I among them, but in bed last night I kept thinking about the story, which is really about a journey from darkness to light, from unconsciousness to consciousness.

"The main characters go through all sorts of ridiculous turmoil, but what they are striving for, longing for, is to reach the highest step of humanity: not just to be loved, but to love in return; not just to be understood, but to understand."

"And it was written before Marianne Williamson. Amazing."

"Now, don't be cynical."

"I'm not, really. I just have a terrible time passing up a fast line."

"So I've noticed. Where was I?"

"Loving and being loved . . ."

"Right. Anyway, Prince Tamino is on the verge of a nervous breakdown. He is being pursued by serpents, he has a leg up on Hamlet in the fear of death department, and the love of his dreams, Pamina, has been abducted by a truly devilish letch. He has even lost his weapon, and the magic flute is given to him to guard him in danger."

"Sort of the pre-Mace device."

"You're doing it again."

"Sorry. I'll just chew. This is getting good."

"Well, I am doing a magnificent job of simplifying the libretto, if I do say so. Anyway, the lovers are living these tortured, fear-driven lives and they keep missing one another by not trusting, not seeing through any of the traps and deceptions put up by jealous courtiers as well as their own anxiety, so they run in circles almost dead from unrequited passion and heartache.

"But what happens to Tamino and Pamina is that finally, in a state of absolute terror, though not at the same time, they faint from fear. And when they awaken it is, symbolically, as if they had been reborn. He conquers his fear of death and she, who has clung to a memory and vision of her lost mother, becomes a mature woman. When you strip all the silliness of the production away, it was quite a tale to tell in the eighteenth century."

Annie put down her fork and looked at him. Tears filled her eyes.

"What have I done? It couldn't have been that boring."

She shook her head. "No, no. Oh, Oliver, that was so beautiful. It was about us, wasn't it. They reminded you of us."

He wiped his mouth, her words cutting through his glibness.

"Yes. I guess it was. Amazing piece of equipment the unconscious is; I really didn't know quite why it had been spinning in my brain until you told me."

"Are you terribly afraid of dying?"

"Bloody right! Bad genes floating all around my family tree on both sides. Everyone toffed off long before their time, whatever that means. But yes. My sister died of kidney failure at twenty-three, which was probably the worst of it all. I have been haunted by the fear of death all my life."

"My mother died on the kitchen floor at forty-five. I just outlived her Thanksgiving Day."

"That's your birthday? It's my favorite American holiday, and now I know why. Happy birthday, Annie." He raised his glass and they toasted. "I'm sorry about your mother. Is your father still alive?"

"No. He died just . . . well, soon after you and I met. It was sudden. Maybe that's why I'm here, I don't know. The Princess Pamina syndrome, too much loss."

She paused, not sure if she should move forward, knowing that if she did, it could bring them back to reality. "Oliver, there's so much we've talked about, but so much we haven't. I don't want to spoil one second in this romantic bubble, but you should know this. Probably the main reason I decided to come was that my husband has been having an affair with . . . your Pot Person — I just can't say her name. He ended it just a couple of weeks ago and he wanted me to go to Japan with him and try to rebuild our relationship. I just didn't seem to be able to hop right back in the old saddle, so to speak. Of course, you may already know about this; I may seem really naive."

"I did know." He put down his glass, keeping his eyes on her.

She stiffened, not having evolved to Tamino and Pamina's near perfect state. "My God! Was that why you . . . because you thought I must be neglected and needy?"

"The truth be told, Annie, I didn't know anything about it until after we had mesmerized one another. I was, of course, a tad curious about the mystery woman whom I had just fondled passionately and invited to join me in London, maybe for the rest of my life! Ivy told me at dinner that night."

Annie gasped. "Did you . . . I mean —"

"Annie! How big a bloody fool do you take me for? You haven't had enough disappointment in the relationship wars to be so suspicious."

"I don't have to; I'm Jewish. It's genetic."

He laughed, and she could see the fear leave his face.

"Look, I've known Ivy Clare for a very long time and while I might enjoy her ferocity and make a profit on her work now and again, she is hardly the sort of person one confides in. She also would have gone right around and told your husband, which wouldn't have done me any good whatsoever. Satisfied?"

Annie sighed. "Yes. I just had a little lapse. I do have moments of anxiety-induced acceleration, where I just completely speed up whatever possible doom-and-gloom scenario is on my plate. Most of the time I do it inside my head, and rapid eye movement or something would be your only clue. I haven't actually had an episode in quite a while, but that's because so many really awful things have been happening that I haven't needed any additional excitement, so —"

He reached across and put his fingers, smelling of smoke and aged Scottish beef, on her lips. "I love you. I love you completely," he said, stopping her mid-sentence and crumbling her hastily built wall of resistance.

There was nothing more terrifying or more wonderful that he could possibly have said. Tears ran down her cheeks and over his fingers.

She had never told any man but Mickey that she loved him in this way, and no man but Mickey had ever said those words to her. If she said them back now, she was really in that Ferris-wheel cage again, bobbing to and fro, or fainting dead away from fright like the Magic Princess. She could not do it, even though she knew that it was true. She loved him, too.

They drove on, stopping each night at a new place on the blustery coast; checking in politely and pouncing on one another the moment the room clerk closed the door behind them. They kept waiting for their desire to ebb, but it did not.

They strolled down rocky, deserted beaches and ate fresh salmon and herring and boiled potatoes with dill, and steaming pots of porridge, and drank Irish tea, talking all the while, talking as if they were the last living talkers and must utter every last syllable as their legacy to the world.

"I know I speak rather roughly, lots of working-class slang and all. I wasn't raised that way. My father was a barrister and my mum was a brilliant musicologist — hence, the opera. But I grew up in that time when wild working-class boys were making their mark in London theater and the art world. I ran with that lot, actors who are now either very famous or long dead, and pop artists.

"I started as a set designer, but the world around the theater didn't really suit my nature. I could never debauch on the grand scale and I was basically a solitary sort.

"When my sister died, I lost the heart for it all. But I still prefer the energy of creative people and a bit of gritty talk. I don't much care for the upper crumbs, though they do buy art, they do, they do.

"I have one child, Ian, by my first wife. He's twenty now and the center of my life. I never loved his mother, but she got preggers and I married her. She's a fine woman and we're great chums. She lives in Spain now, married to an airline pilot. My son is here studying painting, which absolutely tears my heart with joy.

"Elena, my *real* wife, was an art historian. We lived the whole London life for a long time. We wanted children together desperately, actually. But I couldn't. Something off in the sperm count, so Ian is even more precious.

"It ate away at us, but neither of us wanted to adopt one. It just seemed too frightening to have some total stranger set down in your life one morning.

"But it did something to Elena, or maybe it would have happened anyway, and she began to withdraw. First she stopped teaching. Then she stopped lecturing. Then she wanted to live in the Cotswolds and raise some sort of bloody hound-dogs!

"I agreed, and we moved, and I was commuting, running hither and yon. I had lost everyone close by then, parents, others. She really was, besides my child, all I had.

"One Friday I came back from my work week in London and she was out back with her dogs and she turned and smiled at me, and her eyes had gone. I don't mean literally; she wasn't standing there with bare sockets or such. I mean she could no longer see me. She smiled at me with vacant eyes.

"English women can turn like that, you know — we have a fine long tradition of well-bred British belles of a certain age waking up one morn a bit potty; not harmful to others or themselves, but gone eccentric, none the less. I was no longer real or necessary to her.

"My parents had left me their house in South Kensington, a wonderful house, or it is now, as you have briefly seen.

"Well, I had grown up there and it held the ghosts of everyone I loved. For years I rented it out, but I couldn't reenter it until I left Elena. I moved in and went to work on it. I did most of the renovation myself — an old set designer at heart, I suppose.

"I cried every bloody day. I exorcised it and I reclaimed it. I had really just finished when I went to California and met you."

They stopped for lunch at the Roman Camp Hotel and walked the ruins of the old Roman path hand in hand, and drank Bloody Marys by the marble fire in the salon, and ate venison with juniper berries all alone in the pretty French dining room.

Everywhere they went they seemed to be the only guests, the only vagabonds; as if all the doe-faced room clerks and apple-cheeked waiters were there just for them. There was no interloper to break into their cocoon of ecstasy, their private excavation of one another's past.

"How do you feel about ruined abbeys?" he asked, wiping cauliflower hollandaise from his upper lip.

"I probably feel just fine about them. I've never seen one."

"Why don't we drive back through Yorkshire and not go on into Edinburgh. I promise you won't be disappointed.

"Yorkshire is absolute perfection in early spring when everything jumps back into bloom. The fields are the color of emeralds and fresh limes and coated with new life, lambs and calves and fawns and chicks running everywhere. Flowers popping up right before your eyes. It's almost sickeningly Mary Poppins. It's my favorite place in England — but the abbeys are just as magnificent in winter. They are incorruptible by season or anything else."

Annie smiled. "I'd love to. There's a small hotel in York that I'd like to stop by. I've always wanted to write about it."

"I know the one. The owner's a chum of mine."

She turned toward him. "When we get to York, I must call home."

"Yes, I've been waiting for that."

They had been in York for two days before Annie made her call. She had been gone for almost two weeks and had only phoned once, just before they left London. Sometimes she would reach out for the phone, the way she always had when she was away, reaching out for the haven at the other end, tales of daily life humming reassurance of her place on earth through the receiver.

Now things were different. Her children lived their own lives and their safety was no longer either her direct responsibility or under her control. Her husband was off on a pilgrimage of his own, her father was dead, and they no longer had any job commitments or investment concerns to keep tabs on.

This, she realized, was the terror of freedom. She could now vanish from her own life for weeks at a time and not only was it perfectly all right, but no one really noticed the difference. Her hand still reached out for the connection.

Since their arrival in York, however, she had hesitated, sensing that once she picked up the phone, the door to their enchanted cottage would be blown open, filling their sacred place with bellowing clarity. It was Oliver who finally convinced her.

"Annie, I cannot stand another furtive glance at the telephone. Make the bloody call and do us both a favor. The tension is worse than whatever's waiting on the other end."

"Easy for you to say," she said, picking it up. "What time is it there?"

Oliver pondered the slip knot between them and California.

"It's too early. Let's see Rievaulx, have a bite of lunch, and then do it."

"Good." She grabbed her camera and was out the door before him.

She had never seen anything so purely, mystically perfect as the ruined Abbey of Rievaulx, rising out of the snow-covered ground like a phantom ship; a creation of its own, no longer a part of, a remain of, anything. She did not believe it could have ever been more spiritual or more beautiful when it was whole. It looked like the abbey's soul, the truth within the building. She closed her eyes and prayed that her soul, everyone's soul was like this — an essence of being.

They were the only visitors and they moved languidly, Oliver guiding her eye to details only seen by a serious observer. His love of this wonder moved her deeply, and her feelings for him tumbled forward, dazzling her.

As afraid as she was of these new emotions, they were irresistibly delicious. All the experiences of the last ten days were just too maddeningly delectable to deny. She had never had so many positive sensations in a row. The truth was, she realized, standing against a cold stone wall and looking across at Oliver above her on the rim of an arch, that she was far more comfortable with bad feelings than joyous ones. It had always been easier for her to feel anger, sadness, resentment, fear, jealousy, and self-doubt than joy, ecstasy, and happiness. What a truly dreadful and depressing thing to have to admit forty-five years into her life! Well, it was time, way past time, to stop dabbling on the bank and plunge into the stream. What philosopher had written about life as a river, about not being able to step into the same water twice? Well, she had even gone him one better; she would get to the other side without stepping into the actual wet stuff at all!

How terrible to have missed so many years of floating and splashing.

She watched him make his way back to her, astonished that her feelings had led her here; not her head and not her fear, but some more powerful and playful and braver part of herself that she had finally claimed, or reclaimed. Whatever happened to them next, this was worth it. She would never regret one moment of this time with him.

Oliver's face was rosy from the cold and his hair was blown forward across his brow, making him look sweet and impish.

"Let me take your picture," she said, and he grinned at her.

"Very well, but let me take yours first. Too bad there's no one about to capture us together."

"We'll just have to tape them." She held up her camera and he stopped walking, looking awkward the way most people do when someone is looking at them through a cold and impartial lens, capturing their image in the intractable and revealing way of photos.

She looked at him through the tiny eye; a big man reduced by the frame, reduced in his vibrancy and humor. But his eyes were bright and clear, smiling at her, filled with his heart, filled with his love.

* * *

"Good morning, the Wilder residence. How may I help you?"

"Juanita?"

"Mrs. W! This is fontostic! I been thinking all morning you was gonna call."

"Juanita, what is this 'Wilder residence, how may I help you' thing?"

"Oh, I seen it on the TV on one of my soaps. The housekeeper, she answer the phone like that and I think, that's so cool, gives my Wilders more class. If some producer should call up for Mr. W, it looks good, like we're not feelin' any pain."

Annie laughed. "Well, I appreciate your concern, but don't you think it's a little bit, I don't know, too formal for us?"

"Maybe so. I tried it out on Mrs. O'Brian, Mr. Jackie, and the kids so far, and they just laughed at me, so you may be right. I'm waiting until some new person calls to see how it goes. I'll give it another week."

"Sounds fair enough. How are you? Is everything okay?"

"Sure. Toby called from school. He got a cold, just a little one, no big deal. He's taking a dramatic class and he likes it, so he's more happy. Ella told me all about her boyfriend from Austria —"

"Australia."

"I say it okay."

"You said it fine, but it's a different place. Austria is in Europe and Australia is . . . well, I don't quite know how to tell you where it is. It's on the entire other side of the planet."

"No way! You mean like the North Pole?"

"Not quite, but almost as far from New York."

"My Ella going to live in this Australia, like going to outer space or something?"

"Well, it's not that bad, it just feels that bad."

"Boy, this must be some guy. Must be a god like my Pomfi."

"Ella seems to think so. Did she send pictures yet? She promised me she would. We'll all get to meet him in March."

"She say me that. That's cool. Oh, so anyway, she happy. She busy like crazy trying to get ready to go over there and everything."

Annie took a breath. "Has Mr. Wilder called?"

"That's why I been going so crazy since yesterday! He call from Tokyo. Is that close to this Australia?"

"Closer than California, but I'm not exactly sure how far away."

"Well, he's calling almost every day, because you didn't tell him where you were going after London, he says. This make me very upset, Mrs. W, cause it means you and Mr. W are not being together and I don't like to even think about that. But anyway he is calling many times and I'm telling him that I haven't talked to you; but last night he call me very excited. He say, 'If Mrs. Wilder calls, tell her I've found Leonard Lewis.'

"Mr. Lewis is in Japan and he saw Mr. W on a Japan TV show and called him and he say he's in hiding and not to tell nobody, but then Mr. Lewis say to him, 'Have Annie come. I'll talk to Annie, but no one else. She the only one I trust anymore.'

"So he need you to call him, 'ASAP,' he say. What means that? I don't hear that before. He say his producer in Tokyo has booked you a seat, first class! He say to tell you and you must go there ASAP. What a relief you called! I prayed to the Virgin, and my cousin, she do a reading for you and you called!"

Splash. She was in the river now. The rapids churning everything around and around. Hope (they had found Leonard Lewis!) and loss. Her bliss was ending; she would have to leave Oliver and venture back into her former, and now unfamiliar, real life, waiting somewhere downstream.

She looked up and saw him sitting in a chair, his reading glasses low on his nose, his book in his lap, watching her over the rims, the sadness back in his sexy blue eyes.

"Juanita, I'll call him right away but if I can't reach him and he calls you back, have him give you all the flight information and tell him that I'll call you again as soon as I get back to London, which should be in about . . ."

She looked over at Oliver. He was holding up his fingers. Fingers that had just come out of her, fingers that she had caressed and sniffed and sucked and let travel her body and take over her being.

"In about four hours. Tell him I'm on my way."

"Mrs. W, one sec. So what this 'ASAP'?"

Annie laughed. Juanita never gave up, or lost interest in learning. Juanita knew how to live for today. "It is an acro — an abbreviation for 'as soon as possible.'"

"No kidding? I never hear this one. I like this. I am using this immediately. I use it on Pomfi. 'You pick up those dirty socks ASAP.' This is terrific."

"Juanita, will you call the kids for me? Tell them where I'm going, but not why, and that I'm fine and that I love them very much."

"Okey dokey. But I know how to say that stuff. They know it anyway, even if I don't fill in the blanks."

"You too, Juanita. I love you, too."

Juanita paused. Annie had never said that before in words. Had she embarrassed her? Why did she feel she needed to say it now?

"I know that also, without filling in the blanks."

"I'll call you later even if I reach Mr. W."

She hung up and crossed to Oliver. He put down his book and reached out for her, and she curled up on his lap and put her arms around his shoulders, holding on tight. She put her head against his neck and kissed the soft, lemon-smelling skin in the crease between his collarbone and chest.

There were parts of men's bodies that were as soft and silky as babies' bodies, and kissing them felt the same, mother love seeping through woman love, the boy inside the man, melting the raw threat of invasion.

"I knew something was happening, I just felt it," she said, and held him closer, already saying good-bye.

"What is it?"

"I can't tell you. I swear I would if I could and I'm not trying to be mysterious. I can only say that it's vitally important that I go to Japan and that it has nothing to do with my marriage."

"Sounds pretty bloody Mickey Spillane for a cute little Hollywood wife."

She pulled back and tried to get up. "That wasn't very nice."

He held her. "No, it wasn't."

"Let me go now. I have to get dressed and call Mickey."

"So that's it? Thanks for the tour and I'm off to Japan?"

"Oliver, you don't mean that."

He let her go, almost pushing her off his lap. "Go on. Go on. Lock the bathroom door and clean it all back up."

She stumbled and almost fell back against him. She had never seen him angry and she did not know what to do. How easy it would be, she thought, to have a fight and just march out, slamming the door on their love affair, heading off like Nora, fleeing one miniature house for another.

"Oliver, please don't. Let's not do this. I don't want to leave you like this."

"Like what? Is there a nice neat American way to do this? I hope not."

"Oliver, I must go there for *my* future, with or without Mickey. Did you think that I would never have to go back and deal with the rest of my life?"

"I'm not some frothing fool, Annie! It's just rather abrupt. I wasn't prepared."

"Neither was I." She tried to reach out to him, but he stood up and pushed past her, looking in his jacket for his cigarettes.

"Well, at least I'll be able to have a bloody fag in peace for a change." He lit the cigarette and she saw his fingers trembling.

"Oliver, don't hurt me. Don't say things to hurt me, please."

"Why not? Better you see my dark side, see the broody bellicose swine under the tender drooly chap who's been whizzing you around in some adolescent wooing frenzy. It should make your flight back to Mr. Hair Spray so much easier."

"Oliver, I'm not going back to Mickey. I'm going because it involves the money that was stolen from us. *All* of our money! Please, oh please, don't try to cheapen this. I'm not leaving *you*. I can't bear the thought of leaving you. . . . I have to. I just have to."

He crossed his arms over his chest and watched her. She was afraid that he would cry and she would not be able to go.

"So, exactly what are we talking about here? What does this mean? I'm hanging all the way out here, my dear, and I have been since the day I saw the back of your curly red head. I can't stay this unfurled much bloody longer; it's just too big a risk for someone like me, such a lonely old sot; and when I decide to wrap my sails up, Annie-girl, I wrap them tight and for good. I don't want to have to, but I can."

"I don't want you to! I don't know anything else except that I don't want you to and I will be back. I promise."

He stamped out his cigarette, the smoke threading the air between them.

"How long?"

"One week. I'll be back in one week."

It rained on the drive back and they drove in silence for a while, listening to the thud of the wipers on the windshield and to the thoughts inside their own heads. Coming back from any holiday was always wistful, an ending of experience; but this felt even more poignant, because they lacked the stability and commitment to reassure themselves that they would do it ever again.

He pulled up in front of his house and turned off the motor.

"Well, Cinderella, time to let the coach turn back into a gourd."

She turned toward him and took his hand, sniffing his fingers as if memorizing the smell, and held them against her lips. She held on to his hand, pressing her cheek against it. She did not want to open the door and let go of him, of what they had shared. She knew that even if they decided to spend the rest of their lives together, they would never have exactly this again.

He reached over and stroked her head, as if knowing her thoughts. He lifted her face and kissed her, so gently and so sweetly that it took her breath. She felt his love enter her, in an almost physical way.

"Oh, bloody Christ," he said, pulling away. He put his head on the steering wheel and his wide, husky shoulders shook with sobs. "I never thought it would be this hard to let you go."

She reached over and stroked his shaggy head, kneading his hair with her fingers. "One week," she whispered, and he turned his face and she saw his fear.

She needed to tell him. It wasn't fair to leave him without saying it back. "Oliver, I've never said this to any man but my husband in my entire life, so please know how hard it is and what it means to me to tell you." Her voice felt thick and it was hard to form the words. Tears slid down her cheeks, running across her lips, slowing her down. "Oh, God help me, I love you. I love you so, I can barely stand it! Please know that, please remember it while I'm gone."

He reached over for her and they clung to one another, squeezed together in a small, unprotected space, a perfect circle from their beginning.

Oliver opened the front door and Annie followed him inside. She had not reached Mickey and she was an hour overdue on her call to Juanita.

He stopped in the hall. There was light coming from his study at the back of the house and the sound of the television echoing through the darkness.

"That's funny," he said, not moving forward.

"What?"

"Ian's supposed to be in Spain with his mother for winter break and he's the only person with a key."

Annie smoothed her coat, their car scene still clouding her senses. She was not prepared to meet his son.

"Shall I wait upstairs?"

"No, no. Just stay here for a moment. Let me find out what's going on."

He turned and smiled at her and she smiled back, knowing that they were saying farewell, that their private place was about to be encroached upon by others. Even a son would alter everything.

She nodded and he moved forward. "Oliver, I think I will run upstairs and call home."

"All right," he said, without stopping.

She had not seen the upstairs of his house on their brief stop before Scotland and she wandered down the hall past Ian's room and the guest room, which for some reason she felt had belonged to his sister, until she came to his.

It was so like him, she thought, switching on the light and standing in the doorway. Virile and straightforward. One wonderful Moroccan rug, plain, polished maple floors, an enormous abstract painting over the white-sheeted double bed, a phone and books stacked on an ornately carved wooden cabinet that looked Indian or Persian. She took a deep breath, smelling him in the room. She was sorry now that she had not held him in this room. In this special house where he had finally buried his dead.

She sat down on the mattress next to a picture of his son, who looked exactly the way she imagined Oliver had looked at twenty or so, and picked up the phone.

"Wilder residence. How may I —"

"It's me, Juanita!"

"Fontostic! I just talk to Mr. W. He give me all the flight info. He figure out that the plane leaves from London at ten o'clock England time. Is that cool? If not he say you gotta call and rebook yourself for tomorrow."

Annie looked at Oliver's clock. It was shaped like a cow and had little plastic feet and big old-fashioned numbers on the dial. It was just past six. She could make it.

"No, that's fine. Just give me the information and then call him right back and tell him that I'll be on the plane. I'll call you from Tokyo."

"It's cool. I handle everything. Then I pray like crazy and have my cousin light some candles, and everything gonna be good."

She wrote down the details and hung up the phone and sat for a moment. Her bag was still in Oliver's car and she was ready to go. He had not come up to find her and she was not quite sure what to do. She picked up her purse and walked into his bathroom. A large black terry cloth robe hung on a hook, and she buried her face in it, breathing him in.

She switched on the light over the sink, startling herself with the harshness of her reflection in the yellow-white brightness. It was as if someone had pulled a veil off her, clearing the gauzy filter through which she had viewed herself for the last fortnight.

She had gone from a lifetime of glaring at herself in an unmercifully hard and unforgiving light to a kinder, gentler vision born in the slightly out of focus nebula of romantic bliss.

She had reentered too abruptly and resurfaced without adjusting her body to the change in pressure. She took out her makeup kit and went to work repairing her face, trading her blurry diving mask for her more familiar social one. She powdered her nose and relined her eyes and painted her lips and blushed her cheeks and brushed out her hair.

She turned and went back into his room, saying little good-byes as she passed, making her way back down the hall.

The voice on the television was familiar. A sort of slightly affected voice, an American trying to sound British. Dick Cavett, she thought. "The little blond raisin," Molly called him. Molly's name brought her life back to her. Lina and Jackie and her children, and Loretta and her brother, and Mickey.

Oliver was talking to someone. She heard another voice, a woman's voice. Some woman was in his study with him. It was definitely not a young man's voice.

She did not quite know what to do, but she kept moving forward toward the light at the end of the hall, toward the Cavett and the other voices. She could not understand quite what they were saying. The woman was upset. She heard fragments.

"I'm coming apart. I am having a total breakdown over this!"

Over what? Over Oliver? Was she some woman of Oliver's that he hadn't told her about? *Oh, God, don't let it be that. Don't let me leave with that in my head.*

She reached the doorway. Oliver was standing in the middle of the room, obscuring her view. The woman was sitting on the couch, crying into a handkerchief. Oliver moved when he heard her, and Annie saw the woman's hands. She would know those hands anywhere. Ivy Clare was sitting on Oliver's brown leather couch.

CHAPTER XVI

MICKEY WILDER SAT FORWARD on the ice-cold metal slats of a Hibaya Park bench and pulled the wrinkled, word-processed pages out of his windbreaker. He had read them so many times in the last week he knew the text by heart, but rereading the damn thing made him feel more connected to her: "The Tokyo Tango" by Annie Wilder.

This is why I'm losing her, Mickey thought, folding the pages of his wife's article and stuffing them back inside his windbreaker. *I never even read the fucking thing!* He shivered, the cold making his eyes and nose run incessantly and keeping his throat so dry he could barely swallow.

He picked up his coffee container and pulled back the lid, letting the steam cover his chapped, pancake-plastered face. DUNKIN' DONUTS, the cup said, in cheerful pink graphics. The malling of the universe.

It didn't even matter where you were anymore; everything was everywhere. Walking from his hotel to the shoot he had passed four Kentucky Colonels! They even had Colonel Santa nailed to a crucifix in some Yuletide displays. Why not? Why the hell not. They had everything else; Häagen-Dazs, Brooks Brothers, Mrs. Fields', The Gap, McDonald's, Timberland — why not Colonel Christ?

Most of the young Japanese were so trendy and Americanized that unless you saw them bowing, they could be citizens of anywhere.

Well, that wasn't entirely true. In fact, now that he thought about it, maybe it wasn't true at all, beneath the surface. Under the attire they were as foreign as the crew of the fucking *Enterprise*. The worst part, in terms of working, even on a car commercial, was that no one ever said what they really meant, or told you what they really wanted.

Yes meant no, for chrissakes! What could you possibly do as an actor with that kind of direction?

And no one under any circumstances would ever admit they didn't understand something. Never. It was a daily version of the story Jackie had told on Thanksgiving, and two weeks of it was more than enough. He had never been so tired.

This was the worst place to be alone that he had ever been in his entire life. The last time he had been here, Annie had been with him. She had waited patiently on the set or wandered around Tokyo all bundled up in her awful down coat, the one he always teased her about because it looked like she was wearing a comforter. "But it's so warm!" she said, her small, freckled face barely poking out of the top of the damn thing.

His wife, waiting in the wings, pushed back by grips, ignored by the sponsors and the producers, the only wife at dinner, the only woman not working on the film.

"I think I'll try to write something about being here," she said, and what did he do? He said, fine, great, and went back to being the center of attention. *He had never even read the fucking thing.* She had given it to him and he had scanned it and told her it was good, and that was that. He had never even really read it, and she had gone home and put it in their Japan file and proceeded with the slow and steady emptying of her nest and never even tried to publish it.

He had thrown the file into his carry-on, with his scripts and guidebooks and camera, and the pages had fallen out into his lap on the airplane. Just seeing it had been painful, but reading it was worse, because it was good. It was really good, and it was so *her.*

All of the frustrated and never expressed parts of her that she had somehow lost confidence in along the way. She had allowed herself to be ever so politely pushed into the corner, out of the key light and into his shadow. And he had done nothing to help her.

He had never even really read the fucking thing.

Tears of cold and anguish mingled together, crisscrossing his cheeks. What had he done? What had he gone and done to his wife? He was all alone in a place that they had once been together, where her support and humor, her tilt at all the absurdity, had kept him safe in a bizarre and opaque land, surrounded by people who covered their mouths when they laughed and never spoke a spontaneous word. Certainly not his or Annie's kind of crowd.

He remembered a dinner with the sponsors of the miniseries and Annie and some of the other actors. Annie was the only woman, and he could tell that her patience was running out.

The actors were trying to out-Japanese the Japanese and everyone was being superpolite and terribly pretentious. Annie told him later that she felt as if they were all talking through gas masks. Annie leaned forward and asked the president of the whole megacompany: "What is the weirdest thing that you have ever eaten?"

All the actors and the executives froze, waiting for the big boss to react, and the translator went to work and there was this moment of intense unease, and then he laughed. He laughed and laughed and threw his little gray head back and slapped his knees, and then all the salarymen laughed and the actors took off their gas masks and laughed, and finally the boss replied, grinning like the Buddha himself: "Baby bees."

Around the table Annie went, questioning all his executives: "live silverfish," "roast snake," "crocodile eggs," "ocelot," "live baby squid," "rat embryos."

Then the actors joined in; but the Japanese won hands down, and Annie's beaming, freckled face filled his heart with pride.

Such a spunky little broad, always walking close to the social edge but never falling off. She had instincts, his wife did. He had moved her from her real home, her place of strength; her children had left, her career had faltered, and he had betrayed her. In some perverse way, when he wasn't being insanely, ravenously jealous of whoever this prick in London was screwing his wife, he was almost happy for her, happy that someone had come forward to validate her again, to pay that attention and help her through.

He had read her article so many times now that the pages were all crumpled and frayed and stained from the sweat on his fingers. It was the only thing that belonged to her that he had to hold on to now, the pages and his wedding ring and his terror of losing her now that he had his sanity back and understood what he had risked.

He reached into his pocket for a Kleenex, and a roll of paper fell onto the dry, icy ground. He leaned down and retrieved his pack of temple fortune papers, picked up at one of the shrines he had visited with his "assigned guide."

"You will not hear from her, but she will come to see you." He had gotten that one before Leonard's call. "You will fall seriously ill, but will never fail to get well." He smiled. Thank God Annie hadn't gotten that one! He remembered her in Kyoto at the shrine set up on wooden stilts, where Japanese schoolgirls wrote all their troubles down on some kind of dissolving paper and dropped the paper into a wishing well, hoping all their worries would dissolve with the paper. Annie had practically written the Bill of Rights, standing there, guilelessly scribbling down with her little hotel pen everything she had ever worried about or been afraid of.

"Annie, no one is *that* anxiety ridden! You're going to plug the whole thing up."

She had kept right on writing, thrilled by the chance to fend off all her worst fears for herself and her family.

Kyoto had been their treat at the end of filming. They had walked everywhere and seen everything. They had sat for a long time on the steps of the famous Ryoan-ji rock sculpture garden, surrounded by serious tourists and Zen-heads, all staring at the long rectangle of raked sand with fifteen stones placed in an apparently random design.

The rock sculpture garden was one of those paradoxes where one minute they sort of got it and thought the thing was really spiritual and uniquely beautiful, and just a blink later they thought it was all total bullshit. They had reacted almost as if they were one being to everything they saw in Kyoto. And they had laughed so much, watching Japanese *Hollywood Squares* at two A.M. in their hotel room and making love on a tatami with a movie running in the background that went on for hours, lulling them to sleep; a movie where an army of men trudged through a blizzard in knee-deep snow, trudged silently on for hours, coming from nowhere and arriving nowhere.

"Imagine selling *that* to Paramount," he had said, and she had not even laughed, she was so intent on figuring out the symbolism.

She was always so serious in her desire to understand everyone. If she could figure out the psyche of these people, then she would be safe among them; she was always trying to control things that way, making the feared things harmless.

Where the hell was she right now and how did she feel? Did she feel as lost and frightened and lonely as he did? Was that prick treating her well? Was she okay?

He would know soon enough. He looked at his watch. She would be there in just a few hours. God, he could feel his heart skip just thinking about seeing her. It was almost as if they had just met, but met the way grown-up lovers meet, with all that rush of excitement and tremulousness; not the sort of gradual sliding into place beside one another that they had done.

It was as if they were beginning all over, starting from an entirely different launching pad. But it was not the same as their real beginning, because they had never come together for the first time as grown-ups. He had never really thought about that. Would they have been attracted to one another, fallen madly in love, if they had met in college or later? What about if they had just recently met? It was impossible to know.

Now she was arriving like some mail-order war bride, returning to a place they had been in better times, or at least different times; a time when the thought of their marriage ending, of either of them slipping off the edge of their bond into the arms of others would have seemed as preposterous as any shocking change in a life support system.

He had to get a grip on this new truth before Annie arrived. She was not coming because she missed him; she was coming because Leonard Lewis wanted to see her. She was coming for their money, not for him. He must give her some room and some time. He must not push her. He had certainly made it clear enough before he left that he wanted to come home to her, that he still loved her.

But even so, he had not quite understood the depth of his need for her, what being without her, the thought of her really leaving his life, felt like. He had not truly experienced the loss of her until she was really gone and he was really alone in a place that held her presence, the fizz of her inside his head, but not the comfort of her real self.

He thought of a birthday card Jackie had given him one year. On the front was a very young, very sexy blonde holding a birthday cake covered with candles. "On your birthday," it said, "you can have your cake or you can have Edith, but you can't have your cake and Edith, too."

Well, he had tried. Yes he had. Prophetic as the damn card turned out to be. He had almost succeeded, maybe would have succeeded if it hadn't been for the damn underpants, and if his hallway hadn't been carpeted — if it had been like the floor in the Nijo Castle, the nightingale floor, which was designed to squeak like the birds to warn the guards of enemies approaching the shogun. If he had only heard Annie in the hall.

What was he saying? What the hell was he thinking? If he had gotten away with it, if he had gotten to act out every scene in his Ivy repertoire without his wife finding out, then everything would still be okay? What kind of an asshole was he? Did he really believe that it was only a matter of getting caught?

No fucking way. It had happened for a reason, and what had happened to Annie had happened for a reason also, not just because she was suspicious about him.

What kind of marriage would they have ended up with if he had heard the squeak and shoved Ivy into the closet or something? It would have tainted everything honest and good between them. It would still have ruined their marriage. No. It was better this way. If she still loved him, if she could trust him again, it was better that they both knew what they had done. They could walk back toward one another now on a freshly mowed and leveled playing field. The ball would be put back into play by an impartial referee.

Annie called the point-keeping that went on in marriage "marital mileage plus." Every time she showed up at some Hollywood event or entertained people like Stan Stein, she always said, "I've got about fifty thousand miles coming on this one." Well, they had now just about used all of their bonus coupons. They had both cashed in big tickets and evened the score. He had hurt her and she had hurt him.

So, okay. She was coming for whatever reason. Leonard had told him to have her go to the hotel and wait for further instructions, so hopefully they would have some time together. He had two more days of shooting on the series of commercials and another week's work on the soap opera.

War Zone was starting to run there and it looked like it could be a big hit. They would be all right. They would be fine. Stan Stein had faxed him a script for a new series and the part was terrific. It had been one helluva fall and winter, but they would come through it.

The script girl was running toward him, her pretty, moon face blue with cold. One more setup and he could go back and take a long hot shower and wait for Annie.

He stood up, feeling suddenly weak, almost too tired to move. Jesus. He was trying to pep himself up, but his body was telling him something else. So much damage had been done to Ella and Toby; they would never be the same as a family again. He had lost the respect of his children, he had lost the trust of his wife. He was dangling in midair like some fucking Kabuki puppet.

The girl ran up, stopping at a polite distance and bowing to him. He smiled, recognizing the bow from his bowing pamphlet as "the polite bow," a bend at an angle of thirty degrees to greet guests on very polite occasions. It was more respectful than the fifteen-degree "casual bow," but not as flattering as the coveted forty-five-degree, "most polite bow," which was used to apologize or to "revere somebody or honor persons of importance."

Mickey finished his coffee and followed the girl back to the bright yellow car gleaming by the central fountain — which kept freezing over and having to be melted with blowtorches and pails of boiling water. It was okay, the bow; that was where he was in his life, somewhere around a thirty-degree angle, trying to bow from the waist without bending his neck, bowing because it was a must for "a smooth social life and human relations," bowing with good eye contact before and after the bow and, of course, bowing without falling over in a heap.

There was one thing about his positioning that he was sure of, the most important part of the bow according to his pamphlet. It must be done with sincerity of heart. He would try for a better angle with Annie. He would go for the forty-five-degree big-timer. He would look directly into his wife's big green eyes and keep his aching back straight and his frozen feet together and go for it. And he would do it with a daunted but truly sincere heart.

CHAPTER XVII

LOOK, WE'RE LIVING in the Age of the Sociopaths; there are slimeballs lined up from Newark to Nogales ready to tell us what we want to hear. It's harder and harder to find any truth, even within ourselves. Too many 'experts' telling us too much contradictory information. We all have little puzzle-pieces of our own truth, all mixed up with millions of fragments of universal truth, but no one has the time or energy, let alone the clarity, to sit down and put the damn puzzle together."

Annie was dozing, the voice moved across the aisle, floating in and out of her restless, midflight sleep. Maybe the entire conversation was in her dream. She liked the image, puzzle pieces; good title for a book, a book about a woman — someone like her, for example. The Puzzle Woman, she would have to remember that, she would have to write that down when she woke up.

She should make herself wake up and write it down, because when she didn't she never remembered. How many good ideas had she lost in her sleep? Too many, but she still didn't want to wake up; if she woke up she would have all those hours to separate her from Oliver's house. She did not want to think about it anymore. She was just too tired and confused. Pieces of the truth crammed into her pockets, without a chance of being put into place anytime soon.

She turned toward the window and curled her legs up. It was cold, even with two blankets, but at least it was a sleeper seat. She shook her fingers, which had fallen asleep, and put her hand up under her long full skirt, trying to keep warm. All those poor people in coach with no place to stretch their legs. She always felt guilty when she flew first class, but not guilty enough to go back and give someone in coach her seat. Phony liberal bullshit, she murmured to herself, invading her own semiconsciousness. Couldn't she even be nice to herself when she was sleeping?

She sank deeper, back into dreams, and the voice across the aisle gave way to the ones inside her mind. She was in someone's house. An old Russian woman holding a great big juicy dill pickle was coming toward her and Mickey.

"Here, try this, it's my specialty," she said, and held it out to Mickey, who shook his head.

Annie took the pickle, trying to be nice, and bit into the crunchy, bulbous head. "It's delicious," she said to the woman, who ignored her, focusing on Mickey and making her angry, so angry that she took the pickle and threw it on the ground, smashing it with her bare foot. The woman motioned for them to follow, not noticing the murdered pickle. Mickey pushed in front, leaving her behind.

They entered a dark narrow dining room where two slick male tango dancers were strutting back and forth. "Now they will fight," announced the woman, who was no longer old nor Russian but had turned into Ivy Clare.

The men picked up swords and approached the table, laying the blades down like knives and pushing them back and forth at one another.

"What a disgrace," the woman said, and Annie moved closer, not understanding.

"You have embarrassed yourself," she said, and left the room. Annie moved toward the men, who were tangoing off with one another, their faces turned away from her.

"Excuse me please, what did I do wrong?"

The men ignored her and she followed them as they tangoed out and down a long red tunnel. She was afraid of the tunnel, but she followed, calling to them, "Please tell me what I did wrong!" They reached the end and she ran after them, begging them to wait.

They turned, they were no longer tango dancers but had become Mickey and Oliver, and she stopped, not knowing where to go.

"Don't leave me here all alone! Please tell me!"

They twirled one another around in perfectly synchronized turns. "It wasn't you," they said, and disappeared around the corner.

She ran to the end of the tunnel, frightened of what she would find, but when she reached the end, there was nothing but a wide white, sandy beach.

"There is nothing to be afraid of," she said to herself, realizing that she was not all alone. She looked down and saw a little girl with cowboy boots and bright red ponytails. She reached out and took her hand. "It's okay, I'm here," the child said to her.

"Excuse me, Mrs. Wilder, we're going to serve breakfast now. Would you like to wake up?"

Annie jumped, startled by the intrusion. "Sure," she mumbled, still groggy, but preferring a chance to brush her teeth and prepare for arrival to finding herself dropped onto the ground without notice.

She hated this part of the trip. She liked the taking off part, but not the *getting* off part. She sat up. Her mouth felt sour, her head hurt, and her bladder ached.

She lowered the footrest and searched for her boots, which had disappeared under her seat. Panic slipped across her. What if they're gone? What if I have to hobble off the plane without my boots and there's no one to meet me and I have to take that airport bus all the way in without my boots and it's too cold, standing in line waiting for my suitcase. Oh, my suitcase! I can put on some other shoes. She touched her boot. Okay, just accelerating a tad, just your usual airplane anxiety, just stand up, move around, take some deep breaths.

She slid her swollen feet into her boots and pulled herself up. She was still half asleep and slightly unsteady. She picked up her purse and made her way up the aisle to the bathroom. God, they were almost there and she hadn't prepared at all for meeting Mickey, let alone sorted out her final scene at Oliver's. She would have to think it through during breakfast. She should have at least a few of her puzzle pieces in order.

When Annie returned to her seat, her breakfast was waiting. She slid back in and refastened her seat belt and picked up the orange juice. Her body clock was trying to tell her that it was not orange juice time, no matter what British Airways thought, but she wasn't listening. She gulped it down, nausea rising up to meet it. She managed to swallow a bite of some sort of French pastry and two sips of coffee, which she used to wash down some aspirin. She put her head back and closed her eyes again.

She saw Oliver and Mickey tangoing toward her. What the hell was that dream all about? Her dreams had been amazingly pleasant and noncontroversial for the past two weeks. She had experienced a sort of time-out from her usually vivid and complex dreamscape. She cleared the picture, and Ivy Clare's face appeared. God, what a way to leave one another!

Ivy Clare sitting on Oliver's couch, crying. She had stopped dead, completely stunned by her presence. . . . *Focus, Annie . . . try to remember exactly . . .*

Ivy Clare glared at her. No one spoke. Annie felt the room spinning, whirling her around in the Ferris-wheel cage, returning her to confusion.

"What the hell is *she* doing here?" Ivy Clare's voice.

Oliver moved toward her, reaching out to brace her as if he could see her disarray.

"I don't think that is really any of your business," he said, holding Annie up.

Ivy Clare jumped to her feet, startling them both. Annie flinched, as if expecting her to leap upon them.

She stood there towering over Annie, her eyes flashing contempt.

"Well, this is just great! When did this little insanity begin? Don't tell me I set it all in motion that day she came for her damn pot!"

"Ivy, I want you to behave or you'll have to leave. Annie's been through enough and she is certainly not to blame for your difficulties."

Annie felt herself coming back together. He was protecting her; Ivy wasn't his lover, too.

The big woman stiffened and Annie braced herself again, not

knowing what to expect. Ivy Clare took one step toward her and then, almost as if someone in an invisible control booth at the back of Oliver's study had pulled a lever, she backed up and collapsed on the couch, sobbing hysterically. "It *is* her fault! It's always the fault of women like her. Miss Goody-goody, perfect little wifeys. They never risk anything! They just slop around in all of their smug, wifey bull-shit, driving their men out to find something really alive, and every single damn time, they win! No man has the balls to stay out of the bag; they all run right back in the minute it gets too wide open. I hate her! I hate all the stupid women like her! She won. She's got it all! She's got Michael back and her family and now she's even got you, and what do I have? Some broken pots and a broken heart!"

Annie felt dizzy again. She had never been at the center of any emotional storm, and the power of the woman's rage frightened her. There was also something else. She was talking about *her husband!* It was the first time that she had ever considered the possibility that Ivy Clare really loved Mickey. She had not thought that this was a woman who could love anyone. Somehow she could handle the idea of her sleeping with Mickey better than the idea of her loving him. That was too invasive, especially having to stand there and hear about it.

The contempt Ivy had for her filtered in, too; mingling with her own guilt and the long-covered feelings of worthlessness. Was Ivy right? Was she really just a pampered, selfish child-bride, who didn't deserve her good fortune and had consequently been punished for it? Annie shook the thought out, remembering what Loretta had said to her: "God has better things to do than single out nice little red-headed girls for punishment." No. She was not going to let this woman undermine her again.

"I'm losing my fucking mind and it's all her fault!" Ivy Clare jumped up, and before Annie could move, she lunged, knocking her over and pinning her down. Oliver grabbed Ivy's shoulders, trying to pull her off.

Ever since she was a small child, Annie had always hated to be held down or physically confined in any way. She grabbed Ivy Clare's large-boned wrists and pushed her sideways, climbing on top of her while Oliver watched helplessly.

She did not need his help. Her claustrophobia and righteous indignation were pumping her up like locker-room steroids. "You stop this! Just stop it! You're too damn big to have a temper tantrum. I'm going to sit on you, just like I used to sit on my son when he had one. Calm down now! Stop this!"

Oliver stood over them, a referee who had lost control of the match.

Ivy Clare screamed, tossing her wild hair from side to side and trying to buck Annie off. "Get the fuck off of me, you little bitch!"

Annie held tight, straddling her and holding her arms down.

"Stop it. Get a hold of yourself!"

"I'll fucking kill you! You don't deserve him. He needs a real woman. You can't make him happy. I can make him come five times in a night. I bet you couldn't equal that in a month, you dumb little cunt!"

Annie held on, surprising herself. "Hush!"

Ivy went on, kicking and bucking, trying to shock her off. Annie stayed on, keeping the image of Toby as a child in her head, straddling his small tortured body, his face turning purple with indignation. "Get off me!" he would yell, banging his head against the floor, while she held firm, letting him have his small internal earthquake, ensuring that he would not hurt himself or anyone else.

Amazingly, Ivy let go the same way little Toby always had. The fight left her and she stopped resisting. Her body went limp. She was crying again, but these tears seemed more real to Annie; she could feel her sorrow, so similar, it seemed now, to her own.

"I have nothing to show for my life. Nothing! No one likes me. I don't even like myself. I've lost the only decent person I've ever had in my entire lousy arrogant life. I drove him away, like I've driven everyone else away."

Annie let go of her arms and climbed off. It was unnerving to hear a woman like this crack through to herself. She didn't hate her anymore. It actually felt better to think that Mickey had not chosen a totally heartless person to betray her with.

"You'll be okay, Ivy."

The woman opened her silver eyes and looked at Annie.

"I didn't mean what I said about you. I'm just so jealous. I want everything that you have, and I'd take it if I could."

Annie laughed. "I don't think you'd really be interested if you'd been living my life for the last few months. I'd be careful what you ask for."

Ivy stared at her. "He never loved me. I just swamped him — a decent guy like that, he never had a chance. I could ensnare him for a while, but you can't make someone love you. Even if I hadn't blown it big time, he would have left sooner or later, because he never stopped loving you. And now," she looked over at Oliver, "you probably don't even want him back; just my luck."

Annie looked at Oliver, whose eyes were melancholy again.

"There's someone else for you, Ivy. There will always be someone else for you. You know that." Annie got up and crossed to Oliver. "I have to go now or I'll miss my plane."

He nodded, not daring to look at her. Ivy Clare was running her peasant hands through her tangled mane.

Oliver leaned over her. "I have to take Annie to the airport. Why don't you have a hot bath and a drink and get some rest. We'll talk in the morning."

She nodded and let him pull her up. Annie moved back into the hall. She did not know what more to say.

"Annie?"

She turned, her name sounding strange and unfamiliar in the other woman's voice.

She turned back. "Yes?"

"One thing I'd like to know. Are you going back to Mickey now?"

Annie saw Oliver turn away, as if physically ducking the question. "I'm going to meet him. We have many things to discuss."

"That's not what I asked you."

"I know, but it's the best that I can do."

Ivy Clare nodded, crossing her arms in front of her the way she had done that first afternoon, before Annie knew anything except that somehow she could not afford to be compromised by this woman.

"I know you don't have to or anything, but maybe someday you'll tell him that I'm not such a rotten bitch under it all."

The request was so outrageous that Annie laughed. "That's what I call chutzpah, Ivy Clare."

Oliver walked around her and opened the front door, emptying them both into the cold, starry night.

Mickey was asleep when she came in. She had the bellman leave her bag by the door, not wanting to wake him. Mickey did not wake well. He bolted up as if suddenly poked, and then he carried on, disoriented and frantic.

She stood in the shadows and looked at him. He had fallen asleep on the couch in front of the television set. Some Japanese reporter was wandering around a museum filled with toilets, explaining something to the viewers in an animated voice and pointing at the various arcane plumbing pieces. One that truly excited him seemed to be made out of gold. A gold toilet? A toilet museum? Only in a country with no deficit.

The room was dark; the only light came from the set and cast shadows on her husband's face. He was all dressed up, his hair still damp from the shower. On the table in front of him was a vase with a dozen long-stemmed tulips, her favorite flowers, a bottle of champagne, and a note in Mickey's artless scrawl: "Darling Spots, welcome to Tokyo." She smiled. He had fallen asleep waiting for her and she had spoiled his surprise. She took off her coat and sat down in a chair next to him, relieved to have a few minutes more to prepare for their reunion.

She felt uneasy, like a double agent shifting back and forth, one man for each part of her cover.

He turned on his side, his face closer to her. In the dimness, his thinning hair hidden by the shadows, he looked like his boy-self. How many times had she watched him sleep? She had even taken childhood naps with him on Ida Mae's bed. The most amazing thing about her time with Oliver had been finding herself able to sleep next to someone other than Mickey. It had felt more disloyal to fall asleep next to him than to suck his cock.

She slipped out of her shoes and leaned back against the cushions. She was starved, and dying for a bath. She turned back to the television, leaning over and changing the channel. There was some BBC program in English about Japanese women staying single, not wanting to repeat the lives of their mothers. The birthrate was falling and women were starting to rebel against their treatment at home and in the workplace.

Here it comes, Annie thought, remembering the article she had tried to write on her last trip. She had not been able to prove it then, but her feeling had been that feminism would hit Japan by the mid-nineties, and even if it did not arrive with the force of the American land and sea assault, even one catamaran in Tokyo Bay would really shake up Japanese society for a long time. They simply did not have the flexibility in their cultural arsenal to absorb millions of angry women demanding their own weapons of choice.

Now it was really happening. Women not marrying, living with their parents and spending their salaries on package cruises and designer accessories, smoking and drinking and sleeping around and refusing to stay home and have babies, chafing at centuries of being perfectly behaved and polite to every man in sight.

This could be truly interesting, Annie thought, wishing she could turn up the volume.

"I have a good income," some pretty young woman was saying. "I like going out and to travel. Why should I stay home waiting for an exhausted husband?"

Mickey turned over. Why indeed, she thought, thinking of how many nights of her life she had spent exactly like that.

She stood up and tiptoed across the small living room, picking up her cosmetic bag and disappearing into the black marble bathroom.

Thank God he had a Western room with a normal bath and real furniture. Not like last time! It was all very exotic and interesting to be in a Japanese-style suite — for about six hours. She turned on the tub, remembering the two of them standing in the middle of the floor, no furniture in sight, not knowing what to do, where to sit, or how to ask anyone if they might roll out the mats or beds or whatever they were supposed to sleep on.

She was not much of an adventurer at heart. She might as well admit it. Every time someone they knew came back from trekking in Nepal, or some equally exotic spot, with their travel tale — "No electricity for two weeks . . . didn't change clothes or shower for ten days . . . freezing cold . . . horrible food . . . had to use a flashlight to find the toilet . . . insects as big as mice . . . hiked twenty miles a day with fifty-pound packs . . . got some dysentery, BUT *it was the greatest vacation of our lives*" — she was politely horrified. She had never found any part of vacations that involved fear, danger, disease, filth, or physical discomfort appealing. For that she could have stayed in New York!

If she was going somewhere and paying a lot of money, she ought to be comfortable and clean and well fed. She felt the same way about spas. Why should she spend a fortune to eat five hundred calories a day and be awakened at five A.M. to climb mountains and do calisthenics with total strangers, when she could stay home and deprive herself for free? Daily life seemed the more appropriate place for self-denial and military discipline. If she was going to pack clothes and spend money, she wanted a break from all those lettuce dinners and leg lifts.

She turned on the tub, squeezing in a tube of pine-scented bath oil, and took off her clothes. Thank goodness Mickey had always been the same way about vacations, and Oliver, Oliver was way over the top from them both. This was a guy who knew how to enjoy himself. He had given her permission to let herself go more than usual, and she had taken to it with gusto. This was not a good boy, who asked for eggwhite omelets and flossed between meals. Being with someone like Oliver had been adventurous enough for her — as dangerous as a safari in Zimbabwe, to be with a man who still smoked cigarettes and drove eighty miles an hour and globbed whipped cream on his crème brûlée.

He was slightly perilous, but she had felt perfectly at ease and safe with him; or was that just because she had no ties — would she feel so calm and relaxed about it if she were his wife? She turned off the tub and stepped in, the heat moving up her stiff, tired legs, filling her with pleasure. She leaned back, closing her eyes.

What was she thinking? This was hardly some game show, she the giddy housewife in the studio audience, hesitating before her choice, Door Number One or Door Number Two. In fact, never before in her entire life had she really thought that she had made choices. Her life had sort of formed around her, letting her slip off the numerous hooks that conscious options involved.

Well, life with its Cheshire sense of irony had brought her up to speed on that little delusion. She was now standing in the middle of the live audience, the microphone thrust before her nervously grinning choppers, forcing her to deal with possibilities. Door Number One or Door Number Two or . . .

"Hi," Mickey stood in the bathroom doorway holding two glasses brimming with champagne.

She opened her eyes and sat up, slightly shy under his gaze. "Hi. I didn't want to wake you. You looked so peaceful."

"First good sleep I've had since I've been here. I can't seem to break the jet lag. Thank God, they're dubbing me and it doesn't matter how I'm reading the damn dialogue."

"I brought you some sleeping pills from England, the ones you like."

"Thanks," he moved toward her and handed her a glass.

"You're my best sleeping pill. I only sleep well when you're next to me."

She took the glass, her arm covered with soap bubbles, like some old Hollywood movie. The thought made her laugh.

"What's so funny?" He looked hurt, as if he had expected a more gracious response.

"Oh, you, all dressed up, handing me champagne in a marble tub, my arm all bubbly — sort of retro-Gentlemen-Prefer-Blondes or something. All I need is a pair of high-heeled mules with ostrich feathers and an enormous diamond ring."

Mickey turned and held out a pink terry cloth robe. "No mules, no diamonds, but I can provide a very nice dinner, if you're not too tired. We have a lot to talk about."

She put down her glass and stood up, not meeting his eyes. She felt embarrassed, self-conscious, with his eyes on her. It was he, her own husband, who now felt like the foreigner. She slipped into the robe, feeling a deep longing, a void in her heart, Oliver retreating from where she had held him during their time together. Door Number One had turned into Door Number Two and she stood there, dripping bubbles on a marble floor, unable to remember what she had wanted or what she should do.

"Has Leonard called back yet?" she said, veering the conversation away from the danger zone. She picked up her glass and padded to the sink.

"No, but he knows you couldn't be here until tonight, so I'm not concerned."

"Do you think maybe we should stay here and wait?"

She saw his face in the mirror; he looked hurt again.

"Annie, I haven't seen you in three weeks. We need to try and talk to one another. I'm shooting twelve hours a day. These guys are like fucking automatons; they never quit. Once Leonard calls and you go off, I may not really be with you again until I get home. I've still got a week on this damn soap and we're taping three episodes a day! Believe me, he'll call back."

She turned and looked at him. He looked vulnerable, in a way that she did not remember him ever looking before. This was her husband without any camouflage.

"You're right. Just let me get dressed. I'll be ready in ten minutes."

He laughed, sipping his champagne, and she thought he looked relieved. "Ten minutes on what sundial? I'll work on my lines for a while."

He left her alone, facing herself in the fluorescent light of the foggy, marble-rimmed mirror. The end of a series of hotel bathroom mirrors, her face reflected back at her from varying angles, now with another man waiting on the other side of a closed door.

"So, I'm playing an American gangster who is smuggling young girls out of Japan for the Yakuza. They have this innocence in the way they construct the shows. It's like they steal from all of our soaps, but when they convert everything it just comes out, well, it comes out like children were doing it. You know what I mean? It's like a bunch of really smart kids were watching a grown-up show and then writing their own version.

"I have no idea what in the hell is going on in the plot until I go back to the hotel and watch the tapes on television! They don't seem to care what I say. I just babble on. Yesterday I came right from the car shoot and I hadn't had any time to study the scene so I just recited the Gettysburg Address and they thought I was fantastic!

"My translator tells me that next week I get killed in a shoot-out trying to get my girls onto a boat for Singapore. *And* they're paying me in cash!"

Annie licked the soy sauce off her fingers. He had been talking nonstop since they left the hotel. It was a form of anxiety-release that she was well familiar with, it usually being her way of coping. They had switched roles partly because she didn't know what she could possibly say to him. She could hardly prattle on about *her* last two weeks.

She wiped her hands and picked up her sake cup and sipped, feeling the warmth of the liquid move down her throat. Love for her husband had lowered her defenses. He was trying so hard to woo her back. He looked scared and almost frantic, and his loneliness was so powerful, she could physically feel it between them.

She had absolutely no idea what to tell him or how to be here with him. No matter what she did now, she was betraying someone, including herself.

A portly man with a shiny, pockmarked face and two silver front teeth came up beside them beaming down at her. "Oh, the Wilders, what a fond coincidence!"

Mickey stood up and shook the man's hand. Annie could not remember who he was.

Mickey saw her face. "Annie honey, you remember Mr. Matsuki. He was involved with the miniseries we filmed here and he came to see us in Montecito last summer?"

Annie nodded, vague memories of a pack of Japanese people running around her house taking pictures of everything — Juanita, Portia, the Pats — came back to her.

"Oh, yes, of course. How nice to see you again."

The man grabbed her hand, holding tight. "You are always in my heart, because my wife was made pregnant when we visited your home. You are the good fortune for my son."

Annie laughed. "Well, that's wonderful! Glad to be of service."

The man turned to Mickey and grabbed his hands, releasing Annie. "This is most wonderful coincidence, to meet with you like this! I am very passionate to produce a program about the Japanese Brazilians who have come into Japan to work. For myself, I am very crazy about these people. I would like to make the program to be seen in America, too, and it would be an honor if you would be our narrator. Because my wife became pregnant the night at your home, we have named our son Michael, and you would bring good luck to my program."

Annie nudged Mickey under the table.

Mickey bowed, extracting his hand. "Well, that's most kind of you. You have my numbers in America. Please let me know if the project proceeds. If my schedule permits, I would be honored."

The man gave him a thirty-degree bow. *"Arigato. Domo arigato."*

The man bowed to Annie and hurried off.

Annie smiled at him. "Why is it we all start talking that weird formal way with these guys? He's telling you that he and his wife made a baby in our living room or somewhere, and you're talking to him like he's Hirohito."

Mickey sat down and dipped a piece of yellowtail into his soy sauce. "I don't know, it just comes out that way. You do it, too."

"I know. But not the way you do."

"Well, it could be that I'm just more pretentious and phony than you are."

"Did they really shack up at our house? How could I forget something like that?"

Mickey chewed, shaking his head. "I think what he meant was that after they left us, they went home and did it."

"Oh, pretty vivid for an almost total stranger, don't you think?"

"Yep. But that is one crazy guy. He's the nephew of some billionaire gambler who ran up a tab in Vegas of nine million dollars. He was part of a group called 'The Whales' who were so elite they were allowed to accumulate huge debts in Vegas and Atlantic City. They'd play baccarat for a hundred thousand a hand for eighty hours straight without sleeping."

"He looks so ordinary and kind of sweet."

"Yeah, especially since they found his uncle in his hot tub with a hundred and fifty stab wounds in him."

"You're kidding!"

"Even *I* don't watch that much television."

"The Japanese mob, how romantically sinister."

"Well, I must tell you, I'm not eager to work on anything he's involved in, no matter how harmless it seems. Who the hell knows where the chains link."

She picked up her chopsticks. "Nice metaphor, Mick."

He leaned over and kissed her cheek. "God, how I've missed talking to you. I feel like we've just met, sort of falling in love all over again, but at the same time, it feels so comfortable — really alive, but not nerve-wracking."

"I know," she said. He took her hand.

"Don't leave me, Annie. Please don't leave me."

Exhaustion landed on her, protecting her from his plea.

"I'm wiped out, Mickey. All of a sudden, I'm just really beat. Can we go?"

He motioned for the check. "Sure, but we haven't even begun to talk about things."

"Tomorrow, we'll do it tomorrow. I just can't handle it tonight. It's been a very long couple of days."

She saw his face change. *Please let it go,* she whispered to him silently, and he seemed to hear her, because he stopped and threw his credit card on the table.

"Okay. Tomorrow it is."

When Mickey opened the door to their room there was a fax on the floor. Annie picked it up and opened it.

"Mrs. Wilder — It was an honor to reacquaint with you this evening. If you will be so kind as to return to the car entrance, I will be waiting to escort you to the meeting with Mr. Lewis. Needless to say, come alone and tell no one. Faithfully, Matsuki."

Annie handed the paper to Mickey, who seemed more upset by it than she did. She looked at her watch. "Obviously, his running into us was no coincidence. He followed us. I'd better go." She yawned, wishing she'd had more tea.

Mickey was pacing back and forth. "I don't know about this. How can I let you set off with some gangster into God only knows what? This sounds much more ominous than Leonard's phone call."

"Mickey, it's *Leonard.* Besides, I have to do this, it could mean getting our money back! He's obviously being very careful. He has a helluva lot at stake — like thirty years in prison or something."

She was suddenly not tired at all. She could feel her adrenaline kick in, probably left over from her bout with Ivy Clare.

"I think maybe I should slip a Valium in my pocket just in case they blindfold me and put me in the trunk or something."

Mickey looked alarmed again. "Annie, I pleaded with Leonard to let me go, but he absolutely refused. I don't want to send you like this. Maybe we're being really foolhardy; maybe we should call the Tokyo police and have someone follow you."

"No, no, Mickey! I'm sorry. I was just accelerating out loud. Believe me, Leonard and whoever's helping him would pick up on that before we hit the first stoplight. Remember what we went through to order a California roll without fish eggs? Can you imagine trying to explain *this* to a Japanese policeman? No, I'm going. I can handle it. Leonard was one of my best friends; he wouldn't hurt me. . . . Besides, it will build character. If I can do this and not hyperventilate, who knows what may be possible? The first redhead on the space shuttle, or maybe even bungee jumping." She tried to smile. Maybe she was more nervous than she thought she was.

Mickey sighed. "Oh, great. The woman who can't take off or land without crossing her fingers and saying the Lord's Prayer becomes the Mata Hari of Montecito."

They faced one another, using the teasing the way they always had as a delicate bridge between aloneness and belonging.

He put his arm around her and she let him, resting her head against his shoulder, sniffing in his Mickey smell, a smell that had been a part of her senses, but one that she had, in the last two weeks, almost forgotten. They were quiet, feeling the alienation of their altered closeness, two weary, middle-aged married people who had been through a lot together.

"Honey?"

"Yes?"

"Promise me, when you get downstairs, if your gut feeling is bad, you'll come right back up here."

Annie sighed. "I promise. But the thing is that sometimes, in a situation like this, your unconscious can give you a false message. I read a book about that. There's your *real* inner voice, but there's also your *false* inner voice that can pose as your *real* inner voice because it's still coming from your blind spot and so it tricks you. So you think it's your true inner voice, but it's not. Which is why so often therapy doesn't work; because you go in vulnerable and confused about all those voices telling you this and that, and you may be choosing the therapist from your blindest spot. So, I will try, but —"

"Annie!"

"Okay. I know."

She reached for her purse, wondering if she should pack an overnight bag. This was, after all, not a movie, where Michelle Pfeiffer or someone was carried off against her will but always had clean hair, white teeth, and fresh clothes. If she wore two pairs of underwear and several shirts, layered up, she could just shed them as they got dirty. Mickey watched her, knowing she had shut off, already into her departure. "What are you thinking?"

"Nothing. . . . I just want to brush my teeth and maybe take an extra sweater and some yen. . . . Can you give me some just in case I need to take a bus or train or something? This is coming together. I'll be fine."

She turned and smiled at him. She realized that she was not entirely averse to this adventure. Since she had gotten on that plane for London and surrendered herself to what existed moment by moment, she had in some way edged herself forward. Maybe she would never jump off a bridge with a rubber cord around her ankles or climb Everest or go rafting on some raging river, but she did feel braver and more open to life.

He watched her disappear into the bathroom, swallowing a sharp, acrid lump of new fear. Not only was she going forth without him into possible danger, but she was going differently. She had changed, and what that might mean to their marriage was even more frightening to him than the ominous night that now stretched before them.

When Annie came through the polished brass and glass doors separating the deserted lobby of the Seiyo Ginza Hotel from the porte cochere, a black Mercedes limousine was waiting for her.

She was relieved, her fears of car trunks falling away.

She waved to the invisible person or persons within, not sure what to do.

The doorman was watching her with less than typical Japanese inscrutability. Why wasn't the car moving toward her? Had she done something wrong? The car backed up away from Annie.

The driver must not want to be seen, she thought and started walking toward the car. The car waited until she was right beside it. The glass was tinted dark green and she could not see inside. She bent down and tapped gently on the window, which lowered almost immediately.

"Please," the chauffeur said and motioned for her to get in. Annie opened the back door and slid in next to her newest acquaintance. "Mr. Matsuki, we meet again," she said, feeling slightly shy.

The small, pitted head bobbed. "Please allow me to apologize for the dishonesty. It is a most unusual situation. Precautions were necessary to protect Leonard-san."

Mr. Matsuki's paunch strained against his shiny brown suit. His thick black hair was parted in the center and weighted down with some kind of grease. He was wearing a large diamond ring, which was embedded in the folds of his small fat pinkie.

This was not who she would have expected. Leonard was so elegant, it did not seem possible that he would have anyone like this munchkin anywhere near him. Leonard was the kind of man who made his cleaning lady wear a black uniform and a doily on her head to defrost the freezer. But then again, she would never have figured Leonard for a thief, and there *was* his choice of Bambi.

Annie fastened her seat belt.

Matsuki grinned at her, revealing his two silver teeth. Why the big diamond ring and the cheesy dental work? Maybe they were white gold or platinum even? Maybe she should try to think about something more relevant.

He reached into his pocket and pulled out a pair of strangely shaped sunglasses and handed them to her. "I apologize. But it is important that you do not know where we are going."

So far she was getting off easy. No Sessue Hayakawa type, recently freed from fifty years in prison for war atrocities against American POWs and no trunk or blindfold.

She put on the glasses. They were entirely opaque. She could not see a thing. "Mr. Matsuki, would you be offended if I took advantage of my blindness and had a little nap? It's been a very long day."

"Please," he said, most likely as relieved as she was to skip what would certainly be self-conscious small talk. She wanted to save her energy for Leonard. She closed her eyes, too hyper to sleep but grateful for the time to think her thoughts.

"Mrs. Wilder, we have arrived." Annie opened her eyes. She had actually relaxed enough to doze off.

"You may take off the glasses." She handed them back and undid her seat belt. The chauffeur came around and opened her door. She was in a large stone courtyard. A black van with no markings and painted-over windows was parked in front of them.

Mr. Matsuki took her arm and led her to the van. She stopped. Unmarked vans were an entirely different deal.

"Please, it is for your own protection as well that you do not know where we are."

She tried to swallow. No one would ever believe this.

Mr. Matsuki opened the door and hopped up, reaching out his stubby arms for her. Much to Annie's relief, there was no one in the back of the van but the two of them. She could not see the driver or anything else. They bounced along, not speaking. His affability level had changed the minute they stepped into the van. He was now very somber.

She tried to look at her watch, but it was too dark. She figured that they had been driving for about ninety minutes, putting them somewhere beyond the suburbs. From the courtyard, she assumed that they were on the grounds of an estate of some kind and were driving from the security entrance to the main house. God, this was all too bizarre.

The car stopped and he handed her back the glasses. She put them on and let him guide her out of the van. She tripped, grabbing on to her pudgy little abductor and lurching forward.

They went up some steps and down an exterior corridor and through what seemed to be an interior courtyard with possibly a fountain — she could hear water trickling — then up a stairway, the sound of her feet shuffling and floundering between them. Finally they stopped and she heard a door being opened.

He led her in. He did not speak this time, but reached up and removed the glasses. A man was sitting with his back to her, in the shadow light of a large slate fireplace.

Matsuki bowed. "I hope your journey has not been too adverse. I hope we meet again. My wife sends her regards." He bowed again and left her without saying a word to the man in the shadows. She took a deep breath, squinting into the dim firelight at the figure.

The man stood up and turned toward her. Annie thought she recognized Leonard's stately, slightly round-shouldered presence but she was too nearsighted to be sure. The man was not, however, wearing one of Leonard's interchangeable navy blue pin-striped suits, but a long, flowing Japanese robe.

"Leonard?" Annie said, moving ever so slightly closer.

"Put on your glasses, Annie," the man said in Leonard's low, steady voice.

Annie slipped her glasses out of her pocket and onto her face. She was cold and disoriented from the trip and her blindman's buff expedition across the grounds. When Matsuki had taken the glasses off, all she could think of was how grateful she was to have her sight. She promised herself that she would never complain about anything ever again, even though she knew that she would.

"Omigod! Leonard! It is you!"

"Come, sit down by the fire. You must be frozen."

Annie nodded and walked toward him, wishing she could take her boots off. She sat down and stretched her hands out, letting the fire warm her.

The somber, spindly man sat back down in his chair, facing her. He smiled. "Annie. It's so good to see you. I've missed you."

She looked at him, a man she thought she knew. "You look different. You seem so . . . foreign."

"It's the clothes, perhaps. I do think the style fits me, don't you? I never did belong in California, never had the look or the casual manner. I was always overdressed and far too formal. I do believe that I have finally found my true self. Inside good old Leonard Lewis, CPA, was this pristine Japanese intellectual just waiting to come forth."

Annie lowered her hands and exhaled. She had been so shocked by seeing Leonard that she had forgotten to breathe out.

She had to pay attention.

He stood up. "Forgive my manners. Let me take your coat and I'll have some tea sent up."

Annie slipped out of her coat, handing it to him reluctantly. The pockets were crammed with essentials.

"Don't take it too far. I may get cold again."

He laid it down on a table by the door of what she now assumed was his study and pushed a buzzer on the wall.

"I know you must have many questions. I promise I will answer them all, but first let's have some tea and sherry and talk awhile. I have missed you, Annie. You really were one of the lights in my dim little life."

Leonard walked back and sat down in his chair. Annie was so uncomfortable now that she had to tell Leonard if she was going to be able to concentrate.

"Leonard, may I take my shoes off? My feet are swollen from the plane and I stubbed my toes several times coming up here."

He smiled, his new enigmatic Asian-style smile. "Of course. I'm so sorry for the cloak-and-dagger, but it is necessary."

Annie pulled off her boots, too happy with relief to be self-conscious about the tackiness of the activity.

She tried to lean back in the chair, but the edge of the pillow dug into her side, and she shifted her weight. Leonard watched her, still smiling. She turned around and tried to push it up, but it felt dense and strange. She tried to lift it out from behind her, but it was too heavy. She would have to stand up and turn completely around.

"Leonard, I know I'm being a pain, but this is one weird pillow. Maybe I'm coming down with Epstein-Barr or something, but I can't seem to lift it. It feels like a sack of rice."

"It *is* a sack of rice."

Annie gave up, shifting her weight so that the ridge dug into her lower back. "Cheaper than down, right?"

"Not exactly. They're part of a very old tradition."

"So are nail beds, but I wouldn't want to sleep on one."

"Once you get used to them, you would never sleep on any other pillow again."

Annie wiggled her toes. She was calmer now and beginning to reconnect with her anger and righteous indignation.

"Look, Leonard, I mean no disrespect, I am truly happy for you to find someplace that brings you peace of mind and all, but to be perfectly frank, I have no intention of staying here long enough to trade in my snuggle cushions for a couple of Uncle Ben's sacks. I am only here to see you. I have come a long way, and the last several weeks have not exactly been a bouquet of cherry blossoms. Lina and Mickey and I have been through a lot and I think I'm ready for an explanation and an answer to really just one very simple question. Where the hell is our money?"

A soft knock. "Come in," Leonard said, and the door opened. A maid tiptoed in, carrying a tray filled with tea things and little pastries and a decanter of sherry. She put the tray down on the table between them and backed out of the room.

Annie waited, hoping she hadn't come on too strong too soon. Now that Leonard thought he was Japanese, it might offend his new sensibility. Confrontation was a definite Nipponese no-no.

She tried to lighten the mood. "I like Mr. Matsuki, though he doesn't seem to be your type at all."

Leonard pressed his fingers together in prayer formation. "He works for my benefactor."

"Oh. Well, that explains it. Your 'benefactor,' is he in finance, too?"

Leonard smiled his new smile. "Let's just say he's got his spoon in a lot of pots."

"Do any of the *pots* contain your clients' worldly goods?"

Leonard leaned forward and poured tea and sherry with Zen-paced precision. Annie watched him, trying to copy his manner and slow herself down. He put several of the lovely little sweets on a plate and handed them to her, placing her teacup and sherry glass beside one another.

"Arigato," she said and popped one of the treats into her mouth. She chewed, feeling her face change. What was it? Something completely revolting. . . . Maybe they were poisoned or laced with knockout drops. Leonard was looking at her.

"Red bean sweets. Don't you like it?"

She shook her head, unable to swallow the disgusting glob.

He picked up a napkin from the tray and handed it to her. "It's okay, Annie, put it in this."

She held the napkin over her mouth and spit out the deceptively yummy-looking treat. Her body shivered. "Yick! Leonard, that was mean! You know me better than to try and sneak something like that into me!"

"I apologize. I guess I'm overeager to share my new world with someone. These are the finest red bean delicacies. I had hoped you might at least find them . . . interesting."

"Interesting it was, Leonard. Oreos it wasn't. Next time, let me decide in a more informed way." She sighed. "Sorry, that's not quite fair. It's my fault. I should have asked you what was in the damn thing, but it looked so pretty, I got a little lax; anyway, why are we talking about this? Please answer my question."

Leonard rose and walked to the fire, standing with his back to her for a moment. She was afraid that she had hurt his feelings. She really was flattered that he had sent for her specifically, that he trusted her and was so genuinely glad to see her.

She would usually have been much more polite and tried considerably harder to reassure him, and inquire as to the state of his health and Bambi's, and generally discount the reality of her reason for being there. The change in her was startling, rather like finding something — a mole or bulge — that you had never noticed on yourself before.

Leonard turned and faced her. "It's not that simple," he said, and she felt fear return. People always said things like "It's not that simple," when they were going to give you bad news.

"Why not?" she said, her voice less commanding.

"Let me try to start at the beginning and tell you the whole story."

Annie pushed the grain behind her, shifting the lump digging into her back from the left side toward the center. "Good idea," she said, sipping her tea, still trying to get the bean taste out of her mouth. Hadn't she read somewhere that in the Philippines they put sugar on avocados? Must be the same culinary model that would sweeten beans, when a little salt and salsa and lime would be so much better. . . .

"Annie, you look so miserable," Leonard said, moving away from the fire.

She didn't want him to stop.

"No, no. It's nothing, just the leftover bean paste and this, uh, pillow. Please just tell me!"

He reached behind her and lifted the brocade-covered sack out and dropped it on the floor.

"There. Now take a sip of sherry; it will clear your palate. Do you want to use the ladies' room first? You've had a long drive."

She nodded, feeling more like Baby Snooks than Mata Hari.

He helped her up and led her across the room to a carved teak door. "Go through there; you'll find it."

She opened the door and found herself in a hallway covered with photographs. There was an old-fashioned series of pictures of men with spectacular mustaches. "Members of the International Mustache Club," a caption in English said.

She kept walking. She seemed to be in a hallway leading to something more grand and less personal than a private house. Maybe it was some kind of conference center or retreat.

Ahead of her she saw three doors, all marked in Japanese and English.

MALE TOILET, FEMALE TOILET, DISABLED TOILET, the English signs said. She must be in some kind of complex, but the less she knew, the better her chances of getting back to Tokyo in approximately the same shape in which she had left.

She chose the *female toilet,* relieved to find the usual variety with no porcelain sexual characteristics. Good old Leonard, he even remembered her bladder.

She sat down, closing her eyes.

The return of their money had come to represent freedom. It gave her the right to a choice about leaving Mickey and moving to London with Oliver.

Without the freedom of some income, she and Mickey were really bound together. How could she leave him broke and jobless? How could she go forth in such a state herself? They would owe it to one another to stay together and start over, the way they had in the beginning.

What was she thinking? Was that how she was going to make a decision about her future, like some perverse game of Monopoly? If she collected at Park Place, she rode off into the sunset with her lover, and if not, proceeded directly to jail? Was that how she now saw her future with her husband? Wasn't it all just so pat, another way of not taking responsibility for making her own decision? If money was all that was keeping her with Mickey, it was damn well time to admit it. Well, money was not that simple; money and fear always had to be tied together like campers in the two-legged race.

She wiped herself and stood up, hurrying now, afraid to break the fragile new connection between herself and her old and trusted adviser, her good old reliable Leonard, who was now someone more remote than an alien — a friend who had changed.

Nothing, Annie thought, padding back down the strangely-adorned hallway, was lonelier than being with someone you had been close to and having the cord of connection slashed in half. She had been through it before with good friends: suddenly the intimacy is breached; one person has traveled too far down an alternate path, leaving the friendship stranded.

She sat back down. Leonard was standing in front of the fire waiting for her, that new, closed smile on his old Leonard Lewis lips.

"I'm all yours," she said, ready for the truth.

Leonard picked up his sherry glass from the mantel and finished it. "All right. I must ask you one favor: let me tell you all the way through without interruption. I know how hard it is for you not to ask questions, but you will have fewer to ask if I can just tell you the whole sordid story. Some of it you may already know or have figured out, but please bear with me."

"My lips are sealed. I use Elmer's on them now; works like a charm."

Leonard chuckled. "Oh, Annie, you always made me laugh. Too bad I was never attracted to women like you but always to white trash like Bambi; everything could have been so different."

Annie struggled with her promise. Not interrupting, if he was going to keep adding little sidebars like that, was going to be really tough.

Leonard refilled his sherry glass. Annie sipped her tea, choosing a clear head.

Leonard sat back down in his chair and leaned forward.

"It all started two years ago at Stan Stein's New Year's Eve party when I walked in on Bambi and Stan in the master bathroom.

"I didn't actually walk in. I entered the bedroom looking for my coat because I'd left my pipe in the pocket, and I saw them reflected in one of his damn mirrors. They did not see me and I left the room.

"I have always known, of course, what everyone thought of Bambi, and the rumors that she had been a call girl and that was how we met. The truth was far less dramatic. She was working as a salesgirl at Frederick's of Hollywood and I was dragged in there one day by Lina; she was looking for a peignoir for a play she was in, and Bambi was there. She didn't wait on us and I don't think Lina ever saw her, but I did. I don't know what it was about her, but she absolutely hypnotized me.

"When we left, she slipped her phone number into my pocket and one late night after a client dinner, I called her and went over to her apartment and that was it for me.

"I'd always had certain, well, problems with performance. I'd been to sex therapists and analysts and tried all kinds of treatments but nothing had helped until that night with Bambi. It was like a miracle. I was completely cured!

"I suppose I connected her to being able to perform normally as a man and, well, I think you can understand how powerful that was, and of course, she certainly knew it. This was a girl with nothing but a certain kind of trashy prettiness, a good body, and pure rat cunning.

"Anyway, I married her, and I thought we were very happy. I did trust her, even though I knew she came from truly primitive stock. When I met her she was about to be arrested for kiting some checks and credit card fraud. I covered her debts, attributing it all to bad luck and no education.

"I loved her; what can I say. She lit me up. She made me feel incandescent. Look what my life was like, Annie. I spent all my time with creative, flashy, larger-than-life people of enormous talent and charisma. I tidied up after them. I handled all the boring, mundane details of their fascinating lives.

"Enormous sums of money passed through my hands every single day, and I saw *everything,* far more than their shrinks.

"I paid the bills for their liaisons and their plastic surgery. I leased the yachts, bought the Bentleys, hired the butlers, listened to their woes, hid money when they were getting ready to leave their mates, held their hands when they lost parts or had projects canceled or found out they were HIV-positive or whatever.

"I was the invisible man; good old reliable Leonard, everyone's sounding board, everyone's joke. Don't think I didn't know that you all laughed at me, maybe not meanly, but snidely just the same. But you all needed me and you all trusted me and I trusted all of you, too.

"I had no children, no real friends; my clients were my world; my clients and Bambi were my entire life. I never said no to any of you no matter how absurd the request or how unfair the demand on my time. But none of it was about *me*. I was just this shadow man, always backstage holding the star's robe, grateful for a kind word or a peck on the cheek.

"I know what you're thinking. You're thinking that I was pretty damn well paid for a stagehand. Well, you're right. I certainly did fine. I was no victim of unfair trade, but it still ate away at my self-image.

"When I married Bambi, she brought me a luster, my own personal bit of the spotlight. She brightened up every room we walked into, and whether or not people approved of her style, she was *not* boring! Certainly not the type any of you would have expected dull old Leonard to run off with. She made me more intriguing as a person and as a man. 'There must be more to Leonard than meets the eye,' I heard one of my clients say to Mickey at a party one night.

"So there we were, the ultimate odd couple. Me so formal and reserved and quiet and methodical and all, and Bambi, well, you know how she is. I adored her. I gave her anything she wanted. I took all those awful trips. I let her furnish that house I couldn't afford to begin with, in that revolting Versailles powder-room motif. God! I was obsessed!

"When I saw her with Stan Stein, not one of the handsome young actors or even some distinguished mogul, but that crass, repulsive panderer, it almost killed me. I began to pay more attention to her comings and goings. I listened in on her calls and played back the message tapes on her private line, and I started to follow her. Day after day for almost a year I let this madness creep over me, and every single day I found another betrayal, another end to my innocence.

"I kept a list of her conquests, and quite a list it was. Male and female, young and old. My Bambi had slept with *all* of my clients, my lawyer, my doctor, my hairdresser, my mechanic, everyone important in my life.

"Eventually, the only people left who had not, to the best of my knowledge, slept with my wife, were you, Mickey, and our Poland Water delivery man, though why not him, I can't say.

"I went on behaving as if none of this was true. I often thought of telling you and Mickey, since you were the only people left that I could trust, but somehow I knew that once I said it out loud, I would really have to accept it, and that would mean the end of everything.

"You must try to understand that! It was not just the end of my marriage, but of my entire world! I would have to sever all of my relationships! Everyone that I had given my heart and soul to, worked like a dog for, had betrayed me!

"I don't remember quite when the idea to start converting everyone's stocks and C.D.'s and limited partnerships and all into bearer bonds actually came into focus. I started with Stan Stein; he was the first. I found that in knowing something that none of my hotshots knew and in forging their names on things, I gained power. I became more like them, and it was a tremendous high.

"I may still have been the shadow, but now I was the ominous shape reflected giant-size on the bedroom wall, causing terror in the hearts of the frightened insomniacs. So, I started with Stan and it just snowballed.

"I won't bore you with the technical details, but I must admit I was quite ingenious and none of them suspected anything. I paid dividends with overlapping funds, kited checks, and borrowed on credit cards, switching funds back and forth. Certainly, I knew I couldn't go on for much longer. Tax time was coming and bills were piling up.

"By the beginning of November I had converted almost a hundred million dollars into bearer bonds, which I could cash and which couldn't be traced like currency.

"Now, I am going to tell you something that you *must* believe. I never, ever intended to keep any of the money! I was only going to scare everyone, teach them all a lesson.

"What they did to me was wrong. I was their friend. I had never betrayed one single confidence or overbilled one hour of my time! I did not deserve to be cuckolded like that with the one woman they all knew was my whole life! They all had lots of choices, but I only had Bambi.

"I had it all planned. I was going to leave town quietly and wait to be missed. 'Where's Leonard?' one of the Iagos would say. 'I need this, I need that — the Mercedes dealer called and said my payments hadn't been made for six months — where's Leonard?' One would call another. I would wait. Bambi would become frantic. They would all call her, one after the other. By the second or third call, they would begin inquiring — 'Do you think he might suspect something?' 'Leonard?' she would say. 'Don't be ridiculous.'

"When I felt the frenzy had risen high enough, I would send my letters. I had actually spent weeks of nights and weekends writing the letters, pouring out my hurt and anger. When they had had a sufficient amount of time to reflect, repent, and feel the loss of what I had given to their self-absorbed, spiritually freeze-dried lives, I would return their money, less, of course, my usual fees and a percentage of the interest, which I felt was a fair price for their duplicity and my being robbed of my profession and my wife.

"It was with this relatively modest sum that I had planned to leave the country and start a new life here among my karmic brethren.

"Now you may be wondering why I had these connections in Japan. I will say only that in the course of my investment excursions, I have met many Japanese executives of enormous wealth and power and I have from time to time done favors for these men. My benefactor in particular had a colleague who got into some difficulty with the gaming authorities in America. The Japanese have a higher code of morality; they never forget a favor and they always repay their ethical debts.

"What I did not figure on, in my blind, obsessive, and completely polarized thinking, was that anyone would call the FBI! I just simply never entertained the thought, which was grandiosity, no doubt. I was so focused on them all whining and panicking because I was gone, that I believed they would be singly devoted to finding me. This miscalculation, of course, changed everything.

"I had been slowly transferring the bearer bonds in my briefcase every time I went to Tokyo on business, which during the last year was almost once a month. My benefactor's uncle runs a small private bank in Tokyo and I had a large safety deposit box, actually I had two. When I left Bambi, I took one set of keys with me, but in my haste and confusion I left the duplicate set in my basement computer room. They were well hidden and Bambi never went into that room, but I imagine that she was highly motivated and she must have found them.

"By then she was under an enormous amount of pressure. The clients were threatening and harassing her, the police and the feds were following her and watching the house, and I was gone, having left her a note explaining that I knew the truth and would never return to her. Far worse, I am sure, I had canceled all of her charge accounts and credit cards and emptied our joint bank accounts.

"Her fake suicide attempt was a desperate move to win my forgiveness. She must have known I would hear it on the news.

"You see, when my secretary informed me that two men who looked like detectives had come to the office, I knew someone had called the authorities and I had to accelerate my disappearance considerably. I was in San Francisco when the media broke the story, but I already had a new passport and I had absolutely no difficulty leaving the country. Then I zigzagged, not heading directly to Tokyo. By the time I arrived here I had an entirely new identity, even a driver's license.

"Then I made my most serious mistake. When I arrived in Japan I called Bambi. I can only say that curing oneself of another person is neither a linear nor a controllable activity and I had a moment of weakness. She did, of course, try everything she could think of to get me to tell her where the money was and, of course, where I was, 'for my own good,' she said. I did not, but I realize now that she must have traced the call through the phone company."

Leonard sighed.

"When I went to the bank to retrieve the bonds, knowing that returning them immediately was my only hope of avoiding a life as a fugitive — they were all *gone!*"

Annie gripped the arms of the chair, fighting to hold her mouth shut and keep her promise.

"This is what I believe happened. I am convinced that Bambi found the duplicate keys and told Stan Stein about them. When she traced the call — probably at his suggestion — he must have put it together. He knows my benefactor and his uncle; they have gambled together all over the world.

"Stan Stein must have gone to Bambi's and slipped in without the feds seeing him and taken the keys. Here was a way to walk off with a hundred million dollars, scot-free! He was one of the *victims* and I was certainly the only suspect!

"I know that he arrived in Tokyo and signed my name at the bank. He even knew what time of the day the executives and regular staff, who might know me, would be at lunch. He just walked out with the whole portfolio! I may have done a foolish and stupid thing, but I am not an immoral man! I never would have kept the money."

Leonard stopped, sighing deeply. "Annie, I need you to be a witness to this truth. It's too late for me, but you must tell my story to the authorities. Stein must be punished." Annie felt so sorry for him that she almost could not ask the next question. Besides, it was pretty clear. Either Stan still had the bonds and they could be found, meaning the FBI would believe her version of Leonard's story, or all of it was lost.

"Of course I will. I'm so sorry, Leonard. I wish you had come to us. What a terrible burden to carry all by yourself. Everything could have been different."

"Ah, that is just your Western background talking. Everything is always exactly the way it must be."

Annie refilled her cup, which was probably not a great idea, bladder-wise. "Leonard, I really only have two questions. Mickey had a meeting with Jackie and Stan, and Stan said that he had only given you a small amount of his money. I thought he had piles more, so why would he risk this?"

Leonard popped one of the vile sweets into his mouth, savoring the taste and making Annie wince.

"He lied. I should know. He was flat broke, and he had enormous gambling debts; even though *War Zone* was profitable, none of his other series were making it. He was leveraged up the gazoo and a greedy, venal gonif besides."

Annie smiled. "Is that a Japanese word?"

"Oh, Annie, don't make it any harder than it is."

She sat up straight as if physically preparing for what might be the final acceptance. "Okay, I'm back to my first question. If Mickey and Lina and I were innocent, why did you take our money, too? It isn't fair, Leonard. We were worthy of your trust."

Leonard wiped his mouth. "Oh, forgive me! I should have told you about that first! I kept your money separate. I wanted you to keep earning the interest, but also, it was a while before I knew that you three were not betraying me, too. Actually, Lina was a problem. Bambi went to her house a couple of times and I feared that she was like all the rest; I snuck into her condo the second time and found that they were just meeting with some psychic, so I put her money with yours. It's in a separate account in a bank in the Bahamas. I have all of your documents and the account codes and safety deposit keys right here. I'm so sorry I couldn't tell you sooner, but it was just too risky, and actually would have put you all under suspicion and created an enormous amount of animosity toward you. Once I left, I didn't dare contact you. Please forgive me."

Annie jumped up and flung herself into Leonard's lap, covering his damp, pale face with kisses and hugging him tight.

"Leonard, I would at this moment forgive you anything! God bless you, Tiny Tim! May old acquaintance be forgot! Thank you!"

Leonard put his head against her breast and cried like a lost child, and she held him, comforting them both.

He would never really know what he had set in motion in their lives; an avalanche of comeuppance. They had headed off down their old reliable bunny hill and skied right into the mother of all back-mountain danger zones. Sheer icy trails and a flood of blinding white reality. But what she felt for herself was, grateful. She did not understand why, but she was and she realized, holding him to her in this bemusing and incomparable situation, that even if the answer to her question had been the one she had so feared, she would still feel the same way.

CHAPTER XVIII

ANNIE REENTERED the hotel the next morning, clutching an envelope with the documents and keys required to reclaim their worldly goods in one hand, and a rare pine bonsai, a gift from Leonard, in the other. She was so tired she almost staggered.

She opened the door to their suite, stuffing the folder up under her arm, not wanting to put down the documents even for a second. Mickey was gone and there was a note for her on the desk: "Honey, had to leave, please try and call the set. I'm frantic about you!"

She put down the folder and carried her little tree into the bathroom, placing it beside the soap dish on the rim of the tub. She turned on the water and stripped off her clothes, carrying them into the bedroom and laying them on top of the dresser.

She opened the minibar, took out an orange juice, and pushed the phone button for room service, ordering what must have seemed to the order-taker an insane amount of food. She returned to the bathroom, turned off the water, and stepped into the tub, sinking slowly down into the water, sighing in pleasure.

She was not quite ready to call Mickey, even though all she had thought about from the minute she kissed Leonard good-bye was telling Mickey about her adventure and their good news.

She had promised that she wouldn't tell Lina anything until she got home, so Lina would have to hang out there a little while longer. Leonard was leaving for his "new life," somewhere in some remote part of Japan, and he didn't want to risk being followed.

Leonard had given her a confidential file for the police to support his Stan Stein theory, but she was told not to open it. She didn't really want to, anyway. All of this intrigue was taxing her reserves.

She opened her eyes and looked at her tree.

What a strange and pathetic art form, she thought, as the warmth of the water soothed her frazzled and exhausted being. What did it say about the Japanese character? Who would take a tree designed by nature and God at their intersection and stunt it, dwarf it? They took living things and thwarted their natural growth, turning them into artificial and manipulated forms of what they could have been.

It *was* an art and it had a mystical, odd beauty about it, but it was a dissembled beauty, a freak's seductiveness; the beauty of any anomaly of creation.

Was it a metaphor for what had happened to the Japanese people? The form of their rituals and the need to conform stunting the human being behind the ceremonials?

Were they a culture of human bonsais, never allowed to fully explore themselves, or was she just too American to understand the differences in their natures?

Maybe she was being too hard on the Japanese, she thought, picking up a lavender-scented soap and rubbing it across her chest. Maybe everyone was a sort of bonsai, pushed and formed by their families, their fears, and their responsibilities into varying degrees of undersized versions of their potential selves. It certainly seemed true of everyone she knew. It was certainly true of her.

She slid down into the water, covering her ears with her fingers, submerging her head, floating in her own lidless lily tank, thinking about Leonard and Bambi.

She surfaced and opened her eyes. The little tree sat in its funny tub, and she felt sorry for it; like a Chinese concubine with tiny broken feet, never to leap or dance, the ability to run from, or run toward, stunted forever.

It had become, from the moment Leonard placed it into her hand, a symbol of her worst and darkest horror: to die before she found how far up she could grow.

"I have found my true self," Leonard had said. But she hadn't really believed him. It hadn't sounded honest to her; it had sounded like the words of a still isolated and desperate man who had sacrificed everything and had taken the only road left.

She did not want to do that with the rest of her life. After all, she was not an embezzler, a fugitive, or a concubine; she could still run toward something. But what about that speech she had given Mickey? The false inner voice and the real one. How could she be sure?

The buzzer rang and she stood up and reached for a towel. She wrapped it tightly around herself and climbed out. She would call Mickey and have her lunch. She picked up the little pine thing and carried it with her into the living room. It was a symbol of something very important and it had been given to her for a reason. She didn't like it, but she needed to honor it.

Mickey was standing in the doorway.

"I thought you were room service!"

He came in and reached out to her. Instinctively, she moved back, surprising them both.

"I'm all wet," she said, feeling her face flush.

He looked tired. "That's how you open the door for room service?"

"Mickey, the towel is bigger than the *waiters!* Besides, they're all women, at least the ones I've seen. I was just going to call you. What are you doing here?"

"Miracle of miracles, we finished an entire day ahead of schedule, and try as they might, they couldn't come up with any reason to keep me there. I have two whole hours free before I have to be on the soap set." He sat down and took off his cap and sunglasses. "I was so worried about you I couldn't think straight."

She sat down beside him and curled her bare legs up under her. "Mickey, I have lots of amusing anecdotes and everything, but the most important part is — wait a minute." She reached behind her and picked up the folder, which was waiting patiently for her attention under the shade of the bonsai.

"Here, open it."

Mickey took the folder from her and pulled out the contents.

"We have everything back! I mean we will when I walk into that bank in the Bahamas. He never took our money or Lina's. He just took all the money of everyone who was sleeping with Bambi, which was approximately the entire population of Caracas, but that's a different story.

"Poor Leonard! He never meant to keep any of it. He was just so angry and hurt that all of his clients and everyone he trusted had betrayed him. He just wanted to teach them a lesson. We were the only ones who didn't betray him, so he gave it back to us; I mean he was going to give all of it back, but Stan Stein came here and took it all. Stan took all of the money! I have to tell everything to the FBI, because Leonard is going to completely disappear forever."

"Annie. Give me a minute. I can't absorb all of this so fast! Stan stole all the money? Jesus!"

"You won't believe the story."

"I already don't — I mean, I do, but we've obviously got a lot to deal with here. *Stan Stein?*"

She nodded. "He lied to you. He was broke."

He wanted to be horrified, or at least intensely curious, but he wasn't. The anxiety over their life's savings had been their only neutral territory. He watched her. He loved her like this, fresh from the bath, no makeup on, her hair damp and slicked back from her face, her skin pink and soft and sweet-smelling.

"We're going to be okay."

"Are we?" he said, startling them both for the second time.

He hadn't meant to say anything so provocative and personal. He was much too weary, and somehow the fabulous news was not energizing him. It no longer seemed relevant to his life. He felt numb, torpid, and unable to connect to anything but the presence of his wife on the couch.

The buzzer rang and she stood up. "Now, *that's* room service." She shuffled to the door and he closed his eyes, listening to her trying to be pleasant in that same voice that she hated him to use. The waiter, a man this time, wheeled a table entirely filled with food into the room. Mickey opened his eyes.

"Expecting company?" he said, watching her pull the cart closer to the couch.

"I was ravenous and usually the portions are so tiny. Have you eaten? We could dent the deficit with what it cost."

"Pass me the thing that looks like a club sandwich."

She handed him the plate and picked up a bowl of vegetable soup and sat back down. She eyed him while she ate her soup. It tasted funny, not like regular vegetable soup, or rather not like her vegetable soup or Molly's, or that terrific minestrone that Loretta used to make.

Mickey watched her. He bit into a glob of turkey, and mayonnaise squirted out onto his chin. "What?"

"Nothing," she said, carefully putting her bowl back on the tray and reaching for a plate with French fries and a fish cake of some kind.

"Annie, take the damn club sandwich."

"No, I'm fine."

"Annie, for chrissakes, how long have I eaten with you? I know you really want the club sandwich, so give me whatever that is and take it. I don't care what I eat right now. I'm not even really hungry. I'm just keeping you company. Here."

"Just give me one section. That's all I want."

"Take it."

He pushed the plate over to her and took the fries and fishballs from her.

"Thanks." She was still looking funny.

"What?"

"Nothing."

He picked up a handful of fries and dumped them into the empty slot where one section of the club sandwich had been.

"Don't you trust that I won't eat all the French fries?"

"Well, no, why should I? You always get haughty about it and you always eat *all* the French fries."

She picked up the club sandwich and took a bite. It tasted funny, too. Not like the great big healthy ones at Maisy's or that little diner on Sixth Avenue that she and Ida Mae and Ella always went to, where they used some really fantastic bacon without any fat on it and big thick slices of tomato.

"What now?" He popped a fishball into his mouth.

"Nothing. I'm just being a picky eater. I'm doing what I always advise readers not to do, comparing what you eat on the road with what you get at home. I know better. If I'm dumb enough to order American food here, I should just make do."

Mickey moved his plate away, smiling at her. "Do you believe what we're talking about?"

Annie finished off her section of sandwich and picked up some fries. *They* tasted funny too. It was the oil. Could they have fried the potatoes in the same oil as the fishballs? It served her right for ordering all of this fattening junk to begin with. She would have been better off picking up a bucket of fried chicken at one of the Colonel takeouts if she was feeling food nostalgia.

"Annie, where are you?"

She licked her fingers. Maybe there were anchovies in it? "I really need to get some sleep."

"Okay. Let me put you to bed." She nodded and let him help her up. He led her into the quiet, dark bedroom and pulled down the covers. She walked toward the closet, forgetting where she had put her gown.

"Here, honey," he said, and pulled it out of the drawer. "I unpacked for you."

"Thanks." Only Mickey of all the men she knew could pack and unpack for his wife.

She reached out for the gown, but he held it against his face. "Let me put it on you," he said.

She tightened, not knowing what to do, only that his request frightened her and pushed in on her in some deeply private way.

"Okay," she said, not meaning it. She undid her towel and let it fall.

"Oh, baby, my lovely baby," he said, moving toward her as if he had never seen her nude before. She wanted to cover herself, but she resisted, seeing Oliver in another hotel room forever ago, asking her to take off her clothes for the very first time.

Mickey moved toward her and put his arms around her, letting the soft silk fall between them. "I want you, honey, I want you so much. I feel like a boy, like we've never made love before. Oh, Annie, honey."

He buried his face against her neck, kissing her along her pulse line, making her shiver. She could feel her heart beating against his lips. His hands moved down her buttocks. Ivy Clare's face flashed behind her eyes. "I can make him come five times in a night. I bet you couldn't equal that in a month. . . ."

"Annie. Oh, baby, I've missed you so much."

He held her closer and she could feel his erection against her. She wanted to be where he was, but she wasn't. She just wasn't.

He let her go. "What is it?"

She bent over and picked up her gown, slipping it over her head. "Too many thoughts in my head. I'm sorry. I just can't switch gears that fast."

"I see," he said, and she knew that he was angry, even though he had no right to be.

"I guess after Mr. Sports Car got through shifting you all over England, your gears are a little sluggish."

"Mickey, don't you dare."

"Why not? Do you think that because I had an affair, your having one doesn't hurt? Mine's over. I love *you*. I came back to *you*. Do you think this doesn't tear me up? That I'm not allowed to feel jealous and angry and obsessed about you fucking someone else, because I did it, too?"

She moved past him to the bed. She didn't quite know what she felt about his question. "We sound like an hour on *Oprah*."

"Answer me without being cute."

She sat down on the bed and pulled the pillows into a huge pile, thankful they were not filled with rice.

"Look, Mickey, I don't have an answer for you. You've gotten to live out your entire drama on your terms. Now you're all resolved and repentant and in love with me again and horny and everything and I think that's wonderful, but it's all about *you*. What *you* feel, what *you* need. How lucky for you to know!

"I don't know what I feel or what I need, and nothing is resolved for me. I think I deserve as much as you got — my own internal timetable. I'm not a performing seal. I can't just jump up on the ball and smack my little flippers together on cue because that's what you're ready for.

"I've spent my entire adult life meeting other people's agendas. I just don't seem to be able to do that anymore, even if it would make everything a helluva lot easier for both of us. Believe me, if I could, I would, pal. It's what I feel most comfortable doing."

He grabbed her shoulders, pulling her toward him. "Why can't you fucking hear me! How many times can I apologize! I love you! It's over with her! I've never cheated before and I never will again — I swear to fucking Christ! What do you want from me? Anything, I'll do anything! Can't you just let it go? In forty years of a love relationship one fucking affair isn't such a big deal! And now we're even. If I can forgive you, why can't you just cut it out and come back? Or is this about something else? Are you punishing me for years of little things? My success? Forgetting our anniversary? How long is the fucking checklist!"

She pulled away, wrapping the soft sheets around her.

"Mickey, I know you're trying really hard. I don't want to hurt you. I'm not trying to do that or get revenge. I can't help this! It's not that I don't love you, either."

She had not meant to say that. Suddenly tears filled her eyes and her throat, as if a small piece of plumbing inside her had broken.

"Oh, God, Mickey, I know what it is! It's not that I don't love you anymore, it's that I love someone else, too! I have never loved anyone but you and now I do! I don't want to, but I do, and I can't go back and pretend that it hasn't happened. I don't know how to love you with Oliver there. I have no way of combining all of these feelings. I thought having the money back would make it easier, but it's much worse! Now there's no place to fool myself. No place to hide from this!"

He bent down, his anger released, and picked up her towel and carried it back into the bathroom, an act so unlike himself, a man who left a trail of towels and robes behind him, that it alarmed her. She sat up. "Mickey? Are you all right?"

He had closed the door, but she could hear wracking sobs, men's tears; so different from the way women cried, as if each one was a surrender of something they needed to survive.

She got up and went to the bathroom door, turning the knob slowly. He had not locked it and she went in. He was standing by the sink, the towel against his face. She sat down on the edge of the tub, knowing enough not to try and touch or comfort him when he was that upset. Even when they were kids, he had hated to be comforted or touched when he was in any way hurt or vulnerable.

She sat with him, the sound of his muffled sobs mingling with the strange quiet of hotel bathrooms, a restless quiet, filled with undersounds from vents and drains and hallways.

He put the towel down and reached for a tissue. Pancake makeup was streaked across his face, making him look older and slightly feminine.

He blew his nose and wadded the damp tissue up in his fist, slamming it into the tiny little trash can — a perfect Japanese receptacle, Annie thought, small, and conducive to having few secretions and being very neat. It reminded her of the girls at the Tokyo train station with the little white gloves and funny wedge-shaped hats who piled onto the arriving trains and swept everything clean the moment the passengers disembarked. Why couldn't they be like that now — why couldn't they just sweep the aisles of their confusion, tidy it all up and get on with their lives.

He looked up at her, his eyes red and swollen. It absolutely devastated her to see him cry. It seemed to take everything from him; it brought him none of the release that it brought her. Men seemed to truly hate to cry or to throw up; both somehow represented losing some part of the control that they believed essential.

She had seen Mickey cry as a grown-up about the same number of times that she had seen him vomit, less than a handful, and she could clearly remember the details of each dissimilar but somehow connected event. She had been unnerved by each one because they had so traumatized him and because she was so helpless. She couldn't go near him when he was in any way out of control; it made him furious, and he would lash out at her as if her attempt to comfort or help further weakened him.

"So, I guess this is it, kid," he said, crossing his arms over his chest the way Toby did. "If you love this guy, that's the big finale. I don't have any more dialogue. I'm writing myself out of the script."

Her head felt as if someone were squeezing it; pressure and sharp, stabbing pain pushed into her skull. Why couldn't she have just kept her mouth shut, like he had done! It wasn't fair that she should have to be bullied into making this choice now. Why couldn't she just have lied?

"I guess you're giving me an ultimatum."

He wet a tissue and rubbed at his makeup in small angry strokes, petulant, Annie thought. A spoiled child not getting his way. Men were so unerringly predictable! Every man she had ever known, with the possible exception of Oliver, were like software. Once you learned their codes you could punch in the correct response every single time.

Women were not at all like that, even the most seemingly uncomplicated ones. She never ceased to be amazed at the originality and unpredictability of female reactions. Maybe it was because they were always, in some way, trying to change, even if they didn't consciously know they were, while men were mostly trying not to, even if they consciously thought they were striving for enlightenment. Mickey was reacting exactly the way she would have predicted (if the opportunity to make such an observation had been given to her).

"Hey, look, I'm not perfect and I'm not *you,* though God knows it causes you endless disappointment. I can't play this role. I don't have it in me to wait around while you prance all over Europe picking daisy petals — 'I love him, I love him not.'

"We've got our dowry back, so to speak, which gives me a little room to breathe, and I want to make some changes and move on. I can't do any of that with our relationship hanging on the line like last week's laundry!

"We could be starting the very best years of our lives together. The kids are grown, we have some security and freedom, and we're still young enough to enjoy ourselves. We could really have some fun and do wonderful work, maybe even together. I've been thinking about that a lot."

He wadded up another tissue and tossed it into the can. Annie followed its trajectory, as if the mounting pile of refuse had some deeper meaning.

He came over and sat down beside her on the tub.

"You remember that article you were trying to write when we were here last time? Well, I had it in my Japan file and I've been reading it over and over, and I keep thinking that the reason I'm losing you, have lost you it seems, is because I never validated you enough. It's a really brave piece of work. Actually, I envy it.

"I don't think I've ever been secure enough about my own career to really nurture yours, so I let you do the copping out and make the compromises.

"I don't know, maybe that was what you needed. Maybe if I had been pushing you it would have been too much pressure; but I really blew it. I failed you. You as Annie, not as my wife or even as my best friend. I stopped seeing you as you, and I lacked compassion for your struggle.

"I keep thinking that if I had another chance, I could help you find the way to fulfill yourself. I know you hate what you've been doing. I know that it's been easier for me to just pat you on the head and tell you how great it is that you have this little career and can still do everything that you do for everybody else. I guess in some ways it was convenient for both of us; I kept you where I wanted you, and you had whatever excuse you needed for not taking bigger creative risks.

"Funny thing is, that at this point you have the potential of going all the way up with whatever you want to do and I, well, I've had my run.

"I pretty well know what's in store for me. I've had my fifteen minutes, and even so, it sure as hell wasn't the fifteen minutes I had dreamt about. I'm never going to be Brando or De Niro or even F. Murray Abraham.

"I'm gonna do what they send me, some of it okay, some of it shit. If I'm lucky I'll get another series that clicks, but we both know how rare that is, and if not, it's a few movies of the week here and there, some theater and commercials, foreign films by indie companies looking for a poor man's version of whoever's hot and my type. I've peaked, Annie, and I know it.

"All I have of any value to fall back on and make that very tough truth okay is you and our kids, and I've pretty well fucked all of that up. So forgive me for a little pouting. I know I'm responsible, but I just can't take it. I'm not as strong as you are, and I never have been. I don't know what to do but finish up this shit and go home and divide everything up and disappear somewhere and lick my wounds."

They looked at one another, the loss dangling between them like a clown on a high-wire. It was not possible to let it all fall, but there was nothing out there to hang on to.

"Oh, come on, Mickey," she said, knowing she was about to make the entire situation worse but needing to find a way back to the platform. "You're handsome and talented and famous and you're in a seller's market. Women will be karate-chopping one another out of the path to your door and you probably have your most interesting work ahead of you.

"I know you really believe what you're saying, but it's just self-pity and hurt feelings talking. If we split up and Oliver and I don't work out, which is certainly a strong possibility, my future is a helluva lot bleaker than yours will ever be, and I sort of resent you suddenly taking the martyr's role here. That's my turf and I've earned it.

"A middle-aged woman has a much gloomier future alone in this viper's nest we so quaintly call modern life than you can even fantasize about, and no amount of Stanislavsky could ever prepare you for what may be ahead of me. So don't do this, please. I really do understand how you feel and I care too much about you to let you go off like this. Besides, it makes me mad. I shouldn't have to be sitting here feeling 'poor Mickey' right now. God only knows how much I don't want any of this to be happening."

He sighed and looked at his watch. She held her breath. She had been prepared for an outburst of righteous indignation. Maybe they were both just too tired.

"Shit! I've got to go in ten minutes and I haven't even showered or changed yet."

He stood up and began to undress. She got up and started for the door. She really had to sleep for a while now; the pressure in her head felt as if her entire forehead might just pop off her face.

"I've got to get some sleep. Can we finish this when you get back?"

He kicked off his pants and reached for his socks.

"Sure. We should have dinner and try to celebrate. I still haven't heard any of the Leonard details."

"Okay," she said. "Sayonara."

She closed the door behind her and rolled onto the bed. They had helped the clown back to the ground, neither of them quite able to risk reaching the other side of the wire. How could they say good-bye? It was almost like saying good-bye to themselves.

When Mickey came back she was still asleep, and he sat beside her in a chair in the dark, watching her. Flashes from the past . . . his father in the hospital the night he died, Mickey waiting beside him, praying that he would wake up, throw off the coma sleep for just a minute and allow him to make contact one more time, to tell him that he loved him, that he would miss him, to at least say good-bye.

Mickey sat, long after Ida Mae had gone home with Jackie and Annie had left. He sat there waiting for one last flicker of eye contact that would have to last him forever.

He stayed all night and his father neither died nor opened his eyes, and finally he went home without any closure. The phone was ringing when he opened the door, a nurse telling them that his father was gone, and he slammed his fist through the bathroom door, outraged at having been denied his rite of passage.

Why did watching his wife sleep make him think of his father's death? Maybe because this was like a death, not even like one, it *was* death. Only much, much worse, because when his father had died and he had punched a hole in the door, Annie had been there to hold him and help him through.

As long as he had Annie, he could get through anything. This was beyond death. This was . . . what? The void, the big fucking black hole in his cosmos. The primal loss at the core of his being.

He sat until he fell asleep himself, and when he woke up she was gone, the way his father had been gone when they had raced back to the hospital. The bed was empty and he was gone forever.

He got up and went into the living room. She was sitting at the small hotel desk, the stack of documents arranged neatly before her.

She turned and smiled at him. She looked almost radiant, which made him feel like crying again.

"Hi," she said. "Did I disturb you?"

"Nope. Something about sleeping in a chair, it doesn't take too long for your body to speak its mind."

"What time is it?"

Mickey pulled up his sweater sleeve. "Almost eight!"

"Great, we can still eat."

He swallowed hard, not knowing for sure that he could bear sitting across from her without making a scene. "What are you doing?"

"Oh, I'm organizing the documents for you to sign. One of us can retrieve everything, but I need your signature on a whole pile of stuff."

He nodded. "Rack them up."

She picked up a pen and began handing him documents. They did not talk and he did not ask any questions, which annoyed her. He always left all the tedious details to her and Leonard, the message being "I don't have time for any of this, *I'm an artist.*"

He finished and handed the pen back to her. "What's the time frame on this?"

She sighed, knowing where this would lead. "Well, I think I should get down there as soon as I can."

He scratched his head. He was still groggy and his neck was stiff from sleeping sitting up. "So, like, when?"

"Like tomorrow morning."

"I see. Are you going direct?"

She looked up at him. "No. It's not possible. Besides, my ticket's booked through London. When I get there, I'll figure out how to make the connections. I don't even really know where the Bahamas are, and then I have to get ahold of someone at the FBI and tell them the story. Stan Stein has to be arrested before he disappears with all the money."

He was not going to cry and he was not going to pull her up out of her chair and shake her back into their marriage.

"Sounds like quite a load for one small redhead."

She picked up the papers and put them back into the folder. "I'll just ignore that hugely sexist and patronizing remark."

"Sorry. It's the London part."

Tears filled her eyes and she stood up, reaching out to him. "Oh, Mickey, please, give me some time. Please don't make me decide about us now."

He held her, sniffing in her warmth, wishing that he had lifted his father up and held him close, sniffing in whatever a dying man smelled like, even if it was not at all like his father's usual nicotine-and-Aqua-Velva smell.

"Just go, Annie. I'm sorry, I can't handle this. We'll have dinner. We need to talk about the details, and what we tell the kids, but I want to stop this agony. You go deal with this and I'll finish up here, and we'll meet back in Montecito and work out the divorce."

They let go of one another. It was the first time they had said the words.

She nodded, the tears splattered across her cheeks, running between her freckles, giving her face a mottled, blurred look.

"All right," she said and carried the folder holding the tangible struggles and achievements of their adult lives back to the safety of her purse.

He was being stubborn and childish and he knew it, but he could not alter this course; he simply could not stand this. If turnabout was fair play, he was a very bad player.

No one watching them at dinner, talking softly, laughing once in a while, eating from one another's plates, would have suspected that this was a couple who were rewinding themselves, two jacks about to spring out of their brightly colored boxes, leaving the surprises of their lives together — the anticipations, hopes, goals, and strivings — inside.

They had been so closely bound for so long that when they burst forth, it would be without a clear understanding of the consequences of their actions. Consequences can never be understood in the present. Consequences are bottom-feeders, snaking through the hidden grottos of married life, leaving only slithering ripples in the present. Consequences feed on the future, and so they ate and they talked in the present of their marriage, because that is where they were — still bobbing on the surface, far removed from the feeding frenzy about to begin way, way down below.

CHAPTER XIX

One of Helen Gurley Brown's secrets for fabulous-looking skin is to "Put on a shower cap and grease your face. Fill your bathroom basin with cold water. Dump in two trays of ice cubes. Using a snorkel, stick your face down below the water surface and stay there as long as you can."

ANNIE EYE'S were getting heavy. The plane was only half filled and no one was sitting next to her. She put down her newspaper and lowered the back of her seat. She raised the foot rest and tucked in the blanket tight around her feet. She did not want to think anymore. She just wanted to sleep.

She closed her eyes, visions of herself snorkeling in her bathroom sink floating by. What always impressed her was how anyone thought of something like that. Did Helen wake up one morning and the idea of oiling up, putting on a snorkel set, and sticking her head in a tub of ice water just come to her?

Could you do things like that when you lived with other people? Wasn't it hard on the back, bending over like that, not to mention boring? Somehow it didn't seem worth it. Annie curled her legs up and turned on her side.

She drifted off into the sluggish half-sleep associated with airplanes, trains, car trips, and afternoon naps. She could hear people talking, a stewardess bringing a drink to the man across the aisle, ice rattling in a glass, the captain asking them to refasten their seat belts.

Inside the restless dozing, she felt a small slanting shift off the center of herself. Cold sweat curtained her, shrouding her half-consciousness with premonition, a jettisoning of her senses. *Something was wrong with her.*

Holy God, something was *really* wrong. She tried to sleep through it, cruise past it without having to confront whatever was happening to her body. Cramping, terrible pain, squeezed into her pelvis. She pulled her knees in tighter and tried to breathe deeply; wetness, thickened wetness decanting from deep inside her, spilling out onto her thighs.

She sat up, tearing at her seat belt despite the warning lights and the little bell dinging every few minutes. She grabbed her purse and lurched forward in her stocking feet. She clutched the bathroom door handle and closed herself in. The pain was almost unbearable.

She pulled down her pantyhose. Her panties and stockings were soaked with blood. *God. Please.* Thick purple clots were stuck against the nylon like leeches. Blood gushed forth, unstoppable. She punched the lever on the supply cabinet, spilling thick sanitary napkins out onto the floor, and frantically scooped them up, bent in half, the pain blinding her. She did not know what to do first. Think, Annie, dammit. Think. *God, help me.*

The plane hit an air pocket and she stumbled forward, hitting her head on the mirror. She saw herself reflected in the green fluorescence of the glass. Her face was gray and covered with sweat. *Please.*

She pulled off her pantyhose and underwear and threw them in the sink, bracing herself with one arm and rinsing with the other. The plane bumped, and the trickles of water, one hot and one cold, like drops in the desert, vanished into the heavy clotted mess before her.

She gave up on the stockings and worked on the pants. Blood was now pouring down her legs and onto the floor. She ripped open a sanitary pad with wet, shaking hands and pushed it between her legs, holding it with her thighs. She scrubbed her pants, the pain making her sway toward blackness. She scrubbed until the clots were gone, wrapping the panties in hand towels, squeezing out as much moisture as she could. She stepped into them, holding on to the sink while the plane bucked under her, bracing herself like a cowgirl at the county fair.

She opened as many pads as she could find and stuffed them into her panties. Her feet and the floor were covered with blood. She couldn't let anyone see this! She leaned forward, holding a wad of towels in her hand, and started to clean. The pain came again, a wave so powerful that she gasped, losing her balance and crashing into the door.

A knock. "Excuse me, are you all right in there?" A woman's voice. Thank God it was a woman's voice. She hated to ask for help. She never asked for help. People asked *her* for help! That was *her* job. She helped, she rescued, she showed up with Band-Aids and Tylenol.

"I'm fine," she said.

"Are you sure?" the woman, Japanese, Annie thought, asked.

"I'm sure." Family lies used anywhere.

Something shifted again inside her and she slumped down into her own blood, hitting her head as she fell.

She could hear voices outside, confusion. Concern. They were asking her things, asking her to open the door, but she couldn't move. She crouched in her own effluence like an animal birthing. She slipped in and out of consciousness. She was not an animal, she was not giving birth, she was dying. She had felt herself slip away; as if the cement that held her together inside the deepest and most delicate part of her being had been just ever so slightly shouldered off its foundation. She floated in and out of herself on waves of agony.

All of the crazy fears she'd ever had of dying — in the Florida Keys she had thought of being eaten by a crocodile walking down the path to her room. BEWARE OF CROCODILES the little sign had said, right there on the guest's footpath. In Hawaii she was always looking up at the palm trees, waiting for a coconut to come crashing down and drop her in her tracks. She worried about planes exploding, and carjackers, and each disease of the month, but she had never worried about bleeding to death in the toilet of a 747.

Something inside of her had broken apart, just like her mother. Something inside her mother's head and now something inside her womb. Fate would have the last laugh. This was God's timetable and she was going to be taken, just like her mother.

She heard low moaning sobs that seemed to be coming from the ceiling. It must be her, who else was in there up above her? Could it be her mother, watching this happen to her? She reached up toward it. "Momma please, Momma, don't let me die now. Please, Momma, don't take me now, not now. Don't let happen to my babies what happened to me. Please, Momma, let me stay. Help me. Help me!"

Something gave way; the door was gone. Someone was lifting her up and carrying her. She saw faces, shocked, nervous faces looking down at her. "It hurts," she heard herself say. "Bleeding. I'm so sorry," she said.

People were running around. She heard the same woman's voice over the intercom. "We have a medical emergency in the first-class cabin. If there is a doctor aboard would he kindly step forward and identify himself."

Her body was shivering, she could feel her teeth clicking up and down.

Someone was leaning over her. She tried to keep her eyes open. A kindly Japanese face smiled at her. "I am a doctor. Can you show me where it hurts?"

She nodded, using every ounce of her strength to place her cold, clammy hands over her violated uterus. He moved her hands away gently and replaced them with his own warm ones. Everywhere he touched was fire inside her. Tears spilled down her cheeks.

"It hurts very bad?"

"Yes."

"I have something for the pain. It will be okay soon. You know you have large fibroid?"

She nodded. "Yes, but it's harmless."

She tried to focus on him. His face looked so serious. "It has become necrotic. You must go to a hospital and be operated on as soon as possible. Very serious. You are losing much blood. I will call ahead. Is there someone to notify?"

Necrotic. She knew that word. "Dead." It had something to do with corpses. "Necropolis" was a Greek word, "city for the dead," cemetery. Her insides had died.

Who could she call? Who would know what to do with her and her dead womb? She saw Mickey standing in the doorway when she left in the taxi. She saw Oliver standing at the gate when she left for the plane. She was being punished. Loretta was wrong. God did know that she had lost her moral way. One little redhead right up there with Hitler and Ted Bundy.

"Can you hear me? Who should we notify? Someone must authorize," he said.

Pain shot through her and she winced. He patted her arm. "Just hold on for a moment." He left her and she curled up tighter into a ball, fighting to stay present. Sleep was now not a welcome release, a respite from her hyperactive head, but the beginning of her end.

The doctor knelt beside her and pulled up her bloody skirt. People stood over her. She was no longer human. Strangers flanking her while a man stuck a needle into her bare ass; she *had* become a thing, creaturelike and dependent, beyond self-control, beyond embarrassment or protocol. Manners did not matter in the death house.

The shot hit her, heat rushed through her body, and she unclenched her teeth. "My brother," she whispered. "Call my brother. Dr. Martin Miller, in my purse, in my phone book. Tell him to come. Tell him . . ."

She reached out for the doctor's hand. She could feel herself slipping away. "Promise me you won't let them give me any blood without my brother."

The doctor took her hand. "I promise."

"I'm going to die like my mother," she said, seeing her mother float by over her head.

"No, no, don't say. You will be fine."

She did not believe him. She was sliding under and could not be sure she would ever come back. "Tell my children I love them. Toby and Ella, tell them, I'm so sorry."

The drugs rushed her, pulling her down, a beach wader caught in the riptide. Under she went, spinning round and round, down and down and down.

CHAPTER XX

SIX MONTHS LATER

JACKIE WILSKI swung onto the Ventura Freeway and let Vivaldi take his mind out. This he would miss — these Fuck-you-too drives up and down the coast between L.A. and Santa Barbara. That was one thing he couldn't do as well back East. The Long Island Expressway didn't count, since you spent all your mental energy trying not to hit one of the holes — ass- or pot-. You could never just let your thoughts fly.

Of course L.A. wasn't much different these days; all the fucking cities were falling apart. Too much oligarchy for too long; too many special interests flexing for the sake of flexing. The whole fucking country was being bullied by a bunch of Cro-Magnons with good intentions. What was lacking in the whole mess was a rational overview. What had he read about a gay volleyball league? Did gay people play volleyball differently than straight people? Why couldn't everyone just stay in the stuff together. Where would any of it end? Sooner or later vegetarians won't eat in restaurants with carnivores, and we'll end up with forty different Olympic games and twelve thousand political parties and no country that anyone would really give a shit about. And now that the boomers have taken over the White House there isn't even a fantasy left of some kindly and wise father-figure coming along and organizing the playground.

The truth was that what everybody really wanted was someone to follow, someone bigger than they were to show them the way to Santa's house. Take away that need, and all the cult leaders, shrinks, Samanthas, and religions on the planet would vanish in a microsecond.

Lately he was proving his point over and over again and he loved it. (Everyone loved being right.) But all the mendacity and media blather had taken their toll. It was certainly part of the reason for selling his production company, getting out of the tabloid TV business, and going back to New York. Too many angry, polarized peanutheads, all believing theirs was the only way. Too many Joey Buttafuocos becoming international celebrities simply by being more repulsive than the schnook next door.

His life and his brother's had changed so much in the almost nine months since last Thanksgiving, he could hardly grasp it. He swallowed. God, who would have thought that his life would be solider and happier than Mickey's?

He had money and freedom to do whatever the fuck he wanted, and he was no longer lonely all the time and chasing rainbows — fading rainbows with big tits and heads of colored air. Thank you, Dr. Rhinehart, for setting me fucking free!

Could he be the same guy who had roared up the coast last November, filled with rage and bitterness and bargain-basement self-esteem? How was it that the most growth he had undergone in his entire fucking life happened *after* he quit his analysis? Maybe he would turn out to be nothing but an insecure little putz in a pretentious suit who really couldn't produce anything better than *Under the Covers,* but at least he would try.

The day he left Rhinehart's office he had gone into a shoe store somewhere in the Beverly Center mall; he was just sort of free-falling, and spending money always helped reconnect him. He loved pulling out the superelite Black Am-Ex card; "the Darth Vader card," Annie used to call it, sort of the pocket version of his Mercedes — eat your hearts out, suckers — another symbol of his insecurity.

He was waiting for someone to help him when he noticed an old woman sitting across from him. She was long past sixty, squat and lumpy, but she was wearing a stiff black punk-style leather jacket that seemed to have nothing to do with the rest of her. The jacket was stretched over a large, football-shaped hump that pitched her forward, making her various chins and stomach creases push against one another.

She was trying on black pumps or something like that — "pumps" was the only female shoe word he knew. She had several different pairs in front of her and two samples stuffed onto her bloated little feet. Her ankles were swollen and hanging over the tops of the shoes. She was completely focused on her feet.

"Which pair do you think looks better?" she asked, startling him. He was not used to strangers, especially leather-clad, humpbacked old women, speaking to him in public places. He looked down at her shoes, trying not to show his distaste. Every pair looked exactly the same.

"They're all nice," he said, hoping that would be the end of it.

She shook her head, stretching out her tree-trunk calves and twisting her ankles sideways. "Don't ya think the silk is a better black than the faille?"

He had absolutely no idea what she was talking about.

"I'm not much of a ladies'-shoe expert," he said, wanting to leave but trying not to offend her. She pulled herself up and trudged to the mirror. Her hump was so big that she was almost bent in half. Jackie was mesmerized by the sight of this creature, barely able to stand up, taking the choice of the Best Black Pump as seriously as if she were a fucking shoe model or the new Marlene Dietrich about to make her film debut.

He had a horrifying urge to shout at her, "What the fuck difference does it make! *No one* is going to give a shit about your ugly old feet!"

The woman made her way up and down the store, asking the opinion of everyone as to the best fit and "best black."

Jackie waited for her, sitting quietly with his hands on his lap. It took her more than twenty minutes, until the shoe man, who was either going to convince her or choke her to death, said, "The black silk, trust me," and she agreed.

Jackie got up and followed him to the counter, pulling out his black card.

"I want to buy these for that woman," he said, ignoring the raised eyebrow and sardonic curl at the sides of the shoe slave's mouth. He paid, picking up the box and walking back to the old lady, who was powdering her nose and putting on fresh lipstick as if she were Cindy Crawford on her way to a late date.

"Here," he said. "I want to give you these as a present."

The woman looked up at him as if he were handing her a pile of cow turds.

"What is it?"

"Your shoes. I, uh, bought them for you. Please, it's okay."

He handed her the box and walked out, never looking back, afraid that she might leap forth, a feminized Quasimodo, and chase him around the mall.

By the time he got into his car, he knew why he had done it. He was in awe of her self-esteem. That humpbacked old woman, long past the point where anyone would look at her except as an object of curiosity or pity, had far more self-esteem than he did. *It only matters what you think you're worth.*

Funny, he had never really connected that bizarre encounter with his beginning to truly change; but it was the brass key, for sure. No more glass keys for the Jacko.

The Glass Key, Veronica Lake and Alan Ladd: "Be careful he don't give ya a glass key, the kind that breaks off in the lock." The story of his life as a grown-up. Every time he thought he was getting closer to understanding himself, the damn key broke off in the lock. He never got the fucking door open. Maybe now he wasn't in the room, but he was sure as hell in the open doorway.

He turned up the volume. The *Four Seasons* — moving along toward autumn again. This Thanksgiving sure as hell would be different. Joe Miller gone, and Annie. Poor Annie.

All that part of their lives was over now. Stan Stein was no longer a thorn in his side, a reminder of the kind of programs he could have been producing if he had had the balls, and Mickey was no longer a big TV star, making it easier for both of them to heal their relationship.

Every once in a while, like when he read something about Samantha's bounce into the big time, or one of his exes called, trying to use him for a contact or a loan, he would feel a moment of prickly, icy fear; would he revert? Most of the time, though, he was too happy and sure of his new course to let the demons dance on his rocky little head anymore, or at least not for long.

Jackie saw the Montecito village turn-off ahead and slowed down. This would be the last time he ever did this. No one left there now but his brother, waiting alone in an empty house.

It was the house of his brother's fame, where the highest highs and lowest lows of Mickey's entire life had taken place. If houses had souls, as Loretta believed, then this house was a real mixed bag for the new owners. Hope and loss, Annie had always said, was what life was. Well, that sure as hell was what the Wilder's house was about; though he could say the same thing about Loretta and Martin's house and his house, too.

Jackie slowed down at the village stoplight, letting a baby-faced blond man in a blue jogging suit cross the street. The guy was pure Santa Barbara. One of the Winthrop The Third types from the Burnham Hills Country Club set, the kind of soft-faced sons-of crowd that always looked to Jackie to be a little low in the testosterone department. Maybe they annoyed him so much because they belonged to a world that would never accept him.

He picked up the phone and punched the memory code.

"Hello?"

"Hi, Loretta, it's Jackie."

"Oh, thank God it's you, I thought it was the damn breather again."

"What breather?"

"Some creep has been calling the home line all morning, but I didn't want to turn it off until you called. He's been driving me crazy."

Jackie laughed. "Well, is it at least an exciting breather?"

"No. It's a really boring breather. Sort of nasal and wheezy and he doesn't say anything."

"Good, no competition. Well, I'm almost there."

"Gee, you made great time! I called Mickey, but all the phones are turned off."

"Yeah. This is going to be tough."

"Are you going right from there to the airport?"

"I think Molly and Billy are having a little good-bye brunch, then I'm going."

"Call me at my office before you leave. I'd like to talk to Mickey, and Bennie wants to say good-bye to you, you deserter. You're the first one of us to go back home."

Home. Jackie liked the way it sounded. "I wish I could get Mickey to come."

Loretta sighed. "Too many memories. Selling Montecito is enough for now."

Jackie pulled into the driveway. He swallowed, feeling the old lump move back up his throat. "I'm here, and having a lot of trouble swallowing."

Loretta sighed. "Deep breaths and don't clench your teeth. Gotta go."

He put down the receiver and eased his car forward. No more show-off entrances. No more Portia hobbling out to meet him with little Juanita trotting beside her; no more Toby and Ella, flushed from shooting hoops or running on the beach, shouting, "Uncle Jackie!" Why was life such a predictable fucking cliché? Well, it just was, but that didn't make it easier to deal with.

Mickey was sitting on the step talking to Billy. The Pats were gathered around them like a small flock of pug-nosed ducklings. Jackie turned off the engine. Mickey waved, and he opened the car door, wiping tears with his free hand. He was not going to cry; he was not going to leave as baby brother — he was going to leave as his brother's friend and equal. That was what they both needed now; it was their going-away present.

CHAPTER XXI

OLIVER TAYLOR spooned two large teaspoons of sugar into his oversized cup of café au lait and leaned back in the little bistro chair, surveying the Maisy's scene. He picked up his cup, so American in its cheerful excess, and took a long, foamy sip. The place was exactly as Annie had described it.

He winced, aware of the empty space across from him that so demanded her small, freckled presence. It would never stop hurting. He was too old now for any new loss to ever heal. Too old and with too few illusions about the future.

A slender blond woman wearing a slightly tattered straw hat and some sort of floral nightdress floated toward him, looking to Oliver's classically trained eye like a modern-day Ariel on her way to the forest. It had to be Molly O'Brian, as Annie had word-painted her for him — hours of ecstasy on the Scottish coast, painting word portraits of the people and places in their other lives.

He stood up and the sprite in the straw hat waved to him, gliding forth in scuffed white ballet shoes as if she were attached to invisible strings holding her ever so slightly off the floor.

"Oliver, I presume?"

Oliver extended his hand, covering hers completely.

"So nice to meet you, Molly. Annie described you immaculately. I would have picked you out in the middle of a concert at Prince Albert Hall."

"Well, I suppose that's a compliment since y'all are English and far too well mannered to mean it any other way."

"An absolute compliment." He paused and reached into his pocket for a cigarette. "Will this horrify you?"

Molly giggled. "Only if y'all don't share."

He smiled and offered her the pack. "I cannot tell you what a thrill it is to have someone to enjoy a fag with. Everywhere I go in America, I feel as if I might as well be slipping a worm into my mouth."

Molly leaned forward and Oliver lit her cigarette. "I totally sympathize. However, I would suggest that you find another term. Saying to Americans that y'all want someone to 'enjoy a fag with' is bound to get you into some kind of trouble sooner or later."

He laughed, lighting his own. "Absolutely right. Thank you for the slang check. I haven't been here for some time."

The waiter approached. "Hi, Mrs. O'Brian. The usual?"

"Yes, please, and bring one of those luscious little pecan shortbreads and an extra fork."

Oliver smiled at her. Everything he knew about Southern women had come either from Annie's descriptions of Molly or his numerous viewings of Vivien Leigh in *A Streetcar Named Desire,* which might not even count since she was really British.

Molly leaned back and crossed her legs, staring at him coyly under the protection of her bangs. "Well, I understand now," she said, taking a long, deep drag.

He felt his cheeks heat and the tight, choking feeling at the edge of his sorrow. "What?"

"What my Annie succumbed to."

He picked up his cup, not quite trusting his voice.

The waiter returned, setting down her order.

Molly passed him a fork. "Y'all looked like a pecan shortbread type to me."

He wiped foam from his lip. "Right!"

Molly picked up her cup, her pinkie sticking out like a genteel attendee at the Mad Hatter's tea party.

They were quiet for a moment, neither of them, for all their dissimilar but powerful social poise, quite sure how to proceed.

Oliver stabbed at the pecan bar with his fork. "I suppose you want to know what I'm doing here."

Molly stubbed out her cigarette and put her napkin neatly on her lap. "Oh dear man, I do think I know what y'all are doing here."

"Well, I was in L.A. on business and it just seemed, since you knew them so well and it was you who called me and all, that maybe you could help me finish with this."

Molly slipped a chunk of shortbread into her small pink mouth. "I doubt if we ever finish with anyone we have loved along the way, but I will be happy to try and fill in some of the pesky little sinkholes that keep us baying at the moon in the dead of night."

He smiled at her. "Ariel as seen by Tennessee Williams."

Molly grinned, showing her gapped front teeth. "Oh, I do like that image. I am going to tell my Billy that, make him appreciate me more."

"By all means," he broke off another piece with his fork. "Fantastic. Only Americans bake things like this."

"Annie and I did it better. We re-created their recipe but without the almond flavoring. I do prefer vanilla."

His face contracted and he put the pastry back on his plate.

He washed down the sweet with his coffee and sat back in the little chair, dwarfed under his bulk; a big man forced into a kiddie seat. "All right, let's just do it. Can you tell me exactly what happened?"

Molly put down her fork and wiped her graceful fingers on her napkin. "First, let me apologize for having you meet me here, rather than at my house, Southern hospitality and all, but my kids are all home today and Billy's got some client meeting going on and I just knew that would be even less conducive to our conversation than a coffee shop."

Oliver picked up a cigarette, and handed her another.

"Thank you. I do prefer this. I've not been too connected to the world of the others for some time now."

Molly took the cigarette. "Besides, it gives me a chance to smoke in peace without all my nicotine nazis at me."

Oliver lit her cigarette.

"You know, she didn't tell anyone about you."

"I know." His mouth tightened.

"No, y'all don't really. I mean, you don't know what that says. Annie was a terrible liar and an even worse secret-keeper. She was about as transparent as Saran Wrap. *You* were that precious — from the first moment."

Tears filled his eyes. "Look, Molly, I may have made a mistake. I don't know if I am up to this after all. I never loved anyone the way I loved her. I still can't even begin to figure it all out; it was — *we* were so powerful, so fast, and then she was gone forever. I'm like some bloody crash survivor — I'm still wandering around the wreckage looking for my car keys."

Molly put down her fork. "Forgive me. I don't mean to sound so glib. It's just the way things come out of my silly mouth."

Oliver tried to smile. "I know. We Brits do it, too, an irony for every occasion." He fondled the rim of his saucer, caressing it, Molly thought, as if it were Annie.

"I've never talked about what happened or about her to anyone. No one I know ever even met her and that is *the very worst of it*."

Molly watched him. "Do you want me to tell you about it?"

He sighed so deeply that a feather of smoke floated up from the bottom of his lungs. She waited.

"Yes," he said softly. "Please."

"Now, I'm not real good at details, but I'll do my best. As you know, Annie was on her way back to y'all after seeing Mickey in Tokyo. She'd told Mickey that she loved you, and he had gotten all male about the whole thing and told her that was it, forcing her hand, so to speak, and she left.

"She also had all their documents and things and the responsibility of getting back to the FBI to stop that reptile Stan Stein from riding into the sunset with everyone's dinero and all, but she was going back to London to see you first, when about midway she started to hemorrhage, and by the time the plane landed at Heathrow she had lost an enormous amount of blood, not to mention all of the revolting mess caused by her tumor blowing up or whatever it did. She was almost gone when they landed.

"Just think of being all alone way up in the middle of the sky and having something like that happen to you! Well, thank the good Lord there was a doctor on board, a very nice Japanese gentleman that I actually met later on. He turned out to be an internal medicine specialist, so at least she wasn't putting her life in the hands of some podiatrist or plastic surgeon, or someone not so familiar with the internal problems of the midlife female."

Molly slid another bite of shortbread into her mouth, savoring it for a moment. "Now, this part is a little sketchy, but it seems that Annie told the doctor on the plane to call her brother, Martin, and not to let anyone but Martin give her any blood. She kept saying that Martin was a vampire and had lots of great blood, and I don't mean any irreverence, but I did have quite a giggle fit when the little Japanese doctor told me that. Annie and I always kidded about how Martin looked like Dracula. That was pure Annie. Even in the jaws of death she kept her vision.

"Anyway, the doctor found Martin's number in her carry-on and called him right from the plane, and Martin, God bless him, packed several pints of good blood, and a police escort got him to the airport and on a flight to London. He actually arrived almost the same time that Annie did, or what was left of her."

Molly put down her fork. Her cobalt-colored eyes narrowed and flooded with tears. "Poor Annie-pie, she had lost so much blood by the time they landed, the doctors gave her very little chance. She was really too depleted to be operated on safely, and Martin had to give the consent because she was unconscious.

"Her brother had to make the decision without Mickey, because they couldn't reach him. Martin called me and I called her brother-in-law and her children. Oh, my sweet Lord, I can't tell you what that was like! Those kids truly adore their mother, and the whole family had been through a lot without this. 'You must be on the first plane to London, your momma is very ill and needs you to be there!' I told them. I tried not to scare them half to death, but these are two astute New York City kids; they knew it had to be really bad for me to call them.

"Off we all went, flying in from everyplace. Mickey was the last to be notified and I don't even know how the dear man got there — walked right off the set of his soap opera. The Japanese do not understand anything absolute like 'My wife is dying and I'm leaving.' I truly believe they expected him not to go. He told me they all but grabbed on to his legs and physically prevented him!

"Mickey doesn't know this, but Martin asked me if I knew anyone in Annie's life named Oliver and I said no, because I didn't then, and when I asked why, he said that the last thing she said before they wheeled her into surgery was 'Tell Oliver I love him and not to be sad.' Then she said, 'Tell him I came back. . . .'"

Oliver pushed back in his chair, bridling his emotion. He had known it would be hard, but not this hard.

Molly wiped her eyes. "I probably shouldn't have told you that.

"Well, the rest is pretty simple. They practically refilled her body with blood, and they took all her goodies out: ovaries and uterus and whatnot. She had peritonitis and they had to cut holes in her tummy and drain all the poison. I saw her in intensive care and I may tell you, I could barely find my poor Annie between all the tubes and things. There was very little hope by then. Mickey and the kids took turns; no one left that hospital for a week; we just cried and prayed, and real life stopped.

"The British doctors were wonderful. They let Martin assist. Even though she was unconscious, they knew she trusted him, and he never left her — talked to her all the time — we all did, actually.

"I must say I thought it was profoundly moving that she had asked for Martin; really doing the most sensible thing given her condition, but also sidestepping a choice between you and Mickey.

"And then one morning, after we had all about given up, she opened her eyes, and Ella and Toby were there and she smiled at them. Ella said it was like a miracle. All of a sudden color flushed her face, like a rush of life. 'Hi, my bunnies,' she said, as if she was picking up the carpool all those years ago, and then slowly, day by day, she came back to life.

"It was another week before they upgraded her condition from critical to whatever up from that is. She really had the stuffing sucked out of her; it was almost a month before she could even stand up by herself.

"All in all, she spent almost two months in the hospital. One in England and then, when we could move her, one in Los Angeles.

"For her family it was really as if the planet stopped spinning. Everyone's lives just screeched to a halt. Toby dropped out of Brown, which of course he was happy as a lizard on a tile roof to do anyway. Ella put off her move to Australia. You cannot imagine the terror in those dear hearts.

"The only good thing about it all was that it allowed Mickey to repair his relationship with his kids, though that's another story.

"So, now, I guess that brings it full circle. Fate does have a way of intercepting our heart's desires, doesn't it?

"When Annie finally came home, she was different, as y'all can well imagine. The doctor from the plane told me that she kept saying that she was going to die like her mother, and she came as close to the edge of the lake as one can, but she didn't die! She damn well didn't! And she let go of a lot of that fear and guilt that she had been carting around inside her little curly red head forever."

Molly picked up her cup and took a sip, trying to figure out how much more Oliver could stand. He was silent, his big hands threaded together, making him look terribly masculine and engagingly tormented. Now Molly appreciated how hard it must have been for Annie to let him go.

"We never talked much about you once she came home, but I knew she was thinking about you a lot. I could tell by her pauses and the way her mind would wander off, or she would stop herself in the middle of a story, just before it got to some reference that included you, or some memory.

"If I can be so bold as to offer my interpretation, I think that by the time she was strong enough to keep anything in her head but the effort to just stay alive, well, by then she was back here with her children and her husband and her family and her real life, and after almost dying and all, I guess it was just too wide a chasm to cross back to you.

"For a woman like Annie, it would be too selfish to do that to the people who loved her and had given up so much of their own lives to see her through.

"It's been over six months now and she still isn't nearly back to normal. She has really had a time and so have her husband and her kids. Something like that does bring people closer, especially in a family like the Wilders with so much love running everywhere.

"So they sold their house and recommitted to their marriage. Frankly, I would have been shocked to the heart of my Southern soul if they had done anything else."

Oliver stubbed out his cigarette. He needed to go somewhere and be alone now. Molly uncrossed her legs and leaned in closer. "I have a letter for you. It's entirely my fault that you haven't gotten it yet. In all the confusion of the hospitals and helping pack up their house, I just totally forgot about it, so please don't think it was her not caring."

"A letter?" He seemed to repeat the words to himself.

Molly nodded and reached into her purse, pulling forth a thick white envelope with his name scrawled in blue.

Oliver reached out, almost grabbing it from her. He held it in his hands, realizing that he had never seen Annie's handwriting. His eyes burned with smoke and sorrow. He put the letter in his jacket pocket and took a deep, leveling drag on his cigarette.

"I do appreciate your coming like this. It must have been rather awkward for you."

Molly grinned at him. "I'd love to say it was, but the truth is, I am much too curious and basically deviant not to have relished the opportunity of meeting the fabled Oliver. Lord knows, I never got any good stuff out of Annie."

"Well, it's nice to know that she didn't trade me about like recipes or such."

Molly stopped smiling. "Mr. Taylor, I don't know you at all, but I must tell you that nothing remotely like you ever happened to my Annie-pie before in her life. It was a very big deal, and besides almost dying she will most likely also never fully recover from not seeing y'all again. This was not an easy decision for her to make, and like all great big grown-up decisions, the rest of her entire life will reverberate with the road she has chosen.

"I'm not taking anything away from your hurt, but what she was faced with losing was far more than what you were putting into the pot, and I think you do whatever happened between you a great disservice by discounting it.

"It doesn't make it hurt less, dear man, to try and make your relationship less important either from her end or from yours, as I am sure her letter will show, but then again, not having read it — being a trustworthy and sphinxlike friend — I can only speculate."

Molly picked up her purse and winked at him. "It was a true pleasure to meet you, sir," she said, and glided out, her ballet slippers skimming the floor.

Oliver threw some bills down on the table and eased himself off the silly chair. He needed to go to a private place and read the letter.

When she had not come back or called or sent a note, he had indulged in every melodramatic emotion available, railing and blaming and raging at her and at his own blind stupidity. He had stormed about in an obsessive and semiviolent state, calling her home and hanging up — having his assistant phone under various pretenses — but she had vanished, leaving him howling in helplessness until the morning, almost a week later, when he had seen the small item in the *Times*: "Wife of American TV star collapses on British Airways flight from Japan."

The story gave few details and withheld the name of the hospital. His first feeling was an enormous flood of relief that at least she had not just turned away and forgotten him, that she had been on her way back.

The next, which lasted until Molly O'Brian had called him, was mortal fear that she would die. He must find a way to be big enough not to forget that — his gratitude to the gods that she had survived. Unlike so many others that he had loved, *she* had survived.

The hardest part, as unbearable as if she had died, if not more so, was knowing that she was out there, living and breathing and being Annie, and he would never have her again.

She was gone forever, but she was not dead, and he would have to go on as if she were, fighting as with any addiction or obsession the almost uncontrollable desire to storm into her cozy, renewed life and throw her over his shoulder and take her away with him forever, no matter what the cost.

She was alive and he had lost her anyway.

He walked out into the blazing brightness of the California sunshine — Hockney light, unlike any other — and headed toward the beach. He would walk down to the Montecito beach, the one Annie had described, and he would sit in the sun and read her letter.

This would be his own private farewell, and he would have to learn to live with not having really said good-bye to her in person.

Dearest Oliver,

Well, a funny thing happened on my way back to London — See? I told you I can never pass up a fast line. Actually it was not at all funny, but it was just about the best excuse for not showing up short of the plane crashing or being hijacked by Shiite terrorists that anyone could come up with.

I know that Molly has talked to you, so I will not burden you with a recap of all the gory details (and trust me, they were). I keep wondering if I am sort of like a castrated man now, since they have removed all the special things that made me a woman. I know it's not a very sexy thought to share with one's lover, but a rather profound and disturbing one nonetheless.

The removal of all that equipment that we women so complain about upset me far more than I would ever have imagined. I guess still having all the machinery chugging along inside held the whisper of possibility, the illusion of youth, of still being able to create life.

Please don't laugh at me, but in England I did have the fantasy of having your child; two creaky old softies creating something wonderful. The other thing is, I really did believe that I was going to die, and on that airplane I saw my mother floating above me from the floor of the little toilet cubicle like one of Chagall's angels and I thought, she's trying to stop me from going to Oliver. I sort of remember promising her that if she let me live, I would go home where I belonged. I'm not entirely sure about this, but it keeps coming back in my dreams.

Am I making any sense? Oh, Oliver, my darling, please know that my decision to go home with my husband was not because I stopped caring for you! I will never stop loving you, never. I am superstitious enough (or maybe it's California New Age eking its way into my gray matter), but I do believe that we must pay attention to what life brings forth. What my life brought forth was a very dramatic obstacle to prevent me from reaching you, too enormous a warning light for me to just ignore. I really am, after all, a pretty conventional woman. My children and my husband have always been the most important things on earth to me. Not that I'm unique in that, but in the end, it really is where I belong.

Do not think for one moment that that makes losing you, if in fact you are still there to lose, any less painful. You were the most incredible gift to the middle of my life that I could ever have imagined. You were *my* Magic Flute, and I will keep what we shared close inside me for the rest of my time on earth.

I have no idea where my life is headed now. Mickey and I have been toying with the idea of doing a film project together with Mickey's brother, Jackie. I would write, Mickey would direct and star, and Jackie would produce. The story really is about what happened to us with Leonard Lewis. But first I must concentrate on being able to walk two blocks without having to lie down!

I won't even say that maybe someday we can be friends or anything like that, because I know that it's not possible. If I couldn't hold you in my arms and kiss your luscious lips, I would rather not see you at all. Oh, God, my darling, I do really think right now that my heart is going to just crack in half and break all up inside me!

I had planned a far more remote and formal letter, one that would make this easier for both of us, but it just doesn't seem to want to come out that way. I told Mickey in Tokyo just before I left that it wasn't that I didn't still love him, but that I loved someone else too, and I simply did not know how to love both of you.

Well, my sweetheart, I am learning. My husband has been incredible, and my love for him is stronger now in many ways than it has been for a long, long time. It may even be that you are mixed up in there too, that loving you and not having you has melted over into what I have to offer Mickey.

If that is true, then I wish the same for you. I wish you someone lovely, that you can apply the joy and passion that you so freely offered me to what you feel for her.

God bless you, my darling, and please, please, forgive me.

Annie

Oliver climbed down onto the black jagged rocks and huddled between them. Sounds were coming from somewhere deep inside of him, down where he had always imagined his soul to be. Funny that he had never imagined his soul to be in his head or near his heart, but on the top of his belly. He had never made sounds like these and they frightened him; so raw and primitive, an almost violent wailing.

Annie, Annie! Her essence pounding inside his head, driving him mad with the frustration of unfinished love.

"Oliver."

The howling stopped. He whirled, his face running raw with tears, covered with drops of mucus and saliva, a wounded man-beast in the twilight. He was hearing voices. Not voices — *her* voice.

Through his clouded eyes he saw her standing above him, so pale and fragile now, her freckles standing out on her white skin like painted dots. The breeze was blowing her dress around her, a flax-colored silken dress, and she looked like an angel, a Renaissance angel from one of the frescoes in the Orvieto cathedral. He blinked, expecting to clear the image, the phantom projection of his longing.

The angel moved. "Oliver?"

He stumbled forward, bumping against the spike-like rocks, oblivious to his disarray, trudging toward hope.

She waited for him. Quiet and solemn, serene, he thought, nothing like his memory of her, which was always filled with funny faces, legs akimbo, tension flickering through her.

He scrambled up the bluff, panting and wet. "My God," he said, wiping at his face, trying to bring her into focus.

She smiled and reached into her pocket and handed him a Kleenex, and he laughed at this, laughed loud, but in the same strange way a howling laugh, harder and darker than his real one. "Always prepared for possible secretions."

She brushed her hair back out of her face.

"I had to," she said, and he nodded, blowing his nose.

"I tried not to. When Molly told me you were here, I was already miles away. We're moving, and I just kept unpacking dishes but . . . I just couldn't. . . ."

He was crying again. "I'm glad you couldn't. Over and over I've railed at the gods for one more meeting, at least to say good-bye properly. It's the unfinished part that makes it so bloody unbearable."

She sighed, tears falling across her cheeks and running over her lips. He took her hand and helped her down onto the bluff and they sat on the edge, looking out at the setting sun.

He held on to her hand, gently caressing each finger, memorizing the veins and freckles.

She shuddered.

"Are you cold?" he asked, then, "You're so thin."

"A near-death perk, quite a diet plan."

"Annie, not funny." He wound his fingers through hers, caressing the tips.

"I know. I don't seem to be able to talk about it without really bad jokes coming out. I still feel sort of like Robocop, but I'm much better."

They sat for a while not speaking or looking at one another, as if they were afraid of spoiling their good-bye, dishonoring their feelings with chitchat or forced emotion.

Finally she withdrew her hand, leaving a damp, empty place between them. "This is probably the longest I have ever gone in the presence of another human without talking. I like the way it feels. I think this may be the new me."

She smiled at him so forlornly and with so much love in her eyes, he felt again as if he would just have to gather her up and take her off with him. "You have changed," he whispered. "You're very released now, the core is still."

"Really?" she said, looking disturbed, an old Annie face returning. "I'm not so sure I like this — a little too Camille for my comfort."

"It's nice," he said, turning to face her, needing his eyes to be all over her now. "It's the way you are after we make love. It's very sexy."

"*Made* love," she said, her voice trembling, "*Made* love."

He jumped to his feet and pulled her up, pressing her against him. He could not bear this; he could not let her go. He understood now, swaying by this foreign sea, how lovers went mad with grief and killed themselves, flung themselves off cliffs into the mother's mouth of ocean.

Annie held him. It was exactly the same as the very first day, feeling his presence inflaming her, releasing feelings she did not know were part of her, feelings so blissful and terrifying that she had no choice but to follow them.

She had made a terrible mistake. She had believed that after everything that had happened, she could come and say good-bye to him in person — just one last touch, one last sniff of his special smells and then she would head onward into this new serenity or whatever it was. She would go forth having completed their circle, but all that she now wanted was to have him lift her up into his arms and carry her away forever.

"My darling, I have to go now," she said, unable to move.

They clung together, wailing into one another's bodies, mourning the end of their love as deeply as if they had seen it murdered, physically hacked to pieces by others.

The sun was disappearing behind the oil rigs and he let her go.

"Now," he said, "go now, Annie, go fast and don't turn back or I swear to Christ, I won't let you."

She reached out, desperate to kiss him, panicked that she hadn't kissed him good-bye.

He moved back. "No, Annie. I can't."

She wrapped her arms around herself, shivering with loss. She was still so weak she could barely stand. She felt faint, dizzy with need.

"Go now, please."

Mickey would be there, waiting for her; new house, new horizons, sun setting on this one.

"You have my letter?" she asked, and he nodded, and she turned away, her arms still pressed tight, holding herself back, holding herself in. "It's okay, Annie," she whispered, seeing her mother's ghost floating above her in the airplane bathroom. She swayed, letting go of herself, breathlessly scrambling upward. She needed her arms around herself to keep moving away from him. "Go, Annie, go." She reached her car without looking back. Her heart was pounding, and she held herself tight again, patting her heaving chest. "Home, Annie, go home." She hesitated, as if listening to something inside her heart. She closed her eyes, and she danced, just a few steps, tuneless and stiff, but hopeful. She danced.

When he stopped crying, Oliver Taylor walked back down the rocks to the sea. He waited there, the water tapping at his feet, until the last sliver of sun lowered in the sky. *Good-bye, Annie,* he said to the sun, which reminded him of her hair, and he tore her letter into tiny neat pieces, letting them float in the breeze, falling one by one into the salty green water and vanishing into the tide.